CALYPSO

An Eleri Royals Novel

EBONY OLSON

EBANDMUSE
PUBLICATIONS

Published 2020

Published by

EbandMuse Publications

Sydney, Australia

ISBN: 9780648500094

http://ebonyolson.com/

Chapter One

I WAS WET!

Actually, wet might have been an understatement. I'd walked five kilometers in torrential rain. Two kilometers of that in heels, which seemed like a feat in itself. I'd taken my heels off when my second blister busted, and the pain became unbearable.

Not that I was unhappy. I was damn near elated. The date my mother had set me up on was horrible. The asshole son of one of her colleagues was a self-entitled and arrogant son of a bitch. When he tossed me out of his car forty minutes ago because I wouldn't put out, I'd smiled and waved goodbye.

Why? Because doing my mother the favor of dating her colleague's son had bought me a two-week holiday in Hawaii. That's why I didn't care how sore my feet were, or how wet I was skipping towards the late-night Pitstop Cafe. The fact I resembled a drowned rat couldn't steal my happiness either.

The Pitstop is a heritage-listed building in the middle of nowhere but on the main road to everywhere. Close to ten years ago, it opened as a cafe with a seven-eleven service station attached.

Bouncing to the doors with a smile on my face, I was daydreaming about the bikini I should buy for my vacation in Hawaii. That was the only reason I went on this date from hell. Once I was under cover of the awning, I attempted to wring myself of excess water. The glass doors slid open, and the buzzer sounded to let the employee know he had a customer.

Joshua, a high school senior and night shift employee, stepped around the corner from the cafe. His blue eyes going wide as I stepped inside the doors, Joshua's pouty mouth moved, but no sound came out.

Under normal circumstances, I would have no idea who Joshua was, since he was two years behind me at school. But I tutored him for my two senior years. Even a quarter of the way into my second year at university, I continued to mentor Joshua. So, we knew each other well.

"Band-aids?" Smiling at Joshua, I pulled my dripping, sable-colored hair back off my face. That was my one regret tonight, wearing my hair down. Catching my reflection in the glass windows, I looked like the psychotic dead girl from 'The Ring.' Instead of crawling out of the television, I was walking through the door.

"The second row from the back," Joshua answered, then dashed around the corner back into the cafe.

Okay, I guess I've looked better, but I wasn't used to that reaction. Looking behind me as I squatted to get a packet of band-aids, I realized I'd left puddles in my wake. As if on cue, Joshua appeared, setting up a wet floor sign before moving towards me as he mopped the floor.

"Sorry. I did try and squeeze all the water out before I came in."

"It's okay. I've been mopping all night." Joshua smiled, holding out a dry towel. "Give me your coat. I'll hang it in front of the fire in the cafe."

Lowering my handbag and heels to the floor, I unbuttoned my ivory duffel coat and swapped him for the towel. "Thanks, Josh." Gracing me with his natural smile, Joshua went back to the cafe. He'd changed a lot in the last four years. No longer the cute kid, Josh had filled out a little and was previewing the handsome man he'd become. At eighteen, Joshua wasn't there yet. There was still a boyishness about him that made me think of him as a kid.

After using the towel to dry my face, hair, and legs, I grabbed the band-aids with my stuff and walked over to the counter. Retrieving my comb out of my bag, I slicked my hair back into a ponytail. Joshua still hadn't come back, so I took out a make-up wipe and my compact and cleaned all the make-up off my face. The mascara smudged black around my eyes, but I cleaned it until it looked like eyeliner.

"Now you look like yourself," Joshua teased, coming to serve me on the other side of the counter. Picking up the band-aids, he scanned them. "Need anything else?"

"A hot chocolate and something hot to eat."

"Kitchen in the cafe is already closed, but there are a few hot dogs left if you want that?" Joshua offered, pointing to the hot dog machine.

I eyed him. "Two hot dogs would be awesome, as long as there is cafe quality hot chocolate to go with it?"

Grinning, Joshua rang up the hot dogs for me. "Grab your food and come next door to get warm." He handed me my change, his eyes dropping to my cleavage before he moved around to the cafe.

Glancing down, I found my nipples high beaming through the sapphire silk of my dress. As far as dresses go, it was conservative. It showed more leg than anything else. But when you've walked barefoot through torrential rain in Autumn, your body tends to showcase that you are cold.

Wrapping the towel around my shoulders like a shawl, I grabbed my hot dogs. With my handbag over my shoulder, heels in one hand, hot dogs in the other, I moved round to the cafe. If I'd been paying attention, I would have noticed the voices coming from the cafe before I walked around. I didn't.

At first, all I noticed was a table with seven men sitting around it playing cards. An assortment of hoodies, leather jackets, and sport team jackets hung from the back of the chairs. It didn't faze me. The Pitstop was a favorite hangout for a lot of the local youth during the week. Usually, they'd all be at a party by now on a Friday night.

It wasn't until one of them lifted his head to watch me, and the others followed suit, that I became unsettled. Most appeared to be decent, but at least half of them could pass for members of a drug syndicate in a Hollywood movie.

At the far end of the table, were the last set of eyes I expected to see hanging in a service station cafe on a Friday night. Crystal blue, those eyes were almost a perfect match for my dress. Thick long lashes surrounded those eyes as they dropped to scan my appearance. My gaze lowered to his perfect cupid's pout, enclosed in a couple of days' worth of scruff.

Pulling my focus back, I took in the olive skin and the mop of unruly black hair. He wore a long-sleeve heavy metal shirt with a hood. While generous in size, the clothing couldn't hide his broad shoulders and physique. Biting my lip, I turned my focus forward, ignoring Aaron Wish, the catalyst of my raging hormones. Now, the only part of me that had managed to stay dry all night was as drenched as the rest of me.

Like Joshua, Aaron had been a scholarship student - the poor kid at a costly college. Rumors claimed him to be a local drug lord, womanizer and voted most likely to become an assassin. Despite this, I'd crushed on Aaron Wish something fierce from age fourteen. A year ahead of me at school, I want to say that when he left for university, my crush went with him, but it didn't.

As an Excelsior student - an advanced learning student - I chose to leap ahead with my university studies. This meant taking two first-year units each semester for my two senior years of high school.

So, instead of Aaron vanishing from my life, we'd ended up having two university units together. Last year we had all the same subjects and one class together each semester this year.

The saving grace I had, was that Aaron Wish didn't even know I existed. Sure, he remembered me from school, but I hid up the back of my classes at university, so no one even knew I was there.

Joshua slid a mug of hot chocolate across the counter to me as I reached it. "There you go, Caly. Go sit by the fire and thaw yourself out."

Putting my money on the counter to pay for the drink, I gave Josh a warm smile. "Thanks, Josh." Taking a sip while I waited for the change, I then dropped it all in the tips jar.

"You're too generous, Caly," Joshua sighed. When our math teacher suggested Joshua get tutoring, he'd had to admit that he couldn't afford it. His scholarship only covered the school fees and uniforms. So, I'd volunteered to tutor Joshua for free. In exchange, Mr. Downs wrote me a glowing recommendation for early entry to Eleri University. Despite no longer being bound by that deal, I'd grown to like Joshua and wanted to see him get into medicine as he hoped.

The table by the fire was far enough away from Aaron Wish and friends that they'd hopefully forget I was there. Putting my back to the group, I took a large mouthful of my hot chocolate. Retrieving my mobile from what I was grateful was a water-proof handbag, I pressed call.

"How'd the date go?" Penny, my best friend and roommate, answered on the second ring.

"It was a total bust. The bastard ditched me halfway between Charlie's and the Pitstop Cafe because I wouldn't blow him." Taking a big bite of my hot dog, I moaned at getting some decent food.

"That asshat! It's pouring rain, and he left you in the middle of nowhere at night?"

"Yep," I answered around my food. Unladylike, I know, but I was cold and starving. Charlie's was a five-star restaurant that barely served enough to satisfy a gold fish's appetite.

"Shit! Where are you now."

"Pitstop. I've busted my favorite pair of heels, I've got blisters the size of Mount Olympus, and I'm drenched to the bone. But I have a holiday to Hawaii secured in the bag."

"No wonder your mum had to bribe you to go out with such a prick."

"Agreed. Can you pick me up?"

Penny groaned, "God, Caly. If you'd phoned an hour ago, I'd be in the car in a heartbeat. But I went over to see Simon. There is a party on at his place, and I'm about three drinks over the limit already."

My head dropped in disappointment. "Well, shit!"

"I'm sorry, hon. Can you afford a cab?"

Not really. "Yeah. I'm guessing you're staying with Simon tonight, so I'll see you in the morning."

"Okay, hon. Let me know when you're home safe." Penny was the motherly one out of the two of us. Wild but caring.

Hanging up, I took another bite of the hot dog as I contemplated how I was going to get back to campus tonight. It was over a thirty-minute drive from the Pitstop. Slumping down in my chair, I pulled out my iPad and searched the bus timetable using the cafe's free Wi-Fi. The only bus that came by here towards the campus for the rest of the night was still another hour away.

With some free time up my sleeve, I logged onto my blog site and wrote a new post while I devoured my food. Hitting the publish button, I finished my hot chocolate and called my mother.

"Caly, I didn't expect to hear from you until tomorrow," my mother's voice came over the line rushed.

"I expected to get your voicemail. Aren't you at a conference in Singapore?" My mind raced over the schedule I'd memorized for my mum's whereabouts this week and the calculation of time difference between countries.

"I'm just walking into dinner. How did the date go?"

"He wined me, dined me, then dumped me by the side of the road when I wouldn't let him sixty-nine me. I've already blogged it, so you can read it when you get a minute."

My mother's heels stopped clacking across the marble floor. "Are you safe?" She asked with genuine concern. My mother was a high-powered businesswoman in the world of biochemical engineering. She'd given birth to me between replying to work emails and directing her team via phone calls. She worked from home for two weeks, and then I went to work with her.

"I am. I broke those Jimmy Choo's you got me for my birthday last year, but I'm safe. The blisters are worth a holiday to Hawaii."

Releasing a small laugh, the echo of her high heels striking marble started up again. "A deal is a deal. Tell me the dates in summer you want the flights booked and where you want to stay, and I'll get it organized."

"Summer is too far away. How about during winter break?"

"I'm heading into dinner. We'll catch up next week and discuss it then. Love you."

"Love you too, mum," I replied as the call disconnected. With a sigh, I looked at the time and then checked my cash flow.

Despite my family being well-off, my mother insisted on me earning my way. This meant I was very strict with my budget with what I made from work. Don't get me wrong; I wasn't doing it tough. My mother paid for my student fees and dorm costs. But all day to day expenses were mine. For that reason, I budgeted enough each week for coffee's and transport to work, or to go to the bar with my friends.

There was enough cash for the bus ticket home and a least one more hot chocolate. Getting up, I made my way back to the counter, which, unfortunately, took me close to the table of men.

Keeping my eyes on my destination, I didn't let the shenanigans at the other table catch my attention. Glancing up from the book he was reading at the counter, Joshua smiled when I stopped in front of him. "Hot chocolate or something stronger?"

"Unless you sell Bourbon, it's hot chocolate." Putting my money on the counter, I picked up his book. "Mary Shelly's Frankenstein?"

"Set reading," Joshua informed me.

With a nod, I placed it back down so he wouldn't lose his page. A masculine laugh burst out behind me. The way it heated my body better than the fire had made me cringe.

"What's so funny, Ayah?" One of the guys asked.

"There's a blog called Blue Balls that I started following in high school. It's by a girl who calls herself Nymph," Aaron chuckled. "It started off as a blog about all the ways her boyfriend used to try and get her to have sex with him. They broke up a few years back, and now it's about her dating life."

It was like instant freeze, holding my breath, realizing he was reading my blog. My mum and Penny knew it was my blog, but I'd never told anyone else. The desire to get my stuff and wait at the bus stop was overwhelming, but at the same time, it impressed me that he liked it.

"Is it dirty?" One of the guys asked.

"Sometimes, but it's not graphic sex or anything," Aaron answered. "It's still all about what guys say or do to get girls to have sex with them. Like tonight."

Now, I wanted to melt in a puddle of embarrassment as he started reading.

"I went on a blind date. Normally, I would never do a blind date. Let's just say someone coerced me into it, and no matter how bad it went, I was still going to be the winner. So, I went on this blind date with a guy in his mid-twenties. He's the son of a successful businessman. He's good-looking, well-educated, and wealthy. I couldn't understand why this guy needed to be set up on a blind date. Accepting he may be too busy to meet women; I went along thinking I would at least enjoy a nice evening."

Chuckling again, Aaron took a sip of his hot beverage as he scrolled the screen on his phone. "He arrived on time, was dressed well, and even opened the car door for me. So far, so good. He took me to a posh restaurant. Not my scene, but, obviously, he was trying to impress. He insisted on ordering for me; instant turnoff, and then proceeded to talk about himself and how good he is at everything. I was bored before the entree arrived."

Joshua pushed my mug of hot chocolate across the counter, along with my change. He was also listening to Aaron and captivated. "After two hours of listening to this guy talk himself up, and replays of American Psycho happening behind my eyes, the waiter arrived with the dessert menu. Finally, the night was looking up. The desserts at this restaurant were orgasmic. So, considering it was the only orgasm I was getting tonight, I was all for dessert. You know what Ego did? He told the waiter we wouldn't need dessert. He followed this up by leering at me over the table and saying, 'You're hot. You don't want to ruin it by eating desserts.'" Aaron burst out laughing.

His friends made combined hissing and sounds of imminent danger. "Ouch!" One guy laughed. "I'm surprised he's still walking."

Aaron started again. "So, we leave the restaurant. I plan to say goodnight; I understand why no one will date you, good riddance when he pulls the car off onto a side road. Ego then proceeds to remove his seatbelt, unplug mine, and push his seat back as far as it will go. Unzipping his pants, Ego pulls out his Johnston, and tells me to climb aboard."

"This guy is an idiot!" someone exclaims. The others murmured agreement, and I nodded. Chuckling at me, Joshua leaned over the counter to hear better.

"Needless to say, I refused his offer. Both for moral reasons, and the fact that he was either flying at half-mast or, in my experience, was not god's gift to women. If you get my meaning. Ego then informs me that if he shells out, I need to put out. When that didn't work, he tried to negotiate for a blowjob. On my refusal, Ego acknowledged he'd settle for a happy ending."

"Jesus! This guy should stick to paying for it," Aaron's friend laughed.

"When I failed to meet his demands for me to 'take care of his needs,' Ego, ever so politely, climbed out of the car. Coming around to my door, he took my upper arm and forcibly removed me from his car."

The crowd grew quiet. "I don't like where this is heading, Ayah." One of the more dangerous looking guys warned.

Aaron put up a placating hand. "Don't worry; I've already read it through. She's safe, or she wouldn't be blogging about it already." The big guy sits back, crossing his arms in suspicious patience.

"Where was I? From his car. He grips me rather tightly and tells me to get on my knees or walk home. Now, I must tell you, Ego hadn't bothered putting his little fellow away. It was still poking out like a hitchhiker's thumb. Yes, it's cold, and we were getting rained on, so I'll give him some shrinkage allowance. But it had been warm inside the car, so not that much."

By now, all the guys are holding up their thumbs and snickering. "Give the girl my number. Shrinkage need not apply," the big guy leans in with a grin. His eyes lift to me, and he winks. With a chuckle, I pick up my hot chocolate and take a drink while the big guy lets his eyes check me out.

"So," Aaron shakes his head with a laugh, "on my knees or walk. All ladylike, I lift my knee rather forcefully. As he falls to the ground cursing, I politely decline. The queen of England would nod approval at the grace in which I handled the matter.

Collecting my bag, I enjoyed the walk home. Of course, who do I trip over on the way? Lancelot. The one place I wasn't wet from the rain, I am now." Putting his phone away, Aaron chuckled.

"Is Lancelot her fuck buddy or something?" Joshua asks.

Spitting up my mouthful of hot chocolate, I quickly covered it as all eyes turned in our direction.

Frowning in consideration, Aaron leaned back in his chair and shook his head. "No. He's the one guy she's never talked about more than a mention here and there."

"So why call him Lancelot?" Joshua considered. "Lancelot was Guinevere's affair. I would think they must be sleeping together, especially with her saying she tripped over him."

Aaron smiled, shaking his head. "He's been on the scene since she was with her ex-boyfriend. She called him Lancelot for being her temptation, not because they hooked up. He's always mentioned in passing," Aaron clarified.

The big guy was watching me again. "Speaking of ladies out walking by themselves at night... what's a pretty thing like you wandering around in this weather for?"

All eyes turned to me. "My roommate had a few too many drinks at her boyfriend's party tonight and decided to crash there the night. I'm going to wait for the bus and get back to campus so I can sleep in in the morning," I bent the truth.

"Except you work the weekends," Joshua corrected me. If there weren't a counter between us, I would have kicked him in the shins.

"Yeah, but I'm closer to work if I stay on campus, so I get to sleep a bit later. Plus, I get my bed to myself instead of sharing with some jock who thinks he's entitled."

"Hey, I am entitled," one of the guys at the table pouted in humor.

"Not to me, you're not," I winked. All the guys laughed.

"What about me?" The big guy asked.

"What about you?"

"Am I entitled?"

Opening my mouth to answer, Joshua beat me to it. "Dude, no. Caly is spoken for." Blinking at Joshua, I didn't refute it. Picking up my mug, I started walking back to my seat.

"Of course, she is. She's too fit not to be," the big guy complimented. "I can still give you a ride home."

Chuckling, I saluted him with my mug as I walked. "Thanks, but the bus doesn't require me to get on my knees and worship, so I'll take that option, thanks."

All the guys chuckled and returned to their card game. Taking my seat, I opened an eBook to read while I waited for the bus. About ten minutes later, chairs scraping across the floor caught my attention. Aaron and his friends were leaving. They all made their way outside except for Aaron and the big guy. Instead, the big guy came to stand beside me. "My offer for a lift is still there. No expectations. I don't like women being out and susceptible at night. Bad things happen, even on busses."

"Thank you, but my mother taught me never to hop in a car with a stranger." He was being nice, not sleazy, so I gave him a friendly smile.

He returned my smile. "You're friends with Josh?"

Tilting my head, wondering where this question was leading, I nodded.

"And you live on campus?" His smile grew when I nodded again. He looked over to where Aaron was straightening up the tables. "Ayah?"

"Yeah, man?" Aaron stood up, looking our way.

"Give Caly a lift back to campus. I'll sleep better knowing she made it safely."

"No, really-" I tried to object.

The big guy put his hand on my shoulder. "Josh will be in the car for most of the ride, and Ayah lives on campus, so he's going there anyway. Aren't you Ayah?"

Aaron folded his arms across his chest, face stern. "Yeah. I'll get her home safe."

The big guy smiled. "Thanks, dude." He patted my shoulder. "Names Dwayne, by the way. Josh can give you my number if you ever stop being spoken for." With a wink, Dwayne walked out.

Aaron's soul-eating eyes were still focused on me. "Pack up. Josh is closing up. We'll wait in the car." The lights in the shop area went out a second later. Biting my lip, I shoved my iPad back in my handbag, along with the Band-Aids I was going to need for work tomorrow morning. Grabbing my coat off the chair, I pulled it on. Collecting his leather jacket, Aaron yanked it on, his eyes still on me.

Swallowing the massive glob of saliva filling my mouth, I picked up my empty mug and took it to the counter.

"Leave it. The morning shift will deal with it," Aaron told me.

When I turned around, Aaron was holding my bag and shoes in his hand, analyzing the broken heel.

"You are very dressed up for a house party. Don't know many girls who would kill a pair of fancy heels and walk in the rain to the bus stop, rather than take the couch."

Taking my bag and Jimmy Choo's from him, I shrugged off his interest. "I'm not the average girl."

Aaron squared himself to face me. "Caly Zilla, popular, but

always reserved at school. You dated one of the most popular boys in my year and were top of your class. You're rich but rarely showed it, right down to you even working as a tutor to give yourself spending money. And, you were an Excelsior student," Aaron listed off. "You were a year behind me at school, and yet, you've been at uni since I started."

"There a year before, actually," I corrected.

"I'm in my third year, and you are in half of my classes."

"I know." My face and neck became hot. I wasn't sure if I was blushing because Aaron noticed me, or because I'd acknowledged seeing him.

Aaron's eyes lit up. "Let's go wait in the car."

"Does this lift carry the expectation of a blowjob?"

"No expectation, but I wouldn't turn one down if you feel the need to say thank you," Aaron teased.

Rolling my eyes, I followed him out to the car park. Opening the door to a two-door sports car, Aaron pressed the lever for the front seat to slide forward. "Josh needs to get out first, so you'll have to take the back seat."

"There is an irony in that comment, I'm sure," I scoffed, stepping forward.

With a smile, Aaron slid the seat into place, locking me in the back of his car. Closing the door, he walked around, dropping into the front seat. "You look good in the back seat," he winked.

"You probably say that to all the girls you get in your back seat."

Aaron grinned. "Do I look like I fit in that back seat?"

No, no, you don't. At well over six feet, Aaron Wish stood a head taller than me, and his shoulders were twice my breadth. I wasn't short, but Aaron made me feel it in his presence. Taking a deep breath, I decided to divert the conversation. "So, did you become an assassin like your classmates predicted?"

Smiling, Aaron pressed the button for the engine to start. "Can't fit many weapons or bodies in the trunk of this car."

"How does a guy on scholarship afford a car like this?"

Aaron's smile faded. "It was a payout from the job I did through school."

"God, I wish I could afford a car."

"The rich girl complaining about money to the scholarship kid is ironic," Aaron huffed.

"I'm pretty sure the scholarship kid owning a car worth more than my annual income, is questionable."

Aaron met my eyes in the rearview mirror. "Life giveth and life taketh away."

My smile faded too. My hand went to the necklace at my throat. I couldn't remember a time I hadn't worn the locket. Even at school, where jewelry was banned, my mother got special permission for me to wear it. It was a gift from my father to my mother. I'd never met him, had no idea who he was. As far as I knew, he was gone from her life before I was born. The locket was all I had of him.

The passenger door opened, and Joshua slid in. Doing up his seat belt, Joshua smiled at me. "Catching a lift to campus?" When I nodded, Joshua's eyes flicked to Aaron. "She's the reason my grades are good enough to get into medicine next year; keep her safe."

Meeting Joshua's eyes, Aaron huffed. "I know. I will."

There in the dark, illuminated only by the dashboard light, I saw a resemblance in their facial structures that I'd never noticed in daylight. Aaron was all dark and brooding compared to Joshua, who was light and upbeat. Joshua was more auburn in his hair, and his skin a little paler, but their silhouettes and eyes were a perfect match.

"Are you two related?" I asked as the meaning of that clicked in my head.

Aaron smiled. "Josh is my baby brother." Putting his arm across the back of the passenger seat, Aaron looked at me as he started reversing. "He's been telling me all about you for years."

Chapter Two

T<small>AKING</small> the long way to the campus, we crossed the Eleri river to get to the dodgier part of town to drop Joshua home first. The Wishs' lived in a townhouse, in an area dubbed the Lego village because all the houses looked the same. If only it weren't on the edge of a part of town, I wouldn't be caught dead in at any time of day, let alone night. Which is to say, I would most likely end up dead if I ever did try to walk down the road here.

"Climb in the front, Caly," Aaron directed as Joshua climbed out of the car. Shutting the door, Joshua bolted through the heavy rain for the front porch.

Taking my seat belt off, I slid forward on the seat. Slipping my legs between the chairs, I moved the rest of my body into the front. The skin on my lower body felt the breeze of movement. Considering the flowing skirt of the dress, I might have exposed more than the dress intended. An idea confirmed by the sparkle in Aaron's eyes as they lifted from my legs to meet my face. Biting my lip against the hungry look in his eyes, I turned my attention to my seat belt and waved goodbye to Joshua.

"So, you tutor Josh?" Shifting gears to pick up speed, Aaron's hand brushed against my thigh.

Moving my legs, I adjusted myself on the seat to be more comfortable. After all these years, I was alone in a car with Aaron Wish, the igniter of my hormones, and haunter of my wet dreams. If I had a sex dream, he was usually the star. The heated black leather seats were not the cause of the sudden rush of heat between my thighs.

"Yes." Feeling that heat radiate to my cheeks, I squirmed in my seat. "This will be the fourth year."

"You don't charge him?"

"I do. Josh brings me a large juice from Boost to every tutoring session since I left school."

"That doesn't count, Caly. You charge forty dollars from every other student for an hour. You work with Josh for that long and have never charged him."

"I used to charge that. I enjoy tutoring Josh, and he's the only person I tutor now."

"Do you enjoy Josh, full stop?" Aaron asked.

My eyes widened in surprise. "Josh and I meet in the hospital cafeteria every Saturday afternoon. How exactly do you think I'm going to be enjoying him in such a public venue?"

Forehead furrowing, Aaron glanced my way. "I thought you were meeting at the university library?"

Relaxing back in my seat, I smiled at how out of date Aaron's information was. "That lasted a month after I started university. It's two busses for your brother to get there, which is unfair to him. Since I finish work at the same time your mum starts, Josh catches a lift with her, and then he catches the direct bus to work."

"That's right; you work at the hospital." Aaron looked over at me.

"Yeah, in the radiology department. I got a traineeship in my first year. Before I officially began university, I'd already completed ten subjects. Four each of my last two years at high-school, and then two units in summer school. That meant I could study a reduced load during semester time and work a part-time roster. I work Thursday nights, Saturday and Sunday mornings."

Aaron's grip on the steering wheel tightened. "You got the Technologist Traineeship last year?"

The fact that he knew the job title, coupled with his reaction, made me shrink back in my seat. "You applied for it, didn't you?"

"Yes," Aaron gritted. "I need twelve months of experience to get accredited when I finish my degree. If I got the traineeship, then I would have graduated eligible for accreditation. Instead, I'm working at the university bar. Accreditation positions are competitive, and preference always goes to Eleri kids. So, now, I'm probably going to finish my degree and end up working the bar for another four years."

"You're doing the nuclear medicine major?" We were in the same year but only had a few of the same classes.

Eyebrows jumping, Aaron's eyes devoured me. "You're not?"

"Diagnostic Radiography."

Aaron ground his teeth. "I not only got passed over for a first-year student, but you're also doing a lesser degree."

"Hey! Academically, we're the same. I was an Excelsior student too, asshole."

"Call me an asshole again, I'll pull over and let you walk home," Aaron muttered.

Glancing around with wide eyes, I took in the fact we were

still in Riverside. I'd never make it home again if he dumped me here. "Should I call you Ego instead?" Quoting the name, I'd used for tonight's date on the blog.

That made Aaron smirk. "I'd at least take a girl out three times before I started expecting her to put out."

Hoping to defuse the situation, I smiled, getting an idea. Pulling out my phone, I went to the blog opening the contents page. "Okay, so who are you like?"

"What?" Glancing down, Aaron caught me scanning the list of pseudonyms used for my dates.

"You read this blog; you must have an idea of how you would behave. Which of the blogger's dates are you most like?"

Aaron laughed. "Okay. Out of them all, I'm a combination of three. There was an intelligent guy last year. Study something."

"Studitious?"

"Yeah, him." Watching me open that posting and pretend to read about those series of dates. Aaron shook his head. "Then, there is the bouncer from the bar before Christmas."

"Bounce?" I asked with an internal cringe. Both of those guys were two of my favorites. Studitious was intelligent, and an all-around nice guy, but there was no chemistry. He didn't even seem that interested in sex. Bounce, on the other hand, had the entire physical package. There was lots of sexual chemistry, but the intellectual stimulation wasn't there. I'd called him bounce, not because of his occupation, but that's what he'd call out during sex. 'Bounce on me, Baby, that's it, oh god, yes, bounce on my big dick.' Remembering some of the sex marathons I'd enjoyed with that gorgeous hunk of man, I swooned.

Watching me as I pretended to read the blog post, Aaron laughed. "Enjoying that one, are you?"

"Not as much as the blogger did," I replied to his tease. But, seriously, the sex was mind-blowing. "Is this your way of telling me you're good in bed?"

Aaron winked. "And so, the third would be the professor."

For a heartbeat, I froze. Clicking on the first Professor post, I pretended to scan. "She dated one of her teachers?"

Eyes on the road, Aaron tilted his head. "He didn't teach her class; at least, I don't think he did."

No, the Professor didn't teach any of my classes. He wasn't even a professor, but a Ph.D. student who taught at the university. During that first summer school session after high school, I'd fallen for that man. Enough so, that I'd lost my virginity to him. "And how are you like this one?"

Glancing out of the corner of his eye, Aaron licked his lips. "I want what I shouldn't."

My brows furrowed at his comparison because it wasn't like that between the Professor and me. Putting my phone down, I turned my body to slant towards him. "How?"

Seeing me adjust my position, Aaron focused his attention on the road. "The Professor spent months resisting her, scared of risking his future on her. In the same way, there are things I want in my life. But with my background, I could jeopardize the future I've always wanted if I go after them."

Blinking unsure by his meaning, I dropped my eyes to the phone. "I didn't see anything on that blog about the professor's thought process."

"It was implied." He kept his eyes on the road.

Opening my phone, I read the last post about the Professor. "No, you're wrong. The Professor made the first move, but the blogger ended it. It sounds like her feelings for him scared her. She was young going into the relationship and hadn't expected to get in that deep as quick as she did."

"You got that out of your quick read of a few posts?"

"The thing about these sorts of blogs is that our lives and our experiences color our interpretations of them."

Slowing, Aaron focused his gaze on me. "Is that your way of telling me you're terrified of getting your heart broken?"

"Aren't we all?"

There were mere inches between us, and I was giving him the perfect opening to kiss me. Even if he didn't, it was going to fuel a whole lot of fantasy fun-time for me from tonight onwards.

Whipping his face forward, Aaron hit the brakes and spun the wheel. Another car ran a red light as the force of Aaron swerving threw me to the side, smacking my head on the window. As our vehicle turned, we narrowly missed a collision.

Looking up at the lights as if to reassure himself, he did have the right of way, Aaron took a deep breath. Putting the car back in gear, Aaron moved us out of the intersection and continued driving. I was too busy holding the back of my head in pain to care about anything else.

"I'll check your head once we get to campus, but I'm not stopping to get carjacked or worse."

"Totally understand," I gritted. "It's the night for me getting injured."

"You already got hurt tonight?" Head swiveling in my direction, Aaron seemed concerned.

"Twice. I'm sure I've got a few bruises from a creep manhandling me earlier. Then, I got massive blisters trying to walk home. I only stopped at the Pitstop to get Band-Aids so I could wear my work shoes tomorrow. Josh encouraged me to stay, and once I was out of the rain, I didn't want to go back out in it."

"Josh encouraged you to stay?" Aaron asked, looking confused.

"He's always so kind and genuine with me. I feel safe with him. Most guys, they're only interested in looking, groping, or screwing me. They pretend to be nice or interested to get in my knickers. I don't get that with Josh."

Aaron smirked. "If I told you he's thought about banging you nine ways from Sunday, would that change your opinion of him?"

"No. Josh is a teenage boy." Lifting my hands, I grabbed my boobs. "If he hasn't thought about me naked or unloading all over these, then I would question his sexual orientation."

Oversteering a little, Aaron blinked out the windscreen with wide eyes.

Biting my lip, I removed my hands from my D cups. "Sorry."

Aaron shook his head. "No, please. Feel yourself up all you need."

"Really?" Running a hand up my inner thigh, I pushed my skirt up out of the way. "Cause it's been a rough night, and I could use the tension release."

"Always the quiet ones." Turning into the car park, Aaron worked his way down the gears with a grin. His hand brushed my thigh again as he pulled into the resident car park, but this time, he didn't make it casual.

Turning off the ignition, Aaron applied the handbrake and ran his hand up my thigh, chasing my hand. As his hand caught mine only a finger's breadth from the junction, I trapped his hand with mine and met his eyes.

Sitting there, his hand where only two others had ever touched me before, we looked at each other. Aaron's palm was so hot against my cold skin, I could already feel what it would be like for his hands to be roaming my body. With his face only inches from mine, I could taste his hot breath. My skin was already primed for the way his scruff would scratch, especially if he went down on me. Trembling as my desire coiled tight, I bit my lip to prevent the moan as I damn near came just staring into his eyes.

Pupils dilating until his iris was near invisible in the dark, Aaron's eyes widened as we shared air.

With control, I pushed Aaron's hand back down my thigh. "Thanks for the ride," I breathed a little too heavy. "I'll see you around." Opening the car door, I cringed at the torrential rain blowing into the car. Picking up my bag, I slid out from beneath his hand.

Remaining silent, Aaron swallowed hard. Closing the car door, I crossed the car park to the stairs that would take me up the hill to my dorm.

Reaching the cover of the door to my dorm, I breathed out. Part of me hoped Aaron would come after me and show me how he could bounce me. The sensible part of my brain said that it would be a bad idea. Aaron Wish was the very definition of a bad boy, and I had never been easy.

"Caly," Aaron called behind me.

Halting in opening the door, I paused wide-eyed for a moment before I turned to watch Aaron approach. Having pulled the hood of his black shirt up to cover his head, Aaron looked ominous in the dark rainy night. In his hands, Aaron held my broken shoes. Stepping under the cover, he gazed down at me, and without a word, he held up the shoes for me.

"Thanks," I murmured, taking the shoes. Our eyes locked with each other again. Inviting Aaron up was on the tip of my tongue, and his eyes told me he wanted me to offer. When he opened his mouth, I prayed he didn't ask because I wouldn't say no.

"Give me your phone."

Not expecting that request, I frowned at him. He held out

his hand, waiting. Confused, I unlocked my phone and gave it to him. He typed something in then handed it back.

"You ever get manhandled again and are stuck getting home, you call me. I'll come to get you. No expectations."

Checking my phonebook, I noticed a new number under L. "Lancelot?" My heart pounded in my chest, fearing he'd figured out my code name for him.

Aaron gave me a quiet smile. "Knight in shining armor; the man of temptation... you know."

"Guinevere was forced to marry King Arthur. She loved Lancelot. Out of loyalty to their king, they tried to refuse their love, but in the end..."

"Love conquers all?" Aaron asked, amused.

"I was going to say love drowns us all. Look at every great romance in history. It all ends with death and heartache." Touching the locket around my neck, I then swiped the rain from my forehead. "Love is a force of nature, and nature is the most destructive force on the planet."

Eyes on the locket, Aaron scooped it up in his palm. "Once bitten, twice shy? Did Phillip dumping you before he went off to college scar you that badly?"

Rolling my eyes, I shook my head. "I never cared for Phillip like that. It was a relief when he finally dumped me." Taking my locket back, I tucked it down the front of my dress.

Taking the hint, Aaron backed up a step. "Only call if you're desperate. I'm not a taxi service."

"I wouldn't abuse you like that. Thanks again for the lift." Unlocking the door, I walked in without looking back.

On the top floor, I let myself into my room, locked the door behind me, and without turning on the light, went to my window. The black shadow that was Aaron walked to the stairs down to the car park.

Stopping at the top of the stairs, he turned as if returning to my dorm. Only five steps back, he stopped again and pulled his phone out to answer it. Giving my building one last look, Aaron turned and disappeared down the steps.

There were two types of dorms on campus. Only a few years old, my building offered apartment-style living. Aaron lived in the older style dorm. They were four-bedroom adjoined town-houses with shared bathrooms. The most significant difference, of course, was the price. Over a hundred dollars difference a week. It was almost a natural divide between scholarship and fully-funded students.

With a sigh, I pulled out my phone and sent Penny a message to let her know I was home safe. Stumbling into the bathroom for a shower, I hissed when the hot water washed over the head wound. Cringing, I remembered the near-miss, something both Aaron and I forgot about by the end of the car ride. After I dried, I put antiseptic cream over my busted blisters and crawled into bed with my laptop.

Lancelot.

I realized tonight I've never really talked about Lancelot. I think that's because I could never explain my attraction. For sure, he's physically appealing, but that was never what captured me about him. It's his eyes. Guarded, secretive, and oh so naughty. He's not the guy most girls would take home to meet their mothers, and yet, I don't have that hesitation. I'm sure if I introduced my mother to Lancelot, he'd probably remind her of my father.

Lancelot has a fire in his eyes; an unquenchable hunger for something I can't identify. That fire is contagious. It makes you hunger for him, to be near him, to kiss him, to feel him, and when he touches me... there is no word in Heaven or on Earth to describe what he does to me.

Tonight, I realized that may have been what started this blog all those years ago. My boyfriend was whispering dirty things in my ear, while the hunger in Lancelot's eyes across the room hypnotized me. Then and there, it wouldn't have mattered what Blue Balls whispered or how he touched me. He was never going to light my fire as Lancelot did with a single glance.

It is with this sudden understanding that I go off to sleep tonight, wondering, is that why I gave up the Professor?

Four hours later, I woke before sunrise to find my blog blew up overnight with comments from my followers. Ignoring them, I pulled on my sweats before racing out the door to get my morning five-kilometer run done. By the time I got back, I had to rush getting ready for work. When I picked up my phone to leave, I had a message from my mother.

I saw your blog posts. Both of them. We will talk Wednesday night.

Oops. Saying Lancelot was like my father wasn't the best move where my mother was concerned.

Chapter Three

"CALY," my mother smiled as she embraced me in a warm hug. "How was your week?"

"Good. Busy. Yours."

"Same." Gena Zilla, my mother, smiled withdrawing. Build wise, I was my mother all over. More top-heavy than anywhere else. My mother also had the same love for food. For this reason, she'd raised me to love running. She said I'd thank her for it later, and with my appetite and love for feminine clothes, that moment had arrived.

In her late forties, my mother had aged well and was still beautiful enough to be a model. Her honey-blond hair was short in a nineteen fifties style bob. The tastefully applied makeup highlighted her peridot eyes and high cheekbones. "I bought you something." Collecting the large bag off the floor, Gena handed it to me.

With a Cheshire grin, I sticky beaked inside. There were two shoe boxes, Sophia Webster and Louboutin. "Best mother ever!"

Satisfied, Gena took her seat at the table, watching me look at the tissue wrapped parcel. It was clothing, but I would wait until I got home to look at it. Taking my seat, I slipped the bag under the table with my handbag. "So, the date?" Gena started, opening the menu.

"You read the post," I dismissed.

"Yes, but you always summarize for your posts. Quite often, you leave out any identifying details," Gena analyzed without looking up at me. "Did he hurt you?"

"A few bruises. I hurt Derrick worse."

"As you should have. Your father would be very proud of you." Her smile morphed from real pleasure to the fake smile she presented to her colleagues. "Which brings me to our next item of conversation."

"No," I challenged. "Still on that disaster of a blind date. There was a holiday that needs discussing before we get railroaded."

Lifting her eyes, Gena closed her menu. "Of course. Do you know when you wish to travel?"

Closing my menu, I retrieved a Post-it note from my handbag, passing it across the table. "All the details. Dates to leave, when I need to be back by, and where I want to stay."

Gena's genuine smile returned. "Done." Taking out her notebook, she stuck the sticky note inside. I knew my mother. She would take whatever I gave her and hand it to her assistant to deal with. So, it was easier for everyone if I just put it on a Post-it.

"Ladies. Would you like to start with drinks?" The waiter asked with a smile.

"Two Gentlemen Jack's, please," Gena ordered for me. "And table water."

The waiter looked surprised. "With coke?"

"Did I ask for coke?"

"No, mam." The waiter bowed his head and wrote the drink order.

"Ice in mine, please," I requested.

"Caly? Really? I taught you to drink better."

"You taught me to drink responsibly."

Gena smirked, "Do you know what you will eat?"

"Cheese and garlic pizza for the entree. Then, a chicken Milanese salad - entree size - for my main. Then, a sticky date pudding with double butterscotch sauce for dessert, please."

"Small or large pizza?" The waiter asked with bright eyes and smile.

Looking at my mother, I let her make the call. "Large," she answered. "I'll have the Niçoise salad for my main. Then, the salted caramel cheesecake with caramel brandy sauce.

"Cream or ice-cream with the cheesecake?"

Smiling up at the waiter, Gena batted her lashes. "Both. Thank you."

"Of course." The waiter looked impressed and walked away.

"So?" I raised a brow.

"So?" Gena asked, confused, then caught up. "Ah, your father." She sat a little straighter. Not that her posture wasn't already perfect. "It interested me what you said about Lancelot reminding me of your father."

"It was a feeling, not a fact. I don't know the man to know otherwise, remember?"

Gena waited while the waiter placed down our drinks before continuing. "Not knowing your father is for your safety, Caly, not out of spite. I loved him, but he lived a life that put anyone close to him in danger. When I discovered I was pregnant with you, I ended the relationship to protect you."

The life he lived. She used past tense. "Wouldn't people suspect if you dated each other before you became pregnant?"

My mother fidgeted with her fork. I'd never seen my mother fret. "We kept the relationship quiet. With my work and his, we were barely seen out and about together. I never told your father about you." Gena took a large drink. "With everything that happened, it was a good decision. I don't regret it."

"So, he's dead?" I asked. This was the most I'd ever gotten from my mother.

"Your father was a dangerous man, Caly. He had a chip on his shoulder and felt he had something to prove."

"Meaning?"

"That anyone knowing you were his daughter would put your safety at risk." Gena watched me absorb what she was telling me.

A thought occurred to me. "When I was seven, and that man came into the playground?"

Gena studied her drink intently. "I'm not sure. I never told anyone who your father was, so I couldn't be sure if he meant you harm. My family name is a danger to you as it is. However, you said he just asked you your name and if he could look at your locket. I worried, but nothing ever ensued, so I left it alone."

"A huh," I agreed, taking a large sip of the whiskey.

What I never told my mother was the man asked who gave me the locket, and what I knew about it. He'd looked surprised when I explained my daddy gave it to my mummy. He came back again two weeks later. After everyone made a fuss about him coming to the school and talking to me the first time, I didn't mention the repeat visit.

The second time, he waited until my nanny took me to a playground. He had a little boy with him, and the little boy started playing with me before taking me over to meet the man. When he asked to see my necklace again, I told him everyone got upset when he looked at it last time. He said the locket was magical, and he wanted to show me how to use it.

The man opened the locket and ran his finger over the blue sapphire heart embedded in the back of the lock. 'Do you know what a knight is?' He asked.

With a nod, I told him about King Arthur and the knights of the round table, it made him smile.

'If ever someone scares you, or you're in danger, press this heart. A knight will find you and return you to your mother. Understand?' I nodded. Closing the locket, he tugged on the chain. 'If anyone ever makes you fear for your life, I want you to pull the chain from your neck. Pull it hard, so the links break. An army will come to save you.'

'What if I'm far away?' I'd asked.

'I have men everywhere. I'll always be able to find you.'

"For you to say Lancelot would remind me of your father worried me," Gena admitted, calling me back to the present. "Why did you think that?"

"He's from the other side of the river. He's at university with me and trying to get ahead in life, but I don't think he's fully escaped Riverside."

Mum sighed, "No one ever really escapes Riverside." She gulped down the rest of her whiskey. "Before now, Lancelot has been a distant crush. I got the feeling that has changed."

My mother's ability to see through me always unsettled me. Of course, it made me feel loved too. "He gave me a lift home Friday night after Derrick left me stranded."

"Did he kiss you?" I shook my head. Gena shook her head, amused. "He touched you, though?"

The reminder made my cheeks flush with heat. "I opened the door for more, but when Lancelot made a move, I don't know, I chickened out."

Assessing me, Gena lifted her brows a bit higher after my admission. "You're worried reality will ruin the fantasy. I get it." Gena poured us both a glass of water. "So, what happened Monday in class?"

Slumping a little in my chair, I pouted. "Nothing. Lancelot didn't even acknowledge me. It was like Friday never happened. He did give me his number on Friday night, but told me it was only if I ever got stranded somewhere again."

"Have you messaged him?"

"To say what?"

"Thank you; you're hot; I want you... anything, Caly," my mother breathed out exasperated. "He gave you his number to put the ball in your court. You said you're the one who chickened out when he made a move. He was leaving it to you to pursue him if you wanted it to go somewhere." Gena reached over, touching my hand. "It's not like you to back away from something you want. What happened, Caly?"

Taking a deep breath, I took a moment to analyze why I walked away from Lancelot. "I feel like it would be inviting trouble into our lives. Not just for me, but for him too. I can't explain it."

"Would you like to hear my theory?"

"Of course."

"I came to an understanding some years ago that you have a commitment phobia. Possibly, that is my fault. I've never had a committed relationship since you were born. I worry not having a male role model in your life has handicapped you in affairs of the heart. So, I suspect, you know that Lancelot may be the man to challenge your fear of love. That's why he's always been a distant crush. It's why when the chance presented itself, you shut it down."

Absorbing what Gena said, I finished my whiskey. Our

entree arrived, and the talking stopped while we both ate our first slice of pizza. Once we'd both eaten a couple of slices, Gena dabbed at her mouth with her napkin, then studied me. "Message him. Ask him for a drink later."

"He works Wednesday nights at the uni bar. Student discount night, so it's rather a busy night."

"Perfect. You can call Penny and have her meet you there after dinner."

"I can't afford to go out drinking this week, mum."

"I'll put five-hundred on your student account if you go to the bar tonight," Gena bribed.

"This guy could break my heart, mum. Why are you pushing this?" Frowning, I wondered why she was suddenly bribing me to interact with guys. "You've been rather keen for me to start dating someone of late. What's going on with that?"

Gena huffed. "You live your life in a textbook. I want you to step out and live in reality for a while. I want you to have fun, fall in love, and yes, get your heart broken a little. That's living, Caly."

"I date, I go to parties, I..."

"Admitted on your blog that Lancelot has been the fire in your loins for years, and no other guy stands a chance. He's a piece of cake you've been admiring, but too scared to eat for fear of ruining how pretty it looks. You need to take a bite of that temptation and see if it tastes as good as it looks. If you don't, you're going to let every other decent chance of a relationship fall to the wayside. You'll spend your life pining after something which may not even agree with your palette."

Sulking back in my chair, I stared at the remaining pizza, wondering if my mum was right. The waiter came and served our salads. "Are you finished with the pizza?"

"I'll get it in a doggy bag, please," I requested.

Mum waited until the waiter left. "If you're scared to make the first move, don't. Just put yourself in his way and see if he's willing to go after you."

Knowing Gena wouldn't let this go, I took my phone out of my bag and texted Penny. "I've asked Penny to go to the bar. I'll put myself in his way. If he ignores me again tonight, we agree to drop this?"

My mother smiled. "Agreed. Maybe change before you go. Something a little lower cut should do the trick," Gena gestured to my top.

"Jesus, mum. If I put the girls on display, Lancelot won't be able to get near me through all the other drunken guys trying to drool on me. Plus, I think he's a legs man."

Gena smiled. "Well, you've got a nice pair of those too."

Two hours later, I followed Penny and Simon into the Tower Bar. There were several uni bars, but the Tower Bar was the best for live music. It also happened to be the bar Aaron worked at for the past three years, so it instantly became my hang out. I'd taken mum's advice and changed out of the dress I'd worn to dinner. Now, I sported a pair of slim-fit jeans, a scoop neck top that always fell off one shoulder, and ankle boots. Heels in this bar resulted in stomped toes.

Student night was also a night for local bands. Tonight, featured a grunge group with a female bass guitarist who wore a bikini top with a short denim skirt. Simon's eyes nearly bugged out of his head. Penny helped him put them back in by putting his hand on her boob. "You can touch these," she reminded him.

"And I'm the luckiest guy here to be able to," Simon smiled before pulling her in for a kiss.

A cheerleader for the university's football team, Penny had a fantastic body. Her breasts were a seventeenth birthday present from her mother. Only C cups, which she felt more comfortable in then the A cups she spent her teens hating. Wearing boots, skin-tight jeans, and a halter top, which showed her six-pack, Penny left her blond hair hanging long down her back. She worked hard for her body - gym sessions twice a day plus cheerleader training - she deserved to show it off.

"I'm going to the bar," I announced to the tongue tangled couple. Meandering through the crowd, I waved and said hello to a few people I knew but kept walking. Reaching the neon-lit, chrome, and glass bar, I ended up missing where Aaron was serving by about two meters. Not that I could see him until I got to the bar. He'd been bending down, grabbing drinks from the fridge until I got there.

"What can I get you?" The guy who was serving where I stood asked.

"JD and coke in a bottle," I said a little louder than necessary. With the loud music from the other end of the room, it would be acceptable to pretend I was concert deaf.

"Caly!" Julianne, my friend from high school, yelled from further down the bar. Aaron's head turned towards Julianne, then swiveled in my direction. Meeting my eyes for a half a second, Aaron went back to serving as I acknowledged Julianne. Looking back up the bar as he swiped the student's card, Aaron saw Julianne wave me over, but he didn't look back at me.

My heart sank a little. Maybe Aaron was only kind last Friday because of Joshua. Sure, he was willing to take it if I offered, but he probably wasn't interested passed that.

"Here you go." The barman put my drink in front of him, and I handed him my student card. The best thing about our university was you could go anywhere on campus and use your student card to pay. I came to the bar with my phone in one pocket and my student card in the other.

"Thanks." Winking at the cute bartender, I took my card back and slipped it in my pocket. The bartender gave me a generous smile before I took my bottle of drink and weaved my way to the other end of the bar to Julianne.

"Hey," I greeted when I got there.

"Hey. You flying solo tonight?" Julianne was with another two student nurses that I recognized from the hospital.

"I'm here with my roommate and her fella. They are macking on somewhere down near the band."

"Want to hang with us?"

Happy not to be stuck as a third wheel, I joined in with the conversation about work.

Occasionally, Aaron would look up the bar, as if checking where I was, especially every time I bought a new drink. Julianne and her fellow student nurses were partying hard tonight. At some point, I got dragged into their drinking rampage. Not enough that I was blind; I knew my limit. That was five bottles of JD for the record.

After I finished my third drink, I went to break the seal. I'd held it as long as I could, but I was pretty sure I'd be visiting the bathroom hourly now. The nurses had already been pairing up for the toilet for the last hour, so I'd survived longer than most.

When I got back to the girls, they had already refreshed their drinks. Stepping closer to the bar ready to order another, I found Aaron looking down at me. "Water?" He asked.

"Bottle of Jack, thanks."

"Each bottle is the equivalent of two standard drinks, and you've drunk three over the last two hours. Get water."

"I'm responsible, Aaron. I know my limit."

"Yeah, well, as the bartender, I get to make the final call." Turning, Aaron grabbed a bottle of water, placing it on the counter in front of me and putting his hand out for my card.

"Did you swap tills just to cut me off?" I asked, handing it over.

"I didn't like seeing you bruised last week," Aaron countered. Swiping the card, he charged my account.

"I'm horny," I told him, smiling when Aaron's brows nearly disappeared into his hairline. "I've gone out drinking weekly since I started university. I'm horny as all hell, but I've not had sex since before Christmas last year." Aaron just blinked at me. "If I were the sort of girl who got drunk-fucked, that wouldn't be the case, would it?" I quirked a brow at him, taking my card back. "I can take care of myself. Go father someone else." Turning my back on him, I stepped back into the circle of nurse students, keeping my back to him.

"You got an early class?" Julianne nodded at my water.

"Wish decided I'd had enough," I grumbled.

Julianne quirked a brow. "Really? Give me your card?" She asked, handing me her drink. With a chuckle, I handed it to her.

Skirting her way to midway down the bar, Julianne ordered a JD and coke. Pretty as she was, Julianne batted her lashes, and the bartender didn't look at the photo on the card.

Turning my focus to Aaron, I waited until he looked my way then sculled the bottle of water. Smiling, I put the empty bottle on the bar. Peering at my behavior, Aaron lowered his brows above his eyes. Returning to our circle, Julianne handed me the bottle of Jack. Giving her back her drink, I pocketed my card, keeping eye contact with Aaron while I took my first drink of it.

Jaw clenching, Aaron glared at me. With a wink, I turned back to the group.

"Aw crap!" Julianne's face fell a minute later.

"What?" I turned to see what she'd seen. Aaron was leaning over the bar talking to one of the bouncers, Bruce, or Bounce if you read my blog. Looking my way, Aaron pointed me out. Nodding his head, Bruce started towards our group.

Glaring at Aaron unimpressed, I held my arms out to the side. "Really?"

Shrugging one shoulder at me, Aaron was clearly annoyed at me, subverting him.

Shaking my head, I was now pissed with him. Giving him the finger, I crossed through the middle of the group. "Catch you at work."

There was a rule in the uni bars. If the bouncers had to escort you out, they barred you for a month. The bouncers knew me, hell, Bruce knew me intimately, so I'd have no chance of sneaking by them. The unspoken get out of jail free card was that if you left of your own doing, you were just out for the night.

Making my way through the packed bar, I aimed myself at the closest door. Bruce was following but slowed by the crowd of students. At the exit, I stepped out. Jeff, the bouncer there, stopped me. "No drinks outside, Caly."

"I'm going to stand here and finish my drink." Smiling, I put the bottle to my lips, sculling it down. By the time I'd finished, Bruce was standing at the door.

"Get home safe, Caly." He held his hand out for the bottle.

"Give Aaron a message for me?"

"Sure," Bruce lifted a brow, realizing I knew the bartender who kicked me out.

"Tell him I just lost his number."

Smiling, Bruce shook his head. "His bad luck," Bruce's eyes scanned me.

"Fucking oath, it is." Grabbing Bruce by the front of his shirt, I went up on my tiptoes and kissed him. Bruce didn't hesitate to make it a very lustful pash.

When I pulled back, Bruce's eyes were full of laughter. "Was that for Wish too?"

"Not anymore." Laughing, I skipped down the stairs. I didn't do overprotective guys or guys that tried to tell me what to eat, drink, wear. I was my own person. You either liked me for who I am or don't bother.

When Penny stumbled in an hour later, I was at my desk studying. "What happened to you?" Penny asked, looking me over.

Already showered, I was in my pajamas. "Aaron fucking Wish," I grumbled.

Penny lifted a brow. "He was working the bar tonight. What happened?"

"He tried to cut me off. A friend went and bought me a drink to circumvent him. He called a bouncer to throw me out."

Penny's mouth dropped open. "No way? How much had you had to drink?"

"Three."

"Pfft! That's nothing for you."

"I know," I sighed. "So, I walked myself out, then came home and thought I'd get a head start on next week's readings."

Sitting at the end of my bed, Penny considered me. "Aaron's not normally such a stick in the mud. Did you turn him down or something?"

Meeting her eyes, I looked at her like she was insane. "Do you really think I'd turn Aaron Wish down?"

Chuckling, Penny started shaking her head. "No. You've been crushing on him for years. You'd drop your knickers the first time he asked."

"And there you have it." Turning my attention back to my notes, I huffed in frustration. Penny was the only one who knew about my interest in Aaron. She'd thoroughly supported my obsession. He wasn't her taste, but she could appreciate how yummy he was.

"Okay. Well, you got Aaron's attention finally. Maybe he cut you off to get yours."

"He already had mine."

"Yeah, but you hide it pretty well."

"Too bad, he's pissed me off now. He might have finally cured me of him," I grumbled.

"Maybe that was his intention," Penny shrugged. "Night."

Surprised, I considered Penny's retreating form. "Night." Maybe that's what Aaron had hoped for by pissing me off. Sitting back, I stared at my notes, realizing the possibility of that statement.

Taking my phone off the desk, I searched through to find the entry for Lancelot. Without any hesitation, I deleted the contact. Turns out, his flavor cake wasn't to my taste after all.

Chapter Four

WAITING FOR CLASS TO START, I read over the notes I made from the readings in preparation for today's lecture. Professor Stilton had given up trying to get me to come closer to the front. While the academics knew me, they worked out, I didn't like them calling on me in class. In class, I sat up the back and listened. After class or during consulting hours, I discussed any questions I had with my academics.

There was still ten minutes until the lecture started. The other students were standing around, talking, or finding their seats. That's when someone walked up and loomed over the top of me. Looking up, I blinked in confusion while Aaron snatched my phone off the table. "What the..." I tried to grab my phone back.

"Did you delete my number?" Aaron asked.

Refusing to answer him, I glared at him.

"Unlock it." Aaron held my phone out to me.

Snatching it back, I shoved it under my leg. "Fuck off," I murmured and returned my attention to my notes.

"Did you delete my number?" Aaron growled.

"Yes." Glancing up, I ensured no one was overhearing this conversation. "I don't need a knight in shining armor."

Aaron huffed. "Don't be childish. Let me put my number back in, just in case." Standing with his hand outstretched, Aaron waited for me to be a good girl and hand him my phone.

"Go away, Aaron. I got the message last night. You're not interested. Fine. So, drop the chivalry act and piss off."

Keeping my eyes on my notes, I refused to look him in the eye. His eyes were my weakness, and even though I was still angry, I wasn't willing to risk it. In my peripheral vision, Aaron ground his jaw. Bending forward, Aaron snatched the pen out of my hand and wrote his number on the top of my lecture notes.

"Put it back in your phone, Caly," Aaron growled, dropping my pen again. "I don't want the guilt of something happening to you because you didn't call me when you could have." Walking off, Aaron made his way to his seat halfway to the front.

Picking up my pen, I drew a box around the phone number. As Professor Stilton entered, I caught Aaron watching me while he was talking to a classmate. Drawing another box below his digits, I colored it in, making it look like I was scrubbing out his phone number. When my eyes flicked up, Aaron stood arms folded across his muscular chest, strong jaw set in anger. The girl he was talking to stepped closer and put her hand on his bicep. She was batting her eyelashes so much Aaron must have thought one got stuck in her eye.

Shaking my head, I focused back on my notes. Whatever game Aaron was playing, I didn't have time. He wasn't short of female attention, so he could play with someone else. Plenty of women wanted a dominant, over-protective boyfriend. Especially, a boyfriend that looked like Aaron Wish.

Realizing I was doodling in the margins of my sheet, I groaned in frustration. Taking a moment to breathe deep, I shut Aaron Wish out of my head. When I opened my eyes, I refused to even look in Aaron's direction. Instead, I focused on Professor Stilton and his lecture.

After the lecture, I made my way to where my practical class would start in an hour and sat down to prepare. The body moved into my peripheral vision and sat next to me without asking permission. My eyes didn't need to confirm it was Aaron; I could feel him. Ignoring him, I continued to write little notes to myself in the margins of my page.

With a huff, Aaron stole the pen from my hand again. "We wouldn't work. Different sides of the river and all that."

Annoyed, I shut my notes. "Really? Because you came to school on this side of the river. You now live and work on this side of the river. I don't know much about you, but I'm pretty sure you intend to stay on this side of the river."

Bowing his head, Aaron caressed my pen. There was no other word for the way he stroked it, letting his fingers play over the casing. Swallowing the spit in my mouth, his fidgeting was distracting. My body very alert, as if his fingers were moving over me like that, I bit my lip.

"That's true. That still won't make us work, Caly."

Snatching my pen back, I gritted my teeth on my body's reaction to such a minor thing. "Work how, Aaron? I'm not interested in something long term. I don't do long term. I'm more about whatever works right now. As soon as it stops working, it stops."

"You're talking friends with benefits," Aaron frowned.

"No. I date. Occasionally, long enough to become physical, but that's few and far between."

Aaron's brows went up as he nodded. "Yeah, you said last night. Months since you've had sex, and you're horny."

The way he said it made me blush a little. If only he knew that he took my usual level of randiness and multiplied it by a factor of ten. Grabbing my chin, Aaron turned my face to his and placed a barely-there kiss on the corner of my mouth. My heartbeat skyrocketed at that restrained and straightforward intimacy. There and gone in a flash.

Opening my eyes, I watched Aaron pull away to squat in front of me so he could meet my eyes. "Thanks for the offer, Caly, but I'm not going to be another notch in your lipstick case. You want to bang a guy from across the river for kicks, I can give you Dwayne's number."

"That's not..." I tried to argue but swallowed at the look Aaron was giving me. So much hunger in his eyes, like he wanted to devour the world, with me included. Looking away, I shook my head. "He's not my type."

"What is your type?" Aaron asked, using my chin to bring my eyes back to him.

You! I dropped my gaze to his perfect lips. "Guys who like me for me. Not their expectations of me." Lifting my gaze back to Aaron's, I took a breath. "I don't like being told what I can't do."

The middle of Aaron's brow furrowed. Picking my phone up off the ground next to me, Aaron offered it to me. "Put my number back in your phone, please?"

Placing my hand on my phone, I grasped it, but I didn't try and take it back. "No, Aaron. I don't need a knight in shining armor. I'm quite capable of saving myself. Thank you." Refusing to back down, I eased my phone out of his grasp.

Letting my phone go, Aaron stood suddenly, grabbed his bag, and walked away. When our prac class started thirty minutes later, Aaron wasn't there. He came five minutes later and stayed well away from me.

"Michael?" I tapped on my boss's door. "Do you have a minute?"

Looking up from his computer, Michael checked his watch. "You're earlier than normal tonight."

"I wanted to make sure I caught you."

"Oh, no. You're not quitting, are you?" Michael sat back, waiting.

"God, no! I have, however, scored myself a holiday to Hawaii in a couple of months and wanted to apply for annual leave."

Michael's brow lifted. "How long are we talking?"

"Two weeks."

"Do you have two weeks of leave accrued?" Michael asked, opening his timekeeping system on his computer.

"I haven't taken any leave since I started this job, Michael. I have nearly four weeks accrued now."

"Oh." Frowning, Michael took a deep breath. "I have no reason to deny your leave, Caly. I'll have to find someone to cover you. I can use it as a trial for whoever we look at for replacing Sienna."

"Sienna is leaving?"

Michael nodded. "She's trying for a baby."

"Oh."

Michael sighed, "Unfortunately, right now, our purse strings are tight." Watching me, Michael tilted his head, and his expression cleared a little. "Is everything okay, Caly? You look a little put out by Sienna leaving."

"It's just... I was only talking to a third-year Nuclear Medicine student last week who was keen on a traineeship here. It seems serendipitous."

"You're suggesting we try this student in your position for the two weeks you are away. If they're a good fit, I can offer them a traineeship?"

Was I suggesting that? Despite Aaron rejecting me, I knew he needed a traineeship to graduate accredited. "It couldn't hurt. He's top of his classes and a hard worker."

"I thought you were top of your class?" Michael teased.

"I am, but he was always right on my heels. Now that we've both gone into our specializations, he gets to top the classes I'm not in. We are neck and neck in the one class we do together now."

Michael sat forward, both brows up. "You're impressed by the boy?"

What wasn't impressive about Aaron Wish? Looks aside, he'd worked his ass off to get out of Riverside. Knowing helping Aaron helped Josh, I shrugged. "I've seen him work hard to get to where he is. I tutor his younger brother, who is very much the same and hoping to get into medicine next year. Sadly, even with a scholarship, Josh probably still can't afford to do medicine. If Aaron can get accredited as a graduate, then he can help out with the uni costs. Then the hospital will benefit from two exceptional guys. Being born on the other side of the river shouldn't stop you from having the life you want."

Michael assessed me for a moment. With a loud exhale, he sat forward. "Okay." Pushing a notepad and pen across the desk, Michael nodded to it. "Give me his name and number, and I'll ask to meet him."

"So, I can have my leave?"

"Yes, Caly. Go hula your way through your winter break. Just make sure you come back healthy and not pregnant." My eyes widened, horrified. Michael lifted a shoulder and dropped it. "It's happened more times than I count."

"Okay..." Fishing my notebook out of my bag to find Aaron's number, I chewed my lip. "Can you not tell him I recommended him?" Michael lifted a brow at me. "He applied for my traineeship last year, and I don't want him to think I recommended him out of pity. He's good, he should believe he got this on his own merit."

Smiling, Michael took the pad and pen back from me. "Sure. Apply for your leave. I'll approve it before I finish up today."

"Thanks, Michael." With a smile, I turned to leave.

"Caly," Michael called me back. "You'll have to train him before you go. Any issues there I should be aware of?"

My smile dropped for a moment, thinking about having to work with Aaron after he rejected me. After a moment, I gave him a quiet smile. "No, Michael. There's no issue with this guy."

Quirking a single brow, Michael nodded before returning to his computer. "I'm leaving in twenty minutes, so best get logged in."

Chuckling, I went out to the office to log on and put in my leave. Twenty minutes later, Michael came out, closing his office and walking towards me as he put on his jacket.

"I've approved your leave and put in the business case for hiring a casual to cover your shifts. I've then followed that up by putting in a business case for another trainee to replace Sienna. She's a senior technologist, so the board will be happy to pay the lower wage instead. Once I get approval, I'll call your friend," Michael informed me.

"Friend might be a huge exaggeration, Michael."

"Caly, I remembered Aaron from the interviews last year. It was a close call between the two of you. I wanted to give the offer to Aaron. He was older, and this job would have benefited him more."

"Oh." My stomach dropped; my great boss, who I'd always enjoyed working for, hadn't wanted to hire me.

Michael put up his hand to encourage patience. "I've not regretted that the committee outvoted me, and I hired you, Caly. Nevermore so, then twenty minutes ago when you jumped on the opportunity to help not one, but two boys out."

Stepping closer, Michael dropped his voice. "I was born in Riverside and adopted when I was ten by a couple here in Eleri." Stepping back, Michael put his finger to his mouth, letting me know it was a secret. Then, he winked and left. Stunned, I sat there, blinking for a second. My name getting called snapped me free, and I spent the rest of the night too busy to give it a second thought.

"So..." Penny raised an eyebrow at me.

"So?" I asked, panting for breath.

"Um, you caned yourself out there." Penny pointed to the track where I'd just finished my morning run. "I've watched you run every morning since we started university. I've never seen you do sprints, and what was up with the stairs?" Her arm swung to point to the grandstand on the far side. When sprints hadn't zapped the energy from my body, I'd bolted up and down the steps.

Shielding my eyes from the sun, I gazed at the glass windows of the gym that overlooked the outdoor track and field. Penny told me Aaron worked out every morning, so I had no doubt he was there. "Sexually frustrated," I wheezed as I bent over to suck in a breath.

Penny started laughing. "Aaron's in the gym if you want to go hit him up."

Gasping, I shook my head. "No, he told me yesterday that

he's not into me." Picking up my water, I took large mouthfuls to help bring my breathing under control.

Mouth falling open, Penny checked me out and shook her head. "Nope, something wrong with that guy if he doesn't want to tap that."

It made me smile. "Doesn't matter. I'll have to work with Aaron soon, so it's for the best."

Taking a breath of exaggeration, Penny scanned the field. "Okay. So, it's Friday. You need a date." Her eyes focused on someone, and her grin exploded. "Perfect. Come with me."

Throwing her gym bag over her shoulder, Penny started to walk down the track. Pulling my jacket on, ready for my body temp to cool, I followed her. Sashaying up to where a few of the jocks were stretching after their warm-up run, Penny smiled. I probably should've been doing that too.

"Morning, boys." Jocks were Penny's type. Frankly, I think it's why she became a cheerleader. Simon stood up out of the huddle and came over to kiss her.

Deciding to take the opportunity, I started stretching. After a few whispers and a lot more snogging, Simon went back to his huddle. Penny came to stand by me while I finished my stretches. "Any of them catch your interest?"

Okay, a scouting mission. Looking the guys over, I shook my head. "You know I don't do jocks."

Penny rolled her eyes. "You're impossible. I'm heading back for a shower. You coming?"

"Yeah, but I get the shower first. You take forever," I teased as we started walking.

"I take the appropriate length of time for a female with style and poise to make herself presentable."

Walking around the corner of the sports center, we passed

the entrance to the swim facility to get to the path back to the dorms.

"You take two hours if you have to wash and straighten your hair."

"Says the girl whose hair hasn't seen a hairdresser in the past six months," Penny snickered.

"They always want me to...ugh..." My breath rushed out of me as I was crash-tackled to the ground.

As we passed the entrance to the swimming pools, a guy running crashed straight into me. Sprawled face down, under him, on the pavement, I struggled to breathe.

"Shit!" The guy grunted on top of me. "I'm sorry." He quickly climbed up to standing and put out his hand to help me.

"You brute!" Punching the guy in the arm, Penny then shoved him away from me. "What the hell were you thinking?" Offering me her hand, Penny hauled my ass up. While she glared at my assailant, I assessed the pavement burn on the palm of my hands.

"I am truly, really sorry. I wasn't looking..."

"That was obvious," Penny scolded.

"I'd just finished my morning swim and got a message one of my programs was working." The guy showed us his phone as if to prove it. "I've been trying to get this to work for weeks."

When I attempted to move, I hissed as pain shot through the front of my hip. Touching my hand there, I felt the dampness. Cringing, I shifted the waistband of my leggings to see the bleeding graze and bruise bloom on my hip. The pavement burn was covering the bony protuberance of my pelvis. "Farkkk!" I cursed under my breath.

"Oh my god! Look what you did to her." Penny punched the guy in the arm again.

Cringing a little, he rubbed where she'd punched him

twice now, but dropped down to look at the damage. "I'm sorry, it's more plasma than blood, so nothing to get too stressed over."

"Nothing to get stressed over, you say? That will scar, won't it? You've scared her," Penny was haranguing the guy.

Looking down at the top of his dark hair, I met his brown eyes and tilted my head intrigued. Taking my hips in his hands, he screwed up one side of his face. "This might sting a little, but it will help," he warned right before he blew - with his mouth - across the seeping wound.

"Oh, Jesus!" Grabbing hold of his broad shoulders, I leaned on him for support. Yeah, it stung, but it did something else entirely to my nether regions.

Lifting his face, the guy gave me a quiet smile as he stood up, keeping his hands on my hips to support me. "Did that help?"

"Ah, yeah. It kind of did." It took my mind off the hurt is what it did.

"I'm Brad Meadows." His smile grew a little bigger.

"Caly Zilla."

"Let me buy you breakfast to say sorry?"

"You have a program to check on," I reminded him.

Brad's eyes widened in horror before he glanced at his phone. "Shit. Um, I have to go." Stepping backward, Brad grabbed up his gym bag. "Again, I'm sorry. You live on res, right?"

"Block H," I answered with a small smile.

Nodding, Brad ran off towards the university. He was a quick runner. Stepping up next to me as we both watched him run across the road towards the main campus, Penny chuckled. "Pretty hot!"

Confused by the change in subject, I frowned. "It's freezing this morning." Giving me a sly smile, Penny looked back at the retreating physique of Brad Meadows. "Oh. Yeah. He was, wasn't he."

Penny just kept on smiling as we started walking, albeit a little slower, back to our dorm. "He's no Aaron Wish, but he could take your mind off that wishbone of his."

"Penny...!"

In the shower, I hissed at the sting of water on my pavement burn. Searching our at home first aid kit, I failed to find anything to help. Giving up, I got dressed and took my laptop out to the kitchen to eat breakfast.

Sitting at the small table, I read through some of the comments on my blog site. They were kind of standard. Some guys were telling me to date them. A few girls were saying how they've experienced a similar thing. A few men telling me my blog was sexist and offensive and called me a whore. The other readers usually told them where they could shove it, so I never bothered responding.

The only comments that caught my attention were by 'Sin Rocks' and 'The Watcher.' Usually, these two were in complete agreement. In the comments for my post on Lancelot, they disagreed for the first time ever.

Sin Rocks: *Ditch. Lancelot. Now!*

The Watcher: *I disagree with you, Sin. What she has with Lancelot is obviously very intense. You can't walk away from that sort of connection without a whole lifetime of regret. I'm curious though, Nymph, why, if it is this intense between you two, that you keep seeing other people?*

Sin Rocks: *TW I would say Lancelot is unable to make her his priority. It sounds like he finds her only when he wants her. If that is the case, ditch him, Nymph. You deserve someone who will worship the ground you walk on.*

Sighing, I replied to the comments.

Nymph: It's not that Lancelot is using me, nor me him. It is the fact that it's never been the right time for us, or maybe, it's because we are both terrified of getting hurt. We know what we want in life and aren't afraid of going out there and getting it. But when it comes to each other, the exact opposite is true. It's frustrating, but a part of who we are.

As for your question TW, about why we still see other people? The answer is simple. It's lonely to sit at home waiting for the person you want to find the bravery to take a chance on you. When it came down to it, I couldn't tell him I wanted something serious either. I've never had a man in my life for any length of time, so I'm not sure how relationships work. It's a foreign concept for me.

Taking my bowl to the sink, I washed it up. When I came back to check my email, I already had a reply to my comment.

The Watcher: I understand, Nymph. I grew up in a single-parent family, and there was no one for my remaining parent after the other passed away. I have an idea of how relationships work, but not a working reference. In saying that, I've reached that point in my life where I want to try it. Maybe, it's time you should too.

Smiling at the answer, I decided not to comment further. Instead, I closed my blog and checked my emails. The fact was, it didn't matter now, did it? Aaron had made it clear yesterday he wasn't interested. So, the potential for anything happening there didn't exist anymore. Of course, I couldn't say that on the blog now. Aaron read the blog, and he'd have to be stupid to miss the timing. With a sigh, I packed up my gear and headed to the library.

With my reduced load, I'd managed to secure two days a week of no classes where I could focus on study. Today, Friday, was one of those days. When I got home late in the afternoon, there was a small package and card at my dorm room door. Picking it up, I noted my name misspelled on the envelope.

Stepping inside, I dumped my bag and opened the package. Inside was an apology card and a tube of antibacterial healing cream.

Dear Kaly,

Terribly sorry for being such a klutz this morning. Let me make it up to you with dinner tonight? The cream should help prevent scarring.

Again, I'm very sorry.

Brad

With his phone number scribed underneath, there was no missing that he was keen for a chance to make it up to me. Flattered by the gesture, I picked up my phone and texted him, making sure to correct his spelling of my name.

Me: *Busy this week. Next Friday? Caly*

My phone pinged half a minute later.

Brad Meadows: *I'll pick you up at six. Dress casual.*

Maybe, getting swept off my feet this morning was serendipitous.

Chapter Five

"He's getting frustrated." Penny chuckled.

"I don't care." Keeping my back to the bar, I'd made sure I'd gone to the furthest end of the bar from Aaron tonight. It'd been a week since he got me thrown out before he accused me of only going after him to slum it. Not that I was harping on his rejection, but the distance between us was for the best.

Penny was loving it. "He's now looking at you between every customer."

Rolling my eyes, I took another mouthful of my drink. The first hour I was at the bar, I'd watched Aaron move around behind the bar. It's not like I was the only girl admiring the way the tight shirt of the uniform showed off his gym earned body. Yes, he'd rejected me. But that didn't stop me from getting myself off on the thought of what could have happened in his car the other week.

An hour ago, Aaron came down this end to grab something while Penny had been there purchasing her drink. On spotting her, Aaron followed Penny moving through the crowd to find me. At that point, I'd turned my back away from the bar and stayed that way.

"Some of the guys are up the front near the band," Simon yelled to us. "Coming?"

"Okay," Penny smiled, slipping her hand into his.

The last thing I wanted to do was hang out with Simon's friends. They usually spent the night trying to cop a feel. "Julianne is over the other side. I'm going to say hi."

Giving me a thumbs up, Penny disappeared into the crowd.

At the bar, I ordered a fresh drink. When Aaron looked down at me, I smiled, took my bottle, and made my way to where Julianne encamped with her friends. "They let you back in?" She smiled.

"Yep. Probably having my drinks counted again, though, so I'm pacing myself."

Looking towards the bar, Julianne laughed. "Yeah, that's more than likely the case."

For the next hour, I hung out with Julianne and her friends until they decided to head into town to go dancing at a club. Declining the invitation to join them, I went to the bar to get my last drink for the evening and find Penny.

Cutting through the crowd, I made sure I went to the far end from where Aaron was serving. While I waited, Aaron glanced over to where I was standing with the girls moments before. When his head lifted to try and see where I went, I pursed my lips, trying not to laugh.

"Caly," a male voice remarked surprised.

Turning to my right, I found a familiar face standing there, waiting for his order. "Brad. Hey."

"You here with friends?" He asked.

"Yeah, they're up in front of the band. It's not that good a band."

"They suck, actually." Brad gave me a broad smile. "My group is out on the deck if you want to join us?"

Lifting my brows in surprise of his offer, I smiled. "I'm sort of shy around strangers. Thanks for the offer, though."

Taking his bottle of beer from the bar, Brad looked out at his friends then back to me. "I could hang in here with you for a while if you want the company?" It was an absolute sincere offer.

"That sounds good."

"Bottle of Jack?" The bartender asked with a smile. Nodding, he fetched it for me.

"Hitting the hard stuff tonight?" Brad asked, looking at my drink as I took it from the bar.

"No, this is my usual drink."

Looking impressed, Brad traveled his eyes down my body to my hip. "How's the graze?"

"Better, thanks. That cream worked a treat. Do you want a look?"

Brad's eyebrows jumped. "Ah, yeah."

Turning to face him, I lifted my top to my midriff then tugged the band of my jeans down on that side. Bending down, Brad put his face close again. Taking my hips in his hand, he checked out the scabbed-over and mottled flesh.

"It's worse than I thought it was. It must have bruised pretty bad to be that color still." Before I could respond, Brad blew across it again. Sucking in a breath as my eyes closed, I bit my lip and lifted my face a little at the sensation.

Opening my eyes, I locked on Aaron's sapphire blues, watching. He appeared less than impressed, and I wasn't sure if that was at the injury or Brad blowing me.

Standing straight in front of me a moment later, Brad

blocked Aaron from sight. "You've let me blow on you twice now in a week." A wicked smile was filling his face.

Smacking his arm, I laughed. "I bet you told all your friends that."

"I did. I told my mates I saw a beautiful girl and crash-tackled her to the ground. They were all very impressed." Lifting his beer to his lips, Brad took a mouthful, his eyes drinking me in.

"So...Friday?" My body heated under that gaze.

"Yes, Friday." He grinned. "Do you have a curfew?" Brad asked with a slight tease.

"I do. I work the early shift on weekends, so I like to be in bed by twelve at the latest." Chuckling, Brad shook his head as if scolding himself. "What?" I asked with a grin.

"You said you like to be in bed by twelve, not asleep," Brad grinned. "I read into it a little bit."

My smile grew. Brad was a naughty one. It usually took me a while to warm up to guys, but I liked Brad already. "So, what are you studying?"

"Software engineering. I'm doing my Ph.D.," he informed me. When we met, I'd guessed he was several years older than me, and I'd been right. "How about you?"

"Diagnostic Radiology," I revealed. Brad's brows lifted. "So, you're an engineer? I hear you guys party pretty hard."

Brad's eyes sparkled. "I've heard you medicine types party as hard as you study as well."

Instead of answering each other's questions, we stood there, smiling at each other. A moment later, Brad stepped forward and cuffed my neck in his hand. Using his thumb to lift my face, Brad pressed his mouth against mine. He nipped my lips, slow and gentle, but with absolute confidence that I'd wanted him to kiss me.

My stomach flipped, nerves lighting up all the way to my toes. It was a perfect first kiss. Withdrawing, Brad smiled down at me for a second, his eyes glassy, and pupils dilated. Holding my gaze, he removed his hand and retreated a step.

"What was that for?" I breathed, still intoxicated with the lust burning through my bloodstream. That kiss was everything I always thought kissing Aaron would be.

"First kisses are always awkward. I figured it was best to get it out of the way." His eyes lit up as he leaned forward until his mouth was at my ear. "Plus, it doesn't seem right to have blown on you twice and never have kissed you. Very ungentlemanly to behave that way."

I couldn't help the devilish smile I gave him when he stood straight again. Brushing his knuckles across my jaw, Brad chuckled. "There she is."

"Who?" I asked, but I could guess what he meant because I know what I imagined when he looked at me.

"The naughty Caly," he murmured. He looked at the beer in his hand with a sigh. "I might be a little too far gone to behave with you tonight. So, to save the embarrassment of trying for more than I should right now, I'm going to join my friends again. I look forward to seeing you on Friday when I'm sober and can be a gentleman."

"You're a gentleman now," I countered.

Brad's smile grew, his eyes holding the glassy inebriated look. "Yes, and I'm going to leave now before Mr. Hyde gets control because he does love how you gasp when I blow on you, Caly." Knowing how much I loved how I felt when he breathed on me, I bit my lip. Letting loose a small growl, Brad leaned down and kissed right where I was chewing my lip. It was a quick kiss, but enough to make me release my hold on it. Stepping as if to move past me, Brad placed another kiss right in front of my ear. "I'm a good guy, but I'm also a bit of a demon. Don't say I didn't warn you."

Something hard and cold pressed against my breast, right where my nipple was. With widening eyes, I gasped. My nipple hardened and fired electric impulses straight to my pleasure center.

Blinking down, I saw Brad was holding his beer bottle right against my breast. Looking up, I wasn't able to hide the lust glazing my eyes from Brad's sharp gaze. He'd done it on purpose to see what I'd do. The decent thing would have been to knock the bottle away and scold him. Instead, I enjoyed it.

The growl under his breath told me my response thrilled Brad. Shoulders pulling tight, Brad walked for the door to the decked area. Taking a deep breath, I finished off my drink and stepped forward to put the empty bottle on the counter.

Standing on the other side was Aaron. His eyes were narrow, his lips thin and pursed. With that one look, Aaron managed to dampen my high.

Part of me wanted to reach across the bar and see if Aaron's kiss had the same effect. To know if it was as good as I always imagined. But I couldn't, not after he'd made his position on us clear. "Night," I muttered as I went to step away.

Grabbing my wrist, Aaron stopped me as I turned to go. Looking back at him, I blinked and tilted my head. Aaron's eyes were on my hip. Glancing down, I realized some of the bruised skin was still visible. Inhaling, I shifted my shirt to cover it. "It's nothing. I got knocked over by someone not looking where they were going and landed wrong."

When Aaron's eyes drifted to my chest, I didn't have to look to know what caught his attention. My nipples were still hard from what Brad had done with his bottle.

"Be safe, Caly," Aaron finally warned. Letting go of my wrist, he took my empty bottle and went back to his job without another look in my direction.

Blinking in confusion, I fought my way through the crowd to Penny and let her know I was calling it a night. Walking across campus to get to the dorms, I pondered the emotions on Aaron's face when I left. Still confused when I got home, I showered and crawled into bed.

Even though I tried not to, the feel of Aaron's hand on my wrist, and his look of concern and anger stayed with me. So, it was Aaron Wish's eyes that made my back arch when I released my pent-up frustration.

Opening the door, I smiled up at Brad. "I'll just grab my jacket," I told him as I stepped back inside. Catching the door, Brad stepped inside our small apartment. "Cozy." He smiled, looking at the shared kitchen, meals, and lounge area. "I thought the residences on the hill were the fancy lodgings."

"It's only a two bedder, so it's enough for Penny and me. The six-bedroom places have larger living areas." Tilting my head, I studied Brad. "You live in the dorms on the lower side of the car park?"

Smirking as if he'd been waiting for me to call it the poor man's side of res, Brad nodded. "I live in Kings Hall, and, before you ask, yes, I grew up in Riverside."

"Scholarship?" I asked as I threw my iPad in my handbag.

"Partial." Stepping forward, Brad took my handbag off my shoulder as he looked over my jeans and V-neck sweater. "You're not going to need this. You'll just need a jacket, your keys, and shoes you can walk over grass in," he advised staring down at my heels.

"Oh. Okay." The directions about what to wear tonight left

me wondering what we would be doing. Taking my bag, I tossed it in my room before pulling a pair of flats out of the wardrobe. When I turned around, Brad was holding up my door frame, scanning my room. Sitting on my bed, I kicked my heels into my closet before slipping the flats on.

Stepping into my room, Brad walked to the shelf above my desk and appraised the photos. "Is this your mum?"

Glancing over, I watched him take down a photo of my mum and me at my high school graduation. "Yeah."

"She's hot!" Brad's brows were high on his forehead.

"I can give you her number if you'd prefer to take her out?" I teased.

Brad smirked. "Nah, I'm into brunettes. Just expected you to look like your mum, I guess."

"I do, but I have my dad's coloring." Standing up, I closed my wardrobe.

Assessing the frames on the shelf, Brad put the photo he held back. "No pictures of dad up here?"

"No, dad. I mean, I have one, but he was gone before I graced the world with my presence."

Brad frowned. "But you're not on scholarship?"

Shaking my head, I tried not to laugh. "You didn't catch my surname when we met, did you?"

"Caly Zilla," Brad repeated, not getting it. When I raised an eyebrow at Brad, his face cleared, and his mouth fell open. "Wait, as in the Zilla building? You're from that Zilla family?"

The Zilla building was a gigantic monument to architecture right on the banks of the Eleri river. The way it loomed over the city of Eleri made it kind of hard to miss. The university had an extensive science research laboratory named after my mother too. With the money my mother donated to science research at the university, I was royalty in the Dean's eyes.

"I'm a crossbreed. My mum is an Eleri girl, and my dad was a Riverside boy."

"Jesus! Your family could buy Riverside, smash it to the ground, and rebuild new suburbia if they wanted too." Brad shook his head.

My grandparents were very well-off, so the combined wealth of my elders could do precisely that.

"Your mother got knocked up while slumming it?" Brad asked without judgment. It was almost a hopeful question, and I knew why. Rape statistics in Riverside were pretty high.

"No. My mum loved my dad. They were together on and off for years. She was in her late twenties when she found out she was pregnant with me."

Studying me, Brad turned the rest of his body to face me. "Guess we are the same then." Reaching out his hand, Brad caressed my cheek. "My dad is Riverside; my mum wasn't."

"Wasn't?" I asked, already knowing the answer.

"Victim of a shooting when I was ten." Brad met my eyes. "Dads up to his third wife. My older brother, Terry, his mother was a Riverside girl. She died when Terry was six. Now, dad's married to a girl the same age as Terry, but he's made sure there will be no more children."

"So, if she does get pregnant, she will have a lot of explaining to do?"

"Yeah. Don't want to be there for that talk." Brad moved closer to me. "You told me about your dad, so I wouldn't feel uncomfortable with you after revealing where I was from, didn't you?"

"It doesn't bother me where you're from, Brad. It matters who you are and where you are now."

Brad leaned closer to my lips. "I'm in your room right now," he murmured as his arms snaked around my waist and pulled me against him. Staring into each other's eyes, I watched his mouth moved towards mine.

Jerking back, but not away, I put my hands on his chest to keep the distance. "Hello, Mr. Hyde. I've got bad news for you. I'm a three-date minimum girl."

Grinning wide, Brad still held me to him. "Three dates until sex, or three dates until anything naughty?"

"The later." Squirming in his hold, I could feel his hardness growing against my abdomen. "I like to know a guy a little bit before the fun stuff starts. In my experience, once sex happens, the talking tends to die off."

"I respect that." Brad started dropping kisses along my jaw. "I also find it hard to keep my hands off you, Caly. Do you have some sort of aphrodisiac perfume on or something? I'm usually a lot better behaved than this."

Breathing was a little hard as Brad's mouth left a wet trail down my neck. "Yes. It's called we're alone in my bedroom, and you're taking advantage."

Straightening himself, Brad looked down on me. "Hmmm, yes. The location may be affecting me. We should go." Withdrawing his palms from my back, Brad took my hand in his. "I hope you don't mind staying on campus tonight?"

Intrigued, I raised a brow in his direction. "As long as it isn't in your bedroom, I think I can cope."

Brad wiggled his eyebrows. "Don't give me ideas. Let's go."

Across campus where the physics buildings were, stood the planetarium on a hill. Lifting an eyebrow at Brad as we went inside, I said nothing else. Sitting down, I got comfortable. Pulling a blanket out of his bag, he draped it over our laps, then we enjoyed the presentation in quiet. It was like going to the movies, except with stars of the astronomy kind.

"As a boy, I spent a lot of time staring up at the sky," Brad murmured to me. "We spend all this time looking for fun and entertainment, yet, we rarely ever look above us. Every night, the universe puts a show on for us. It's beautiful, and it's never the same twice."

Enjoying looking at his profile as he watched the sky, I smiled. He turned his face when I didn't reply. "You should have saved this for the third date. You definitely would have been getting lucky tonight."

Brad blushed a little. "They only do this once a month. While I'm not expecting you to put out straight away, I was kind of optimistic, to not have to wait a month either."

"Hmmm," I considered. "Usually, that admission would have landed you zero chance of scoring with me. But I get the impression it's been a while for you. So, I'm going to take your comment as you just being a sincere guy."

Brad's eyebrows jumped in amusement. "Why do you think it's been a while for me?"

"How quick you get hard around me," I countered.

Blushing again, Brad tried to keep a straight face, but his lips split at the start of a grin. "That's because you are an attractive woman, Caly."

"A huh," I dismissed his excuse. "How long has it been, Brad?"

"For sex?" I nodded. "About four months. I've been too focused on my research since I started my Ph.D. to bother seeking it out. I still wouldn't have bothered, except, I met you."

"Crash-tackled me," I argued.

Smirking, Brad gave me a cheeky shrug. "Serendipitous. The universe thought it was a good time for us to meet." Brad turned his eyes back to the stars. "Which begs the question. Why are you single, Caly?"

Groaning, I glared at the sky. I hated that question. "Oh, I've been dating. Sadly, I keep getting guys who are more interested in getting in my pussy, rather than getting in my head. One-night stands aren't my thing, and even if they were, most of those guys wouldn't interest me."

When Brad burst out laughing, several people around us turned to glare at him. He looked at me, the humor showing in his eyes. "I'm sorry. I wasn't laughing at the jerks you've dated. You said pussy in reference to your snatch, like you would talk about the weather. I've never heard a woman own the word pussy like that before."

Smirking, I leaned into his ear. "I am also quite comfortable with the words, cock, cunt, and fuck," I whispered before sucking his earlobe. Brad let out an audible moan, and those same people turned to look at us again, making me chuckle. "Just not yet." Withdrawing to a safe distance, I kept my attention on the man beside me.

Brad turned his face to look at me; his eyes were pure and primal. "You're not like any girl I've ever dated before."

Meeting that look, I let my smile fall off my face. "I'm hoping you're not like the guys I've dated before."

Reaching out, Brad caressed my cheek. "I like you, Caly. Your beauty got my attention, but it was the way you handled our collision that made me ask you out," Brad admitted. "I've dated a fair bit at uni. It always seemed to be two kinds of girls. The prudes, who would have smacked my face for doing what I did at the bar two nights ago. They are so uptight about guys using them, that they shut down their sexuality to the point of being nuns. The other kind... well, they would have suggested we find somewhere quiet. Those girls don't own their sexuality; they give it away to boost their self-confidence."

"Yeah, but you wouldn't turn her down, either," I challenged.

"I said I was a gentleman, not a saint."

"You said you were a bit of a demon, too," I reminded him. "So, why should I trust you?"

Brad smirked. "A smart girl doesn't trust a man's words. She trusts her instincts and his actions."

"So, I should trust you are honorable because you played the gentleman card on Wednesday?"

Brad shook his head. "My intentions are not honorable, Caly, but I do want to get to know you. Either of the two types of girls I just described would have reacted like your friend at the gym. You weren't angry with me for hurting you. You weren't concerned with the physical outcome, other than you being in pain. You looked at me intrigued, not with hate or interest. I've never had a girl look at me like that before. Then, when I blew across the wound to fire your nerve receptors and help minimize the pain for you, I thought you were going to..."

"Don't say it," I cut in, feeling myself heat all over. "It distracted me from the pain, so you reached your goal."

Stroking his thumb across the line of my collarbone, Brad smiled. "Well, the thing about me is when I reach a goal, all I do is set new goals higher."

"In this case, you mean lower," I whispered, but I couldn't smile, not with the intensity of his gaze.

"No, Caly," Brad scolded. Reaching across my waist to the far side, Brad firmed his grip before pulling me up against his side. "Your pussy isn't enough. I want all of you."

"You're freaking me out now," I breathed as his face came close to mine.

"Good. Because the way I react to you is starting to freak me out too."

"Not that," I breathed, anchoring my hand on his chest to push myself away and get a little distance. "I'm kind of a commitment-phobe. You want to see me disappear really quick, start talking marriage and babies."

Cocking his head as if trying to solve a puzzle, Brad didn't seem offended or put out. "So, you don't do one-night stands. You have a three-date rule, which would make most guys think you want a relationship, but you don't want a commitment?" Brad chuckled. "That's sort of a massive contradiction, Caly."

"It's not that I start dating a guy already determining the length of time we'll see each other. But I also don't start planning permanency either. I take it as it happens."

"What's your longest relationship?" Brad asked, withdrawing a little. It was like my confession had cooled his interest in me.

"The longest I've dated someone is three months. Give or take a week."

Brad's eyes squinted at me from beneath concerned brows. "How many times have you dated someone for more than a month?"

Glaring at him, I cocked a brow. "Are you asking how many guys I've slept with?"

Brad's brows jumped. "God, no. I'm asking how many have even gotten a third date to try and sleep with you?"

"Two," I answered with a sigh. "Two guys have made it to the third date, and the second shouldn't have."

Puffing out his chest, Brad looked like someone asked him to run for president. "So, only one guy has ever tempted you to try something long term before?" When I nodded, Brad's shoulders dropped.

"Have I ruined this before we even finished our first date?" I asked, hoping to god I hadn't. "I've never told a guy my history before. For some reason, I felt the need to be honest with you."

"Ruined it? No. You've told me that the bar is a little bit higher than I'd thought." Withdrawing, Brad gave me my space.

"I kind of feel special now. If anything, I'm even more determined to win you over." Standing up, Brad took the blanket with him and folded it. "Come on. A date requires eating together. Let's go to The View bar and get some dinner."

Smiling, I took his offered hand to help me stand. The View was the more relaxed bar on campus. It was in the main building and one of the two that still served food after three in the afternoon. The food wasn't exceptional. Nachos, chips, burgers. It was greasy but yummy. In my mind, it was a kind of perfect first date food.

Over the next couple of hours, we talked about a lot of things. Our career aspirations, experiences at university, and some of the academics we've encountered. Then Brad told me all about his research project.

At ten, Brad walked me home. All the way to the door to my building. "Before I ask if I can kiss you goodnight, when can I see you again?" Brad asked, taking my waist in his strong hands.

"Next Friday?"

Brad's face dropped. "I have to wait for a whole week? What are you doing tomorrow night?"

"Dinner with the family. My grandparents book my mother once a month. Otherwise, they'd never get to see her."

"Do you ever get to see her?"

"Yes, of course. We meet up whenever work brings mum to town, and she gets the time out from being a boss."

"What about next Wednesday at The Tower again? My friends and I hang there regularly."

Deciding not to play too easy, I smiled. "Wednesday's I'm always at The Tower, but to be clear, that won't count as a date, and I'm not ready to meet your friends yet."

Grinning, Brad moved closer. "So, we can talk a little bit, maybe you'll let me inspect your injury and blow on you again?"

Snickering, I shoved his shoulder. "Yes. I might even let you kiss me again. Just in passing, of course."

"Of course." Giving me a mocking smile, Brad pulled me against him. He brushed his mouth across mine. "In passing." His lips pinched mine, once, twice, and then he kissed me.

Melting into him, I wrapped my arms around his neck, lifting up on my toes to get a little bit more out of the kiss. Brad moaned as my body rubbed against a rather hard part of his. Shifting his hands to my butt, Brad gripped me through my jeans, grinding my pelvis hard against his. When I soughed into his mouth, Brad growled and pulled away. "Fuck, Caly."

Stepping back a few meters, Brad shifted awkwardly around the large bulge in his jeans. "Okay, so I need to leave right now. I'll find you Wednesday, and I'll let you know what time I'll see you Friday," he informed, backing away.

I struggled not to laugh. "Are you okay?"

"I'll be fine after a cold shower." Peering down, Brad then looked me over. "Maybe two."

"Taking care of yourself would be a lot more satisfying. I plan to," I suggested, having to fight hard against laughing, but I couldn't hide my amusement when Brad's eyes lit up.

Brad stopped backing away. "You did not just admit to planning to masturbate when you get upstairs?"

Tapping my finger to my lips, I tilted my head. "I did actually."

Brad looked pained. "You need to go inside now. I am trying hard to behave, and you are doing everything to give Mr. Hyde the power."

"My sympathies, but guys aren't the only ones who get riled up, you know." Turning, I unlocked the door, smiling over my shoulder at him. "Good night, Dr. Jee-kyll," I made sure to pronounce the name correctly. "Thank you for a lovely evening." Stepping inside, I closed the glass door, already knowing what I'd see when I looked up.

Brad had moved forward and was looking at me through the glass. "You've seen the Frederic March adaption of the book?" When I nodded, Brad breathed out hard. "You are damn lucky there is a locked glass door between us right now, Caly."

Smiling, I blew him a kiss. "Good night, Dr. Jekyll," I once again pronounced it correctly, then moved to the stairs. At the landing, I turned and saw Brad watching me, pure primal lust shining in his eyes. Forty minutes later, that look made me climax. Twice."

Chapter Six

B*LOW*

Sometimes you meet people in interesting ways. This guy bowled me over in a way I could never have expected. By the time he asked me on a date, there was no chance I could say no, and it was so worth it. He's down to earth, but he lifts you up into the stars and shows you the world from a different perspective. I like the view from here.

Of course, there is the perpetual fear he might let go of my hand, and I'd plummet to earth with nothing to break my fall. Could he be worth the risk? He's so different from the guys I've dated before. Maybe, he will last longer than a month. We'll see.

Nymph

Sin Rocks: *Hopefully, Blow will treat you like the princess you are.*

The Watcher: *There's a pattern in your dating. I'm beginning to think it's not the guys that are the problem, but you, Nymph. You ditched the professor when things started to get serious between you. Last week, you couldn't tell Lancelot that you wanted something serious. But this week you're on about floating in the stars with a guy you* *only just met. If you couldn't tell the Prof. or Lancelot how you feel, what makes you think you will do any better with any new guy?*

The Penny Drops: *TW, it's a combination. Nymph can't tell Lancelot how she feels because he's not ready to hear it. When she tried to take that step, he shut her down before she could be honest. Blow might be the one to make it work because he will hear it. Even if he doesn't, he might be worth the ride and try. She's still young. There's plenty of time to get serious later.*

Sin Rocks: *I like the way you think TPD.*

Nymph: *You are all right, in some ways. There's only one way to find out.*

My laptop screen shut in front of me. Blinking my eyes up, I found Penny peering down on me. "Forget what some stranger says on there. Come on; it's time to go." She walked off to grab her bag.

With a sigh, I grabbed my handbag before following her to the door. "I'm staying at Simon's tonight," Penny told me as we skipped down the steps to the dorm car park. "There's a party at their place to celebrate the game today."

"Enjoy." I kissed her cheek before she walked to where Simon's car was waiting for her. Turning the other way, I moved to my cousin's Maserati GranTurismo MC Sportline. Leaning against the side of his twenty-first birthday present, Kingsley looked dashing.

Tall, fit, and ash blonde like the rest of the Zillas', Kingsley held his phone to his ear. "...all well and good, Babe, but crying isn't going to work on me. Look, my date for the night has just walked up..." Moving the phone away from his ear and the foul names she was screaming at him, Kingsley laughed.

"Another one of your charming girlfriends?" I asked as I walked up and kissed his cheek.

Rolling his eyes at me, Kingsley put the phone back to his

ear. "Babe, it was nice knowing you." He hung up the phone. "Why are chicks so fucking clingy? You enjoy a couple of nights having amazing sex, and then they start talking about weddings and babies."

"You're generalizing," I warned him.

"You know what I mean." Opening my door for me, Kingsley stepped back. "The reason you're my favorite cousin is that you don't act like a normal chick. That, and the only reason I haven't boned you is that you're my first cousin."

"Charming!" I rolled my eyes.

"Please, you so would have spread those sweet pins of yours for me if we weren't blood."

Observing Kingsley, I leaned on the door, so it was between us. "Fighting with mum or dad this week, King?" I asked, getting his stir shit mood.

He'd been the same ever since we were kids. If his parents pissed him off, he would try and piss everyone else off and start a fight. He never felt he could stand up to his parents, but he could tell everyone else where to go.

"Granddad. He wants me to intern at Zilla Industries here, but I want the Switzerland office. He says I'll screw my way around the Swiss women and not focus on learning the family business."

"He's right," I challenged.

"It's bullshit!"

Not arguing, I raised a brow at him. Kingsley's face softened a little, then a smirk crept its way over his face.

"Yeah, he's right," Kingsley finally exhaled. "But, if I intern at the Zurich office, I get six months' experience that's worth twelve, and you know it."

"Plus, since mum runs the Zurich office, you get to work

with her. That's a lot more appealing than your father looking over your shoulder the whole time."

Kingsley rolled his eyes. "You are too smart for that hot fucking body of yours, Calypso. Get your ass in the car."

With a smile, I sunk into the luxury sports car. Shutting the door for me, Kingsley walked around to the driver's seat while I strapped myself in. Looking out the window, I saw Aaron across the car park, about to hop into his car. Our eyes met for a moment, then Kingsley was in the car with me, and the engine purred to life.

Heavy metal music blared out of the stereo. "Is that Aaron Wish?" Noticing who I was looking at, Kingsley startled me into focusing on him instead. Kingsley had been the year ahead of Aaron, so they'd probably known each other.

"Yeah." I relaxed back into the seat.

Kingsley peered at me. "You slumming it, Princess?"

"Get off it, King. He went to school with us," I scolded. "Stop being a snob."

Reaching over, my cousin brushed my cheek with the back of his fingers. "He's still a Riverside gang banger, Princess. He hangs with Rockford's enforcers."

Rockford was one of the two ruling bodies of Riverside. He'd done a lot to clean up the streets, to give the people of Riverside better options and services. While his motives were sound, his way of getting the job done hadn't been, and everyone knew it. The problem was he was up against Timothy Meadows, the Godfather of Riverside. He was your leading drug runner, gun runner, and just an asshole in general, from what I heard.

"Aaron also hangs with some of the jocks here, though he isn't one," I defended. "He has a varied group of friends."

Kingsley's grip on my jaw made me wince. "I love you,

Princess. You are probably the only woman to whom I'm ever going to say those words. I'm not going to let you fuck up your life on a gang banger. If I find out Wish becomes something more than a way for you to get off, I'll nail his testicles to the wall and make you watch while I feed him to my father's dogs."

Snatching my jaw from my cousin's grip, I glared at him. "You sound more like a gang banger than he does, King."

With a sigh, Kingsley turned his focus to the road and put his car into gear. "I'm a prick, Princess. You know that. Everyone knows that. But I'm the prick who loves you, and I'll do what I need to, to protect you. Even if it's from yourself."

"Mums wrong," I grumbled. "My commitment issues have nothing to do with not having a father but having you as the only male that I'm close with."

"You're close with granddad," Kingsley countered with a smile.

Rolling my eyes to the window, I watched the scenery blur past us as we sped out of the university. "Another misogynist who has started threatening to arrange a decent marriage for me."

"Still, you're granddad's favorite." Kingsley's eyes lit up. "You could sway him to send me to Switzerland."

Glaring at my cousin, I looked at his car as a thought occurred to me. "Sure, but I get your ride while you are there." I stuck out my hand. "Deal?"

Glaring at my hand, Kingsley put his eyes back on the road. He kept his hands on the wheel. "Like hell, Calypso. I had to graduate with my name on the dean's honor roll and get accepted to do my masters to get this baby for my birthday. You go make your deal with the devil to get your car."

Pouting, I huffed back in the passenger seat. "Well, unlike your father, my mother doesn't have to blackmail me into doing well at university. She's also not about to buy me a car that doesn't come with an armed chauffeur."

"It's easier to kidnap you if you are already in the vehicle. That's the only way Queenie got a car. Then again, she was being chauffeured everywhere since primary school."

"You got a car without protection."

Tilting his head my way, Kingsley gave me a look of sad understanding. "I have a car with live tracking data that feeds back to a security officer. That security team reports if my car approaches the bridge to Riverside. I was also taken to the range and taught how to shoot, just like you. On top of that, I had a personal trainer in three different martial arts. I've had to work hard and negotiate every step of the way for this freedom. Be glad you got the mother you did, Princess. I adore Aunt Gena. My mother is a trophy wife who starts drinking at breakfast and falls into bed, unconscious at night. She hasn't looked at Queenie or I since we were born and look how we've turned out?"

Taking a deep breath, I exhaled slowly. "You have a point. Spoilt, conceited, assholes. Though, what did she expect naming you Kingsley and Queenie? You're just lucky I love you both."

Kingsley's grin returned, his eyes glinting in his mischievous mood. "Says a girl named after a nymph. Tell me, Calypso, do you act like your namesake?"

"I may not act like a nymph, but I have the appetite of one," I teased.

Turning onto the expressway, Kingsley floored the accelerator. "You're damn lucky we're related."

I rolled my eyes. Kingsley had been talking trash to me since I turned sixteen. He didn't mean anything by it, and it was nothing compared to how he spoke to the girls that slept with him. It left me in awe. Why would anyone want to sleep with him considering Kingsley was a prick before they ever got to his bed? Yes, he was handsome and wealthy, but still an asshole. The problem was, I knew it was a defense mechanism.

That protective brother act he'd pulled about Aaron? That was Kingsley's way of showing he cared and wanting to make sure I didn't get hurt. Kingsley had been taking care of me since primary school. He said I needed someone too.

Of course, he hadn't always been like this. Three years ago, Kingsley caught his girlfriend banging a guy from Riverside. He'd worshipped the ground Kerry-Anne walked on and spent the night crying on my shoulder. After that, the misogynist asshole with deep-seated hate for all things Riverside was born. Now, the women who'd fallen for his charm called him Kingzilla.

Kerry-Anne broke his heart, and in doing so, destroyed the last belief he had in love or relationships. While I missed the old Kingsley, when he wasn't in a bad mood like he was tonight, I still adored him. When he was in this mood, I wanted to give him a big hug and strangle him all at the same time. Tonight, was going to be exhausting.

Chapter Seven

"Am I the only one who got out on the right side of the bed this morning?" I asked Queenie as we sank into our chairs at the dinner table.

She flipped her ash-blonde hair. "Don't know what you mean?" She scowled. Her brown eyes were glaring at Kingsley.

"Okay..." I rolled my eyes, looking over the table. Granddad was muttering under his breath about disrespectful children. Aunt Karina was downing her fifth scotch since we arrived twenty minutes ago. Uncle Bryce was glaring at Queenie, and my mother was a no-show. Looking down, I checked my phone for a message or call. Still nothing.

"Gena's flight got delayed," Nanna announced. Striding into the dining room, she put the home phone on the side table. "It's just us, so let's eat."

Leaning to my other side, I whispered to Kingsley. "What did you do to Queenie?"

When Kingsley looked at his sister, she hissed at him, which made him smile at me. "You know the clingy bitch I was on the phone to earlier?" I nodded. "That was one of her sorority sisters."

Closing my eyes, I shook my head. "Nice one, King."

"Eh, she was fuckable," he dismissed.

"And what has Queenie done to piss off your dad?"

"He sprung her doing some lawyer at the office, in his office," Kingsley chuckled. "Guy was older than dad."

"Ew!" I cringed at the idea.

"I know, right?"

"If you two are finished? I'll start prayers." Giving granddad an apologetic look, I bowed my head. After he gave thanks - only for the food tonight, the family didn't deserve his good graces this week - we all ate. No one uttered a word through the first two courses. By the time dessert was coming out, Nanna had had enough.

"Caly, how's university going?"

"Good, Nanna. Still doing well and working part-time."

"Are you seeing anyone?" Everyone looked at me now.

Clearing my throat, I prayed this didn't get me in Grand-dad's bad books. "I am actually. We started dating last week, so it's still new."

"Is he a college boy?" Granddad asked.

"He's doing his Ph.D. in Computer Engineering." Giving my grandfather something, I knew he'd be happy with, I hoped he didn't explore it any further.

Granddad huffed with approval. "At least one of my grand-children has good taste in partners."

Kingsley tilted his head to consider me. "Wish can't be old enough to be doing his Ph.D. yet."

"He isn't," I smirked. "He's also studying Nuclear Medicine. I'm not dating Wish. As I said, he's a friend."

Lifting a brow, Kingsley gave me his cheeky smile. "Why,

Caly, you player, you."

Rolling my eyes, I went back to eating my dessert.

"Any chance this one may last more than a few dates?" Granddad asked instead.

"The forecast is looking positive so far." I let my eyes gleam with happiness. "I like this one."

"Good. I expect to meet the boy before it becomes too serious," Granddad nodded, his mind made up.

"Did you meet my dad before he got mum pregnant with me?" I asked to tease.

Knocking his water glass over, Grandad started choking on his food. Nanna and Uncle Bryce went very still. "Your mother never told us who your father was, Dear," Nanna answered first. Her eyes flicked to her son, who gave a short shake of his head.

"You guys know, though," Kingsley observed what I did. "You all closed circle so fast it wasn't funny."

"Stay out of it, Kingsley," Uncle Bryce warned, "you're on tenterhooks as it is."

"Enough!" Granddad recovered. "The man your mother fell in love with at university wasn't good enough. I told them that when he asked to marry her, and they went their separate ways. Your father isn't important. As far as I know, he was a one-night stand. What's important is that you are my granddaughter. You are brilliant, and kind and your mother has raised you well." Granddad fixed his steely gaze on me. With a nod, I returned to eating, and he moved that gaze to Kingsley.

"You know, Granddad, I think you would have married me off to Caly just to have her as one of the family if she weren't already." Picking up his water, Kingsley took a big drink.

"If she weren't already family, I would have adopted her. You, my boy, are not good enough for her, either."

Grinning large, Kingsley loved stirring our family patriarch.

Shaking his head, Granddad went back to eating. "Why all my children had to have such bad taste in partners." Granddad's eyes flicked to Aunt Karina.

Snatching the bottle of scotch from his mother's grasp, Kingsley topped up my glass. "Here, Caly, I think you need this more."

"I'll drink to that," Queenie grumbled, snatching the bottle from him.

"Give that back," Karina gurgled.

"I'll get you a bottle on the way home," Uncle Bryce consoled. "The cheap stuff. You drink it way too fast to appreciate a good scotch anyway."

Karina stood up. She meant it to be a quick and harsh shove of her chair, but with how much she was swaying, she looked sad and kind of pathetic. Zigzagging her way out of the room, Karina hit the door frame on her way out, swearing under her breath.

"That, Caly, my father considered to be good enough for our family," Bryce informed me. "She was high society, beautiful, and all happiness and light. She was perfect until our wedding night. Once Karina had that ring on her finger and the Zilla name to flash at everyone, she stopped being so beautiful, or lovely, or light."

"Why did you stay married?" I asked.

Bryce sighed, "Prenups didn't exist in our days. I divorce that bitch; I lose half of everything."

"It's cheaper to let our mother drown herself to death," Queenie answered, unemotionally. "We'd all hoped she'd have killed her liver by now."

"You know that's our mother you're talking about so coldly, right?"

Queenie raised her scotch to her brother. "Here's to our

mother. She gave birth to Queen and King Zilla. Mercy to all the young women of Eleri, lest the King fucks and dumps them. Mercy to all the men of wealth and stature, lest I ruin them."

Laughing, Kingsley clinked his water glass with his sister. "Let's not forget Caly and her daddy issues."

Grinning, Queenie sent a wink in my direction. "Mercy to all the boys of EU, lest they lose their hearts to the sweet Princess of Eleri."

Lifting my glass, I laughed with my cousins.

Rising, Grandad shook his head as he left the table. "This is what will become of the Zilla name," he grumbled to Bryce.

Smiling, Uncle Bryce joined his father, patting his shoulder. "They are young, dad. You remember what I was like, what you were like. They'll come good." Uncle Bryce winked at us all as he left the room with Granddad.

Nanna stood with a smile. "Go mount your rebellion in the games room. Somewhere your dirty talk won't give your grand-father a heart attack."

"Yes, Nanna," we all chorused. Stealing the rest of the scotch, we wandered down to granddad's billiard room.

"So, this guy you're dating?"

"Leave it alone, King," I warned from the passenger seat. Taking another sip of the bottle of water Kingsley gave me as we left the house, I groaned. I was going to have the worst hangover at work tomorrow if I didn't rehydrate.

"I'm just looking out for you, Princess."

"While I appreciate that, it's still none of your business. I don't get your black book, stay the hell out of mine." Swallowing more water, I whined, "Why did you let Queenie talk me into shots? You could have looked out for me then?"

Kingsley chuckled to himself, his eyes reflecting the lights from the dashboard. "Because seeing you drunk is rare, and you talk a lot more when you are."

"I have to work tomorrow."

Shaking his head, Kingsley watched me down the rest of the water. "It usually takes more to persuade you to drink. Want to tell me what's eating you?"

"Probably the fact that no one is eating me."

Oversteering, Kingsley quickly corrected. "Sorry."

Glaring in his direction, I eased my grip on the door armrest. "Try not to kill me on the way home. Jesus, what is with guys and driving me home of late?"

"I said, sorry. Don't distract me with images not appropriate for a cousin, and we'll be fine."

"Stop thinking of me inappropriately at all, and we would be fine," I countered.

Smirking, Kingsley pulled into the dorm car park. "Not gonna happen until you get old and fat."

"What if I look like my mum when I'm older?"

Kingsley raised a brow. "Then, my wife will be very jealous at family dinners."

That started me laughing. "Wife?"

"Thought you'd like that one." He pulled into a park. "Want me to walk you in?"

"No, I'm good." Opening the door, I sat for a minute to clear my head.

"Let me rephrase. Do you need me to walk you in?"

"Stop looking for a way to try and feel me up." Pushing myself out of the car, I held onto the door to keep my balance.

Watching me get out of the car, Kingsley smirked. "You know me too well, Princess. See you at the fundraiser in two weeks."

Waving, I shut the door, trying not to sway as I moved to the stairs. As I reached the fifth stair, Kingsley drove off, and I slumped against the rail. "Stupid, Caly. Really stupid. You know better than to do shots with Queenie." Sinking my bottom to the step, I removed my heels and sighed as I held my head in my hands.

Moments later, a car pulled into the carpark. Lifting my head, I struggled to see Aaron getting out of his driver's seat. Cursing under my breath, I pulled myself back up to standing, trying my best to walk up the stairs like normal. Ascending wasn't easy. The stairs were moving side to side like the kind you get in a funhouse at the amusement park.

"Caly!" As I lurched to the side and would have fallen, Aaron caught me.

As I collided with his hard body, I cursed again. "Just for note, this is me drunk."

"I sort of figured that. Come on; I'll help you inside."

Slinging my arm across his shoulders, Aaron placed his around my waist. This wasn't comfortable considering how much taller than me he was. We managed five steps before even Aaron gave that up.

"Get on my back." Turning me to face the carpark, Aaron stepped down two stairs. Shrugging, I hiked my dress a little and fell forward. Draping my arms over his broad shoulders, I hooked one leg around his waist. Stepping back into me, Aaron collected my other thigh and shifted his hands behind me to hold my bum.

"Why don't you want to date me?" I sulked as he climbed the steps.

"I'm not in your league, Caly."

"That's a bullshit excuse," I huffed. "I've been into you since I was fourteen, and I had my first dirty thought."

"I know. I saw the way you looked at me at school. You always looked so guilty when I caught you watching me."

"So, why didn't you ever hit on me?" My entire body heated, knowing that he'd known all those years.

"Your family will never approve of me, Caly." Reaching the door to my dorm, Aaron leaned down so I could unlock the door.

"No one is talking marriage," I grumbled.

"That's the other problem. I don't want a casual thing with you, Caly," Aaron murmured, climbing the steps to the second level. "You are too dangerous a liaison not to be worth something more than sex." Aaron deposited me in the hall outside my room. How he knew it was mine, I don't know. Probably wouldn't take much to find out.

Frowning at him, I tilted forward a bit to emphasize my words, but Aaron had to catch me, so I didn't fall on my face. "Aaron, I don't have sex with just anyone. I have to like a guy a lot to sleep with him."

Taking the key from my hand, Aaron opened the door to my flat. Handing me back the key, he placed me inside, but I clung to his arm when he turned to leave. Meeting my eyes, Aaron moved a step closer. When he lowered his luscious mouth to my ear, I couldn't help my hands fisting his shirt.

"Caly, you aren't any other girl to me. You are the reason I escaped Riverside," Aaron whispered. "I was in love with you the moment we met on the playground as children. You were beautiful, but you were also my ticket to a good life for my family and me. I can't use you for sex, and I won't allow you to use me up. Especially when the risk of losing everything I've worked so hard towards is so high."

There was way too much alcohol in my system to understand what he was talking about right now. Besides, I'd got stuck with his loving me from the moment we met. "You love me?" I whispered a little awed.

Grumbling under his breath, Aaron shook his head. "Caly..."

Launching forward, I wrapped my arms around his neck and kissed him. Freezing for a moment, Aaron became tense, but I was too gone to care. Then encompassing my waist, Aaron pulled me tight against him, and he kissed me back.

Remember how I said I'd imagined my first kiss with Aaron and how perfect it would be? So. Much., Better!

Chapter Eight

Music was playing. Blinking my eyes open, I rolled over to silence the noise. Except, I couldn't reach my alarm over the body between me and the side table. My eyes opened farther at the broad naked shoulders I was looking at in front of me.

The body sharing my bed groaned and silenced my alarm for me. That's when Aaron rolled over and looked at me. It wasn't the cocky, satisfied smile of a man who got laid. It was concern shining out of his eyes at me.

"How are you feeling, Sunshine?" Aaron asked, tugging my lip free from where I was repeatedly biting it.

"That's all going to depend on the next few minutes..."

"We didn't have sex. You were way too drunk for that to happen," Aaron assured.

"But I'm naked?"

Smirking, Aaron flicked his eyes down to my covered breasts. "Yes, you are." He sounded way too chipper about that. "For a drunk person, you could strip very well. Moonlighting to pay your tuition?"

Cringing at the idea, I closed my eyes. "No!" Aaron laughed a little more. Opening one eye, I browsed the solid chest before me. "Are you naked?"

Aaron grinned a little more. "Should I be?" Moving his face toward mine, Aaron took my hand in his, sliding it beneath the sheet to his waist. He placed my hand on his hip so that I could feel his boxer shorts. "We didn't have sex, Caly."

"Okay, what did we do?" I braved asking.

Cradling the back of my head in his hand, Aaron kissed my lips lightly. "Some of this." His hand slipped down to skim across my nakedness. "Some of that," he murmured. Tilting his head, Aaron smiled at me. "Then, you passed out, but not before you begged me to stay so passionately that I didn't have the heart to leave." Rolling out of my king-single bed, Aaron collected his jeans from the floor, pulling them on. "I have to get my stuff and get to the gym, or the boys will be wondering where I am."

Holding my sheet to me, I sat up watching him dress. Disappointed, yes, but until I knew what went down last night, I'd take it slow. "So, nothing but kissing and touching?" I checked.

"Relax, Caly; you were unconscious virtually straight away. We kissed once, and then you stripped your way to the room. When I wouldn't take advantage of you, you begged me to stay and passed out."

"Okay. Thank you," I exhaled relieved.

Aaron's arrogance fell over his face like a mask. "I thought you said you didn't drunk fuck?"

Closing my eyes ashamed, I turned my face away. "Normally, I don't," I sighed, annoyed with myself. "Any other person, I wouldn't have offered."

"So, I'm a special case?"

I bit the inside of my cheek.

Placing one knee on the bed, Aaron caressed my face. When I met his eyes, the pain of his rejection still stung as he placed a teasing kiss on the corner of my mouth.

"That's why I stayed, Caly. You're special to me too. I wish the situation with us was different." Stepping away, Aaron left.

Exhaling in one long breath, I held back the threatening tears. I didn't understand what the big deal was. It's not like my family would get him expelled for sleeping with me or anything. Then again, maybe it wasn't about me. It was feasible, the reason Aaron wouldn't get involved with me was something to do with his life. Perhaps, he was a gang banger like Kingsley said, and I couldn't see it because of the way I'd always felt for him.

Jumping out of bed, I went for my run. Needing to get to work on time, I made it shorter than usual. Plus, I was only too aware that Aaron would be in the gym overlooking the track. Hungover and embarrassed about last night, I didn't have the energy for my usual run.

Never had I experienced the walk of shame or that awkward moment when you have sex with a guy you shouldn't have. Usually, I looked for Aaron coming into class. Watching him covertly, I enjoyed the blessing of being able to look upon such male perfection. Saturday night ruined that. On Monday morning, I bowed my head to my lecture notes and didn't look up to see anything but the academic.

This behavior continued all week. At the Tower bar on Wednesday night, I got my friends to get my drinks for me. Brad and I hung out well away from the bar. After he returned to his friends, I decided to have an early night and head home well before I usually did. As the week wore on, my frustration with my behavior only grew. Like always, I dealt with it by running myself harder and faster.

"What is going on?" Penny demanded as I stretched on the track Thursday morning.

"I got drunk Saturday night and might have kissed Aaron Wish." Groaning, I flopped to the ground.

Penny looked confused. "What was he doing at your family dinner?"

"He helped me up the stairs when I got home, and I threw myself at him. He declined the offer."

Penny looked aghast. "What is his damage?"

Shrugging, I let her help me up. "It's for the best. I'm dating Brad, and he's nice and kind of different to any guy I've dated before."

"He's hot too," Penny teased as we walked back to our dorm. "I mean, Wish is gorgeous if you are into tall, dark, and brooding. But Brad is hot and doesn't look like a possible future psychopath."

"Well, we'll see."

As awkward as lectures were during the week, it had nothing on our one shared practical class on Thursday. That was an agonizing three hours of avoidance. Sighing with relief when that finished, I checked my phone to see I had a voicemail.

"Caly, it's Michael. In case I fail to catch you before your shift starts, I wanted to tell you that Aaron Wish will be starting his training with you tonight. I hope he works out."

With a loud groan, I disconnected the call and headed back to my dorm to change for work and get some study done. On the way, I called my cousin. "Princess. To what do I owe the pleasure?" Kingsley answered.

"How do you face up to a chick you had drunken sex with?"

"This is a trick question, right?" Kingsley chuckled.

"No. After you left Saturday night, I ran into someone and sort of threw myself at them. Now, I have to work with them in a few hours, and it's awkward," I confessed.

Kingsley whistled into the mouthpiece. "A. I knew I should have walked you inside on Saturday. B. Look at you having random meaningless sex."

"Well, we didn't have sex. I passed out not long after I performed a striptease in front of him."

There was an awkward pause. "You should call Queenie to ask these questions."

"Why?" I asked, annoyed he would fob me off.

Kingsley blew out his breath. "Look, did you want something to happen with this guy?"

Of course, I did, but I knew Aaron wasn't interested. "No. That's what is embarrassing. The guy isn't into me and has made that clear before."

"So, the guy is gay?"

"No, but he doesn't want to get involved with a Zilla."

Kingsley laughed, "He must have dated Queenie before."

The idea made me growl. If I found out Aaron passed me up but had hooked up with Queenie, I couldn't live with myself. That just made Kingsley laugh harder.

"Look, if it's not going to happen again, apologize and thank him for not taking advantage of you. Leave it at that and pretend it never happened," Kingsley advised sagely.

"You know, I don't know why Grandpa thinks you won't come good, King. You are pretty good at dispensing life advice."

"A huh. Then let me meet the new guy before Grandpa?"

"Thanks, King, got to go." I hung up quickly before getting into that argument with him.

"Apologize," I repeated to myself. "Just apologize." That was my mantra for the day. By the time I arrived at work, I was at ease with Saturday night. Swiping my card, I pushed open the door.

"Evening, Caly, Michaels' looking for you," the receptionist informed me.

"Thanks." Stowing my stuff in my locker, I knocked on Michael's office door. "You were looking for me?"

"Caly, you got my message?" I nodded. "Excellent. Well, Aaron is already here. He's gone to get his staff card and finalize the paperwork with HR. He shouldn't be too far away." Glancing at his watch, Michael swore under his breath as he started packing up. "It's Mandy's birthday today. She's organized a sitter for the kids, so if I'm not home on time, she'll murder me."

"Don't worry about it. Can I get a copy of the training checklist and I'll take it from there."

Moving to his filing cabinet, Michael pulled out some pieces of paper, handing them to me as he headed for the door. "Now, if you need anything..."

"Michael, I'll be fine."

Michael chuckled to himself. "Yeah, you will be. Night, Caly. See you next week."

When Michael walked out, I sighed as I started looking over the list. "Easy peazy."

"Lemon Squeezy?" Aaron smirked as he leaned on the office door frame. God, he looked so damn sexy in his uniform. The navy slacks and white polo shirt made him look professional. I swear his attractiveness got bumped up by five points, and I didn't think that was possible. "Caly?" Aaron chuckled.

"Yes?"

"Do you need lip gloss?" Aaron asked, folding his arms across his chest.

The question confused me. "Why?"

"Because you are going to make your lip bleed if you bite it any harder. Stop thinking of me naked and get your head back in the game."

My eyes went wide. "Sorry." I shook my head. "And I'm sorry about Saturday night. Thank you for not taking advantage of me."

Huffing, Aaron let his eyes roam over me. My uniform did not make any female appealing, so the dilation of his pupils made me chuckle. "Now, whose thinking of who naked?"

"You brought up Saturday," Aaron teased. "I should have taken photographs." When I raised a brow, Aaron shrugged. Closing his eyes, Aaron rubbed the bridge of his nose and then stood up straight.

"So, let's agree to not think of each other naked at work, and get on with the actual work," I suggested.

"Agreed." Aaron nodded, relieved. "What do you want to show me first?" His eyes dropped to my breasts.

With a chuckle, I shook my head and walked out to reception. "Come on, Wish. Let's get you orientated."

"Want a lift?" Aaron asked as we grabbed our stuff from the lockers.

Stifling a yawn, I considered how much longer it would take to get home if I took the bus. "I won't say no."

Smiling, Aaron led the way out to his car. Parking at the hospital was expensive, so he'd parked a few streets away, but I didn't mind the walk in the fresh air.

Aaron's phone ringing disturbed the silence. "Heya, Dwayne, what's up?" Aaron's feet stopped walking. "What? Now?"

Aaron's eyes flicked to me, then he groaned, "I've got Caly with me."

Wiggling my fingers in hello, I remembered the big guy from the cafe who insisted he give me a lift home. "No, we just finished work, you pervert. I'm making sure she gets home safe." Rolling his eyes, Aaron cringed a moment later. "Fine." He hung up. "I've got to make a stop on the way home. Do you mind?"

When I shook my head, Aaron opened the passenger door, holding it while I slid in and got comfortable. Aaron drove quietly, but quickly, only the heavy metal music he listened to for sound. Watching out the window, I frowned when we crossed the river and headed deeper into Riverside. Pulling into a park on the street, Aaron unclasped his belt. "Stay here. I'm not sure what's happening. I'll check it out and then get you home." Aaron was out of the car before I could respond.

Taking a deep breath, I relaxed back in the seat. This area of Riverside didn't seem bad. The apartments were well lit, and there was no one loitering on the streets. All in all, I didn't feel frightened for my life. About ten minutes later, A black Mercedes with dark tinted windows pulled up. A well-dressed man in a suit headed towards the apartment building with two men following him. As he walked in front of Aaron's car, he looked in and saw me. Stopping, he just stared at me for a moment. He was attractive for his mature years, but his suit did not fit in with my image of Riverside.

Murmuring something to his bodyguards, the man continued towards the apartment. One of the guards continued with him; the other stayed in front of Aaron's car. He wasn't watching me, but watching everywhere else around us.

It took another ten minutes for the front door to open again and Aaron to emerge with the man in the suit. They were arguing. Peering overhead, I turned off the door light and cracked my door open a little.

"...on our way home from work when Dwayne called. What did you want me to do? Dump her by the side of the road and keep coming?"

The man held up his hands. "Relax, Ayah. I'm not angry, just concerned. You left her out here in the car, that's not any safer."

"You would have preferred me to take her in to see that?" Aaron pointed back to the door.

That's when I noticed the front of his white work shirt wasn't white anymore. Sitting up, I worried. Was that blood?

The man in the suit sighed. "I see your point. I'll make sure she gets home safely. Do what you can here."

"Wait..." Aaron called worried as the man walked away.

"Help your friend, Ayah. I'll do your job," the suit grumbled as he marched towards the car.

My eyes went wide when he came to the side of the car and opened the door wide before he offered me his hand. "I'm sorry, Miss Zilla, Aaron is preoccupied. I'll drive you home."

While his face was familiar, I couldn't pinpoint who he was or why I wanted to try running home instead. "And you are?"

"Sinclair Rockford," he replied miffed.

I swallowed. "As in..."

"Yes!" Getting sick of waiting for me to get out of the car willingly, Rockford grabbed my upper arm and helped me out. "We need to go now."

As he walked me to the Mercedes with a firm grip on my arm, one of his guards opened the back door. Rockford pushed me forward to force me into his car. Sliding in, I clutched my bag to me and got as far away from him as I could.

Sliding into the seat next to me, Rockford strapped on his seatbelt. Once the guards were in the front seats, we were moving. Observing me, Rockford smirked. "Relax, Caly, I'm not going to steal your bag."

"Oh, you can have that. Just don't touch me." I rubbed where he'd gripped my arm. It looks like I was adding to my bruise count.

Rockford raised a brow in surprise. "You have nothing to fear from me. It wasn't safe there for you. If Meadows tracked the kid back here, then you could be hurt in the crossfire."

"Meadows, as in Greg Meadows?" I asked, feeling the blood drain from my face.

"His son Terry."

"Was that blood on Aaron's shirt?" I whispered.

Meeting my eyes, Rockford sighed, sadness filling his pale blue gaze. "His friend got shot. Ayah is the only one with any form of medical knowledge."

"We have these things called hospitals. Though, I'm surprised you don't have a doctor on retainer," I grumbled.

Rockford shook his head. "It's not about the authorities catching you over here, Caly. It's about getting caught by the wrong people. If the boy seeks medical attention and the authorities get his name, then so does Meadows. He has a sister who Terry could use for leverage. What Ayah is doing is not only about saving the boy, but protecting his sister as well."

"Why is this even still an issue? You have money. You could fix this town."

Rockford looked out the window at the passing buildings. "It's not always about money. People's attitudes have to change. I'm working on that, slowly and surely, but I'm not a miracle worker."

Sick to my stomach, I felt the anxiety eating away at my insides. "Aaron will be okay, won't he?"

Rockford turned his attention back to me. "You care about

him?" When I nodded, his mouth thinned out into a straight line. "Are you and he...?"

"Just friends. I'm close to his younger brother too. I don't want to see either of them hurt."

Nodding as if he knew about Josh and me, Rockford inhaled, then exhaled. "Do you have a boyfriend, Caly?"

"No offense, Mr. Rockford, but if you can breed them, don't screw 'em." I decided to put that horse to bed immediately.

Rockford gaped at me. "I'm sorry?"

"You're a little too old for me," I clarified.

Mouth hanging open for a second, Rockford blinked, then he started laughing. "I wasn't hitting on you, Caly, only asking."

"Oh." I relaxed. "Well, yes. I'm seeing someone."

"What's his name? What does he do?"

"Brad is at university for Computer Science," I informed him as we approached the campus.

Rockford nodded like that was acceptable. "Do you think you'll marry him?"

"Jesus, I haven't even slept with him yet. Let's not put the cart before the horse," I gripped.

"I'm pretty sure marriage used to come before sex."

"That was before women realized they could try before they buy too. Men weren't the only ones who could get the milk for free without buying an entire cow."

Rockford looked to be struggling not to crack up laughing. "I guess that's very true. Your mother never married, did she?"

Blinking at the reference to my mother, I wondered how much he knew about my family. It made sense that he would have excellent working knowledge about the families of influence in Eleri. "No. She fell in love at college, but my grandfather didn't approve of the man and drove them apart. She never stopped loving him, so she never married."

Rockford's smile faded around the edges. "She must have met someone, Caly. Otherwise, how did she get you?"

"I don't know. Gena won't tell me about him."

"Does that bother you?"

"It used to."

"Well, having met you and your mother," Rockford got a tease in his voice, "the man's probably dead." When I looked at Rockford concerned, he shrugged. "Your mother always reminded me of a praying mantis. She most likely decided she wanted a baby, found a suitable man, and once he impregnated her, she disposed of him."

"That's gross imagery of my mother. Thanks."

Rockford smiled as the car came to a stop. "I knew your mother and uncle well when they were younger, Caly. Trust me; I could do much worse."

"If they were anything like Kingsley and Queenie, I don't want to know. I'd need therapy."

"Ah, Queenie. That cousin of yours is more dangerous to a man with a six-figure bank balance than any gang banger in Riverside."

"Been on the receiving end of her attentions, have we, Mr. Rockford?" It didn't surprise me, he was a successful business-man, even if he was from Riverside.

"Let's say a Zilla woman has burned me once too often. I'm happy to avoid it ever happening again." He winked at me as his guard got out to open my door for me.

"You're not what I imagined, Mr. Rockford."

He cocked an eyebrow at me. "Perhaps, we could be friends?"

"Possibly." Giving him a wink, I moved to exit the car.

Grabbing my arm, Rockford studied me, his face serious. "Be careful, Caly. If anything happened to you, your mother would tear this city apart in her grief. No more trips to Riverside."

"Is that your way of telling me to stay away from Aaron?" I read between the lines.

Releasing my arm, Rockford turned his gaze out the window. "Good night, Caly. It was a pleasure to meet you."

Chapter Nine

❦

"Is something wrong?" Stopping walking, Brad made me look at him. "You've been sort of quiet all night and not your usual bubbly self."

"It's not you. I didn't sleep well last night. Kept having nightmares," I admitted.

Taking me to a bench, Brad sat us down. "Tell me about the nightmare."

"I was getting a lift home with a friend, and we ended up in Riverside. Some masked people stopped us. When they dragged us from the car, it terrified me that they were going to shoot him and do something else to me." The memory of the dream made my mouth dry.

"Then we were alone again, and he was holding a gun, pointing it at me. Then he shot me." My eyes teared up, remembering the look in Aaron's eyes when he pulled the trigger.

Observing me, Brad caressed my cheek, his forehead buckled in a frown. "It's just a nightmare, Caly. No one in their right mind would take you into Riverside. You're a walking ransom note, so don't worry about it."

Biting my lip in regret, I opened my mouth and exhaled hard. "I was in Riverside last night."

Brad's eyebrows lowered. "What? Why?"

Gazing down at my knees, I tried to word my revelation safely. "My friend was giving me a lift home from work when his friend called asking him to swing by his place. We did. I don't know what was happening. A man turned up in a fancy car and suit and dragged me out of my friend's car and into his and brought me home. He told me to stay out of Riverside."

Blinking at me for a moment, Brad shifted closer and put his arm around me. "Caly, you're trembling. Did this man hurt you?" I shook my head. "But he scared you, didn't he?"

Out of the blue, I was crying; I hadn't thought I'd been that scared. Sinclair Rockford seemed kind of decent, and I'd made it home safely. Why was I crying about it now?

The thing that had been bugging me all night long was how familiar Sinclair Rockford seemed. My memory told me I'd met him before, and talked to him, but I didn't know why or when.

"I'm sorry. I don't even know why I'm crying." The image of Aaron covered in blood flashed in my head.

"Maybe the movie was worse than we realized."

Looking up, I found Brad holding back a smile. My mouth lifted just a touch, and I liked that he tried to lighten my mood.

"Look, the guy was likely someone your family hires to protect you. You crossed the river and set off an alert on your family's security system." Brad touched one of the diamond earrings my mother gave me for my sixteenth birthday.

Anyone with sense would assume that at least one piece of my jewelry was a GPS. Since the small studs were the same ones I wore every day, it would be a smart guess. The truth was,

I'd never asked if they were, but it wouldn't surprise me to find out his assumption was correct.

"So, your family's security tracked you, found you, and removed you from a place you shouldn't be. I get that he scared you, but if he dragged you back here and didn't hurt you, then he more than likely works for your family." Taking my hand, Brad started walking us towards the dorms. "Come on, let's get you home. You'll feel safer inside your apartment."

At my dorm, we stopped by the door. When Brad moved in to kiss me, I stopped him, causing his brows to bunch and his mouth to tilt down. "Did you want to come up? I don't want to be alone."

Brad lifted an eyebrow. "Is that a trick question?"

With a smile, I led him upstairs to my room. Inside, I made us both a cup of tea, and we sat on the sofa. "So, what are we doing tomorrow night?" Brad asked.

"Not a movie," I teased. "How about trampolining?"

"Trampolining?"

"Yeah, we can bounce all over the place for a few hours, then get some junk food and hang out," I suggested.

A smirk bloomed on Brad's handsome face as he shook his head. "What the lady wants, the lady gets."

Smiling, I leaned in to kiss his lips. It was a tentative kiss, just a touch of lips, a slight pinch, and then I pulled away.

"How about next Friday?" Brad asked, his bright eyes hopeful.

My smile disappeared. "I'm my cousin's date for an event. My mother can't make it and insists I go as part of the family. Sorry. I can do Saturday night?"

Sighing, Brad shook his head. "My grandfather's birthday bash at their beach house in Barr."

Barr was a popular place for wealthy Eleri to have beach

houses. My family had one there. Since Brad's mother was from Eleri, her parents were likely quite well-off.

With a huff, I leaned into him. "Guess we'll have to make the most of this weekend then."

Trying to control his lips from smiling, Brad drew closer. "I guess so." He kissed me, firm and with utter confidence.

Closing my eyes, I moved into him. When he pulled me onto his lap, I straddled his thighs while we made out a little. It was entirely PG. Lips only; we kept our hands locked behind each other, so they didn't go wandering. Yet, I was hot and randy. Part of me wished he'd rip my clothes off and bounce me on that considerable bulge I could feel pressing into my hip.

"I should go," Brad choked, pushing me away from him a little.

"Really?" My brows lifted in surprise.

Brad chuckled at the look on my face. "Caly, it's eleven, and you have work in the morning. We can pick this up tomorrow night."

Pouting as Brad placed me back beside him, I laughed when I noticed the awkward way Brad was moving. Growling, Brad pulled me up into his arms. "Laugh now, Caly. One day soon, I'm going to be burying this inside you." He rubbed his hard-on against me, holding me tight so I couldn't pull back. "Then, you won't be laughing."

Moaning, I swooned with anticipation. "Promises, promises."

Grinning, Brad frenched me, then let me go and left. Before I went to sleep, I might have spent a longer time than usual with my favorite hot pink silicon friend.

. . .

"Caly, about Thursday night?" Aaron started as soon as we were alone on Saturday morning.

"Yeah, let's talk about that, Aaron. About you taking me into Riverside and leaving me in the car unprotected while you play doctor. Or how about you let a stranger drag me from your car and drive off with me," I growled at him.

"My friends needed me, and you were safer in the car than inside," Aaron defended. "I'm sorry about Rockford dragging you around, but he was trying to keep you safe."

"You didn't even come to the car and explain," I fumed at him.

"I was covered in blood!" Aaron yelled. Checking his volume, he lowered his voice. "I didn't want you to see me like that, Caly. I didn't want to involve you."

"Well, I saw you. You stood there and didn't lift a finger when some big-time gang banger dragged me off to god knows where."

"Rockford would never hurt you. He's not like that," Aaron defended.

"I don't care about Rockford. I care that you don't care."

"Caly!" Aaron scolded hurt. "You know that's not true."

"No, Ayah. If Saturday showed me anything, it's that I don't know diddly-squat when it comes to you." Storming out, I avoided being alone with Aaron for the rest of the shift.

After I finished work, I met Joshua in the cafeteria as usual. Following me in, Aaron sat a table away. "He's giving me a lift to work afterward," Joshua explained, seeing the intense glare I gave his brother. "This will be the norm on Saturdays from now on."

"Great!" Opening the workbook for tutoring, I tried to block Aaron out of my thoughts.

"Did my brother do something, Caly?"

Shaking my head, I exhaled to release the tension in my body I still felt about Thursday night. More so the dream, then Aaron's actual behavior. "Don't worry about it. Let's get you into Medicine."

Joshua and I spent the next hour studying while Aaron focused on his studies a table away. Every now and then, I'd look up and find Aaron observing me. Averting my eyes, I'd sneak another glance as soon as I knew he wasn't watching.

When we finished, Joshua packed up while I stood to leave. "Want a lift back to campus?" Aaron offered.

"Safer walking. Thanks." I grabbed my bag. "See you next week, Josh." Turning on my heel, I walked away.

"What did you do to Caly?" Josh growled at his brother.

Needing to get some of my studies done before my date with Brad tonight, I didn't stick around to hear Aaron's answer. Only Penny had other plans.

"We haven't hung out in ages," Penny grumbled. "Let's spend the afternoon doing mani-pedis'?"

"I have to study. I have a date tonight and have barely studied all week."

"Please, you're probably a full month ahead of the entire class already."

"Only three weeks," I defended.

"So, you can take a day off and spend it with your bestie," Penny declared, stealing my laptop and putting it back in my room. "So," Penny came back into the room with her nail kit, "date number three. Is Brad getting lucky tonight?"

"No." My body heated, remembering the kissing last night. "Not entirely lucky anyway."

"So, there will be more dates?"

"Yes." I felt my mood lighten a little. "What's happening with you and Simon?"

Dropping her smile, Penny scowled as her pupils contracted. "Simon's a douche. Little prick slept with a law student Thursday night."

"So, where were you last night?" I asked, confused she wasn't home.

"Banging his best friend and roommate. Loudly. In the room next door to Simon. Craig doesn't have a little prick." When she winked, we both burst out laughing.

"Oh my god, Penny. Are you going to keep seeing Craig?" I couldn't believe she hooked up with him. He'd seemed like such a player every time he hit on me.

"God, no! Craig is a whore. Just thought I'd sample the wares while I was there," Penny declared. I breathed a sigh of relief. Sitting back to wait for my nails to dry, Penny tilted her head to assess me. "I think you're right about the jocks, you know."

"You know I am."

"Maybe I should try a different run of guys. Go the geeks or something?"

"A hot cheerleader dating a geek. The guy would sprog his pants every time you wink at him."

"Hello. You're dating an IT guy, and he's hot. Has he sprogged his jeans holding your hand?" Penny grumbled.

"No, but I reckon he came close when we were making out on the couch last night."

"Wait, you were having a make-out session here on this couch last night?" Pursing her lips when I nodded, Penny scrunched her nose. "You haven't had sex on this couch, have you?"

"No! As if I would risk you walking in and offering to join us."

Penny's blue eyes lit up at the idea, and she swept her bangs out of her eyes. "Brad is pretty hot. Do you think he'd be up for a three-way?"

"If he is, then we aren't going to last long, are we?"

Penny's eyes glittered. "You'll marry Brad."

Time stopped, I froze, my heart pounded in my chest. "What? Why?"

"He's so in your league, but, like you, he prefers to keep a low profile. He's gorgeous, and, I don't know, he makes you smile like the professor used to before you freaked out about it."

Smiling, Penny lifted her eyes to meet mine. "Don't ruin things because I said that, okay? I just wanted to put it out there, so if it does happen, I can say 'I told you so.'"

Blinking down at the midnight-blue nails she'd given me; I considered her reasoning. "I like Brad."

Checking the nails weren't still tacky, Penny was quiet for a moment. Grabbing a tube of cream, she moisturized my hands, her eyebrow lifting. "What about Aaron?"

"That isn't going to happen. Aaron has made his feelings clear, and there is the chance it could be dangerous to get involved with him. I get the feeling he's involved in something that's not good in Riverside."

With a sigh, Penny put her arm over my shoulder. "It sounds like Wish was a fantasy that you've finally grown too old for?"

"Or I needed to get past how gorgeous he is and see the real him?"

"Or you're in denial that you are still seriously into Wish, and it cuts you up that he keeps rejecting you?"

Exhaling hard from that truth, I leaned into her. "Perhaps, but I still like Brad."

"Then get me a badge. I'll join team Brad."

. . .

"Caly," a deep voice called across the car park. Swinging around, I noticed Dwayne standing by a black Chev. He stalked over to me. "Good to see you made it home safely." He smiled, looking me over. "Still spoken for?"

The big guy made me smile. "I am. Just about to go out with the said man."

"What a pity." Dwayne smiled, his eyes glancing over what I was wearing. "That's what you wear on a date?"

Looking down at my outfit, I chuckled. "Isn't it the thing to do everything in your activewear these days?"

"Well, I can think of one thing you wouldn't be doing in it with me."

"Let me guess. Being active?" I gave him my best bimbo look. Dwayne winked, I laughed. "Our date is at the trampolining center."

"That's very down to earth of you."

"I can sit down and eat at a fancy restaurant when I'm too old to bounce around. I want to do fun stuff with my friends and create awesome memories."

"Hey, Caly, are you going to introduce me?" Penny sidled up to me. Dwayne's eyes widened with interest.

"Penny, this is Dwayne. Dwayne meet my best friend and roommate, Penny. Hurt her, and Sinclair Rockford will have nothing on me and my wrath," I smiled sweetly.

Brow's lifting a little, Dwayne's eyes went to my locket. "So, noted."

"So, how do you know this handsome hunk?" What she wanted to know is if he was a prior disaster date.

"Dwayne is friends with Aaron Wish." I smiled up at him. "He's a sweetheart."

"Oh, really?" Penny swung her body slightly. Her way of jumping for joy.

"I've been trying to get Caly to go on a date with me, but apparently she's spoken for," Dwayne fished.

Blinking confused for a second, Penny looked past Dwayne. "Yes, and here he comes now."

Tilting his head, Dwayne lifted a brow and turned to look. On spotting Brad, his smile dropped. "You're dating Brad Meadows?"

To answer his question, Brad walked up and nodded hello to Dwayne before kissing me on the mouth. "Evening everyone," he greeted, then turned to assess Dwayne. "You two know each other."

"Yeah, Caly and I are friends." Dwayne almost growled.

"So, Dwayne, what are your plans tonight?" Penny jumped in, sensing the tension as much as I did.

"I'm hanging with Ayah and some others." Dwayne's eyes still flicking to where Brad's arm was around my waist. "Does Ayah know you two are dating?"

"Should he?" Brad's brows dropped low over his eyes.

"He and Caly have a history."

Brad's hand froze at my waist. Blinking, I felt my eyes widen. "Not that sort of history. We went to school together, and we work together now. I'm closer to his brother than I am with Aaron."

"I can attest to that," Penny jumped in. "Aaron told Caly point blank he wasn't interested, so there's nothing between them."

Mouth falling open, Dwayne double blinked. "He did?"

"We should go," I deflected, worried where this conversation was going. The fact Brad's grip at my waist hadn't eased was telling. "Nice seeing you again, Dwayne."

"You too, Caly," Dwayne nodded as Brad waved and led me to his car. "Ayah seriously turned her down?" Dwayne asked as we left.

Brad was kind of quiet as we slid into his car. "Did Wish really turn you down?"

"It's in the past," I dismissed. Aaron's constant rejection was the last thing I wanted to discuss with him.

Contemplating me, Brad pursed his lips. "I've never known Ayah to turn any girl who looked like you down."

That didn't make me feel any better about myself. "Yeah, well, I've been tutoring Aaron's little brother for over four years. I think Josh told him not to play with me. Josh also told Dwayne I was unavailable when he first met me."

Exhaling a lungful of air, Brad nodded as if that was a relief. "That makes sense. Ayah adores Josh." Brad started the car.

"You know Aaron well?" I was kind of curious. Riverside wasn't that small.

"Yeah, we live in King's Hall together," Brad explained.

Of course, two riverside boys at college on this side of the river knew each other. I could have forehead slapped myself. "Nice ride," I changed subjects, getting comfy in the leather seats of his Lexus. Anything was better than thinking about Aaron or waking up beside him naked only a week ago.

"A gift from my grandfather for getting accepted to do my Ph.D."

"Seriously?" I groaned.

Brad's smile vanished. "What?"

"My cousin Kingsley got a Maserati for getting into his Masters. You get a top of the line Lexus. My mother makes me work for everything I get. I even had to go on a horrible blind date to get a holiday away. I came straight from school to university and started in the summer session. I haven't been on holiday in four years."

Brad looked ready to laugh. "So, you'll appreciate it more when you get it."

"Now, you do sound like my mother."

"So, did you get your holiday?"

The reminder made me relax, sinking into his seats, thinking about the fun in the sun soon to come. "Two months until Hawaii."

"Really? For how long?"

"Two weeks. I'm going during the winter break," I sighed in longing.

Brad tapped his steering wheel. "Sounds like fun."

Watching his reaction, I smirked at the stroppy look on his face. "Are you jealous?"

Inhaling for two counts, Brad exhaled for four counts before speaking. "This is our third date."

"Yes."

"So, things are going well between us, right? I mean, there is no sign this might not last a few months longer?" Brad reasoned. Raising a brow, I waited for Brad to reach his point. "You running around, on a tropical island in a bikini, is going to be torturous if we are still together."

The little flare of jealousy made me cautious. If we were still together, there was the option of joining me. But if Brad expected me to give up this holiday for a potential relationship, we could turn this car around.

My mother always said the hints to how a guy will behave long term are still there in the initial stages. Bad guys camouflage the negative shit while dating. It's our job to identify those small niggles as significant issues going forward. Having told Brad how much this holiday meant, if he asked me to quit it, then what would he expect me to give up for him when we were serious? "Well, could you afford a flight to Hawaii?"

Brad's jaw slackened then quickly reengaged. "Are you asking me to go with you?"

"Not yet, but if this is still going well in a few weeks, could you afford the ticket?"

Brad relaxed a little. "Yeah, I could."

"So, don't worry about it. If this fizzles and dies, you are free of me. If we are still going strong, you can buy a ticket and spend two weeks rubbing sunscreen into my naked body."

Clenching his fingers around the wheel, Brad groaned. "You said that on purpose."

"Yeah, I did. I might be hoping to get to know Mr. Hyde a little tonight."

"Be careful, Caly, or Mr. Hyde is going to turn this car around and drive you straight back to my place."

"Why your place?"

"My roommates are all out at a party tonight."

Leaning closer, I pressed my lips to his ear. "Tell Mr. Hyde, I look forward to seeing what bedspread you have." Brad's pupils dilated. "After our date."

One side of Brad's mouth lifted. "You know how to make a guy crazy with anticipation, Caly."

With a smirk, I relaxed back in the seat. "I haven't even started driving you crazy yet, Brad."

Chapter Ten

WITH A HUMPH, my back hit the wall. Pressing his thigh between mine, Brad rubbed my arousal through my yoga pants, causing me to moan, long and low. Smiling against my lips, Brad snatched my bottom lip between his and sucked hard. Gripping his hair, I reefed his head back as I latched my mouth on his neck. Hands grabbed my ass, and he hoisted me effortlessly to his waist.

"You get me so turned on, Caly." Kicking his bedroom door shut, Brad walked the meter to his bed and dropped me on it.

Before I could say otherwise, Brad pulled his shirt over his head. "Whoa!" My eyes snapped wide on the display of skin.

Brad was hot. His body was that of a typical twenty-something who swam laps every morning. There was no eight-pack, but Brad was trim and fit. Then there was the tattoo encompassing the left side of his torso, back, and front. It looked to be a thorny bush of black roses. But, that's not why I was pulling the reins on.

"Slow, Brad," I managed to say as he knelt above me on the bed.

Brad caressed the side of my face. "I know. I'm boiling in here and needed a little less restriction." Getting that naughty look in his eyes, Brad crept his fingers under the hem of my top. "You look hot too."

Rolling my eyes, I didn't block his hand as his fingers walked along my waist to the base of my ribs. Scooping his hand around my core, Brad pulled me tight against him.

"I like you, Caly," Brad murmured as he kissed across my décolletage. "So, I want to take this slow with us. Get to know each other well before things go all the way. Are you okay with that?"

"Yes," I breathed as his mouth pinched over the mound of my breast. "You may need to remind me of that if you get me too revved up."

"I'll try." He kissed me with such intensity I expected my pants to evaporate from between us. Then Brad's hands moved my top up until we had to break the kiss for it to come over my head.

"One item of clothing tonight," Brad advised as he dropped it on the floor. "And each consecutive time, we'll enable one item of clothing further." Using his hips to spread my thighs wider, Brad lay his pelvis against mine. The feel of his hard bulge pressing into me caused me to bite my lip on a moan. "That's three more dates until I get you naked."

The planning he was putting into this made me laugh. "Knickers last?"

"Definitely!"

"What about foreplay...aw, god!" I cut off on a moan as Brad pressed Mr. Hyde harder into me, and my sex pulsed with need.

"Jesus, Caly. Shut up before I give up being a nice guy," Brad whined.

Laughing, I used his hair to bring his mouth up for a deep, languid kiss. His hands and mouth explored my upper body, but he didn't once grope my breasts. He kissed the flesh above my sports bra - not the sexiest underwear, but we had been trampolining - but that's as close as he went.

For my part, I ran my hands over his gorgeous body, feeling the muscles in his back shift beneath the skin. Scraping my nails down his sides, I fisted his thick dark hair while he kissed down my abdomen. Rocking his hips against mine, Brad rubbed his arousal hard against my sensitive bud.

"Oh my god, stop!" I meant to breathe but yelled when I felt ready to climax.

Chuckling, Brad opened his mouth to say something, but his door flew open, and Brad yanked off me. "What the...?"

"She told you to stop," Dwayne growled at Brad.

"Dwayne, wait." Moving to grab his shoulder and explain, I noticed two other people in the doorway. My eyes went wide at Aaron standing there with another of his friends I recognized from the Pit Stop. Aaron's angry eyes went straight to my breasts. Remembering I was in my bra, I collected my top from the floor and pulled it back on. It was inside out, but I didn't care.

"Dwayne, chill," Brad was trying to calm him down. "I wasn't forcing her."

"He wasn't," I confirmed.

"So, why did you yell for him to stop?" Dwayne asked unconvinced.

"I, ah, um." My cheeks were burning, trying to word the explanation.

"She was about to cum," Brad laughed. "So, was I, for that matter. Perfect timing on that intrusion."

Dwayne's ears burned red as he looked to me for confirmation. Still very embarrassed, I hid my face with my hands as I nodded. Swallowing, Dwayne released Brad. "Damn, I'm, ah, sorry, Dude."

"You weren't even naked together," the guy with Aaron laughed. "Didn't realize you were a minute-man."

"Dude, look at her. She's an inducer," Brad defended as he moved towards me. "What are you all doing home so early, anyway?"

"Party blew. We decided to get a movie and chill here. Sorry to, um, interrupt." Dwayne was looking at me when he said that. His ears were bright red as his eyes scanned me, then he pushed out of the room, taking the tall, built, jock with him. "Stop drooling, Dom. You can't touch her." Dom whined as they moved out to the lounge room. Aaron stood at the door a moment longer, eyes still cold on me.

Taking my waist in his hands, Brad pulled me against him. "You want to say something, Ayah?" Brad asked, a little bite in his voice as he looked between us.

Aaron's eyes jumped to Brad. He didn't say a word, just turned, and left the room, but he didn't shut the door after him. Groaning, I pulled my shirt off to put it back on correctly.

Brad ran his hand through his hair in frustration. "I'm sorry about that." Leaving a little distance between us now, Brad sighed.

"My fault. I just wasn't ready to, um..."

Tucking an escaped strand of hair behind my ear, Brad smiled. "You are so cute when you get embarrassed." The comment made my face flame hotter. Brad chuckled. "I'll walk you home."

"I could stay a little longer. We could kiss and talk."

Brad caressed my cheek. Me. Puddle. On. Floor. "That sounds like a good idea." Kissing me, Brad took my hand and led me back onto his bed. Since he didn't shut the door, we could hear the guys watching their movie. We spent the night laughing as we discussed our lives and got to know each other better between kisses.

"Can I ask about the tattoo?" I yawned, tracing the vine with my fingers. It wasn't feminine. In fact, it was quite masculine with the sharp, dangerous points of thorns and leaves. It almost looked dangerous to touch him.

"Eighteenth birthday present from my older brother," Brad sighed, snuggling closer to me. "He waited until I was drunk off my nut, then took me to his friend, who is a tattooist, and this is what I woke up with."

"Does it hold meaning?"

"Betrayal. My brother despises my Eleri blood and thinks I'm a traitor. I refuse to get involved in the family business, so he branded me for leaving. We both knew I was never going back to Riverside."

Forcing my eyes open to meet his, I observed Brad watching me, his eyes as quiet as the space between us. "I'm sorry. I can't even comprehend how lonely that must be."

"You're an only child whose mother spends half her life in another country."

"Yes, but I always knew she loved me. I have cousins I'm close with who are sort of like perverted older siblings, and if I call my family, they are there for me." Rubbing my head against his chest, I empathized with what he went through. "It would hurt for them to turn on me."

Holding me tighter, Brad kissed the top of my head. "Sometimes, there are families that being part of them is worse than being alone."

There was an ache in my chest for Brad. What he said was valid, but I'd never experienced anything like that. My cousins were the only comparison I could draw, but only because of their mother. Closing my eyes, I listened to Brad's breathing. Considering his childhood, was Brad scarred emotionally, like Kingsley and Queenie? I don't know who fell asleep first, but someone poking my arm woke me up.

Standing over the bed where I lay entwined with Brad, Aaron gestured to the bedside clock. My eyes widened when I saw the time. While I disentangled myself from a snoring Brad, Aaron left the room.

Out in the kitchen, Aaron was eating a bowl of cereal. "I'm driving you to work. Go get ready."

There was no argument from me. I'd miss my bus in twenty minutes by the time I changed. "Thanks."

Leaving their dorm, I ran across the car park and up the stairs to get to my apartment. It took me ten minutes to shower, dress, and race back downstairs, so I was waiting at Aaron's car when he came out.

"You and Brad share the same dorm room?" I asked as Aaron drove.

"Yep." He wouldn't look at me.

"I didn't know." The space between us was dead quiet, but Aaron's fingers relaxed a little on the steering wheel. It wouldn't be that great a leap to think I hooked up with Brad to goad him for rejecting me. "Are you friends?"

Gritting his teeth, Aaron drove in silence, choosing not to talk to me unless it was necessary for the rest of the day.

After work, I caught the bus home. It was strange that Aaron didn't beat me back, but he pulled into the car park the same time I walked up the stairs to my dorm. It was ridiculous that Aaron made me feel ashamed for being there with Brad. Aaron rejected me. Brad and I were dating, and it's not like I knew they were flat-mates.

"Caly!"

Turning, I smiled when Brad jogged up the path behind me. Wrapping an arm around my waist, Brad kissed me for several breathtaking seconds. When Brad pulled back, his eyes were glassy with desire. A car door slammed. Looking passed Brad, I saw Aaron storming into King's Hall.

"I enjoyed last night," Brad brought my attention back to him.

"Me too." Smiling up at him, I blocked the niggle in my mind about Aaron, pushing it away and focusing on the guy who was here. Aaron didn't want me.

"Since you know some of my friends already, would you want to hang out with my friends and me on Wednesday at the bar?"

Well, that could be awkward since Dwayne had already made it clear how he felt about Brad and me dating. "How about we wait until we are sleeping together."

Brad's eyes turned naughty as he lowered his mouth to my nose. "We slept together last night." When he pecked my nose, I felt heat creep up my face. "I wasn't expecting to like it as much as I did. I 'm very comfortable with you, Caly." Pulling me close, Brad kissed the top of my head.

"I enjoyed it too, but I'm not ready for friends." Especially when one of those friends is Aaron Wish.

"Can I at least call you my girlfriend?" Brad murmured against my crown.

"Not yet. We aren't even sleeping together."

Pulling back, Brad met my eyes. "Caly, relationships don't

end and begin with sex."

Body tensing, I bit my lip, my eyes jumping out of my sockets. The term 'a deer in headlights' came to mind at the mention of us being in a relationship.

Caressing my face, Brad sighed. "Okay, let's try it this way. I want us to be exclusive. Is that an issue?"

Considering that I hadn't met anyone other than Aaron, who even held my interest in a long time, was it? It's not like I'd ever dated more than one guy at a time anyway, so exclusivity didn't bother me. "No, that I'm good with."

Smiling, Brad drew my mouth closer. "Good because you may have ignited my first feelings of jealousy, and I don't like how that feels."

My brows drew down, trying to work out how I had made him jealous. Was he still talking about Hawaii? "Jealous of who?"

Brad's eyes wandered to King's Hall. Following his gaze, I swallowed as I remembered the look on Aaron's face.

"The boys know me. We've been friends for years. Dwayne and I went to school together, that's how long we've been friends. They know I would never force a girl. Last night, they came to your protection even though they knew me better than that. Plus, I saw the way Ayah looked at you, Caly. He may have rejected you, but there's something between you two as well."

My toes were very fascinating because I was unable to meet Brad's eyes.

"If you tell me that I can trust you alone with Ayah, I'll believe you. But I want it clear that we are exclusive to each other before this goes any further." Brad tilted my chin up to meet his eyes. "I don't want to lose my heart to you if yours already belongs to someone else."

Surprised, I shook my head. "No, it's not like that. I mean, I've had a crush on Aaron since the seventh grade, but that's all it was." My words tumbled out, trying to explain, then catching my breath, I sighed. "Look, I got drunk once and told him I liked him, then I kissed him. He told me it was never going to happen and gave me some vague reasoning that I couldn't understand. It's been kind of awkward between us since. I'm not in love with him, Brad. You don't have to worry about that. I wouldn't lead you on if there wasn't a chance for us." Brad didn't smile, but he didn't walk away, either. "You can trust me with Aaron. Nothing is going to happen. That boat has sailed."

Brad lowered his mouth to mine again. "Exclusivity, Caly. I want you to be all mine." Brushing his lips over mine, Brad encircled my waist with his hands.

"Time," I breathed. "This is new to me."

Moving his lips across my cheek to my ear, Brad kissed my pulse. "Okay, but I'm not going to touch you again until you tell me you're mine." A small whine escaped my throat, causing Brad to chuckle. Frenching me, he held me tight to his body for several minutes.

"Get a room." Someone grouched walking past.

We broke apart laughing. Meeting his eyes, I noticed they were glistening as much as mine were. "You want to come up for a while?"

Brad lifted a brow. "I'm a man of my word, Caly."

An idea was forming as I started backstepping towards my door. "I don't doubt that for a second, Brad. We can hang out and talk and kiss some more."

Brad's feet started moving to follow me. "So, you want to hang out for the afternoon?"

"Of course," I smirked, unlocking the door.

Brad followed me, a wicked glint in his eyes. "Why do I get the feeling I'm about to meet Miss Hyde?"

Restraining the naughty smile on my face was impossible.

🐍

Two hours late, Penny threw my door open. "Oh my god, Caly." Stopping at the sight of Brad tied shirtless to my bed and the ice cube dropping from my mouth onto Brad's abdomen. Penny's eyes went wide. "Oh. My. God. Caly!" Penny stared while ice water dribbled down Brad's torso, beneath his belt, and lower. As Brad bit his lip and moaned under his breath, Penny smiled.

"Um, Penny? Something you need, or can it wait?" I smirked.

Penny's mouth tilted up to a huge grin. "Ah, it can wait. Please continue."

When Penny continued to stand there grinning, Brad started laughing.

"Penny!" I snapped, laughing.

Startled, Penny realized this wasn't appropriate. "Oh, right, yeah, I'll be out here, or should I come back later?"

"Out there is fine. We were finishing up." Picking up the almost melted ice cube, I put it back in my glass beside my bed and started to untie Brad from the silk ties.

Penny's eyes roamed lower on Brad. "Are you sure he's finished?"

"Yes. Brad has declared he's not touching me again until I agree to be exclusive or in a relationship with him."

Penny chuckled when Brad blushed. "Really? How very eighteen hundreds of you."

Brad shrugged, circling his wrists. "I like Caly. I want a relationship with her. I can wait."

Raising a brow, Penny laughed. "That's good, cause you are going to be waiting for a very long time if that is your criteria." Penny looked at my hands. "Hey, are those my ties?"

"Oh, yeah." Standing up, I handed them back to her. "I wanted to prove my point."

"Which was?"

"That he only said he wouldn't touch me," I replied with a wicked grin. Turning back to Brad when Penny started laughing, I ran my hand along his thigh and over his cargo shorts. "I think he enjoyed it, though." My hand brushed over the tent in his pants.

Brad's eyes shuttered. A second later, he grabbed my hand and pulled me back on the bed, rolling on top of me. "Later, Penny," Brad growled before his lips found mine in a fast and hungry kiss.

"Remember to use a condom," Penny laughed, leaving.

When the bedroom door shut, we stopped caring about the outside world. Kissing me until I was panting, Brad tugged my work shirt over my head, and then his mouth was exploring my body. Keeping his hands on either side of my body, Brad avoided anything inside my bra. Everything else he kissed, sucked and nibbled.

Not as restrained, I ran my hands all over Brad, from his hair to his butt as I pulled him tight against the front of me. At one point, Brad knelt back to look down on me. Taking the opportunity, I tugged his pants open, then pushed them down, so he was in his boxer shorts.

"Are you sure?" Brad asked, eyes dark with lust.

"God, yes," I breathed before unzipping my work pants. Stepping off the bed, Brad dropped his pants. His Hulk print boxer shorts doing nothing to hide Mr. Hyde, who was peeking out the waistband. Grabbing my waistband, Brad helped me out of my pants until I was lying in my underwear.

"We agreed to an item of clothing further each time," I reminded him as he lowered his body over mine.

Shaking his head, Brad smiled. "You are the biggest prick tease I've ever met, Caly."

It was a compliment. The way he said it more than anything told me that. Pressing between my legs, Brad rubbed his hardness against my sensitive flesh. We kissed as we dry humped, moaning, and gasping for breath.

There wasn't much material between us, so it took a matter of minutes for me to bite Brad's shoulder as my body seized. Brad's hands, which had been clenching the quilt to avoid touching me, patted my hair as I relaxed beneath him.

When I opened my eyes, Brad smiled down at me. He looked like he wanted to say something, but I didn't give him a chance. Throwing him on his back, I dropped back to my knees and licked the exposed tip of Mr. Hyde.

"Caly!" Lifting his hands to stop me, I clasped them with mine, then lowered my mouth to suck and lick his tip. Brad didn't need much encouragement. "Caly? Oh, god, fuck!" he groaned before he spurted into my waiting mouth.

Sucking his tip until he relaxed, I made sure it was clean, then I knelt back and licked my lips. Brad watched me, a look of awe on his face. Sitting up quickly, Brad grabbed the back of my head and pulled me down on him to kiss me passionately.

"You didn't have to do that," Brad murmured.

"I know. That's what made me want to do it because you didn't expect it."

Brad kissed me slower this time. "Mine, Caly. Tell me you're all mine."

Kissing his shoulder, I relaxed against his side. "Not yet."

Huffing into the top of my hair, Brad sighed. "I want to see you during the week."

"You'll see me Wednesday," I assured, my fingers tracing the vine of roses on his chest.

Exhaling in frustration, Brad didn't fight it. Instead, he snuggled me closer to him. We stayed that way until Penny banged on the door, declaring she was hungry. "Can't she feed herself?"

"No. Penny is a terrible cook," I sighed against his chest. "I cook a big meal Sunday's, and then we package the leftovers for during the week. Saves either of us taking time out from study to cook."

Sitting up, I placed a kiss on his lips. "Come on, your tummy is growling too." Standing up, I removed a skater dress from my wardrobe. When I turned around, Brad was watching me, and Mr. Hyde was standing erect again. "Really?"

"What did you expect?" Brad teased, standing up and kissing me. "You moved. It affects me every time." With a wink, he started dressing.

With a roll of my eyes, I pulled my dress over my head. "You're just horny."

"Since the day I met you, Caly Zilla." He kissed me a little deeper this time. "Now, you best get out of this room before Penny has to call for pizza."

Chapter Eleven

LANCELOT

He gave me up!

I told Lancelot how I felt about him, and that I wanted something more. He climbed out of my bed the next morning and told me it wasn't going to happen. It hurt; I'm not going to lie. Now, he won't even talk to me. He's still in my life enough that it still stings whenever I see him. I should have listened to you Sin Rocks; then, I wouldn't feel like I misplaced part of me, when I lost him.

Nymph.

Sin Rocks: *I'm sorry, Nymph. You are worth more than a fun time. You deserve to be loved, and for the man you share your heart with to want you outside of the bedroom. I hope you find someone worthy of you.*

Penny Dreadful: *He's an idiot! No more needs to be said. He was a fool to pass you up, and soon enough, he's going to realize how bad he fucked up. Then he'll be sorry.*

The Watcher: *I'm sorry.*

"Well, don't you look spiffy?" Penny grinned when I came out of my room. She wolf-whistled when I twirled for her. "Be careful looking that good around your manwhore cousin."

"He's my cousin." My nose was scrunching at her.

"He's hot and loose of moral," Penny lectured.

When Penny started fanning herself, I laughed. "And where are you going in that skimpy outfit?"

Twirling, Penny flashed more leg than a swimsuit model. "Party with some mates. Don't wait up." Grabbing up her purse, she waved as she moved out the door.

Laughing, I followed her out. "Is this party in a nightclub because that's one hell of a dress for a house party."

"Go enjoy your fancy fundraiser, Rich Girl." Penny waved me off as she headed off towards the campus gym.

That's when I remembered there was a party at the gym for all the gym members tonight. No invite for me since I only ever ran the track. My mind wandered to a particular brooding male, wondering if he would be there. Aaron still wasn't talking to me after finding me in Brad's bedroom. Snapping myself out of my self-made misery, I turned my attention to the car park. Leaning against his car, Kingsley watched me approach with a wicked smile on his face. "Evening, Princess," he greeted, opening the car door. "You look beautiful."

"A date fit for a king?" I kissed his cheek.

"Always." Kingsley shut the door once I was inside. "Have you had a good week?" Dropping into his seat, he belted up before starting the engine.

"Yes. You?"

Kingsley considered my question. "Well, yes, actually." Shifting gears, he sped out of the parking lot and university grounds. "Dad's forced mum into rehab. Quietest the house has been in years. Everyone has been a lot happier."

"That's sad, King."

Kingsley shrugged, but I saw the glassiness in his eyes. "She brought it on herself."

How could I disagree? All my memories of Aunt Karina were of her screaming at the kids or drowning herself in a bottle. There was likely some deep emotional trauma buried under all that bitchiness. Sadly, it was beyond any of her family to reach it. They'd tried; every single one of them. Kingsley spent his childhood trying to reach his mother. He persevered the longest, even after his father and Queenie gave up. Kingsley hoped the longest that his mother would cuddle him, pay any interest in him, or tell him she loved him. In the end, he decided the woman's last words would be of hate when she finally washed into her grave.

Arriving at the fundraiser, Kingsley handed his keys off to the valet. Before leading me inside the iconic Sarita building, Kingsley took a deep breath. "Here we go."

The Sarita family was a wealthy Eleri family who ran international hotels. They contributed to any charity which focused on bringing peace to Riverside. The idea was to build a safer community for both the Riverside and Eleri citizens by getting rid of gangs.

The Sarita's interest was personal. Before I was born, someone from Riverside kidnapped their only daughter. It wasn't about money, but something more illegal, the specifics were never released. The Sarita's refused to compromise their business integrity by agreeing to the demands. So, they never saw their daughter alive again.

It took ten years before they recovered her body from the river. The headlines above pictures of her plastic-wrapped body read 'Shot, execution-style.' Those morbid images sat side-by-side with the last photo of her before she disappeared.

There was some controversy about the Sarita's finding out they were grandparents. That's when it came out the gang held their twenty-year-old daughter prisoner and raped her for years. What I knew was by way of third-hand gossip, since I was only five when her body washed up.

"Kingsley, how good to see you." A man old enough to be my grandfather welcomed us as we entered the grand ballroom. "Is it just you tonight?"

"No, Douglas. Dad is coming in time for the auction, and I doubt Queenie will miss the bachelor's auction. May I introduce Gena's daughter, Caly."

Taking my hand, Douglas Sarita surprised me with the strength of his grip. "And as beautiful as her mother. Your arrival in the world was as controversial as my grandson's. It's good that you are willing to support our cause." Unsure what he meant, I gave him a timid smile and nodded.

Tensing as he excused us so the man could welcome other guests, Kingsley moved us into the ballroom.

"What does he mean by that?"

Sighing, Kingsley led me to the side away from eavesdroppers. "It's speculation, Caly. Don't worry about it."

"What is speculation?"

"Look, your mum turned up pregnant one day and gave birth to you the next. She didn't put a father on your birth certificate and refused to discuss it with anyone. The high society decided your mother was another statistic of Riverside Rape." My stomach dropped out of my insides. "They started a fundraiser for victims of rape all based on the rumor that's how your mother got you."

"But it wasn't," I hissed. "She loved him."

Kingsley rubbed my upper arms. "I know what your mother told you, but you are the only person she's ever told that too. For everyone else, she refuses to discuss it." Staring at his toes, Kingsley rocked back and forth to his heels. "Fuck, I'm sorry, Caly. It's been twenty years, I thought everyone would have something better to discuss."

Frowning, I shook my head, refusing to believe my mother lied to me about something this important. When Kingsley's gaze shined sympathy my way, instead of assurance, I looked past him into the crowd. Gena would not have lied to me about something important like that.

"What. The. Fuck!" I cursed only a little louder than a whisper. My eyes locked on a certain tall, dark, and handsome man who only a week ago I'd spent a lot of time kissing.

Turning around, Kingsley followed my eyesight. "That's Emily Sarita. She's Douglas's grandchild from his son," Kingsley observed the tall, gorgeous blond. "Do you know her?"

"No!" I spat. "But I know the man wearing her like a scarf."

That answer made Kingsley's eyes darken, and his brows drew down. "How do you know Brad Meadows?" When I turned my glare from Brad with his arm around Emily's waist to Kingsley, his eyes became murderous. "Oh, you are fucking me! You're screwing Brad Meadows?"

The people closest to us turned astonished looks our way. Embarrassed and angry, I slapped Kingsley's arm. "Shh. Do you want a megaphone, so everyone knows my sex life?"

"No, but I'd prefer you to go bang Aaron Wish. Hell, marry Wish. Get the fuck away from Meadows," Kingsley scowled.

"Why? He's a decent guy, and he likes me," I argued back, albeit keeping my volume down. My eyes tracked to where Brad was letting Emily Sarita almost rub him down. "Well, I thought he was."

"Why?" Kingsley growled. "You mean other than him being a Meadows?"

Tonight, was one slap in the face after the other. How had I not picked up on the surname? Freezing at the realization, all I could do was blink at Kingsley.

Swiping his hand down his face, my cousin shook his head. He was likely not believing how stupid I was not to have noticed his name before now. "You didn't know?"

Shaking my head, I felt like Kingsley knocked the wind out of me. My sweet, charming, Brad was the youngest son of the most horrid gang leader in Riverside. Brad Meadows was the son of Greg Meadows and the younger brother of the vile Terry Meadows. Brad's tattoo popped into my head. Terry Meadows did that to him. Closing my eyes, I took a deep breath. "He doesn't have anything to do with his family. They branded him a traitor." Glancing where Brad was schmoozing with a group of socialites, I cringed. His arm was now around Emily Sarita's waist.

Kingsley watched me watch them. "Jesus, you've fallen for him."

"I thought he didn't care about the money. I was wrong if he's here with Emily Sarita."

Rubbing the bridge of his nose, Kingsley exhaled. Placing his arm over my shoulders, he pulled me close to whisper in my ear. "They're family. Brad is the controversial child of Mary Sarita, Douglas' daughter."

The hits kept coming. "Brad's mother was the woman who they kidnapped, raped, and murdered?" Tears sprung to my eyes when Kingsley nodded. "So, that would mean, Greg Meadows was the one who kidnapped his mother?"

"No one has proved Meadow's guilt, nor that he had any involvement with her murder." Talking as he walked, Kingsley moved us through the crowd. "The only thing anyone knows is that Greg Meadows is Brad's father, and Mary Sarita was his mother. The how doesn't matter. He is Meadow's son, and I don't care if he speaks to his family or not, you need to end it with him."

"Kingsley," a man called stepping towards us.

Taking a deep breath, I closed my eyes and focused on shoving aside this discussion and my emotions. Killing the conversation, the turbid current of high-society gossip sucked us in.

We swished from group to group. Kingsley never stayed long with any group. The men wanted to talk about business or sports, and the women hit on him or discussed fashion with me. It was all very dull, and my cheeks were hurting from the fake smile I was keeping on my face. Then we entered into the next group, and I found myself face to face with Sinclair Rockford.

"Caly, how nice to see you again," Sinclair smiled, coming forward and taking my hand to raise it to his lips.

Over his shoulder, I spotted Dwayne in his suit, looking like a professional bodyguard. "You work for him?" Dwayne nodded.

Rockford glanced over his shoulder at Dwayne, frowned, and took my arm. "Do me the honor of a dance?" He nodded to Kingsley, who had only now realized I was dance-napped but too late to stop it.

Leading us onto the dance floor, Rockford spun me in to face him. "You look lovely this evening," he smiled as he moved me around the floor with him. Not proper ballroom dancing. Just stepping side to side, swaying really.

"Thank you."

"I heard you are dating Brad Meadows?" Rockford

conversed. Oh god, it's going to be one of those nights. "It's good that you were smart enough not to come as his date tonight."

"There was nothing smart about it," I gritted my teeth. "I would have if Brad asked me."

Rockford met my eyes, and again the familiarity struck me. "His older brother is here. If Terry Meadows sees you two together, he will use you to hurt his brother."

Getting angry very fast, I met Rockford's eyes. "Wouldn't the same happen if Terry sees us dancing together?"

Rockford's brow jumped. His eyes dropped to my locket before he released my hand. Palming the pendant, Rockford rubbed his thumb over the filigreed surface of the metal. "This necklace your mother gave you is worth more than you think."

Confused by the change in subject, I tilted my head to consider him. "It's a magic amulet."

Letting go of the locket, Rockford retook my hand. "Is it just?"

"Not really, I've just been telling myself that since I was a kid..." My mind flashed back to the man in the playground, and my eyes went wide as I focused on Sinclair Rockford. "That's why you're familiar."

Gripping me a little tighter, Rockford forced me to keep dancing. "Don't make a scene, Caly; you can't let people know that we have a history."

Mouth hanging open, I stared at him. "Why? Why, after all this time, are you back in my life again?"

"It is your life choices that are bringing you into my life, Caly." His eyes found Brad still with his cousin all over him. "Bad life choices."

"Brad is the most decent man I've ever met. His family isn't part of his life, so that's inconsequential. Why does everyone have such an issue with him and me?"

"You are a Zilla, and he is a Meadows. The issue would be rather obvious," Rockford's voice was peaceable, but his eyes were a tornado of anger."

"How does that affect you, Mr. Rockford? Did you have a son vying for my attention that I wasn't aware of?" Aaron came to mind, but then I remembered that he'd warned me off Aaron already.

"May I remind you that we are at an event in honor of the last girl who got herself kidnapped and killed in Riverside. The Zillas' are good people, Caly. But if that were to happen to one of their blood, they would not pay the ransom. They would not start a charity in the name of their lost child. They would bring the war to doors of Riverside and annihilate everyone who stood in their way." Releasing me, Rockford stepped back. "My interest is the damage that could do to an already broken people."

"You know, Mr. Rockford, I may be a naive rich girl to you, but I know when someone is trying to feed me a bag of horse shit. Thanks for the dance."

Spinning around, I walked off to find Kingsley. My eyes tracked to where Brad was, and I had to swallow the burn of jealousy, seeing Emily wrapped around him. Should cousins be that touchy-feely? I mean, Kingsley was inappropriate with me at times, but he'd never been all over me like a rash.

Lifting his drink to his lips, Brad paused as his disarmed eyes met mine. He wasn't expecting to see me, and he wasn't sure what to do now that he had. Stomach clenching, I turned my gaze and disappeared into the crowd to locate Kingsley. It wasn't hard. Just look for the biggest group of suck-ups.

"Hey, where did you get to?" Kingsley smiled as I slipped

back in beside him. When I shook my head, Kingsley let it go and placed his hand in my lower back to draw me into the conversation. Shortly after, the announcement for the auction attracted the crowd towards the stage. "Everything alright?" Kingsley murmured as he maneuvered me to where he wanted to stand.

"I've been getting a lot of unsolicited dating advice tonight. I'm sort of over it," I grumbled.

"We worry about you, princess. But, if you tell me to butt out, I will."

Meeting his eyes, I glared, knowing he was lying. "Butt out."

Kingsley smirked. "I'll think about it." The auction began. "Grandad told me to buy something decent. Your mum's birthday is coming up, so if you see something worthwhile, let me know."

"Kingsley," Uncle Bryce came to stand beside his son. "Caly, enjoying your first fundraiser?"

"Yes, it's fantastic," I hid my annoyance at being here in a healthy dose of sarcasm.

Chuckling, Bryce turned his attention to the auction. "Queenie will be around here somewhere. Knowing my daughter, she's scoping out the bachelors for the auction."

"I should go join her since my taste in men is not adequate," I grumbled.

"What did I miss?" Bryce mock-whispered to Kingsley. The auction began, and Kingsley waved his father off to focus.

Uncle Bryce bid on a crate of some impressive wine and won; Kingsley bid on a swim with the sharks' experience. The bidding got crazy with another male in his thirties, trying hard to win it. When the price was astronomical, Kingsley pulled out and let the other man pay through the nose for it.

"That guy glaring at me look familiar to you, Caly?" Kingsley whispered.

Studying the man, I could see something familiar in his eyes, but that's about it. The guy was glaring at Kingsley while he whispered in my ear, which in turn brought the guy's eyes to me. He gave me the same feeling as biting into ice, so I sighed with relief when he turned his attention back to the auction.

"That's Terry Meadows, your boyfriend's older brother." Kingsley gave me a meaningful look, then started bidding on a month worth of massages.

Searched the room with my eyes for Brad, I couldn't see him. Instead, I spotted Rockford. A few minutes later, I watched when he embarked on a bidding war with Terry Meadows for a plot of land along the river. In that instant, I knew that's why both men were here tonight.

"The land was for a college in Riverside, but the city gave up on Riverside ever getting its shit together. The city then sold the land to a private developer ten years ago. After too many employees got caught in drive-bys trying to survey the land, the developer sold it on. Now, the current owner has donated it because it's worthless," Kingsley enlightened me.

"That's sad. The kids of Riverside deserve a higher education that's affordable, like a college."

It was wrong that Riverside kids didn't have more options. If they didn't have the grades for university, then their education ceased. And that wasn't accounting for the small chance of getting a scholarship. The auctioneer called the wrap up with Terry Meadows about to win. It seems even Rockford could only stretch himself so far.

"One point nine million!" Raising his hand, Uncle Bryce bid over five hundred thousand more than Meadows' last bid. With his phone to his ear, it was clear Uncle Bryce was taking a call.

"I have it at one point, nine million. Is there any other bid above one point nine million?" Rockford and Meadows both shook their heads, scowling in my uncle's direction. "Sold to Bryce Zilla," the auctioneer called.

"It's ours," Bryce informed the caller and hung up. Eyeing my uncle, Rockford flitted his eyes to me as the auction continued.

"What are you going to do with a plot of land in Riverside?" I asked.

"Exactly what the city intended it for, Caly," Bryce smiled, giving my cheek a small pinch. "Now, if you'll excuse me, I'll go pay the bill, and then I'm leaving. Don't stay too late. You don't want to see all the spells break, and everyone turn back into vermin and rats."

Kingsley chuckled as his dad walked away. "Now, the fun starts."

The auction changed over to the Bachelor Auction just as Queenie appeared at my side. She was her usual tipsy and exuberant self. "Evening, fellow Zillas," she greeted.

"Who's the victim this year?" Kingsley teased.

"Lucky number three," Queenie twittered. "Phil Crell. Art historian of the museum, single, new to his money, and straight."

"Always important," I chuckled.

"Want me to spot you, Caly?" Kingsley offered. "There has to be a bachelor here who could catch your eye."

Glaring at my cousin, knowing what motivated his offer, I gave him the finger. Kingsley and Queenie chuckled, then got caught up in the auction.

A hand brushed my elbow got my attention. Looking over my shoulder, I found Brad standing behind me. "Excuse me." Stepping away from my cousins, I caught Kingsley eyeing Brad.

Taking my hand, Brad led me out of the ballroom and down

an empty corridor. "I didn't think this was your thing." Brad stopped us halfway down the hall.

"It's not, but Kingsley asked me to go with him. Our family always supports this event," I justified my presence.

"I was going to ask you to be my date, but you said you were busy." Taking my hand, Brad moved a step closer. "You look stunning."

"So does Emily."

Brad's brows twitched, then a slow grin developed. "Are you jealous, Caly?"

"No," I snapped.

Brad's smile grew. "A little defensive, aren't we?"

"Okay, I was a little upset seeing some blonde all over you when a week ago you were asking me for a commitment. But that's before I knew it was your cousin."

"Ah." Brad stepped a little closer. "Caly, Emily, and I aren't related."

"What?" That wasn't helping.

"The Sarita's adopted her father; she's not blood-related."

"Oh, that explains how touchy-feely she is with you," I grimaced.

Blowing out a breath, Brad nodded. "Tell me about it." Closing the distance, Brad placed a delicate kiss to my lips. "Come home with me? We are going the same way, so it makes sense we go home together." He firmed his lips against mine.

A deep throat clearing jolted us apart. Standing a few meters away, Rockford looked less than happy. When his eyes lifted above our heads, we turned to see Terry Meadows approaching.

"Hello, little brother. Who is this sweet thing?" Terry wandered closer to us, two dodgy-looking men behind each of his shoulders.

"I should get back." I retreated another step.

"Whoa, what's the rush?" Terry stepped in my way.

"Let her go, Terry. She's just a girl from uni," Brad dismissed, his eyes flicking back to Rockford and Dwayne behind him.

"Like slumming it do you, honey?" Terry blocked my way again. "Want to get dirty with a Riverside boy?"

"Not my thing," I snarled.

"What getting dirty or..."

"Let her go, Terry. Her date is probably wondering where she is." Boredom and annoyance were resounding through the corridors from Brad's voice.

"Caly!" Kingsley called from down the corridor. Halting, he shoved his hands in his pockets. "I'm ready to go."

"That's your date?" Terry Meadows snickered.

"Yeah, because I have taste," I sniped, shoving past him and marching down the hall to Kingsley.

"You have balls too, bitch," Terry called behind me, "but I'll still fuck you."

Kingsley glared at everyone behind me. "She's out of your league, Meadows. Go back to your skanks and stop trying to catch yourself a pedigree." Unsure which of the meadows he was addressing, I wasn't about to stop and ask.

Placing his hand in the middle of my back, Kingsley turned his back on the scene. He waited until we were in the car to lose his cool. "End it with Meadows tonight."

"No," I gaped at Kingsley astounded.

"He's not good for you," Kingsley growled.

"Have I ever told you how to live your life? You are one condescending prick. You are egotistical, you treat women like dirt, and I know you fucked Penny on my birthday last year. I've never torn you down about it because I know, deep down, very, very deep down, that you care. You care too God damn much, and that's why you hide it and try to protect yourself with this bastard you became. You don't get to demand I give up the first guy I've liked in years because his brother is the big bad across the river."

The car fell silent for several minutes. "It would break my heart if anything ever happened to you, Princess," Kingsley murmured. "I'd no longer be Kingzilla. I'd be the living breathing version of Godzilla to Riverside if any of those bastards hurt you."

"Since I'm not the whoring narcissist in the car, can you give me the benefit of the doubt? I mean, I am pretty picky about who I date." Keeping my voice even, I placed my hand on Kingsley's on the gear stick.

Kingsley spared me a quick look. "It's serious, then?"

"It could be."

Taking a deep breath, Kingsley shook his head. "I'll make you a deal. Take Brad to meet granddad at the next family dinner. If the old bastard tells you to get rid of him, you will end it the next day. Deal?" There was no doubt that Granddad would tell me to end it once he knew who Brad was. That meant I had two weeks to prepare for my grandfather meeting Brad; I'd need to lay some groundwork.

When Kingsley dropped me off, I entered my dorm room to find it empty. Showering and slipping into my pajamas, I picked up my study notes. My brain needed something to focus on, or I'd dwell on the situation of my relationship and never get to sleep.

Chapter Twelve

Blow

'The wind from one door closing opens another.'

Blow entered my life at the same time Lancelot made his lack of interest known. The experience of dating Blow is not the same as any other before, and I crave to see him whenever I stop to take a breath. Is this what it feels like to fall for someone? Acknowledging that scares the hell out of me, but I don't want to make the same mistake I did with the Professor. My mother tells me I need to experience getting my heart broken. But she never recovered from that happening to her, so how can I be brave enough to suffer the same?

All I know is I'm not ready to give this feeling up yet.

Nymph

Gee Zee: *You can't avoid relationships out of fear of what your mother went through. Your experiences will be yours. Learn from someone else's mistakes, but don't stop living for fear of making any. That's what life is all about.*

Sin Rocks: *I agree with GZ. Your mother made her choice, but you are not your mother, and you won't necessarily make the same* mistakes. *My mother always told me you couldn't help who you fall in love with, but you can control what you do about it. Don't fear to live, Nymph, just make wise choices about who you let into your life.*

The Penny Drops: *Chill the fuck out, everyone. Nymph, you were two years younger when you fell for the Professor, and he was your first. You got scared, and you made a choice. Stop dwelling on the past and ride Blow hard. If he brings out your inner cowgirl, ride him until he breaks. If he throws you off, pick yourself up, brush the dust off, and know not to ride that stallion again. Let loose and have some fun, and stop overanalyzing this shit. I blame Lancelot for this. Remember how easy going you were with Bounce? That's the approach you need right now.*

❧

A knock sounded at the door as I finished another week's readings. Closing my laptop, I went to the door and cracked it open. Surprised, I opened the door further. "Brad?"

"Can we talk?" Brad pleaded.

Opening the door, I let him in, shutting it behind him and following him into the small living space.

"I'm sorry I didn't tell you who my family was. I wasn't trying to hide it from you, I didn't want you to judge me by association," Brad launched his defense.

Stepping forward, I covered his mouth. His eye's springing open, Brad observed me. "Are you using me?" Brad shook his head. "Did you come into my life to set up some elaborate kidnapping and ransom?" Brad shook his head again. Lowering my hand, I stepped closer. "Is your interest in me anything to do with your family or mine?"

"No," Brad answered huskily. "God, no." Stepping forward,

Brad swept my hair back so he could cup my face in his large hands. "It's all you, Caly. I'm in love with you."

Surprised by his choice of words, I swallowed. Considering how I felt about Brad, I was sure any hesitation would be acknowledging I felt the same. "Then your family doesn't matter to me. But you are going to have to be amazing to win my grandfather over," I warned. "My family are closing ranks now that they know who I'm dating. It's all going to come down to Granddad's approval."

Wrapping me in his arms, Brad rested his chin on my head. "Do you want to end this?"

Closing my eyes, I had to wonder if he was worth what was coming. "What did you tell your brother?"

"He doesn't know who you are, so I told him we used to have a thing, and that you dumped me for Kingsley."

"He bought that?"

"That some classy chick dumped me for the richest guy in town?" Brad chuckled. "Yeah, he bought it."

"You're the first guy I've dated in years that I can see lasting, Brad. I don't want to let go just because your family are assholes." When Brad shifted his stance, I looked up to assess his reaction.

Brad lowered his face to mine. "I didn't scare you off, telling you how I'm in love with you?"

Swallowing hard, I shook my head slightly.

Grabbing a fistful of my hair, Brad shook his head. "I want you, Caly."

It was time I followed my gut. "Then take me," I whispered.

Crushing his mouth to mine, Brad demanded I surrender to him, so I did. Dropping his hands to my waist, Brad lifted my legs around his hips, then he carried me into my room. Dropping me on my bed, Brad removed his jacket, shirt, and shoes.

Did I mention he was still in his suit from the fundraiser? How was I ever going to resist him looking so debonair?

When Brad stepped towards me, I came to my knees and stopped him. "Everything."

Brad's lips twitched. "Hello, Miss. Hyde." Lowering the zip on his pants, Brad pushed them down, boxers and all.

"Hello, Mr. Hyde," I purred at how hard and ready he was.

Lifting my pajama top over my head, I then lowered my shorts to the ground. Brad's breath rushed out of him. His reaction to seeing me naked made me smile.

Kneeling on the bed, Brad started to lower himself over me but stopped. "You're on the pill, right?"

"Yes."

"You're not going to insist on a condom?"

Crap! The things you forget when you're tired and horny. "Do you have one?" It had been a while, so I was out. "I can grab one from Penny's room?"

"I'm clean, I promise." Brad pulled away. "But let's use the condom to be safe. It will make our wedding night special if that's the first time I take you bare."

My eyes went wide. "Wedding night...?"

"Shh," Brad placed his finger over my lips, a devilish smile on his face. "Get the condom now, freak out about commitment later."

Blinking at him, I got up to raid Penny's stash. Brad smacked my bottom as I passed him, and I smiled at how his soft chuckle heated me up.

He was lying on the bed, stroking himself when I walked back into the room. Making sure to lock the door in case Penny tried to barge in, I slowed my steps, watching him handle himself. I never expected that to be such a turn on.

"I should have told you to get a few," Brad teased.

Holding up my hand, I relaxed my fingers and let the strip of foils drop down so he could count the six.

Brad laughed, "Rather ambitious, aren't you?"

With a shrug, I moved towards him. "I have high expectations."

Caressing my face, Brad kissed me slowly as I leaned over him. Taking the foils from my hand, Brad tore one away while I nibbled my way to his nipples. Putting out my hand for him, Brad placed the individual packet in my palm.

Kissing lower, I opened the pack. I wanted to take him in my mouth, but it had been a while for both of us, and I worried if I did, he might not last the preamble. Instead, I straightened and applied the safety net, making my hands roll it down in a slow and firm stroke.

Brad's eyes rolled back in his head as a delicious moan reverberated out of his throat. "God, Caly, you drive me crazy."

Smiling as I moved my body over his, I aligned our pelvises. His tip dipping inside, I lowered my mouth to his. I didn't say anything; I didn't want to talk right now. I ached to be quiet and enjoy every sound his entering me wrested from him.

Placing his hands on my hips, Brad pushed me down, slow and steady, spreading me open to him. Biting my lip, I inhaled with how much space he demanded to occupy within my body.

We took it slow, neither of us wanting to rush this. Enjoying the feel of each other, we kissed and touched, pausing to explore and draw out the sensations.

I'd never had sex like this. Usually, it was fast or slow, but I never had a guy pull out of me, or still himself inside me, to kiss and touch me. The drawn-out experience meant I came for him twice. The second time, taking him to the pinnacle of pleasure with me and dragging him into euphoria.

"Can I stay the night?" Brad murmured when he rolled off me to let me use the bathroom.

"I expected you would," I grumbled, a little surprised he'd asked.

Brad kissed my shoulder. "Don't be cranky. You're the commitment-phobe. I didn't want to push my luck."

Staring up into his eyes, I found they were light and full of happiness, also red-rimmed and tired. He looked scruffy and gorgeous as I kissed his nose. "For future reference, I like cuddles after sex, so expect to stay the night."

Rolling off the bed, I went to the bathroom. When I came back, Brad was under the covers, snoring a little. Setting my alarm, I snuggled into bed with him. There was a giddy feeling in my stomach, the right sort. One that made you think of cold winter nights snuggled together. Or to dream of white dresses and churches.

My eyes shot open before the 'I do's,' and I silenced my alarm. Brad grumbled behind me. Slipping out of bed, I dressed for my run. As I was leaving, Brad was still sound asleep, and he was not a light sleeper.

After my run, I had a shower then came into my room to dress. Brad was awake, checking his phone. "Sorry, I've got work," I explained as I donned my work uniform.

"What are you doing tonight?" Brad asked, pulling up his knees to wrap his elbows around them.

Meeting his gaze in the reflection of my mirror, I frowned. "You have your Grandfather's birthday party."

"Come with me." The request made me freeze, staring at Brad. "You said your family is already circling the wagons, so they know about us. I want my family to know about us, too," Brad explained. That one stopped me breathing. "My mum's family."

There was no hiding my full body exhalation. "I would, but I have work early tomorrow."

"Pack a change of clothes now. I'll pick you up from work, drive us to Barr and back again tonight," Brad offered. "You can sleep in the car on the way home."

Considering his offer, I thought better of it. "You're going to have to come to dinner in two weeks and meet my grandfather. We should wait to see how he reacts before we go letting anyone else know about us."

Throwing the sheet back, Brad walked towards me. My breath caught at the sight of his gorgeous nakedness.

"I promised my grandfather I'd let him meet you before it got serious," I explained as Brad took me in his arms. "You're talking love and marriage. We've had sex. I'm feeling about you how I haven't for anyone except one other person before. I know what this feeling is, Brad. It's scary for me. If this is going to last, I need my family to support this. So, I'm going to go visit my grandfather tonight, and lay the groundwork."

Brad watched my eyes, assessing my words. "Okay, but the weekend after I meet your granddad, you're meeting mine." His acceptance of my plan tempted a smile on my lips. "Exclusive from now on. And I'm going to start calling you my girlfriend too." I grizzled at that. Brad chuckled. "We're hanging out with my friends on Wednesday night."

Placing my hand on his chest, I tapped my fingers. "My mum is in town this week. I'll be having dinner with her and staying the night at home so I can spend some time with her."

"Wait, I'm meeting your grandfather before your mum?" Brad took a step back, unhappy.

"My mum doesn't know about you yet. We moved forward a little faster than I anticipated."

Brad didn't look impressed. Looking at it from his perspective, I guess it made sense to him he should meet my mum first. But Granddad ruled the family, so he was the important one.

"I'm going to tell her Wednesday, ask for her to meet you while she's in town, and explain the situation to her. If she's on our side, she will help pull Granddad over for us."

Brad's brows and mouth slanted down. "Caly, if your family doesn't approve, what happens then? Because the way you're talking, I'm out of the picture if that's the case."

My eyes prickle with restrained emotion.

Brad saw it. Stepping back as if I'd slapped him, he started yanking his clothes on. "If that's the case, you should have waited an extra two weeks to give in, Caly."

"Brad..."

"Why? Why did you sleep with me last night if you know you'll have to end it in a few weeks?"

"I slept with you because I wanted to, and the time felt right. Why does a female wanting to have sex have to equal marriage and babies?"

Brad's eyes glared at me. Jesus, Kingsley said women got hung up after sex.

"Look, I care about you. I spent last night telling everyone they could stick their opinion of you up their wazoo. For fuck's sake! Do you know even Sinclair Rockford expressed his opinion about a Meadows-Zilla alliance? An absolute stranger told me to end things with you, and I told him to stick it too. So, no, I'm not planning to end this, Brad. I'm planning the exact opposite. But I'd rather do it with the support of those who I care about, then without."

Stepping into me, Brad cuffed the back of my neck and kissed me passionately. Gripping his still-open shirt, I pressed the kiss deeper. After a moment, I forced myself away from him and grabbed up my bag.

"I want to be with you, Brad, so give me space and time to make it happen." Without waiting for his response, I left.

Jogging for the bus stop, the nerves in my stomach made me nauseous. Would I end things with Brad if my Granddad told me to? Thinking of my mum and that she'd never fallen in love with a man again, I knew I didn't want to spend the rest of my life lonely.

Once I was on the bus, I called Gena. "Caly? Is everything alright, Honey?" It was late evening in Switzerland.

"I'm on the bus to work and wanted to make sure we were still having dinner this week?"

"Of course. I'll be home for two weeks this visit. I need to collaborate with Bryce on some things," Gena assured. "Now, tell me why you really called."

"How did you know you were in love with dad?"

Chapter Thirteen

✦

BLOW

This blog's purpose was to act as a homage to all the ridiculous shit my first boyfriend would say to get me to have sex with him. After we broke up, it became about my dating experiences, the good, and the bad. Well, Blow has always known the right things to say to get a woman to have sex with him. What makes it better is that he's been sincere in his words, and backed them up with his actions.

Last night, I doubted the potential of this relationship. Blow showed up and not only put my mind at ease, but convinced me we were worth pursuing. So, now I'm in my first committed relationship since the Professor two years ago. Guess it's time to meet the parents. Or, in our case, the grandparents.

I'll let you know if I still have a boyfriend by the time my family has finished with him.

Nymph.

P.S. I finished dinner with my grandparents. Why do people lie? Why? I don't know what to think anymore.

. . .

Penny Dreadful (Formerly The Penny Drops): Men suck! They lie every time they open their mouths.

The Watcher: Not all guys, PD. Some have things they feel the need to hide.

Penny Dreadful: An omission of truth to hide something important is still a lie.

Sin Rocks: I agree with TW. Not all guys lie, and some lies are to protect you. Still, if the grandparents know some truth, it's worth listening to and getting rid of this guy too.

Gee Zee: I'm skeptical. But you should confront someone with their lie. Hear their truth before you believe another's. There are always three versions of every story. Yours, theirs, and the truth.

❧

"Hey," Brad's voice broke me out of my stretch. Sitting upright, I met his eyes. "I've been sitting over there going over my data for the last hour and a half, just waiting for you to look up or stretch." Brad took the seat opposite me.

"How'd you know to find me in the library?" Stretching my neck, I checked the time. God, I'd been reading and writing notes for three hours now.

"Penny. She told me she's a noisy learner, and you're quiet, so you go your separate ways."

"She likes to study with the television on, and it kills my concentration."

Brad nodded, "Ayah gets all pissy if anyone makes noise while he's studying. He's usually here on the weekend."

Pointing my pen to the private study rooms, I slumped in my chair. "Room three, he has it permanently booked."

"You don't use a room?"

"For assignments, yes. It is more like exam conditions out

here, quiet but still a lot of background noise. Better for me to study in," I explained. "How was the party?"

"Good. How was your Granddad?"

Sighing, I closed my study books and started packing them up. "Unusually quiet."

"You sent me a message that you wanted to see me," there was hesitation in Brad's words.

Chewing my cheek, I shoved my stuff in my bag, looking for the right way to discuss this. "I spoke to my mum. She wants to meet you. She told me to bring you to dinner on Wednesday night." Standing up, I slung my bag over my shoulder. "Grab your stuff; I have to go start dinner."

Brad stood but moved forward, taking my hand. "You're upset?"

Shaking my head, I looked around. "Not here."

Brad's mouth dropped open, his shoulders snapping back.

"It's not that," I assured. "I'll explain as we walk."

Once Brad collected his gear, we walked back towards the dorm. He kept looking at my hands, which were clutching my backpack strap as if he wanted to hold them, but I was on edge today. When we reached a bench well away from everything, I dropped down onto it. Brad sat next to me. "You're making me nervous, Caly."

"My grandfather was all keen for you to come to dinner, happy and chatting," I started.

"Until you told him who I was?" Brad guessed.

"He stared at me like I'd told him I'd murdered someone." My eyes watered, remembering the look on granddad's face. "Even my grandmother didn't know what to say. I told them you and your father are estranged, that you're nothing like that side of your family. Granddad said that he knew all about you because he's friends with your grandfather."

Groaning, Brad scrubbed his hands. "Shit, I should have considered that." Taking a deep breath, Brad looked at me. "He told you?"

Nodding my head, I stood up and turned to look at him. "Jesus, Brad, even my mother knew. Why does everyone know but me?" Brad lowered his eyes to the ground. I swiped at the tears, starting to fall down my face.

"You could have told me," I muttered as I tried to compose myself. "I cannot remember a single time in my life, where my mother has told me I have to do something. Not once. She has always given me my options. Even as a child, I had the option of doing what my mother told me, or going to my room without any toys, but it was an option. Yesterday morning, my mother told me she would meet you at dinner on Wednesday. It wasn't a request or an option."

Looking up at me, Brad watched me, his own eyes were glassy.

Swallowing back more tears, I looked away. On the path, I spotted Aaron, standing there watching. "Jesus!" I murmured to myself and looked to the sky, blinking even more tears away. The last person I needed to see. "It's over, right?"

"So, so, over," Brad groaned. "I was younger when I got caught up with her, but it's never been a permanent thing. We are friends only now, I swear."

"Everyone expects you to marry her. Everyone in that circle. If I was to guess right, after her behavior on Friday night, she still expects it too."

Slumping against the bench, Brad glared up at me. "You're right, she does. It's why Emily was all over me Friday night. What no one knows is six months ago, Emily got plastered and crawled into my bed, telling me she wanted a baby. When I told Emily she was drunk and talking gibberish, she got angry.

"Emily told me she wanted a real connection to our family. Her father's adopted, so she's not related in any way. While my grandparents treat her well, the moment they found out about me, I became the heir to their fortune.

"That's why she was after me. She didn't love me, and she was happy for us to see other people, but she would be my wife. If she had to get knocked up to force me to marry her, she would. Emily was so wasted; she doesn't even remember saying it to me. I haven't touched her again since."

"But you go to those events together, so everyone else thinks..."

"I don't go anywhere with her," Brad argued, standing up. "I would have taken you, Friday night. I went by myself. She hangs off me in public."

Studying his eyes, I was looking for any hint of a lie, but he seemed sincere.

Stepping forward, Brad caressed my cheek, wiping away my tears. "I thought I would be the one getting upset about other men chasing your tail. Emily is so far in the past for me; I didn't even consider her an issue until you saw me with her Friday night."

"You knew she would become one, though? It's why you told me straight up you weren't related."

Catching a deep breath, Brad cleared his throat. "Emily and I lost our virginity to each other, but I never thought it was leading to marriage. She started sleeping with other guys, and I saw other girls. Hell, Emily and your cousin, Kingsley, had a fling for a month, and she started preparing her wedding to him."

"Oh, well, that would have killed that relationship," I acknowledged. "So, Emily is trying to ensure she stays rich by marrying well?"

"It would seem so." Brad moved closer. When his eyes flicked past me, I knew he'd finally noticed Aaron. "Message me what time Wednesday. That's if you still want to keep seeing me," Brad muttered into my ear. "I know I've given you reasons not to trust me, Caly, but I do want this to work between us. For no other reason than I'm in love with you." Placing a kiss before my ear, Brad stepped back to grab his bag and walked over to where Aaron was watching.

"What'd you do?" Aaron asked, straight out.

"The usual. I was born," Brad answered as they started walking back to the dorms. "Why is Rockford interested in her?"

Aaron's eyes jumped to me, then shifted away as he shrugged one shoulder. "How should I know? Rumor says he's banged all the other Zilla females. Maybe he's lining her up for a go."

Shivering at the thought, I picked up my bag once they were out of earshot and made my way back to my dorm. "Did Brad find you?" Penny asked as I came in.

"Yeah."

"You ask him about screwing his cousin?"

I'd told Penny when I got home yesterday, having already heard it from mum. Then I recounted to Penny how my grandfather dropped the bomb that Brad was engaged to be married. What I hadn't told anyone was how Grandad stared at me with absolute disappointment in his eyes. After murmuring about me being like my mother, Grandad left the table. When I'd burst into tears, my grandmother spent the next twenty minutes trying to soothe me.

"Brad told me it finished last year, that they were never exclusive. He also suggested that she's a money-grabbing bitch," I summarized.

Penny closed her book. "So, that's settled? When can I start planning the wedding?"

With a sigh, I dropped down onto the couch next to her. "My family are never going to approve of him now. It was bad enough he's related to the worst family in Riverside, but for them to think he's been using me as a piece on the side." I shook my head. "My family are going to see his interest in me as financial and to gain prestige here in Eleri. They'll never believe he loves me."

Penny took my hand in hers. "Do you believe he loves you?"

Calculating Brad's words against his actions, then subtracting the time we'd been dating, I found it hard to believe. "Not true love, but I believe he cares for me."

"Relationships aren't easy. That's why you've avoided them as long as possible. You care about Brad, and him you. If you want this to work, it's going to take time, patience, and forgiveness. Even you have a past. Did you tell Brad that only the other week Aaron Wish spent the night in your bed?"

"He knows it happened, but not how recently it happened." Taking a deep breath, I sighed. "I see your point."

"Good. Now, I'm hungry. What's for dinner?"

Chapter Fourteen

LIES, *Truths, Risk*

There comes a point where you have to balance one person's truth with others. Then you make a decision on whether you will let mistruths derail your future. People make choices every day that can lead them down any number of paths. Sometimes they choose a track, and halfway down it, they realize that was a mistake.

The thing about life is that there is no going back, no returns, no resubmissions. But you can make a choice to get off that path. See, if you aren't in too deep, there is always another decision available to take a side path. It may haunt them going forward, but if they can justify the choices they've made, why should we punish them for it?

Why should we give up on them? What if, by giving up on them for their past mistakes, we make a choice that sets us on the wrong track?

I'm listening to my gut, and trusting the past is the past. After all, I'm not perfect. While I told Blow about Lancelot, I didn't give him the timeline of recent events. My mother always told me people in glass *houses shouldn't throw stones. Well, I'm standing in a glass house on this one.*

Nymph

The Watcher: *If Blow makes you happy and you can see a future with him, then you should give it a go. Just don't put any pressure on yourself to be perfect for him, Nymph. You need to be who you are, first and foremost.*

Sin Rocks: *There is a risk with every relationship. You need to balance the risk of continuing the relationship. What if he lied, and it's not in his past, and you give him your heart?*

Penny Dreadful: *SR is right. There is a risk in every new relationship. That's why you should always use condoms and make every new sexual partner get an STI screen. Safety first, Nymph. Forget the heavy stuff until you've been together long enough for it to be an issue.*

"You look lovely," Brad murmured as he kissed my cheek

"I'm nervous. I've never introduced a guy to my mother, and we are walking in after judgment has happened." Shivering, I pulled my jacket tighter against the weather.

Brad opened the passenger door to his Lexus for me. "Remember this dinner isn't about you being good enough, Caly. You're her daughter. Your mother loves you and wants to protect you. That's all this is."

"Really? It feels like we are going to a green card interview. If either of us fucks up, one of us will get deported," I admitted as I dropped into the passenger seat.

Bending down, Brad kissed my cheek. "No one is getting deported." Turning my face to his, I kissed his lips. Butterflies took flight in my stomach, so I leaned a little more into the kiss.

Once. We'd only had sex once. Just that first time and I was so hungry for more.

Pulling away, Brad shut my door as that reminder made me frown. The two guys I'd been with before were so keen for more once it happened. They'd see me every night if I'd let them, which I didn't, but they wanted too. Brad hadn't tried for it since.

"What's the confused face for?" Brad asked, starting the engine.

"Ah, um, it's just, you haven't wanted to have sex with me again. I wasn't sure if I did something wrong?" I answered awkwardly.

Brad smirked a little as he pulled out of the carpark and headed for the University exit. "Caly, we've sort of had this whole, 'I'm not worthy' thing happening." Pulling up at a red light, he leaned over to caress my cheek with his nose. "Friday night was the best sex I've ever had. I don't want to get used to it if I'm going to lose it in a week."

"I think you're worthy," I whispered, opening my eyes. "Green."

Sitting straight, Brad started driving again. "We get through this, and I'm yours any and every night you want me."

"Promise?"

Brad's lips tilted up into that devilish smile I adored. "Promise." Reaching out, I placed my hand on his thigh. Smiling, Brad put his hand over mine, then lifted my hand to his mouth and kissed my palm. "We'll be fine, Caly. Relax. We're meant to be."

"You've read Romeo and Juliet, right?" I asked sarcastically. With a chuckle, Brad shook his head at me.

We arrived at the restaurant my mother had chosen. It was her favorite, a little family-run Italian restaurant. Great food, small and friendly. It was also out of the way and would have limited witnesses.

The maître-d' lead us to mums usual table in the back corner. Standing to greet us as we approached, for the first time, Gena wasn't smiling to see me. Then and there, I nearly burst into tears.

"Hey, it's about me, remember?" Moving his hand into the small of my back, Brad kissed my temple.

"Mum," I greeted her, stepping in to kiss her cheek, but not even trying for a hug. "This is Brad Meadows, my boyfriend."

"Nice to meet you, Ms. Zilla," Brad offered his hand.

Gena shook it, eyeballing him. "Brad." Stepping back, mum sat down. No usual bag of presents, none of the twenty-year normality of my mother existed at this moment.

"So, how did you two meet?" Mum started the interrogation. At least that's how it felt. She asked questions about us, or Brad and Emily, or Brad and his family. The questions kept coming like an oral exam, Gena only stopping to order drinks and our meals, and then to eat. By the time we'd finished our mains, I swear my mother knew more about Brad than I had.

"Would you like to see the dessert menus?" The waiter asked.

"Yes, thank you." Mum didn't even spare a glance for the waiter. "Just two, the young man is leaving."

"Mum!" The waiter's eyes went wide, and he scurried away. "You're being rude."

"Am I?" Mum asked with a raised brow.

"Yes, and you know it," I griped. "I've never seen you behave like this, acting like you're better than someone else. You haven't even acknowledged that waiter all evening, and you've put Brad through the Spanish Inquisition. For someone who slummed it long enough to get knocked up by a Riverside boy, you sure are judgmental." Standing up, I took Brad's hand. "Come on, we're going."

"Sit!" Gena growled.

"I don't think I will." Throwing my napkin on the table, I prepared to leave.

My mum's eyes went wide. "Sit down now, Calypso Clair Zilla!"

I sat. It was an automatic response from my childhood. Eyebrows in his hair, Brad started laughing. My mother glared at him, but Brad shrugged. "Sorry, the look on Caly's face was priceless."

Putting his mouth to my ear, Brad ignored my mother. "Calypso, the nymph, hey?" He chuckled as he stood. "I'm going to go to the bathroom and let you two chat," Brad announced to both of us, then looked to me. "If you still want to leave when I get back, we will."

My mother watched Brad walk away while I glared at her. "What the hell, Mum?"

"I'm playing devil's advocate like my father did when I brought the man I wanted to marry home. The difference being, Brad has kept his cool and composure the entire way through."

"The guy you were in love with lost his temper?" I asked, catching on that it was a test.

"Yes. Once he did, my father declared he wasn't good enough and told him to get out," Gena swirled her drink in its glass. "I like Brad. I see what has captured you about him. I don't like who his family is, and what that could mean for you. But it's not like you're going into the Zilla family business one day, so he's got nothing to gain from dating you."

"He's the heir to the Sarita Hotel Corporation, mum; I think that covers money for him."

"It still puts you at risk. He is still a Meadows."

"I'm a Zilla. That makes me high-risk when it comes to Riverside already. Do you think dating a boy who lives and works in Eleri is going to put me at any higher risk?"

"You like this boy?"

"Would he be here tonight if I didn't?"

"He could be a rebound, Caly. I saw your blog about Lancelot. He finally slept with you and turned you away..."

"I'd already started dating Brad before that happened." Gena's eyes went wide. "And we didn't have sex. I kissed him. I may have stripped naked, but I was drunk, and he put me to bed and held me after I passed out."

"It could still be a rebound..."

"It's not!" I snapped. Gena stared at me with both her brows raised. "I've never felt like this with anyone."

"That's the second time tonight you've got defensive enough about this boy to raise your voice at me." Mum adjusted her napkin. "I know better than to push you when you've dug your heels in, Caly. If you say this boy is going to make you happy, I'll support it."

Blinking, I stared at my mum a moment. "Wait, you mean that?"

"Yes, sweetheart. I've wanted you to get serious about a boy for a while now. He's not the boy I would have chosen for you, but if he's the one your heart desires, then I don't have the right to stop it."

Getting up, I wrapped myself around my mother. "I love you. Thank you."

"Don't thank me yet; you still have to deal with your grand-father." The warning made me cringe, remembering the way Granddad looked at me on Saturday night.

When he returned to the table, Brad stood behind his seat,

waiting for me to tell him what was happening. "It's okay, we're staying for dessert," I advised, taking his hand in mine.

Taking his seat, Brad lifted my hand to his mouth and kissed it. I might have swooned, causing Gena to chuckle into her bourbon. Raising a brow at my mother's change of mood, Brad took a mouthful of his Coke.

"So, Brad, I hope you're using condoms," Mum asked as if she was about to start lecturing us on the practices of safe sex.

Brad snorted his Coke through his nose. Mum and I started laughing.

Chapter Fifteen

REBOUND

That term got thrown at me like a smack in the face, and it impacted just as hard. Shocked that anyone could apply that term to this relationship, it left me speechless. It's been two years since my last relationship. The definition of a rebound is jumping into a new relationship to get over the last one. Or following a different line of thought, getting under someone new to get over the old. That's not what happened here. So, why did it hurt so much to hear that word?

Nymph

Sin Rocks: *Because you usually are very cautious about the men in your life. Subconsciously, you know you are forcing this relationship with Blow. What TW said about your being a commitment-phobe got under your skin.*

Penny Dreadful: *Blow isn't a rebound, but you do have Daddy issues. That's why you always go for older men.*

Nymph: *Seriously, PD? How is that relevant?*

Penny Dreadful: *Well, if you are going to become a headcase over something, at least address the real issue.*

Nymph: Not helpful.

The Watcher: I agree, PD. Not helpful. You should be pointing out she is still talking about Lancelot. Doesn't that scream rebound?

Nymph: No. I was never in a relationship with Lancelot.

The Watcher: Lancelot has been a constant in your love life since you started the blog. He may never have been a relationship, but it was clear that he meant something. He told you the two of you weren't going to work, and the following week you were hooking up with Blow. How is that not a rebound?

Penny Dreadful: OMG get over the Lancelot thing. The jerk doesn't deserve her.

The Watcher: Maybe he felt that way too, and that is why he backed out of the race?

Penny Dreadful: That's why he doesn't deserve her. He let her go without a second thought. If he genuinely wanted her, he would have made it work.

Sin Rocks: It sounds like you are conflicted, Nymph. You should take a break from dating for a while until you sort your feelings for both Blow and Lancelot out.

Nymph: SR, I've always valued your advice, but I'm not conflicted. I'm not giving Blow the flick while I sort out my feelings for a guy who didn't want me.

Sin Rocks: Then why did the word rebound hurt you to hear?

Nymph: Because I realized it was the start of the judgment. That it would be the first untrue thing people say about Blow and me together, but it wasn't going to be the worst. It hurt because I know there are going to be harsher words to come. Thank you, PD, TW, and SR for helping me realize that.

It was one of those awkward moments. You're in the shower

with your new boyfriend, legs around his waist, his slow thrusts inside of you. You're on the peak of orgasm when the door opens, and the guy you've spent your life fantasizing about walks in.

"Sorry, Dude. I'm busting," Aaron excused. Walking straight to the toilet, Aaron unzipped and started relieving himself. He couldn't see us through the shower curtain, and we couldn't see him.

Tensing in his hold, I tried to disentangle myself from Brad's embrace. Indicating I should be quiet, Brad thrust a little deeper, making me bite my lip. "Long shift?" Brad chuckled.

Closing my eyes, I tried to keep my moans internal.

"Every man and his dog was at the bar tonight," Aaron answered, finishing up. "How did it go with Caly's mum? Did you get kicked to the curb?"

"Nah, she turned out to be nice." His eyes intent on me, Brad grabbed my ass a little tighter and squirmed his hips inside of me.

"Really? I didn't think she'd go for you, no offense."

The sink tap turned on, and I swear Aaron was brushing his teeth. God, Brad was so deep, and I was so close. The sound of Aaron talking wasn't helping. At fourteen, Aaron developed one of those deep voices that left you in no doubt of his masculinity. It had been driving me crazy since I realized the effect it had on me.

The image of Aaron joining us in the shower playing through my mind, was too much. Opened my mouth, I came harder than I ever had before. Groaning, Brad joined me seconds later. The bathroom fell into silence. Just our heavy breathing, the sound of the shower, and the gurgle of the water funneling down the drain.

Kissing my nose as he withdrew, Brad removed the condom

to wash clean. Then, stepping out of the shower, Brad wrapped the condom and threw it in the wastebasket.

"Things went well. Thanks for your concern," Grabbing his towel, Brad dried off then handed it to me. Wrapping the cloth around me, I stepped out of the shower. My legs were like jelly after having them clenched around Brad's waist.

Aaron stood there, toothbrush still in his hand, no shirt. Both of them there shirtless, I was ready to go again. "Hi, Aaron," I murmured.

Taking my hand with a smile, Brad led the way back to his room. "Night, Ayah. We'll try and keep it down."

Still standing there, Aaron gawked at me until I left the room, and Brad shut the door behind us.

"Do the guys come into the bathroom whenever?" I asked, dropping the towel and climbing into Brad's bed.

"Yeah." Brad rubbed the back of his head. "We may have to work out a signal to let them know you're in there, so you don't have anyone walk in on you."

"This can't be the first time you've had girls stay over?" As Brad climb into the bed, I cuddled into him and started kissing his neck.

"No, it's not, but it was quite random until now." Brad pulled back to meet my eyes. "I plan on this being a regular thing."

When Brad rolled us, so he was on top, I felt him hardening against me. "Again?" I purred.

"Jesus, Caly, with the effect you have on me, I'm never going to get enough of you."

A hand latching onto my upper arm dragged me back as I tried to leave class. Because I sat at the back, I was always the last out.

But not today by the looks. Turning around, I startled when I met my professor's eyes. "Wait a minute, Caly. Someone needs to talk to you." Still restraining me, my professor stepped me a few meters back into the lecture hall.

As I was about to ask what was happening, the emergency exit door clicked open. Getting more anxious by the minute, I swallowed when Sinclair Rockford came inside. No body-guards today, unless they were waiting outside.

"This clears my debt, right," my professor demanded.

My eyes were bigger than saucers, as my heart started racing in my chest.

"Yes, Richard. Consider your debt erased," Rockford agreed.

Letting me go, the professor stepped towards the door. Only then did he hesitate to leave me there. "You won't hurt her?" Receiving an unimpressed glare from Rockford, my professor dashed out.

"Well, that's not going to make the rest of my semester uncomfortable at all," I grumbled. "What do you want?"

"A chat." Rockford indicated the seats at the front of the lecture theatre.

"Mr. Rockford, I know what this is about, and I hate to tell you, I'll date who I like."

"Actually, that's not what I came here to discuss, but since you brought it up..."

"What are you here for then?" Folding my arms, I watched and waited. I wasn't going to listen to a lecture on my dating life from this man.

Raising a brow at me, Rockford gave me a look that should have made me flinch. Unfortunately for him, I'd grown up with my grandfather, so that look didn't work on me. Rockford's lips tilted at my ability to stand up to him, giving me the impression that it didn't happen often.

"The land in Riverside that your uncle won at auction last week." Taking a seat, Rockford indicated for me to join him. I stayed where I was. "I want that land, Caly."

"Why are you talking to me? Go talk to Uncle Bryce."

"I'm talking to you because your uncle wasn't the purchaser. Your mother was, but it's your name she purchased it in."

"What?"

"Now, if I know it, so does Greg Meadows. So, as below the radar as you've flown the last nineteen years, that's all about to change. You in bed with Greg's son, literally, makes you even more vulnerable."

"Does Aaron tell you everything?" Aaron only found out Brad, and I were having sex at one this morning, so I couldn't believe Rockford already knew.

"When it comes to you, yes." Standing up, Rockford walked towards me. Hooking his finger under the chain of the necklace, Rockford lifted the locket out of my shirt. "This won't be enough to protect you anymore; you'll need a detail."

"What? No." Snatching my locket back, I moved away from him.

"Caly..."

"Why?" I finally asked. "What brought you to the playground that day? Why are you so interested in my locket?"

Shoving his hands in his pockets, Rockford studied me. "Your father bought that locket for your mother to protect her. He never told her what the locket was for."

"Then how do you know?"

"I designed and built it."

The fact my jaw was on the floor pretty much gave away that was the last answer I expected from him. Rockford's pale blue eyes were intense as one of his brows twitched upwards.

"I did electrical engineering at university; my master's was in business. That locket you're wearing was the first security chip I made. It was the prototype for all those fancy GPS trackers that came after. Those earrings and watches the Eleri elite buy to protect them started with that locket."

Palming my locket, I stared wide-eyed as I comprehended what Rockford revealed. He was Drofkor Engineering, a multi-million-dollar company built from the ground up.

"To upgrade the locket's software, I need to be in the same vicinity for a period. I was checking its location to do the next scheduled upgrade when I noticed it was popping up at your school. I came there that day sure someone stole it." Rockford tilted his head. "Then I found you, and you explained quite innocently how you came by that locket. You see, I knew you existed, Caly. How could I not? But the rumors were pretty adamant that your mother was either raped or got knocked up with one nightstand. It wasn't until you told me with absolute pride how you owned that pendant that I knew the rumors were very wrong. Your mother would not have told you the necklace was a gift from your father if that wasn't the case."

"So, you know who my father is?" So close to finally finding out his name, I was on the verge of tears.

"Yes." Voice softening, Rockford sighed that one word.

"Who?" I stepped forward, demanding to know my father's name.

Hesitating, Rockford gritted his teeth in anger. "Didn't your mother ever tell you?"

"No. She said it was too dangerous."

Cursing under his breath, Rockford clenched his jaw, glaring at the floor between us. "My interest is that locket. Your father only indebted me with protecting the wearer."

My skin tingled where the locket touched it. It was a sensation that occurred rarely, but often enough that I didn't worry about it. Something beeped in Rockford's pocket. Removing his hand, Rockford took out a small device and looked at the screen.

"Aaron has one of those," I stumbled over the words, recognizing what was in his hands.

"No, there is only one of these, and it's specifically designed to update that necklace."

Comprehending his words, I glared at the device and gripped my locket tighter. "Aaron works for you?"

Rockford put the device away. "Yes."

"All these years, he's been updating my locket for you?" I started putting the pieces together.

His eyes gleamed. "Yes. From the day I brought him to play with you in the playground, so I could update it and show you how to use it."

"You sent Aaron to my school to have a way of updating my necklace?"

Giving a single nod of acknowledgment, Rockford shrugged a shoulder. "He was a smart kid, and he deserved the better start to his life."

"How does Josh fit into it?"

"He didn't until you made Josh part of your life. Aaron asked for his brother to go as well, so in truth, Josh rode Aaron's coat-tails. I would have done what I could to take care of those boys anyway. Their mother and I dated in high school, and when I went to university, she took up with my best friend."

"Aaron said his dad was dead. That was your best friend? Doesn't that break the bro code?"

Scratching his jaw, Rockford considered my question. "My best friend married my ex-girlfriend, yes. Over the years, we've suffered heartbreaks, and we've been there for each other, just as I've supported Louise's sons. The fact that arrangement benefitted my need to access you was fortuitous. That's all you need to know."

The precise wording of Rockford's answer made me think it was a calculated response to omit the truth. Going back over his words, it stood out to me that he avoided calling his best-friend Aaron's father. My eyebrows lifted as it all made sense. "Are Aaron and Josh your sons? Is that why you forbade Aaron from getting involved with me?"

Pursing his lips, Rockford studied my eyes. "You are a job, Caly. I've taught all my men not to get emotionally attached to a job. I also warned Aaron your family would never let him be more than a notch on your bedhead. Something your current boyfriend will find out in due time. The Zillas' are free to slum it all they like, but they only marry within their own social class."

The temptation to hit him clenched my fingers, but there was no hiding the insult or the hurt. Aaron was only in my life because his father made him for business reasons. Now Aaron's rejection hurt me for another reason. Add in Rockford's insinuation that I would use a man for fun but thought myself better than them just pissed me off more.

Angry, I shoved him. "Damn you! It's all your fault!" I raged at him. "The last four years, it's your doing."

Rocking back from my feeble impact, Rockford blinked wide eyes at me. Clenching my teeth to prevent crying, I dug my fingernails into the palms of my hands. "You aren't part of my life. You're not my father, and I'm not one of your lackeys. I will date who I want to date. If my mother wants me to have that land, I will do something worthwhile with it. But I will not sell it to some big-time gangster from Riverside." Grabbing up my bag, I turned to leave.

"I'm a businessman, Caly, not a gangster. I protect the people of Riverside, which is more than any pretentious Eleri elite has ever tried to do. I will build the college for which the city intended. I will give my people something to improve their chances in life, and the first way to do that is to educate them. I want that land," Rockford growled, his voice low and threatening.

Glaring at the exit, I refused to look back and acknowledge him. "I wanted Aaron," I snarled at him over my shoulder. "Too bad that's in the past, or you might have had something to bargain with me. Now that I know he's your son, I wouldn't touch him with a ten-foot pole."

"But Greg Meadow's son is acceptable?" Rockford seethed.

"Greg raped Brad's mother! Brad escaped his dad the moment he could. You can't blame him for how his mother conceived him any more than you can me."

Taking a deep breath, Rockford exhaled. "You're right. I have great respect for Brad Meadows, but he is no good for you, Caly. He's going to break your heart if he doesn't get you killed first."

"Your opinion is nothing to me!" I yelled, frustrated. Stepping towards him, I gritted my teeth, outraged that Rockford thought he got a say in my relationship. "You are nobody to me."

Clenching his jaw, Rockford glared at the floor as if his eyes were lasers, and he could start a fire. "What do you want, Caly. How can I get you to sell me the land?"

Frustrated, I huffed as I grabbed the handle for the door. "You have nothing I want even to tempt me." I stormed out of the lecture theatre.

Aaron was waiting outside. "Caly..."

"Get lost," I snapped, barely able to contain how angry I was, at him, and at Rockford.

His brows hit his hair as Aaron's mouth fell open. "Wait, what? Caly..." He grabbed my arm, but I yanked myself free.

"Don't ever touch me again. I know Rockford forced you to be in my life."

Stepping back, Aaron shook his head, his eyes flashing with hurt. "Shit!" Rubbing his hand through his hair in frustration, Aaron avoided my eyes.

"You're not my friend. You're not anything to me but a fellow student and colleague." As I walked away, I was trembling. What Rockford revealed left me questioning every relationship with everyone in my life. As I ran back to my dorm crying, I realized I was heartbroken.

I'd been in love with Aaron Wish all these years, and I was just a job to him.

Chapter Sixteen

Secrets (Lancelot)

There is a moment when you realize everyone around you has secrets. The secrets may not relate to you, and keeping them is personal or habit, but those secrets can still hurt you. That pain is not always that someone you cared for hid something, or that their secret harmed you. But in their need to keep those privacy concerns, they created a distance between you or broke your heart.

Today, I found out the reason Lancelot walked away from me. His secret is more consequential than I could have expected, so it hurt me more than his rejection. He's not the person I thought he was, and in learning his mystery, my perspective of him changed. My entire outlook has shifted because I'm now thinking, 'what if he wasn't the only one?'

I'm heartbroken. Not because I was in love with a man and he didn't want me, but because his reason for being in my life was a lie from the start.

Nymph

Sin Rocks: *I'm sorry that you are hurting. Sometimes secrets are* *there to protect you. I, too, am hurting today because someone I care about said something to me, which cut to my bone. A secret I'm keeping got thrown back at me. Not to be mean; they didn't know my secret to know any better. But they did it in a way that made me want to hug them. The urge to tell them how wrong they were and how much I love them and want to be part of their life was overwhelming. But the secret wasn't mine to start with, and now I keep it to protect them. So, I took their anger and let them walk away because I love them, and I know my secret would hurt them more today.*

❧

"Caly?" Walking into her office, Gena slowed when she saw me before checking her watch. "Shouldn't you be at work?"

"I called in sick." My eyes felt like I'd lined my eyelids with sandpaper.

"What's wrong? You look like you have the flu," Mum assessed. "Or crying. Did Brad do something?"

Still angry about everything that happened today, I stepped towards my mother. "Why do you assume that it's Brad's fault that I'm upset? It turns out my mother purchased highly-sort land in Riverside, and she did it in my name. It appears this information reached a prominent Riverside resident who wanted that land. He then detained me in my classroom today, so he could threaten me into selling it to him."

My mother's face drained of color. "Damn it! They assured me the paperwork was secure."

"Well, it wasn't, and according to Sinclair Rockford, Greg Meadows already knows too." Lowering herself into her seat as though terrified that there were tacks on it, Gena bit her lip. "Why?" I asked, sitting down.

Gena cleared her throat. "Well, it was meant to be your

twenty-first birthday present. I'll have to thank Sinclair for spoiling that for you." Her eyes assessed me. "Did he divulge anything else to you?"

"Like what, Mum? That you two used to bump uglies?" When my mother's eyes closed, she confirmed my suspicion. Rockford's warning to Aaron was a personal grudge, not a random 'them' and 'us.' She'd broken his heart.

"That was a very long time ago," Gena murmured.

The pain in her response softened my anger a touch. Rockford wasn't the only broken heart. "He was the guy, wasn't he? The one you loved, and Granddad told you to end it?"

"Yes. Back then, Sinclair focused his life on getting his degree and getting the hell out of Riverside. The night your grandfather told him he wasn't good enough for me, that changed. My father felt Sinclair was after me for my money to start his own company." Shaking her head, Gena lifted her eyes to meet mine, emotion glistening in them. "I changed too."

Damn, my mother was still in love with Sinclair Rockford.

"It's why I'm giving Brad the benefit of the doubt, Honey. I don't want to see you end up like me. I may seem to have everything I ever wanted, but I go to bed alone, I wake up alone, and I miss being held, and loved and how good the ss..." Sitting up straight, Gena realized who she was talking too. "Well, I miss all the things that come with being in a relationship with someone you love."

My heart went out to my mum. She buried herself in work to prevent going through that again. "You should try dating again?" I suggested like I had many times before. "After all, you dated my father."

Looking out the window wistfully, Mum sighed. "Your father and I didn't date. We fucked each other senseless whenever we were in the same town."

"Mum! I'm never unhearing that," I groaned, hiding my face in my hands.

"My point remains..."

Holding up my hands, I warded off any more unsavory word-induced imagery. "Got it the first time. Time to change the subject. What am I meant to do with the land in Riverside?"

Rising out of her chair, Gena retrieved a large roll of paper. Spreading it open on the desk, she showed me two impressive buildings built next to each other. "The Caly Zilla Medical Centre and Riverside College. You will deliver the long-ago promised college. Along with that, we will build a medical center with the capability to act as a hospital's emergency ward."

"Why?"

"Because you were so passionate about it when we spoke last month. Remember? You told me how your friend from Riverside couldn't get the work experience he needed. You suggested the need for a medical facility in Riverside. You gave two good reasons. The first is that it would offer the clinical experience to Riverside students. The second was as a triage center that could also provide critical treatment. You felt this would improve response rates and reduce in-transit fatalities."

Tears welled up in my eyes again. "You did this for me?" When I raved to my mother about the inequity, I'd been thinking of Aaron and Josh.

Gena's eyes softened. "It's a good cause, Caly. I discussed it with Bryce. We can integrate business to make it financially viable. It will be good for the people of Riverside, and it will take our community work where it needs to go. It's high time Rockford and Meadows stop being the only names on the other side of the river." Mum brushed my cheek. "Riverside runs in your veins too, Caly. Your contribution to the community should be there." Looking back at the plans, Gena paused half a minute. "What do you think?"

"It's awesome, but a car would have been a good twenty-first present too," I teased.

"Well, it's a two-year build after we go out for tender. So, I'll consider the car for your birthday subject to other requirements."

"Like?"

"We'll come back to that. Let's talk about your community project. We're going to break ground on both buildings at once. The college should take twelve months, and the medical center will take two years."

Staring down at the plans, I grimaced at the drafted plaque. "Can we take my name off it? It seems a little self-important."

"Sure, we can call it whatever you want."

We spent the next hour going over everything we thought needed to be in the buildings. I wanted secure parking for the staff and students with room for growth. Gena insisted on a research lab as a steppingstone into the Zilla medical sciences business. The planning continued until a phone call alerted mum that her car was waiting to take her to her next meeting. "I'll drop you back to the University."

"I thought I'd come home for the weekend, spend some time with you."

A gleaming smile covered my mother's beautiful face. "I'll drop you at the uni and pick you up on the way back from my meeting."

Three hours later, I was waiting in the carpark with my bag packed. Arriving home from work, Aaron pulled up in front of King's hall. As he closed his car door, his eyes narrowed in on the duffle bag full of clothes at my feet. My stomach hollowed out at the sight of him, a sense of betrayal slinking through me.

The town car pulled up as Aaron took one step towards me. Opening the door for me, my mother's chauffeur blocked Aaron from view. When I dropped into the car, my mother took my hand in hers. "Are you okay?" Gena asked as the car pulled away.

Watching the car leave, Aaron retrieved his phone from his back pocket. "Yeah, I'm feeling vulnerable, I guess."

Gena's eyes went to Aaron, glaring daggers at him. "I read your blog post on the way over. What was Lancelot's secret?"

Exhaling hard, I looked out the window. "Lancelot works for Rockford. Always has."

"That's how Rockford knew how to find you today?"

"I guess."

"Hmm," Gena mused.

Turning my eyes to meet hers, I assessed the way she examined me. Shrugging one shoulder, Gena patted my hand. "Don't take it too hard, Caly. Anyone from Riverside living on this side of the river either works for Sinclair or Meadows. That's how it is over there. Be glad Lancelot worked for the Devil of Riverside, rather than the King."

"What's the difference?"

"Having your fingernails pulled out until you sign over the land."

"Well, that should invoke some nightmares, but I'm glad you went with fingernails."

"I've never sugar-coated with you, Caly. The nails are where they would start." My mother squeezed my hand and looked away.

The saliva in my mouth proved hard to swallow. My heart rate was accelerating as I imagined how the rest of how my day could have gone had Meadows got a hold of me.

❧

Friday was my study day. Waking at my usual time, I joined mum for a morning run, then I came home and enjoyed the quiet for studying. Going out to dinner with Brad as planned, I explained I was staying with mum for the weekend and left it at that. The truth was, I hesitated to disclose any more. He was flat-mates with Aaron, and they were friends.

At the end of the night, I didn't go back to his place or let him come to mine. There was something about my bedroom that I considered innocent, having never had a guy in there. I wasn't ready to lose that last vestige of sexual innocence from my life yet. So, we kissed a bit and parted ways.

Saturday, I ran with mum again, then went to work. Since our home was close to the hospital, on the other side of Eleri from the university, I got to work early.

"You came in?" Aaron sounded surprised when he arrived.

"Is there a reason I wouldn't?" I replied, keeping my eyes on my work.

"After you missed Thursday, I worried that you didn't feel safe around me anymore." His shoulders rolling forward, Aaron pouted. "I'd never do anything to hurt you on purpose. Not even for Rockford. In fact, part of my role was to keep you safe."

When I stayed quiet and focused on my job, Aaron huffed out a breath and shoved his hands in his pockets. "Did you move out of the dorm?"

"That's none of your business." Finished plugging in the settings for the scan we were about to perform, I turned to face him. "Did you even want to do Nuclear Medicine, or did you do it because of me?"

"I wanted to do Medicine," Aaron admitted.

"Your marks were good enough, why didn't you?"

Checking over the patient paperwork again, Aaron sighed. "Because Rockford only paid for Josh to go to school while I was there. Without Rockford's support, I couldn't afford Medicine, even with the scholarship. If I studied something else, I could work to help my mum out, and Rockford agreed to keep paying Josh's fees. So, I took a scholarship for Nuclear Medicine. I knew Josh wanted to be a doctor. I thought if I got a good job, I could help him achieve his dream instead."

So, only Aaron was Rockford's son, not Josh. "You used me to get out of Riverside and then continued to use me to get your brother out too?"

Aaron rubbed the back of his head. "I used Rockford's interest in your necklace and his need for someone to have an excuse to be close to you. I never used you, Caly. That's why I couldn't sleep with you; that would have crossed that line."

Damn it, but I couldn't hate Aaron for being opportunistic. I would have done the same in his situation, and he'd done it for Josh. Aaron adored his little brother, and I loved Josh like a younger cousin. Only a month ago, I'd raged to my mother about the unfairness of their situation. Now, she was building a medical center because of them. Turning back to the operation panel, I avoided Aaron's eyes. "This is ready to go. I'll go let the guys know they can bring the patient in."

"Caly." Aaron grasped my bicep as I went to move past him. "I couldn't cross that line because I knew you would have hated me if you ever found out. But if that hadn't been the case..."

"I'm with Brad," I murmured. His face so close to mine, his eyes flicking between my lips and eyes. "There's no going back, Aaron."

Closing his eyes, Aaron grimaced as if I'd stabbed him. When he released me, I walked out. Stopping on the other side of the door, I blinked away the tears threatening to spill.

Getting my composure back, I walked down the hall, where the patient from oncology was waiting.

For the rest of the weekend, we worked well together. We spoke but limited our conversations to work or study. Sunday, Aaron enquired if I was moving home for good. My phone rang at that same time, and I answered it, avoiding answering him. "Mum?"

"Hi honey, it's been a while since we've gone to the gun range together. Would you be keen to do that this afternoon?" Gena spent the morning at the day spa with Queenie, but it sounded like her massage didn't get her frustrations out.

A champion shooter, my mother started taking me to the range once I was old enough, and taught me to shoot. Gena said shooting released her frustrations better than anything away from the bedroom. I didn't want to know how the two related for her.

"That sounds good." God knows I could shoot the shit out of a few targets to deal with my own emotions right now. Gena probably recognized that last night.

"Excellent, I'll grab you a change of clothes and pick you up from work." The call disconnected.

Standing there, pretending not to listen, Aaron waited a minute before he tried again. "Why won't you tell me if you're moving home?" Aaron growled, getting frustrated.

"Because I don't know yet, Aaron. As I said yesterday, it's none of your business." Grabbing up the next file, I went back to work.

When we hit the range that afternoon, I got my best score ever. It's incredible how focused anger can make you.

Chapter Seventeen

LANCELOT

Why do guys think once their big secret is out there, everything will be okay? It's like when someone cheats on their partner and admits it. Once they've got the guilt off their chest, they feel relieved, and they expect you to forgive and forget. But that's not how it works. All you've done is to move the burden of guilt to your partner for them to carry.

In this case, now that I know Lancelot was using me, I'm supposed to forget how much that revelation hurt me. While I understand his motivations, it doesn't mean the situation has changed. I'm still angry and hurt, and I'm scared.

Too much is happening, and it is scaring me. Over the last few weeks, everything has changed in my life. Between my relationship, community projects, my studies, work, and family issues, I'm struggling to keep it together. I need to simplify things, or I'm not going to cope with everything.

Nymph

§.

For the following week, I stayed at home. Mum's driver dropped me off in time for class each day and picked me up in the afternoon. It was like before I went to boarding school and mum went back to Zurich. Each morning, I was running with Gena again, and I used her spin bike each evening to change up my exercise routine.

Wednesday, I stayed on campus to go to the Tower Bar with Penny as usual. Unlike the norm, Penny dragged me out to meet the rest of Brad's friends and insisted we hang out with them all night. Brad was happy, and while I didn't mind, it was very suspicious.

My answer came an hour later when Dwayne turned up with Dom. "Ah, the class of this group has improved by the addition of women," Dwayne proclaimed, pulling me into a hug. "We need to talk," he whispered in my ear before he released me and greeted Penny....with a kiss?

"When the fuck did that happen?" I asked Brad.

Smirking at the smooching pair, Brad chuckled. "Last week-end. They've been on a few dates already, but Penny is holding out on him. Dwayne's smitten," Brad snickered.

The way they looked at each other made me smile. Dwayne seemed like a decent guy. "I go home for one week and come back to this."

Brad pulled me against him. "Speaking of which, you're staying on campus tonight, right?" When I nodded, Brad grinned. "So, are we going to your place or mine?"

"It's my turn."

Brad nibbled my earlobe. "It's already nine. If you want to sleep tonight, we should head off soon. We've got a week to make up for."

Not one to argue with sense, I took Brad's hand. "Let's go then."

In the morning, Brad woke up with me and walked with Penny and me to the track. He went to the pool to do his laps while I ran, and Penny did her gym session.

"So, two months, it must be serious," Penny teased when she found me stretching after my run. "I'm guessing you've done the deed?" When my cheeks heated, Penny performed a cheer, cartwheel, and all. "My god, you've needed to get laid. I'm so happy for you."

"I would tell you to calm down, but the sex is worth much more than that cheer," I chuckled.

That answer made Penny grin. "Better than Bounce?"

"Not even on the same playing field," I sighed then gave her a wink.

Laughing, Penny dragged me back towards the dorm. "I want details. Size, stamina, technique. Dish, woman."

Penny's enthusiasm was contagious, so I was still smiling when I arrived at class on Thursday. For his part, my professor acted as if nothing untoward occurred last week. After noting my presence, he continued with his lecture.

It wasn't until I was walking down the stairs that anything odd happened. Aaron stepped into my path to stop me leaving. "Not that way," he murmured, reading his phone. "We'll go out the fire exit."

Grabbing my arm once everyone else left, Aaron dragged me across to the other exit.

"Want to tell me what's going on?" I snarled, hating that he manhandled me.

"Dom messaged me. Two of Greg Meadows' men are waiting outside the classroom. We can only gather they are here to take you to talk with Greg," Aaron informed me. My hands became cold and clammy, and my stomach fell through the floor. "Let's go hang out in the library until prac class. It looks like they know your schedule, so I'll have Dwayne collect you from the lab and take you to work," Aaron decided. "I can bring you home from work without raising suspicions."

"I'm going home tonight, so mum's driver will collect me."

Observing me for a moment, Aaron pulled out his phone as we entered the library and sent a message. Following suit, I sent one to my mother telling her what happened. Aaron got an instant reply that seemed to appease him. My phone stayed quiet.

It was thirty minutes later when Aaron's phone rang. "Hello?" Listening to what the caller, Aaron frowned. "Really?" A moment later, my phone buzzed.

Gena Zilla (Mum): *All taken care of, Honey. See you tonight.*
Love mum.

Hanging up, Aaron looked perplexed. "The police turned up on campus. They arrested Greg's men for trespassing with suspicion of the intent to kidnap."

Resisting a smirk, I showed Aaron my mum's message. Aaron's eyebrows rose as his eyes bulged.

"Your mother made a call and got SWAT raid a university campus within twenty minutes?"

No longer able to prevent it, I laughed. "Yeah, Aaron, my family have that much clout."

Shaking his head in disbelief, Aaron huffed. "Brad doesn't know what he's gotten himself into with you."

Acid churned my stomach. "Brad grew up in the Meadows' compound. His mother was a Sarita, a family with as much clout in Eleri. From our first date, Brad knew who I was and what I'm about, Aaron. I assure you, Brad knows very well what he's 'in' when it comes to me."

Listening, Aaron smirked as he leaned his mouth to my ear. "From what I heard in the bathroom, being in you is worth cumming for."

Slapping Aaron's arm playfully, I hid my face and the heat creeping up my throat.

Looking around, Aaron stood, making me worry. "Come with me." Grabbing my hand, Aaron dragged me off into the stacks. My heart raced in my chest as I peered over my shoulder to see if anyone was following, but I couldn't see anyone. Finding a dark dead-end I suspected he knew intimately, Aaron stopped and faced me.

"Aaron...?" Capturing my face in his hands, Aaron kissed me. On autopilot, I moved into the kiss. My body temperature soared, and butterflies took flight in my stomach. The kiss was hungry but purposeful. Nothing about Aaron was haphazard. He knew what he wanted, and he was taking it.

Realizing there was no immediate threat except the feelings I still had for him, I broke the kiss. "Aaron, wait..." I pleaded as his lips kissed over my jawline. He backed me up against the wall, his hands gripping my hips.

"I've wanted you so long, Caly. That night you threw yourself at me, it took everything in me to resist you."

When Aaron kissed me again, I melted into him, the words I'd longed to hear so long molding my body to his. Aaron's hand slipped under my top, cupping my breast, his thumb grazing my nipple through my bra. Gasping, I arched into his hand.

"Calypso, you've always been mine," Aaron whispered in my

ear. "My nymph."

The familiarity in the way Aaron called me that stopped me from drowning in desire. "Aaron, stop!" I shoved him away.

Peering at me shocked, Aaron stood with his features still masked in lust. My chest felt tight, my heart racing within it. Blinking as if he'd been in a daydream, Aaron stepped back, his face clearing to realize what we'd been doing.

Swiping at a stray tear, I barged past him. Snatching up my bag from the table, I stormed out of the library.

"Caly, what's up?" Passing me outside, Penny stopped me. Taking one look at my watering eyes, Penny excused herself from her friends and dragged me off to a quiet place. "What happened?"

"Wish hit on me," I whispered. "Why now? Now that I've met Brad, that I care for Brad, that I've assured Brad we are exclusive, why now?"

"Because it took seeing you with Brad, to know what he was losing," Penny offered with sympathy. Not expecting a reply, she cuddled me tight for a good ten minutes. When I pulled myself together, Penny relaxed and met my eyes. "What are you going to do?"

Exhaling, I shrugged. "Too little, too late. I care for Brad."

The furrow in Penny's brow told me that's not the answer she expected. Checking herself, Penny gave me another hug.

Grateful she kept her thoughts to herself and was there for me, I hugged her back, then got to my feet. "I have to get to class," I excused. "Thank you for being my best friend."

Tilting her head, Penny squeezed my hand. "How many times have you let me climb into bed with you and cry over my broken heart? I'll always be there if you need me, Caly." Despite Penny's bitchy cheerleader exterior, she truly was the best friend for me.

Aaron was already in the simulation lab when I came in. He tracked my path, his eyes hard and emotionless. Halfway through the prac, Aaron walked by and dropped a folded piece of paper in my lap. Unsure what to expect, I picked it up and read it.

I'm sorry.

Folding the paper, I took a deep breath and put it away, focusing on my prac. Dwayne was waiting for me outside when the class finished. "I thought the police dealt with the issue?" I questioned his presence.

"Precautionary. Meadows isn't known for giving up after one set back," Dwayne explained.

"Okay." There was no harm in being cautious. The irony that I was letting Sinclair Rockford protect me wasn't lost on me. But as my mother said, better the Devil than the King of Riverside. Besides, I now knew Rockford had protected me since I was six years old, and he did it for my father.

An alert tone sounded. Reading a message on his phone, Dwayne looked over his shoulder to Aaron as he tucked his phone away. He gave Aaron a single nod, placed his hand in the middle of my back, and moved me forward. "Let's get you to work," Dwayne murmured. "You can tell me how to win Penny's favor on the way."

"I think you've already won her favor," I chuckled.

"No, I've garnered her interest. Winning her favor takes a little more effort," Dwayne objected.

"You want to know how to get in her pants?"

"I know how to get in a girl's knickers. Winning favor is getting a girl like Penny to enter a committed relationship with you. It's the step before winning her heart."

"Be careful with Penny," I warned.

"I know, you'll do far worse to me than Rockford..."

"That," I looked at him as we reached the dorms, "but I don't want her to break your heart either. I like you, Dwayne, and I can recognize a big pussycat when I see one."

Dwayne's entire chest shook when he chuckled. "Don't you dare tell any of the guys you called me that, or I will be forced to do something to protect my hard man status."

His humor made me smile. "I need to get changed for work. Want to come up?"

Peering up at my building, Dwayne shook his head. "The last thing you need is Brad or Ayah thinking something happened between us." The comment confused me. Dwayne sighed. "I know you're with Brad, Caly, but I'm Ayah's best friend. I've watched him watch you for years. I know how Ayah feels about you."

Biting my lip, I stared at my feet. "I'm a job. Rockford told me he warned you guys off."

Dwayne cocked an eyebrow. "No, he warned us not to get involved with you with the hope of anything long-term. Caly, Rockford is like a dad to me, so there is no chance I would have hit on you if he put out a no fraternization order. We're here to protect you. Even Rockford knows there is no better place to protect a person than from inside their bed. It's a way to get overnight proximity without having to shiver your ass off in a cold car. Having said that, I'm one of Rockford's closest guards. I have access to what you would call privileged information, stuff that Ayah doesn't know. Trust me; it's more complicated than you being a job."

Close to blurting that I knew Aaron was Rockford's son, I stopped. There was a potential even Dwayne didn't know that. Deciding to get out of there before I said the wrong thing, I started towards my dorm. "I have to get changed."

Chapter Eighteen

"NOW THAT I'VE got you alone... I was hoping to talk to you last night about you and Brad."

I groaned. "Not you too?"

"Look, Brad's in a shitty situation. He's my friend, and he deserves happiness, but you and him? Caly, you've got to know that put a target on your head for so many reasons."

"I've already had this lecture, thank you." Slumping in the car seat, I watched the traffic.

Dwayne tapped his wheel. "Rockford is going to be watching you, Caly. The moment your relationship sparks an issue, he will make sure it ends."

My brows pinched over his words. Frowning at Dwayne, I worried how Rockford thought he could force me to end my relationship. "What are you saying?"

Dwayne gritted his teeth. "That it's not just your life in danger here."

Glaring at Dwayne, I hoped I was misunderstanding him. "Did Rockford threaten to kill Brad?"

"I never heard him say those words," Dwayne denied it.

"But he implied it?"

Dwayne sighed, "Look, Brad knows what dating you could expose you too. He's still doing it. He still pursued you knowing it would be a red flag to his bull-headed brother. Rockford, Aaron, even your family knows this. If you get caught in the crossfire or kidnapped, if someone hurts you or you die, part of the blame is going to fall on Brad. He knew the risk and still chose to get involved with you."

"You can't blame Brad for his brother being a dick."

"He can be when he knowingly put you in danger," Dwayne disagreed.

"He's entitled to want to be happy. Could you imagine going through life like that? Denying yourself love just in case your brother uses that loved one to hurt you?"

Dwayne sighed again. "That still makes his motivations self-ish. You told him upfront who you were, but did he tell you? Did he give you the chance to say, 'no thanks' before he'd seduced you?"

Biting my lip, I stayed quiet. Brad hadn't been upfront about his family, on either side, though, I couldn't blame him for that either. People must judge him all the time.

"That's why he will wear this, Caly."

"What if you are all wrong?" I proposed. "We might be perfect for each other, end up married, have four kids, be happy?"

"Does he know about you and Ayah?" Dwayne got a twinkle in his eye.

"Yes, you know that."

"I meant about today, in the library?" Dwayne was too precise in his attack.

My mouth dropped open a little. "How could you know...?"

Watching Dwayne's eyes flicker to his center console, I snatched his phone out of the pocket. Dwayne tried to grab it, but I moved out of reach. Because he was driving, Dwayne couldn't take his eyes off the road to fight it as I woke the screen.

"You should have this pin code protected," I lectured as I opened his messages and found the one from Aaron.

Aaron: Dude, I kissed her. I mean, I thoroughly kissed her. It was terrific, everything I've been dreaming about for six fucking years, but now she's pissed. I think I've blown any chance with her. Can you tell her I'm sorry? Tell her I was being stupid and got caught up in the moment or some shit.

Dwayne: Dude, don't be apologizing for kissing her, I know how you feel about her. Just don't let Brad find out. He's your best friend, and I don't want to have to take sides.

Aaron: I know, I'm trying so hard to be okay with them together. I think it's all getting too much for her. Keep her safe.

Dwayne: Wasn't planning otherwise.

Shoving the phone into the console, I crossed my arms and slumped in the passenger seat. Dwayne's eyes watched me in the peripheral for a reaction. "Please don't tell Brad. I told him he could trust Aaron and me together."

"I don't have to tell Brad. The way Ayah looks at you told him all he needs to know. Brad may trust you with Ayah, but he doesn't trust Ayah with you, and he shouldn't. Now that you know the truth, Ayah has no reason not to pursue you either," Dwayne warned me as he pulled up at the hospital.

"I. Am. With. Brad!" I enunciated every word. "Aaron missed his chance. Tell him to either be my friend or get the hell out of my life because the other option expired two months ago." Throwing open the door to his car, I grabbed my bag from the floor and climbed out. "Thanks for the lift, Dwayne."

"Caly," Dwayne called to me before I could shut the door, "You know you're in love with him, right?"

Staring at the seat between us, I refused to meet his eyes. "Which one?"

Tilting his head, Dwayne reached out to brush his finger under my chin. "That's the problem."

My eyes lifted. Dwayne was looking at me with so much sympathy, like I'd found out someone ran over my dog. Shutting the door, I went inside, making my way down to radiology.

When Aaron arrived, he went to talk to me, but I couldn't look at him. Closing his mouth, Aaron focused on the job and only spoke to me when he had to. He'd got the hang of things now, and I had no doubt he could do the job by himself when I left for holidays in two weeks.

God, so much had happened in the last two months. This Saturday, Brad would be meeting my grandfather. How wrong that could go made me close my eyes as I felt them start to water.

"Caly? Why don't you take off early, let me finish up tonight?" Sitting down beside me, Aaron rubbed my shoulder.

Shaking my head, I swiped at my eyes and continued writing up the reports. "I'm fine."

"No, you're not," Aaron grumbled. "I've been watching over you since you were seven, Caly, I know when you are fine, and I know when you aren't."

Sitting back, I kept my eyes on the screen. "You know why Rockford came to see me? Why Meadows wants to meet me?"

"Yeah, I do," Aaron ran his fingers through his hair. "Your mother has put you on the map big-time with that."

"We're building the college, but we're building a medical center with a trauma unit too." Aaron was the only person I felt I could talk to about this since he was aware of it. "You see, every member of our family takes on a community service project, a way to give back. My mother did this because I was telling her how the Riverside kids miss out on placements." Lifting my eyes to Aaron's, I saw his recognition of how this all started in those eat-the-world eyes. "I ranted to my mother about the injustice because I care about you and Josh. The benefits it will provide the Riverside residents is huge."

Aaron swallowed, his eyes intent on me. There was energy passing between us, begging for him to reach out and touch me. Whenever we were close like this, I could feel it like sparks passing between our bodies. Exhaling, Aaron stood up, moving away from me. "So, Brad's the real thing?"

Forcing my watery eyes to meet Aaron's, I choked on my answer. "Yes."

With his shoulders dropping, Aaron nodded. "I'm going to go do a final check; then, I'll walk you out to your car." Aaron walked away.

The tears I'd been holding back escaped. For all the reasons my family may not accept Brad, there were more why Aaron would never be allowed. The first was the reason he became part of my life; the second was who his father was. If Rockford wasn't good enough for my mother, then his illegitimate son wouldn't stand a chance. And that's nothing to how Gena would react.

Aaron had been all I'd ever longed for. Had he told me the truth, said to me that he felt the same, but I needed to know about his work for Rockford. Yeah, I'd have overreacted initially, but I accepted it pretty quickly when I did find out. His rejection had stung, and then I'd met Brad. The equivalent of the wind from one door closing, opening another. Now Brad was in my heart just as profoundly, and I wouldn't give him up.

When Aaron walked me out to mum's car after work, we didn't say a thing. As soon as the chauffeur opened the door, Aaron diverted his direction to his vehicle. Pulling out his phone as he walked, I knew, on instinct, he was reporting into Rockford. Aaron was probably passing on the information about the trauma center.

Dropping into the back seat of the town car, I pulled out my phone and called Brad. "Hey there, on your way home?" Brad asked.

"Yes, it's been a long day."

"Work or everything?" A door clicked shut, and I could picture Brad in his room.

"A bit of everything. Has Dom spoken to you today?" I asked.

"He's working some job for Rockford, so I've not seen him around much of late," Brad admitted.

"Wait, are you the only one in that dorm who doesn't work for Rockford?"

"How innocent of you to think I don't work for Rockford."

Frowning into the phone, I sat a bit straighter. "Do you?"

"Nah, but I've considered selling state secrets to him at times," Brad admitted. "I was yanking your chain, but you're stressed about something and not up to that. Want to talk to me about it?"

"Dom saw some of your dad's men waiting outside my class today. He warned Aaron, and they snuck me out the back way," I murmured.

Brad was quiet for a moment. "That's what the police tactical unit was here for today?"

"Yes."

"Caly, that happened before lunch, and you waited until now to call me?"

Shit! "I've been processing everything. Last week Rockford came after me in the same classroom, and today your dad, and I'm just starting to feel a bit insecure..."

"Rockford...what the fuck? Why didn't you tell me?" Brad raged into the phone. The pressure in my chest built up, and I started crying. Brad took a breath. "Caly, not telling me when this shit happens doesn't protect me. Can you tell me what is going on?"

Between sobs, I told Brad about the land in Riverside. the college and medical center. "So, this isn't to do with dating me?" Brad checked.

Squeezing my eyes tight, I remembered Dwayne's warning about how Rockford would react. "No, though I don't doubt they might take advantage of that."

"I don't doubt it either," Brad grumbled. "I want to see you."

"You know where to find me."

"I'm on my way."

Hanging up as I arrived home, I went inside. Upstairs in my bedroom, I showered before pulling my pajamas on. Going back downstairs to the kitchen, I got myself a drink. Standing staring at the large island bench, I jumped a little when the home phone rang, and I had to calm my heart rate before I picked it up.

"Miss Zilla, a Brad Meadows is here for you," offered the security guard.

"I'm expecting him, thank you." Hanging up, I went to the front door. After several minutes, Jack knocked before admitting Brad. "Thanks, Jack," I waved to the security guard. With a nod, he shut the door.

"Is this normal?" Brad asked, pointing to the door.

"Did he frisk you?" When Brad nodded, I laughed. "Jack's been telling me since I was fourteen, he'd be frisking any boys I brought home."

"I'm guessing you didn't get many to come for a second visit?" Brad still looked wide-eyed as he removed his jacket.

"I never had any for a first visit. You're the first guy I've ever let come to my home."

That confession made Brad pause. His eyes raked over me, and a moment later, I was over his shoulder. "Bedroom?"

"Upstairs," I laughed, trying to give directions as Brad stole me away to my room.

Lying in each other's arms afterward, Brad took a deep breath. "You leave for Hawaii in two weeks."

"I know."

"You haven't asked me to come with you," Brad reminded me.

"I was waiting to see how Saturday went. You may not want to know me after Granddad gets through with you," I worried.

Sweeping my hair back, Brad drew my face up to meet his eyes. "Caly, I don't care if the world hates the idea of us. I'm not going anywhere unless you tell me to go." His eyes were sincere as they pierced me with his assurance.

Reaching up, I pressed my lips to his. "Then you better book your ticket, Mr, because I don't care what my grandfather thinks."

Beaming a smile, Brad kissed me. Pulling away, he picked up his phone from the mess of clothes on the floor and called someone to confirm his ticket.

"You'd already put a ticket on hold?"

"Back when you first told me about the trip. I'm on the same flight as you. In coach, but on the same flight."

Filled with a sudden hit of happiness, I pounced on him. Brad returned my passionate kisses until our laughter was moaning.

When the phone rang, I picked it up and sort of moaned a greeting. "Just to let you know your mother has called for her driver to pick her up, Miss Zilla," Jack warned. "In case your friend needed to be leaving."

"He's good, Jack. My mother knows, so you can let the others know my guest will be staying for the next few nights." I smiled down at Brad's raised brow.

"As you say, Miss." Jack hung up.

"A few nights?"

"Tonight, then you may as well stay tomorrow because I'm not letting you out of bed. Then after meeting Grandad, you should come here for protection," I susurrated as I circled my hips on him.

With his fingers digging into my rear, Brad forced me down hard as he thrust up. "I was thinking we should just spend every night together from now on."

"Really?" I chuckled.

Squeezing his eyes shut, Brad mouthed a filthy word. "Yeah, you've finished your studies and just have your internship to go. So, we can alternate staying at each other's places, at least until we get back from Hawaii."

Biting my lip, I enjoyed feeling Brad thicken and throb inside me.

"Then, we should move in together and look at getting married."

My entire world stopped. "What?!"

Peering up at me with that small cheeky smile on his face, Brad licked his lips. I wasn't sure if he was being serious or stirring me again. "You'll be graduating this year, and I'll be finishing my Ph.D. Next year we could marry and..."

Realizing he was serious, I blinked and rolled off him. "We've known each other for two months."

"Hey!" Rolling towards me, Brad used my hip to roll me back to face him. "I love you. I've never felt like this about anyone. I've known you were the woman I'd want as my wife from the moment I first blew on you before I even knew your name."

"Brad," I scolded when he smirked at me. "Be serious."

"I am serious," Brad dropped kisses under my jaw. "I am in love with you, Caly Zilla, and I intend to marry you. I can wait if you need to, but I don't want to wait too long." Rolling us, Brad pressed back into me. "Oh, God, Caly. I can't wait to be doing this as your husband."

Thumping Brad's chest, I crawled out from under him. "Wait, is this marriage all about fucking me bare? Cause if it is, a simple test can make that happen faster."

Raising a brow, Brad pulled me back towards him. "Do you think I'm that shallow."

"No, but that's my point, Brad. Two months is not long enough to know each other well enough to commit to marriage. My family doesn't do divorce."

Brad rolled me back underneath him. "First, we know each other pretty well. Secondly, I have always known I'd know the right woman for me the moment I saw her. My mother believed in love at first sight, and she taught me to believe in it too. Third. We can go to pre-marital counseling, and you'll see how perfect we are for each other. Lastly, they have these things called prenups. There is no way we are getting married without one, my grandfather would have conniptions. So, we may as well accept that will be part of the process."

Staring up at Brad astounded by how much thought he'd put into this, I tried to keep my breathing calm. "Brad, remember how I said this sort of talk was the fastest way to get rid of me? Are you wanting to break up with me right now?"

Fear entered Brad's eyes. "Can't you see, that's why we will work. Every other girl who has wanted me has wanted me for my money. You couldn't give a shit about it. Your cousin is taking over the family business, so you know I'm not coming after you for that. Queenie is my age. I could be wooing her if I was after the Zilla wealth."

Sweeping his hair back from his face, I continued to stare up at him. The marriage talk had freaked me out, but not for the reason it usually would. It freaked me out because it sounded like the perfect idea. But considering the week I was having; I couldn't be sure that wasn't the stress getting to me.

"Hawaii first. If we survive a holiday without fighting or needing time out, then we can look at the pre-amble. But I have exams coming up, so we can't see each other every night. Next term, it won't be an issue as I'll be full-time on placement, but not before winter break."

Grinning as if I'd already agreed to marry him, Brad nosed my neck. "Okay, but we look at moving in together after Hawaii, okay?"

My eyes glanced around my room. "My mother is usually only home one week every month. If that. If we decide to do this, let's move in here. No point in it going to waste."

For the first time, Brad's smile faded. "We'll get our place once we marry, right?"

His concern made me laugh. "Of course."

Kissing me, Brad let me feel his happiness. Piercing into me,

Brad made me call his name in holy reverence, then he moaned mine before collapsing on top of me.

"I should talk about marriage during sex more often," Brad teased in my ear. "You got so tight around my cock."

Cursing him, I tickled his ribs where they were most ticklish.

Pulling away laughing, Brad fended me off. "You loved it," Brad laughed, getting off the bed to go to the bathroom.

"Caly!" my mother called as she threw my door open.

Brad, standing naked in the middle of my room, had nowhere to hide. Thankfully, I had the sheet over me. Gena's eyes widened as she took Brad in, completely. "Well, it seems you do take after your father in some ways."

Chapter Nineteen

BLOW

It's all happened so fast. I've never believed in love at first sight, but from the moment Blow bowled me over, there was a connection. I feel safe with him. He makes me laugh and knows how to ease or distract my anxieties. When I'm with Blow, I can't imagine being with anyone else. For that reason, I've decided he needs to be the one I take the leap of faith with, as far as love is concerned.

Nymph

Sin Rocks: *You're young. There is no need to rush this relationship. Take a breath and keep some time for you. Don't press yourself to believe this is the one because you feel the need to have that connection.*

The Watcher: *I'm happy for you, Nymph. Blow must be one hell of a guy. While I'm sure he feels the same way about you, take time to get to know each other better. Those unknown elements could be the catalyst for a broken heart. As SR said, there is no need to rush this new relationship. Make sure you get to know each other well from the start.*

Penny Dreadful: Yay! I hear wedding bells in the distance! Notice how I said distance? While I'm happy you are finally letting a guy in, you are too young to be settling down. Blow is the first guy you've allowed into your beautiful heart, and we all need a good heartbreak. While Lancelot did that for you, don't discount that the guy who seems perfect for you can turn into Mr. So. Wrong at any given moment. I've had it happen enough times. Ease yourself into this new love.

King of Hearts: So, my friend suggested this blog for a laugh. I've enjoyed the read, but over the last few entries, you've become more serious about the men in your life. You've lost some of that youthful vitality when it comes to dating. While I agree that we all need to get our hearts broken, I have seen it do lasting damage to the ability to trust again. I'd hate to see you lose that innocence, Nymph. Be careful. Also, it took me a while to realize, but you are so busted, Princess! We need to talk.

Penny Dreadful: LOL Welcome to our secret society of Nymph support, KOH.

Gee Zee: Don't start shit, KOH, or I will make your life hell.

Penny Dreadful: LOL, this is priceless. I need to study film and make this into a documentary.

Gee Zee: PD!

Penny Dreadful: Sorry, Zee.

"Oh my god! I could have gone my life without ever seeing that!"

Gena laughed, so did Brad.

Closing the porn magazine in which his father was staring, Brad handed it back to my mother. Watching my mother put the pristine magazine into its protective case, Brad frowned. "I'm going to hate to ask this, but why do you have that?"

"Well, it holds a happy memory for me. A dear friend gave the magazine to me, and we spent the night laughing about it. Your father hadn't become the man he is today at that stage, and was an unknown." Gena tucked the magazine away. "My friend knew your father and thought it was funny when he'd come across him in this magazine. He told me to hold onto it, so I did."

"Considering my age, it couldn't have been long after that my father took over Riverside."

"The following year, or thereabouts," mum confirmed for Brad. "He made big money in the porn industry, came home, and set himself up as a King. Some of the gang bangers took an issue to Greg, thinking himself all that, and tried to take him down a peg or two. Your father wasn't stupid. By the end of it, he'd wiped out most of the gang and took over what they left. After that, well, morals were never Greg's cup of tea."

Deflating, Brad stood up, looking exhausted. "I'm going to call it a night."

"Wait," I stood up, wrapping my arms around his waist. "You're not going, are you?"

Tucking a strand of hair behind my ear, Brad gave me a small smile. "I'm going upstairs to your bed because you know how to wear a guy out, Caly."

"Mother is in the room," Gena groaned as she stuck her fingers in her ears.

It made Brad and me chuckle. Going up on my toes, I kissed Brad. "I'll be up to bed soon."

"I better get some sleep while I can then," he teased with a wink.

"Nice seeing you, Brad," mum called out as he left the kitchen.

"Mum!" I scolded at the twinkle in her eye, Brad blushing again.

"What? It was nice seeing him. I mean, what mother doesn't want to know her daughter is being taken care of?"

Covering my face, I waited to die of embarrassment, which only encouraged her.

"Plus, Brad is nice to view. If you hadn't already snatched him up..."

"Oh my god, you are such a cougar," I accused.

Laughing at me, Gena came around the bench and hugged me. "I'm glad you are happy." Gena took a deep breath. "Are you both ready for tomorrow night?"

Shaking my head in answer, I exhaled hard as I made up my mind. "But no matter what Grandad says, I'm not giving him up, mum. I've asked Brad to come to Hawaii with me."

Lifting a brow at my defiance, Gena pursed her lips for a moment. "Well, I hope my father doesn't feel the need to make the same mistake twice."

"I can make it quite simple for him?" I suggested. "He can accept Brad, or he can lose me."

My mum's pupils dilated. "Caly..."

"What can he do, mum? You brought me up to be self-suffi-cient. I've had to earn my way. So, if Granddad cuts me off, it wouldn't change anything except me not having to go to the estate once a month."

Swallowing hard, Gena knew I was right. What my grand-father held over her head thirty years ago, wouldn't work on me. Lifting up on my toes, I kissed her cheek. "Good night mum, I'm going to sleep in in the morning, so don't bother waking me for the run." I couldn't keep the devious smile off my face.

It made my mother smile. "Play safe."

Eleri boyfriend for the fun of slumming it. I fell for a guy in high school, since then, I met and fell for another guy. My relationship is nothing like what you went through."

Gritting his teeth, Kingsley turned to face me as we reached the next doorway. "They are friends, and you can't choose between them. That's worse!"

"I have made my choice, or Brad wouldn't be here tonight," I hissed back. "Do you think I would cross Granddad like this if I weren't serious?"

With a huff, Kingsley peered over my shoulder. "You are in too deep too quick, Princess. Brad is your first serious relationship, and I know how overwhelming that can be. You get swept away in the passion, the emotion, and the sex, but what you don't see is how it's smothering you. You won't realize it until one day you wake up feeling like you are suffocating. Or worse, you wake up feeling nothing for the person you once thought was your world. You need to take ten steps back and dance through this a bit slower."

"I am not you, King, and I'm not your mother."

"No, you're your mother, and look how well that turned out for her. She's lonely as fuck. Gena isn't interested in anything beyond a one-night stand or call to an escort agency."

Closing my eyes, I tried to block the imagery from my head. "Did I need to know *that* about my mother? And how has what you described any different to you, King?"

My cousin raised one of his brows at me. "Exactly. You may not be me, Princess, but if you don't realize you are drowning, you are going to end up like the rest of us." Moving a step closer, Kingsley molded my face in his hands. "Your mum, my dad, Queenie, and me. Look at us, Caly. Think about the only relationship any of us have ever had."

Staring into my cousin's eyes, I felt mine water. He was

right. They all had only one relationship and never tried for another. My entire family was walking heartbreaks.

Assessing me with his sharp eyes, Kingsley nodded when he saw me grasp his concept. "Now, tell me you haven't set yourself up to be just as miserable."

"It may work," I pleaded. "Could it hurt to try? If it doesn't, then that's our fate."

"The curse of wealth. We can never trust, even our hearts."

"But it wasn't mum's heart that broke her, King. It was Granddad refusing it."

Taking a deep breath, my cousin looked down at his shoes. Exhaling hard, Kingsley placed a kiss on my forehead. "You are right and too smart for your own good, Princess. I'll mourn your heartbreak like it was my own."

"Thanks, King," I replied with as much sarcasm as I could muster.

With a smile teasing the side of his mouth, Kingsley backed up. "Grandad approved me going to Switzerland in July for six months. If I prove I can behave, he'll let me finish my internship there. Otherwise, he'll force me home and give me a junior position. So whatever you said worked. Thank you."

Happy to be back to our usual jest, I smiled up at him. "Congrats, King." I held out my hand. "Keys to your baby?"

His usual smile was finally breaking free as Kingsley kissed my temple. "Not until I leave, Princess." Letting go of my arm, Kingsley walked forward without looking at Brad. "Watch out for Queenie; she's in a mood."

Wrapping his arm around my waist, Brad walked forward with me. "Your cousin knows you are related, right?"

"Which is why we haven't fucked, or we'd be engaged already." Glaring at me, Brad knew that was a dig at him and Emily, but it was also the truth.

"I'm not kidding. I'm the only girl who gets King. I'd marry the bastard in a heartbeat if we weren't related. I love him and have had since we were children."

Brad put his mouth to my ear. "Too bad for him, you're all mine now." When he nipped my ear, I giggled.

"Cut that shit out," Queenie snarled as she walked in from outside. "Bunch of lovesick kids. You couldn't even comprehend the shit you're in." Her eyes locked on Brad, glaring as she walked past us.

"Did I mention your cousin is good friends with my cousin?" Brad murmured as we followed her into the dining room. "I've told my family I'm serious about you and meeting your family tonight?"

Considering being angry, I shrugged it off. Brad's grandparents had to find out eventually. "Well, that's going to make it three against three. So, it will all come down to Uncle Bryce as the swing vote."

"What about your grandmother?"

"She's Switzerland. Neutral in times of war."

Stepping into the dining room, we found Uncle Bryce was already there, his wife still at the Rehab center. "Caly," Uncle Bryce came forward to hug me. "For once, it's not my children under the guillotine."

"It had to happen eventually," I whispered back.

Chuckling, Bryce turned to Brad. "Brad, so nice to meet you."

"And you, Mr. Zilla," Brad shook Bryce's hand.

"Please, that's my father, call me Bryce."

The other doors opened, admitting my grandfather with my grandmother. Kingsley was the first to greet them before taking his seat. "Caly, your mother is late again," Granddad grumbled, hugging me.

"It wouldn't be mum otherwise, Granddad," I smiled back. "My boyfriend, Brad," I introduced, then stepped aside to greet my grandmother.

"Mr. Zilla," Brad held out his hands.

Granddad assessed him. "Well, you look like Douglas in his youth, let's hope you have his morals also."

"Thank you, sir," Brad smiled. "Pop tells me Caly looks like your wife did at the same age, so I'm guessing I have the same taste as him too."

Glaring at Brad's smiling face for a minute, slowly, my granddad smiled. "I guess this squares us up then. I stole his fiancée; his grandson steals my granddaughter."

"Not yet, Mr. Zilla," Brad negated. "The day I marry Caly, you can consider it even."

Granddad's pupils narrowed to pinpoints. Taking Brad's hand, I pulled Brad away from his imminent death. "Best we go sit," I excused. "You had to go straight to marriage?" I whispered.

"Best to make my intentions known."

"Sorry, I'm late." Gena strode into the room, greeting my grandparents before she took the seat on the other side of Brad. I was sitting opposite Kingsley tonight, Queenie next to him, glaring at Brad and me.

The entrees passed without much drama. Bryce and Gena kept Granddad busy talking about the business. When the mains came, granddad put an end to that. "So, what's happening in the world of my grandchildren?"

"Business as usual with me, Granddad," Kingsley smiled.

"Oh, yes? And how many hearts have you broken this month?" Granddad raised a brow.

"Not as many as deserved it," Kingsley replied wickedly.

"Queenie?" Granddad prompted, chuckling, and shaking his head at Kingsley.

"I've spent the week comforting my friend. The man she was engaged to announced he was dating someone else," Queenie seethed.

"Oh, poor thing. I hope your friend kept the ring."

"She didn't have a ring," Queenie snapped.

Feigning confusion, I blinked at her. "The jackass never even bought her a ring? What did he propose with?"

Kingsley was snickering into his dinner. Thank, god, Queenie didn't have laser vision, or I'd have fried in my seat.

"His dick!"

"Queenie!" Bryce scolded.

Rolling my eyes, I huffed. "Oh, please? Every guy proposes with that. If you held them to it, you and Kingsley would have been engaged a record amount of times." Who says this?

Everyone at the table covered their mouths to keep their food in. Except for Queenie; her mouth dropped open.

"Did the man really propose? Or was Emily planning her wedding without the groom's knowledge, as she did with Kingsley?" I challenged.

"Oh, my, god, you had to remind me of that," Kingsley winced. "That girl's determination to marry money deserves admiration. She'd marry Douglas himself if she could seduce him."

"Wouldn't put it past her. I ended our casual affair when she got drunk and told me she was only after me for my family's wealth. She said some other lovely things about the people she's chosen as her close friends. It's all to ensure her status in society," Brad added casually but looked at Queenie. The entire table went quiet.

"When was this?" Kingsley asked.

"Her birthday last year," Brad informed everyone. "You'd just dumped her after finding the mock engagement party invitations. She went straight back to trying to manipulate me."

Queenie studied Brad. "What did she say about me?"

Taking a breath, Brad tapped the cutlery in his hands. "Nothing that I'm ever going to repeat in full, but I know about Slider." Queenie's eyes bugged out of her head. Throwing her napkin on the table, she stormed out of the room.

"Um, is my daughter about to commit murder?" Bryce asked warily. "In case we should prevent her from leaving."

Smirking, Brad shook his head. "No, I don't think so, but she's less likely to believe everything my cousin tells her from now on."

Raising a brow at Brad, I pretended to peer up his jacket sleeve. "Exactly how many aces do you have up your sleeve?"

Brad kissed my cheekbone. "More than I should have," he murmured to my ear."

"Caly?" Granddad prompted after clearing his throat.

"It's been a busy month, Granddad. I've entered my first committed relationship. Become the owner of some highly sought land in Riverside. Been detained in my classroom by Sinclair Rockford, who threatened me to sell the land back to him. Then I had to sneak out of the same class a week later because Greg Meadows tried to have me kidnapped."

Considering the events of the past few weeks, I smiled at everyone at the table. I loved my family and would hate not to be a part of them anymore. "I've spent the last two weeks at home with mum, which has been great. I've missed it, and I'm thinking of moving back there after winter break."

"Really?" Mum asked, wariness in her tone. She flicked her gaze past Bryce and Granddad before coming back to me. "But it puts you so far from campus?"

"Yes, but I do my placement next semester, so I won't be

going to the campus anymore. I'll be at the hospital full time," I explained. "I've already secured my location, so I don't have to leave town. It makes sense to move home and be closer to work." Brad squeezed my hand under the table.

"Can we back up here," Kingsley interrupted. "Is no one else worried about Greg Meadows kidnapping Caly? Or that Sinclair Rockford managed to get her alone? And this is after both sides already made a try for her at the benefit."

"What?" My eyes went wide as I stared at Kingsley, confused. "Rockford danced with me. He didn't try and kidnap me."

Looking to Brad, Kingsley lifted his brow in question. "You didn't tell her?"

Squeezing my hand, Brad shook his head. "She already had enough on her plate. I didn't want to freak her out."

"Tell me what?" I demanded.

Instead of addressing me, Kingsley spoke to Granddad. "Caly went off to the bathroom during the bachelor's auction. I noticed Rockford leaving early, and Terry Meadows following suit. When I realized Caly wasn't near me, I went to find her. They'd both gone for her but found her with Brad. Being with him is probably the only reason she's still on this side of the river."

"But why? Terry didn't even know who I was then."

With his shoulders dropping, Brad sighed. "Terry didn't need to know who you were. You were standing with Kingsley and Bryce, the man who just bought what they were both after. As soon as Kingsley left with you, Rockford followed you out. Terry sent one of his guys to see if you actually left with Kingsley. If you hadn't, they would have tried to snatch you before Rockford could."

Sitting there, speechless, I felt my heart pounding in my

chest. "Terry didn't even know I was dating Brad then. He would have targeted me, anyway?"

Scratching the tablecloth, Bryce looked to my granddad for a cue. Granddad shook his head. Looking next to my mother across from him, Bryce shook his head before he turned to me. "You didn't need to date Brad to get on the Meadows' radar, Caly," Bryce explained. "You were with my son."

"But I've hung out with Kingsley for years?"

"Yes, you are the only constant woman that is hanging out with Kingsley. At sixteen, you became a high-value target to the kidnapping syndicate as a way to get to Kingsley. No one wanted your life turned upside down, and you were already a creature of habit. So, we encouraged your routine, which kept you pretty safe."

Blinking at Brad, I frowned, trying to make sense of everything I was hearing. "You knew Terry came out there for me?"

"Not until after you left. That's when I realized everyone's interest was you," Brad assured. "I knew then that my being in your life wasn't going to change anything for you. You were always a target, Caly. I figured at least if we were together, I could try and protect you when your mum's protection couldn't."

"Mum's protection?" Lifting my eyes to my mother, I found her eyes closed off, not giving me anything. Looking at Bryce, he was staring at Granddad.

"Oh, for fuck's sake!" Kingsley huffed. "You've had a protective detail from the time you were born, Caly. At school, they were embedded as a teacher. Since you went to university, a fellow student. It was the case for all three of us. Luckily for your nanny, you've never been one for clubbing or going to parties, so it's made watching you easy."

My eyes went to my mother and grandfather. "You've had someone spying on me?"

"Not spying, securing," Granddad grumbled. "They have never reported back on any aspect of your life except your safety. They were there to protect you from outsiders with limited interference in your life."

When I went to open my mouth to complain, Granddad gave me one of his looks. My shoulders and head dropped, and I bit my lip. I was in enough shit tonight. If I wanted Granddad to accept my relationship, I didn't need to pick a fight about something I had no control over. My grandfather always told me to pick my battles, tonight, unseen security was not the battle I needed to win.

Chapter Twenty

JUMPING **the Gun**

Families can be complicated, and they can be overbearing. I know they are looking out for me, but my family can take protecting to the nth degree. Almost to the point of controlling your life.

I'm not sure how to feel about the revelations tonight. Or, of the lengths my family is willing to go to, to keep me safe. Or, at least, their version of safe. You see, in my mind, my family's actions, their name, their associations, have caused me the most risk. It makes me worry if I have kids someday, will I behave the same?

Until I am a mother, I won't know how far I'd be willing to go to protect my child. So, unless I am in their boots, meeting the first boy my daughter brings home, they'll have to accept my anger.

If you are wondering. I stood my ground and Blow, and I are still together. Hopefully, my family will back down now.

Nymph

Gee Zee: Parenting is hard. It's not until you are in that situation that you appreciate the way your family tried to look out for you too.

We hope that we handle it better with every passing generation and that no lasting damage is done.

Nymph: *Do you appreciate it, though, GZ?*

The Watcher: *Family can be hard, even more so if you don't get along. That's why we have friends. Friends are the family we choose. I'm lucky enough to adore my mother and brother, and I'm very close to them. My mother has enough to worry about keeping us alive than any girl we bring home. So, I'm never going to go through what you are right now. You stood up for what you believe. Your family should be proud, and Blow should love you even more for believing in him enough to defy your family.*

Sin Rocks: *I'm proud of you for standing up for the man you love, Nymph. I hope it doesn't come back to bite you.*

Penny Dreadful: *My beau is too hot for my mother to care where he comes from. I'll have more trouble keeping her cougar paws off my man than worrying about if she approves of him.*

Nymph: *LOL I get where your mum is coming from PD. He is super-hot! My mother did lament not meeting Blow first, especially after she walked in on us and got to see the full package.*

Penny Dreadful: *OMG, That's awesome! I can't blame her. I so would have taken a ride of that bad boy if he'd thrown me a bone at any time.*

Sin Rocks: *This conversation seems to have gotten off track.*

The Watcher: *And they say guys talk!*

Penny Dreadful: *No talking. Nymph has a bad habit of not locking her door.*

King of Hearts: *Your family is looking out for you, Nymph. You know where I am if you want to talk. In the meantime, learn to lock your door.*

"I'm going to start by saying I'm worried about you." After he'd closed his study door, Granddad gestured to the two-seater lounge in his office. I sat obediently. Sitting beside me, he met my eyes so I could see his concern. "You've had a rather stressful month. How are you coping?"

'By banging my boyfriend until it's uncomfortable to sit down,' was the reply in my head. "I'm not. I'm ignoring it and hoping it will blow over."

"That's not going to happen, Caly."

"I'm not going to let those men scare me. I'm not changing my life, and I'm not giving up Brad."

Considering me for a few minutes, Granddad pressed his lips together once, then sighed. "I wish I could tell you I'm going to make life easier on you, Princess, but I know you well enough. This discussion is only going to upset you more."

Placing my hand on his, I pleaded with my eyes. "Then don't. Give us your blessing and let it go."

Squeezing my hand, he stood and made his way to his desk, opening his top drawer. "I wish it was that simple. Your mother informed me that you feel strongly about this young man. That you would be willing to sacrifice your place in this family for him." Removing a document out of his drawer, Grandad placed it on the desk. "That won't be necessary."

"You'll accept him?"

One of the granddad's eyebrows lifted. "It's a good match. He's the sole heir to the Sarita fortune. Douglas and I have agreed to terms of your involvement."

"Terms?" How the hell did my relationship with Brad affect our grandparents?

"A prenup. If you agree to the terms, then Douglas and I will support this relationship."

"But we're not getting married yet...?"

"It doesn't matter. There is a lot on both sides to protect. Douglas wants to ensure his grandson's financial security, as well as his company. I want to ensure your safety."

Suspicious, I stood up and moved to the table. "What does it state?" When Granddad wouldn't meet my eyes, I knew I wasn't going to like what I was about to hear. I couldn't remember a single time the old man wasn't willing to stare me into submission.

"You won't be entitled to a cent of the Sarita fortune, no matter how long you are together."

Reasonable. "Okay, I don't mind that. You know money has never been my motivation for anything."

"A saving grace when it came to this, I assure you. Douglas was very clear that if it had been Queenie, he would have interfered himself."

That made me smirk, especially when Grandad grimaced. Since Queenie stood to inherit part of the Zilla corporation, money wasn't an issue for her either. "What if Brad and I marry and start a family?"

Lifting his gaze, Granddad considered me. "That's the second time marriage has been mentioned tonight. Something you want to tell me, Calypso Claire?"

Oh, my full name. Now, he wasn't happy. "We're moving in together after winter break. We're thinking of marrying next year or the year after," I admitted, trying to sound sure and confident.

"You've gone from commitment-phobic to engaged in the space of a couple of months?" My grandfather prodded.

His glare burning my way made me swallow hard. Why did I have a bad feeling about the direction this was heading? "When it's the one, it's the one," I tried to justify.

Peering at me, Granddad dropped his eyes to my tummy. "How far along are you?"

"What?"

"I wasn't born yesterday, Calypso Claire. How far along is the pregnancy?"

Trying to lift my jaw off the floor and force it to move in answer was equal to chewing on a jawbreaker. "I'm not pregnant!"

"Don't lie to me!" Never having seen this side to my grandfather before, I jumped back, terrified. "You're just like your mother."

"You just gave your approval of Brad..."

"He's a Meadows!" Granddad snapped. "That's the other half of this contract. If your relationship puts your safety at risk in any way, you will get half of the Sarita fortune. If I discover Brad is in contact with his father or brother, you will get ten percent. If the Meadows' kidnap you, rape, and or murder you, I will take everything that boy is entitled to. And then I will crush Meadows once and for all."

A pit yawned open in my stomach at the graphic imagery now swimming around in my head. Holding in a sob, I tried to shake myself free of my anxiety. My fear had been building since my first encounter with Sinclair Rockford.

Taking a deep breath, I drew up the courage to fight for my heart. "I'm not pregnant. I love Brad, and neither of us is going to sign that. If you don't permit it, then you can disown me. I'm not giving up my happiness like my mother did and spending the rest of my life pining for the man you made me give up." Turning on my heel, I reached for the door.

"Stop." My feet halted immediately. I'd spent my life with my grandfather as my patriarch, so obedience was in my nature. "You are a fierce little thing, Caly. Headstrong like your mother.

But you will sign this, or you will go your separate ways," Granddad concluded.

"I love you, Granddad, but I won't allow you to bully me as you did my mum."

"Oh, I know, Caly. You have nothing to lose here. Can your boyfriend say the same?"

My brows bunching, I turned to face him. Stern features greeted me, and the light of righteousness in his eyes. My grandfather knew he was going to win this battle. All that remained was telling me how my relationship was going to work.

"Let me fill you in. If Brad continues to see you after you refuse to sign this agreement, Douglas will disown Brad. The company will pass on to Emily."

"Why?" I frowned. "Why does this matter to him that he would lose his only grandson, the only remnant of his beloved daughter?"

Sitting in the chair at his desk, Granddad seemed at ease. "Caly, why, if Brad hates his father and what he stands for so much, has he not changed his name from Meadows to Sarita?"

It was a good question, but one I was sure I already knew the answer too. "For the same reason, that when we marry, I won't take his name. In taking Douglas' name, Brad would be a Riverside bastard attempting to be more. Eleri high society would forever see him as a wolf in sheep's clothing.

"Brad doesn't want to forget who he is or where he was born. What happened to his mother is the foundation of Brad's psyche. That's his morality. It is his way of showing everyone that just because Greg Meadows is his father, doesn't mean Brad is his father." Granddad considered me silently. "I love Brad. I love you too." I met his eyes. "Don't make me choose."

Sliding the papers across the desk, Granddad lifted a brow.

"This family will support your relationship on the proviso you sign this prenup today. It protects you both. Not from each other, but from the outside forces that will impact your relationship. Your mother and I have your best interests at heart. Sign the papers, and this discussion will be over."

Tears flowed down my cheeks as I opened my mouth to decline, but my grandfather had one more ace to play.

"Brad already signed. He may love you, Caly, but he wasn't willing to give up his inheritance for you."

Blinking down at the two copies of the prenup, sure enough, Brad's signature was there. "When, how?"

"Douglas had him sign a few days ago after he told his grandfather his plans to marry you once you graduate. Brad told Douglas that you are the love of his life, and he wants to spend the rest of his life with you."

"Does mum know?" I asked a little shell-shocked.

"Who do you think suggested it?" Granddad grumbled. "Your mother will support the relationship, but she is a Zilla. Most importantly, Gena is your mother. She will protect you, first, and foremost. She always has."

Sitting down, I read through the documents. I couldn't go after Brad's money; he couldn't come after mine or any of the Zilla's fortune. There was the Meadows harm clause grandad mentioned, but there was also an heir clause. For every child I bore to Brad, I was entitled to ten percent of the Sarita fortune. "They're screwed if I have ten kids," I muttered.

Pushing a pen across the desk to me, Granddad smirked. "Try having one first, then decide if you want to do that nine more times."

Taking the pen, I cleared my throat. "I hate that you've done this."

"I know," Granddad accepted it. "I can see it in your

eyes, and I hate that you look at me now, the same way your mum has since the day I drove the man she loved away. Fathers do what they must to protect their families. That is something that your mother has come to understand."

Signing the papers, I pushed them away as if they burned. "I'm going home."

"Caly," Granddad mourned my anger. "If what you feel for each other is true, then this piece of paper shouldn't matter."

"If you love me the way you claim, then you'd understand why that isn't true," I debated. "You'd put my happiness above all else." Storming to the door, I stepped out into the hall where my mother and uncle Bryce were waiting.

"Caly." Gena took one look at my eyes and fell quiet. Uncle Bryce put his hand on my mum's shoulder in comfort as I swiped away the tears and went to find Brad.

They weren't hard to locate. Brad was in the lounge with Kingsley and my grandmother. "We're leaving," I stated as I passed through to the entry foyer.

"What happened?" Kingsley worried, especially when I didn't stop to say farewell to our grandmother. The truth was, I was barely holding my emotions together, and I didn't want to fall apart here. Standing, Brad assured Kingsley he'd take care of me. Saying goodbye to my grandmother, Brad followed me out to the car.

"You could have told me about the prenup," I griped once we were in his car.

"I did."

It was true. He'd said our grandfathers would insist. That didn't excuse that he didn't tell me he'd already signed it. "I hate that they will blame you if your family harms me. My family has put me at risk more than dating you does. Yet, nothing is penalizing them if Meadows or Rockford kidnap and force me to sell that land."

"That's because your family will already suffer if they lose you."

"Wouldn't you?"

"I would be heartbroken," Brad agreed, "but that's not losing a child, Caly. It's an entirely different type of grief."

"Like losing a parent when you are a child?" I whispered understanding who he was thinking about in saying that.

Brad reached over, taking my hand. "Yes. It doesn't matter, though, cause I'm not going to lose you, Caly. That's why I signed."

"Did you even hesitate?"

"No. As soon as Douglas said, I sign or walk, I signed."

"I fought it," I admitted. "I don't like that our families forced it on us."

My answer made Brad smirk. "I expected you wouldn't like it. Why do you think I let your grandfather tell you? I did not want to be on the receiving end of your sharp tongue, Caly. I only like that when we're naked. Speaking of which..."

"Brad, I'm angry."

"Does that mean you don't want me to stay over?" Brad queried, barely fazed by my mood.

My anger started to dissipate with every smirk he sent my way. "Just don't put anything in my mouth. You wouldn't be happy with me sinking teeth into," I dared back, his mood infectious.

Mr. Hyde glimmered from within Brad's eyes and smile. "That's okay, Caly. I'm more in the mood for eating you."

Chapter Twenty-One

There are moments in your life where you have to let go and let shit happen. For the first time in my life, I didn't overanalyze a situation. I went with the flow. It felt right. So, I let the tides sweep me away, and boy, it felt terrific.

Right now, I am the happiest I've ever been. I refuse to stop and assess the situation out of fear it will all dissolve into vapor. But I hope it lasts. One thing's for sure, this has been one of the best holidays of my life. As I prepare to board the plane home, I'm determined to bring happiness back with me.

Now, the trick is making it last.

Nymph.

Penny Dreadful: *Lots of fantastic sex will do that to you.*

Sin Rocks: *Does it always come down to sex with you?*

Penny Dreadful: *Pretty much, but in this case, it's scientific. Orgasms produce serotonin, which cures depression and makes you sleep better. The more orgasms, the more antidepressant hormones that are floating through your system. Ergo, lots of fantastic sex will* lead to the frame of mind Nymph is experiencing. Since she's never had regular long-term sex, the scientific reasoning supports me. Nymph's happiness is from spending two weeks sunbaking and banging Blow's brains out.

Gee Zee: By that definition, PD, you have answered Nymph's problem about how to make it last. Keep having lots of great sex.

King of Hearts: If only the sex were enough. While on holidays, you are in a bubble, protected from reality. When you come home, the bubble bursts, and all the orgasms in the world can't protect you from your truth.

Penny Dreadful: KOH, it sounds like you need a week of great sex and orgasms.

King of Hearts: You offering PD?

Sin Rocks: PD has a boyfriend, KOH. Shine your knob elsewhere.

Waking up, I smiled even before my eyes opened. Snuggling behind me, Brad had his arm wrapped around my waist. With his hand buried between my legs, Brad stroked me gently. Mr. Hyde was hard against my back while Brad nuzzled the back of my neck.

"Morning," Brad murmured as I rocked into his hand. Opening my eyes, I found sunlight lit our condo bedroom. The window opposite the bed showcased the view out across the beach to the water. "Our last day in Kauai," Brad murmured.

"Hmm, that means back to Honolulu and shopping before flying out." Gena had given me spending money, so I was looking forward to the shopping before leaving.

"I was thinking, we have a late fight, and our charter won't be here until eleven." Shifting himself, Brad found my damp core. "We should go for one last walk to that waterfall you love before we go."

The smile on my face stretched further. "I'd love that."

"Me too," Brad murmured as he pressed into me.

Before leaving for Hawaii, we spent two weeks apart so I could study for exams, and then I had to pack ready to move home. We'd enjoyed a great two weeks on holiday. We hadn't needed any time out from each other, either. That proved that we could be quite happy and comfortable around each other over long periods. We'd enjoyed our space in the afternoons, sitting on the lounge reading. When I went for a run along the beach each morning, Brad swam laps in the pool. Other than Brad nearly drowning while trying to show off surfing, it had been a perfect vacation.

After showering, we packed our gear before we hiked to the waterfall. When we got there, Brad cuddled me against his chest while we watched the water crash into the lagoon below. "It's beautiful here," I sighed.

"Very different to home," Brad agreed. "Makes me almost not want to leave."

"Reality finds you eventually. We can't stay here forever."

"I know." Brad dropped a kiss to my neck. "I'm glad we came early and had this place to ourselves."

"It's peaceful."

"And less embarrassing," Brad muttered. The comment confused me, even more so when Brad stepped around in front of me and dropped to one knee. My heart jumped into my throat.

"I was going to wait until you graduated, but then I saw the perfect ring. Even then, I was going to wait. But every time we've been here, I've loved the smile on your face, and I knew this had to be the place," Brad explained.

Taking my left hand, Brad held a beautiful and simple platinum engagement ring up. "Calypso Claire Zilla, will you do me the honor of marrying me?"

Blinking down at Brad, emotions swelled to overload. The first tear breached my eyelid, causing me to curse as I swiped it away. Brad's face fell. Taking his cheeks in my hands, I kissed him, pulling him to stand. "Yes," I whispered before I kissed him ardently.

"Wait, yes, you'll marry me?" Brad pulled away excitedly.

"Yes, I'll marry you." Wrapping myself around him, I hugged him tightly.

When I let him go, Brad stepped back and took my hand up, slipping the ring on before he pulled me into a long deep kiss. "Hmm, we need to get back to our room so I can have you again before we check out."

"Good thing I'm wearing my running shoes then." Turning on my heel, I started running back to the room. Brad's footfalls sounded behind me, keeping a comfortable pace until we got back to the condo. As we stepped through the door, Brad snatched me up, pinned me against the wall, and then there was no breath to waste on talking.

"Miss Zilla," Mum's driver, now also mine in her absence, greeted us at the airport.

Slipping into the backseat of the car, Brad and I held hands as we drove to campus. The day before we flew out for Hawaii, I'd moved out of the dorms. Penny was miffed but understood. Brad was moving in next weekend, so he still needed to be back at the dorm for now.

"Who are you calling?" Brad asked as I pulled out my phone.

"Mum, I need to tell her I'm home safe." Waiting as the call connected, I got Mum's voicemail. "Hi, Mum, just letting you know we're back. We had a great time. Can you call me as soon as you get this? I've got some news."

When I hung up, Brad snickered. "She's going to kill you. You know that."

"Not as bad as everyone else will."

Lifting my left hand to his mouth, Brad kissed the two rings on my finger. "I knew I did the right thing bringing the set."

Reaching over, I ran my thumb over the band on his left ring finger. "Do you still like it?" I asked.

Brad looked at the band we'd picked out for him, almost an exact match for mine. "I love it."

"Here, place your hand next to mine. I want to get a photo and send it to Penny. She's going to wring my neck." Arranging our hands to show off the rings, I clicked the picture and sent it to Penny. The response was almost instant as my phone started ringing.

"What the fuck?!" Penny's voice greeted me. "This better be a joke?"

"Nope, sorry," I smiled, hearing the excitement in Penny's voice.

"Oh. My. God!" She screeched.

"What the hell?" A deep voice grimaced next to her, making me laugh.

"Sorry, honey. Caly and Brad eloped. They got married," Penny sang.

"Fuck!" Dwayne's voice was crystal clear this time.

"Where are you going?" Penny sounded confused.

"I have to break the news to someone before they find out from someone else." A door closed in the background.

"Everything okay?"

"Yeah, Dwayne has gone to tell Aaron," Penny explained.

For the first time since Brad got down on his knee, I regretted the spontaneity of our decision. Then I remembered all the reasons Aaron and I couldn't work. The ones he'd told me when he tried to let me down gently, and the ones I knew would be worse.

"So, have you told your family yet?"

"No," I cringed at the idea. "I figured I'd tell someone who would be happy for us first."

"You know they will all think you are pregnant, right?" Penny asked, humored.

"Yeah, I know."

"And that you are going to have to do it properly, here," Penny continued. "There is no way a Sarita and Zilla can get married without the huge fanfare. Legal or not, you're going to have to do the big white wedding."

"Argh," I grumbled.

Penny's laugh was chiming bells. "That's the only reason I'm not killing you, Bitch. Trying to rob me of my grand entrance as your bridesmaid. I'm damn well organizing you a hen's night too. You think I'm missing out on that either; you're wrong." When I groaned louder, Penny continued laughing at me.

Penny was right. The announcement went down like a ton of bricks. My mother remained silent on the other end of the phone for so long I thought we'd been disconnected. Minutes after that, my grandfather called and demanded I come to see him at once. If I'd been a child, I dare say I wouldn't have been able to sit down for a month.

"What do you think you are doing, Calypso Claire?"

"Granddad, we're in love."

"You've known him a matter of months."

"I knew I loved him within a week."

Hard eyes flicked to my stomach and back. "You told me you weren't pregnant."

Peering down at my flat stomach, I frowned. "I'm not!"

"Don't bullshit me, Princess. No one has a gunshot wedding anymore without a baby being the cause."

"I swear to you, I'm not pregnant. Brad proposed, we got caught up in the moment, and since there was already a prenup, there was no reason to wait."

"There is every reason to wait!" Granddad stood, raising his voice. "You are twenty, you are still at university, and you barely know the boy. But reason number one is that you didn't tell your family."

"You forced me to sign a prenup. What other permission did I need?"

"He's a Meadows! He has manipulated you from the moment you met. Within a matter of months, he has tricked you into marrying him and moving in with you."

"Manipulated and tricked me? To what gain? If it were for the Zilla wealth or business, Queenie would have been his target. I offer him nothing of power or privilege except a biased patriarch who thinks he is a king over this town."

The way my grandfather's nostrils flared told me I'd crossed a line. The moment those words left my lips, I wanted to take them back. Granddad never acted like he was above anyone. He was a good man who looked out for his family and believed in hard work.

"I'm sorry I didn't mean that. I love you, Granddad, and I've always looked up to you, but I love Brad, and I've made this choice. There is nothing you can do about it." Sitting down, I waited for his judgment.

"You have always been a level-headed girl, Caly, so my reason for concern is your sudden rash decisions. You are making life choices with barely any thought to the consequences. Those are the sort of actions that lead a girl into bad situations." Taking his seat, Grandad looked over the wedding certificate he'd insisted on seeing.

"In this case, the damage is done. You are married, and as you say, there is a prenup. You will learn why engagements always lasted a year the hard way. I've called and booked the church for your formal wedding. If you want this family to accept this ill-conceived action, you will play by our rules going forward. Go speak to your grandmother to make all the other arrangements."

Rising out of the chair, I shuffled to the door, kicking my heart along the floor as I walked.

"Princess?" Looking back into my grandfather's eyes, my self-esteem bottomed out. "I have always loved and admired you, but today, you disappoint me. Not because you married the man you love, or because he's a Meadows, but because you did it thoughtlessly. You did this without concern about how that would make your mother feel. You are her only child, and you eloped without notice. You owe her an apology."

Stepping out of Granddad's office, Kingsley sat on the lounge by the receptionist. When our eyes met, his angry, mine watering, I couldn't take anymore, and the floodgates opened as I looked away.

Standing up, Kingsley buttoned his suit jacket, then took me in his arms, hugging me tightly. "Did he demand you annul the marriage?"

"No."

"Then, you won, Princess."

"It doesn't feel like it."

"Well, you didn't expect him to wave the white flag and show weakness, did you?"

"You hate me, too," I sobbed into his chest.

"Of course, I do. You broke my heart. All my hard work to change the law about marrying your first cousin turned to dust. Now, I need to face the fact I will forever be the manwhore bachelor of Eleri. The only woman worthy of me fell in love with someone else."

"You'll meet a woman one day who will make you eat those words, Kingsley."

"Well, until I meet her, I will mourn losing you." When I kept sobbing into his chest, Kingsley sighed. "Come on, I'll take you to see Nanna. Queenie and our Grandmother will help you organize your big day until Gena can get back. Since it might be the only wedding I ever get a say in, I'm coming along for the ride. Plus, you need me there."

"Is Queenie going to kill me?"

"God, no! She's over the moon with having this media frenzy to control. So, expect her to have a say in everything that could end up in a photo in a magazine."

"Great!"

Chuckling, Kingsley led me out to his car and drove me to my grandparent's estate. That's how I spent the weekend before my final placement. Getting dragged around bridal boutiques, function centers, and cake shops by my kin.

The hardest person I had to face wasn't anyone in my family. Arriving for placement at the hospital where I worked on Monday morning, I came face to face with Aaron. His eyes were the most emotional I'd ever seen. Like he could open his mouth and swallow the world whole. Lifting my left hand, he glared at the rings. "This isn't you."

"I assure you; it is."

Shaking his head, Aaron ran his thumb over the rings. "You don't do brash decisions, Caly. You plot and plan everything before you do it. Especially the big decisions. You took three months to find your debutante dress. It took twelve months for you to choose the degree you wanted to do before you applied for the advanced program. Jesus, Caly, you research a new brand of toothpaste before you change." Aaron held my hand up in front of me. "This, it's not you."

Taking my hand back from him, I forced myself to meet his eyes. Aaron didn't want me, so I shouldn't feel guilty. "It's done, and it's legal."

"What is?" Michael, my boss, asked over my shoulder.

"Caly eloped while in Hawaii," Aaron snipped and walked off.

"Are you pregnant?" Michael asked.

"No. Why does everyone go straight to that?"

Michael shrugged. "Who's the lucky man?"

"Brad Meadows."

His brows lifted a touch, but Michael didn't comment. "Well, congratulations. I hope he treats you well, Caly."

"Thanks. I'll get started."

When work finished that afternoon, Aaron surprised me by waiting for me. "Brad has organized a dinner and asked me to bring you straight from work."

Suspicious that this was a trap to get me in a room with Rockford again, I retrieved my phone from my bag. As I followed Aaron to his car, I texted Brad as we walked. Brad texted back immediately, confirming he'd made some arrangements. Relieved, I slid into Aaron's car.

Twenty minutes later, we arrived at Gena's favorite restaurant. The same one she gave the Spanish Inquisition to Brad at when she found out we were dating. Aaron was silent the entire drive.

"What's going on?" I asked Brad when he greeted me with a kiss.

"Well, I was thinking," Brad began, drawing me away from Aaron while the waitress showed him to our table. "You were saying all the places your grandmother showed you for the reception were not to your taste. It made me think of this place. It's out of the way, beautifully decorated, and we could restrict guest numbers based on space."

Looking around the small restaurant, I smiled at the idea. "This could work. God knows the food is wonderful."

My agreement made Brad smile. "So, I invited the important people to join us for dinner here and help us decide on a menu."

Checking over the table of friends, I noticed Penny and Dwayne there, with Queenie, Aaron, and Kingsley. "How does Aaron fit into this?"

"Look, I know you two have history, but he's actually one of my closest friends. So, I've asked Aaron to be my best man."

The air rushed out of my lungs. Brad saw it, but he didn't say anything, waiting for me to think it over. "And Kingsley?"

"Well, you said you are very close. It made sense to ask Kingsley to be a groomsman as well as Dwayne."

"That gives you three groomsmen to my two bridesmaids," I pointed out the odd numbers.

Nodding his head, Brad met my eyes. "You're going to need another bridesmaid."

"If you even suggest Emily, I will divorce you on the spot," I declared haughtily.

Surprisingly, Brad smirked. "It's not a good idea for us to have someone either of us has slept with in the wedding party."

Cringing a little, I raised my palm. "Let's rephrase that to sex. Otherwise, it wipes out both my bridesmaids and one of the groomsmen if it's sleeping with them."

My comment made Brad laugh, but I bet that wouldn't be the case if he knew I'd never shared a bed with my manwhore cousin. "My point being. Do you think you can find another bridesmaid?"

Without even hesitating, I nodded. "Julianne was my best friend through high school, and I'd always planned for her to be a bridesmaid. I'm sure she'd love to be with Kingsley for a night."

Content with that answer, Brad pulled me into a kiss. "So, we agree on our wedding party and the reception location?"

"Sure. Let me call Julianne and see if she can make it tonight?"

With one more kiss, Brad walked away, joining our wedding party. Moving back into the quiet foyer of the restaurant, I called Julianne. Over the moon with the request, she told me she'd drive out straight away. Hanging up, I turned to join our guests as Sinclair Rockford appeared in front of me.

"Stay quiet." Taking my elbow, he maneuvered me down the hall and into the manager's office. His eyes were angry as he grabbed my left hand and examined the rings. "Tell me this wasn't legal."

"Entirely legal," I gasped at his grip. When Rockford released my wrist as if my touch burnt him, I stepped back out of reach.

"Are you insane? You married a Meadows?"

"I married the man I love, and it's none of your business."

"Bullshit, Caly! It is exactly my business. Do you have any idea what you've done? Gregory wanted a foot in the Sarita corporation. He kidnapped Brad's mother and held her hostage while he repeatedly raped her. It was never about the ransom. He wanted a child that would be the sole heir of the Sarita billions. Now, you've given him a key to the door to the Zilla fortune as well."

"But Brad turned on his father," I challenged.

"Yes, he did. Do you know why? Has Brad told you?" When I shook my head hating where this was leading, Rockford scowled. Greg was kind to Brad's mother from the moment he knew she was pregnant. At least, when Brad was around to see the two of them together. When he was ten, Brad's mother told Brad the truth and tried to escape with him. Greg executed her in front of Brad. That was Brad's turning point."

Feeling sick to my stomach at the revelation, I stood there. Brad had watched his father murder his mother. No wonder he was happy to have nothing to do with him.

"Greg tried for your mother first," Rockford revealed. "When I found out about his plan, I sent someone to protect her. Greg tried again a few years after Brad was born. I protected your mother again, and that occasion is what brought you into the world."

"You hired my father to protect my mother?" I stumbled through his words. "Did he love her?"

His eyes full of emotion, Rockford's face softened. "She was his oxygen." My hand gripped the locket around my neck. "Once Greg found out that your mother was a mother, he stopped going after her," Rockford continued.

"Because Kingsley and Queenie were born by then, and they would get the business, not me?"

Shaking his head, Rockford reached out and caressed my cheek, his eyes full of sympathy. "Because you were a girl, younger than either of his sons. He got his foot into the Sarita corporation with Brad. He just had to bide his time and let one of his sons put his hold on the Zilla family name, in you."

My jaw tensing, I glared at Rockford. "Brad didn't marry me because his father told him too."

"No, he didn't," Rockford agreed. "Do you know what

happens now?" When I shook my head, Rockford's face turned serious. "You inherit everything. Your children, they'll inherit it from you. Children who will carry the Meadows name." Rockford let his gaze intensify. "At some stage in the future, Greg is going to make his way into your children's life. Then Brad will suffer a tragic accident. Possibly the same one your cousins Kingsley and Queenie will suffer. You will inherit everything. Then, Caly, Greg will come for you."

Trembling beneath the horror of his words, I closed my eyes, tears streaking down my face unchecked. "There's a prenup," I admitted, barely a whisper. His brow pinching, Rockford double blinked. He hadn't known.

"I can't touch his money, Brad can't touch mine, and I only get ten percent per child. If what you say happens. Greg Meadows won't be entitled to shit out of the Sarita family," I hissed. "Granddad understood the game Greg was playing. Our families created the prenup to prevent anyone from benefitting from this arrangement."

Surprising me, Rockford exhaled in relief. His eyes met mine, and I froze. Mind racing back to the photos I'd seen of my mother, to the graduation photo that hung in my Granddad's study. Gripping the locket around my throat, I remembered it was hanging around her's in the picture. It was there for most of her twenty's. She only stopped wearing it when I went to school, and she put it around my neck.

Tears fell faster as I realized how long my father had been in my mother's life. God, how much worse did that make the things that happened between Aaron and me. "Gena knew what this was, didn't she?"

Eyes hesitant, Rockford focused on the locket. "She might have worked it out over the years." Watching my eyes as I observed him, Rockford took a breath. "I would never harm you, Caly. All I've ever done is try to keep you safe."

"I believe you, and now I know why. You loved Gena once. Do you ever regret not standing up to my granddad, convincing her to run away with you?"

Eyes glittering with emotion, a small smile played on Rockford's lips. He dropped his gaze to his feet, then back to my eyes. "For the last twenty years, but never so much as I have for the last twelve years."

Acknowledging his confirmation of my suspicions, I nodded. Moving towards the door to leave, I stopped and considered Rockford. "Do you know what's going on out there tonight?"

"Dinner to celebrate with your friends?"

"It's dinner with our bridal party. Our grandfathers are insisting on us doing this correctly."

"Ayah is in the wedding party?" Rockford raised a brow.

"Dwayne and Aaron are quite close to my husband. Aaron is to be best man," I revealed. Rockford and I watched each other. "You've been protecting me for twelve years, Mr. Rockford, I think an invitation to my wedding is the least I could do."

Stepping closer, Rockford lifted his brow. "Just an invitation?"

His smile slowly grew, reflecting the one that was spreading across my lips. With a small twitch of my lips, I left, greeting Julianne by the door before we both made our way to join the others.

"Where'd you disappear to?" Brad asked.

Aaron was looking over my shoulder towards the door. My stomach burned to ash. I found myself assessing those eat-the-world blue eyes and comparing them to Rockford's. My mother always told me I had my father's coloring. While we all had dark hair and blue eyes, I didn't see a younger version of Rockford when I looked at Aaron. For some reason, I was sort of glad about that.

"I ran into a family friend and was telling him about our wedding plans." Meeting my husband's eyes, I resolved that I'd made the right choice because, in reality, there was no choice. It was a realization I could have used some months ago.

Brushing my cheek, Brad smiled. "You seem happier, did something happen?"

"Yeah, it finally clicked," I told him as I moved closer to him. "I'm married to you."

Chapter Twenty-Two

"YOU READY, CALY?" Mum asked as the car pulled up at the church.

"I'm already married to him, mum," I reminded her with a laugh. Though, yes, I was nervous as hell. Not because I was about to take my vows in the church to make it official before God - as my grandmother put it. But because of the surprise I'd planned.

Tears in her eyes, Gena smiled. "You look beautiful, just like a real princess."

When the driver opened our doors, Penny, Julianne, and Queenie were waiting. My dress was relatively simple. It had a lace bodice and keyhole back, over a flowing satin skirt that tapered down to a small train. No hoops or netting or frou-frou on my wedding dress. Simple, sleek, and elegant, but fitting enough that the rumor of pregnancy could be ruled out.

Brad and I had been married for three months already, living at my mother's and happy. The ceremony was for everyone else. For my part, I was going to make our grandfather's choke for the fun of it, as payback for that prenup.

Entering the outer lobby of the church, Penny and Queenie made a fuss of my dress looking just right. "I'll go in and let them know you're ready," Gena smiled at me.

"Mum," I grabbed her hand. "I need to warn you." I watched my mother frown, a little worry threading into her brow. "I know."

"You know?" Mum looked at me, confused.

Meeting her gaze, I looked over her shoulder. Sinclair Rockford looked terrific in his suit.

Still confused, Gena followed my gaze, the blood draining from her face when she saw her ex. "What are you doing here?" She gasped.

"He knows too, mum. He's the man who asked me about my locket when I was seven. He's known all these years and has protected me."

Eyes wide, Gena blinked at me. "You asked him here?"

"He's giving me away."

My mother's eyes bugged out of her head. "Your grandfather will have a heart attack."

The impact of this small action made me smile. "Yeah, I know."

"Calypso Claire Zilla, you did this to annoy us?" Gena challenged.

"One-word, mum," I met her eyes dangerously. "Prenup! You should have discussed it with me first." Her mouth fell open.

Being cheeky, Rockford moved forward and kissed my mother's cheek. Her eyelids fluttered for a second; then pure annoyance glared out at us. "She looks like you, Gena, but those eyes of hers, you can see she's just as cunning and naughty as her father."

"If you do this, there will be pictures taken, and questions asked," Mum warned Rockford.

Her fear didn't even impact his smile. "I have the perfect answer for them all," he assured mum. "Caly hasn't just asked me to give her away, Gena. She's invited me to collaborate with her on the Riverside College Project. Your daughter and I are now business partners."

My mother's mouth gaped. "Caly..."

Taking a step forward, I hugged her. "I didn't do this to hurt you, Mum. We can do good things in Riverside, but with Rockford on our side, he brings more money and resources to the project. Brad's bringing the Sarita name to the project too. It was the right thing to do."

Her breath hitching, Mum, held me tight. "When did you get this brave?"

"I take after you in so many ways." Mum held me tighter. "He's still gorgeous, Mum, and single," I teased as I pulled back.

"Calypso Claire!" Blushing, Gena flicked her eyes over Rockford appreciatively. "Sit by me after you give her hand to her husband. We might as well make the rumor mill go crazy."

Winking at her, Rockford admired her backside as she sashayed into the church. "You and Brad are leaving the reception and going straight on your honeymoon, right?"

"I won't be home tonight, if that's what you are asking," I snickered. The music we'd chosen started; Julianne entered the church. Penny and Queenie were making eyes at Rockford. While his presence confused them, they were too interested in banging him to question it.

"You look beautiful," Rockford kissed my cheek as he took my hand. "Thank you for asking me to give you away."

Smiling, I couldn't imagine this day getting any better as Queenie entered the aisle. "I want to tell you something I haven't told anyone else," I whispered. Rockford's eyes watched me. "I've stopped taking the pill. Brad and I are going to try for a family straight away."

"Caly, you're too young to start a family," Rockford looked worried. "Why rush things?"

"Well, it's not rushing. We are leaving it in fates hands, but," I swallowed unsure how to express the rest. Turning to face Rockford as Penny started into the church, I pretended to straighten his tie. "I get this feeling, in here," I put my hand over my stomach, "that we can't wait on this. Maybe, it's because of what I do for work. My gut tells me the longer I wait, the more chance things could go wrong."

Rockford caressed my cheek. "You're worried about the radiation exposure causing genetic issues?" When I nodded, he gave me a kind smile. "Well, it's a perfectly reasonable explanation for wanting to start your family young."

Grateful, I could share this with someone, and they'd understand, I hugged him. "Okay, enough of that, are you ready?" Rockford lifted a brow. Taking a deep breath, I nodded, and Rockford took my arm in his as we stepped inside.

Walking down the aisle with Sinclair Rockford was everything I'd imagined. Gasps of surprise filled the crowd, more than the whispered comments of my appearance. Brad smiled brightly at me; he'd been the only person I'd forewarned of my plan. His eyes went to both our grandparents, and he burst out laughing at their mouths hanging open.

My eyes went to Aaron, who looked confused, like Kingsley. The only groomsman who was smiling was Dwayne. He seemed as happy as Larry. "Dwayne knows, doesn't he?" I asked, remembering how Dwayne told me he was privy to inside information.

Rockford turned his eyes to me. "Yes. His father was my best friend. I all but raised Dwayne."

"You didn't encourage him to go to university?"

"He did. Ask Brad," Rockford murmured as we reached the front.

"You look amazing," Brad greeted me as I stepped up next to him.

"We are gathered here today..." The priest began. "Who presents this woman?"

"I do," Rockford smiled, giving Brad my hand. With a wink, he went to sit by my mother. The gossip through the church was like a tidal wave. My grandfather looked ready to murder someone.

"Something I should know?" Brad asked quietly. Smiling large, I winked at him as the priest continued. Everything went as planned. The only glitch for me was when the priest pronounced us husband and wife. Over Brad's shoulder, I saw Aaron flinch.

"You may kiss the bride," the priest smiled.

Reeling me in, Brad went to French me, but I made it quick and sweet. Considering me as I pulled away, Brad lifted a brow. "Shy, Mrs. Hyde?"

Cheeks heating, I wrapped my arms around his neck and kissed him properly. People started laughing. My grandfather cleared his throat, pulling me back, my heart filled with happiness. "Better?"

Brad's eyes were glassy. "Much. I'll show you how much in the limo on the way to the reception," Brad whispered in my ear.

"Photo's first," I mumbled.

Moving me in front of him as the photographer aimed, Brad

murmured so others wouldn't hear. "Best you stand in front of me, Honey." It made me laugh. The photographer loved it.

My grandfather came over to shake Brad's hand, his eyes tense. Taking me in a hug, Granddad put his mouth to my ear. "What is Rockford doing here?"

"He's my new business partner," I advised. My grandfather pulled back to meet my eyes, not buying it. Batting my eyelids, I smiled sweetly. "Instead of a father, a good-looking man of equal age was appropriate, don't you think?"

"I think you are still angry about the prenup," Granddad murmured. Smiling cheekily at him, I moved on to hug my mother.

The reception was fun. Lots of laughter at funny speeches about Brad and me by my grandfather and his. When Aaron got up to talk, I gripped my dress in my hands under the table.

"I've known Caly longer than I've known Brad. We went to school together, but she was closer to my younger brother than me. Caly was the pretty Zilla girl in the year below me. She was kind, respectful, reserved, and studitious," Aaron began.

"I met Brad three years ago when I went to university, and he became my flat-mate. Once we got past his surname..." Everyone chuckled, "we became fast friends. It turned out; we already had a good friend in common." Aaron patted Dwayne on the shoulder. "This soon led to lots of drunken nights, watching movies, and general good times. There are many entertaining stories I could tell you about Brad. There was a socialite so obsessed with him that she turned up at our dorm with a ring ready, demanding Brad propose." Everyone's eyes turned towards Emily, who was pouting in her chair.

"But, that's not the story we are here for today. Brad met Caly by crash tackling her." Everyone laughed. "You all think I'm joking, but I'm not. Leaving the gym in a hurry one morning, Brad bowled poor Caly over. He swears, he didn't see her. Not a single one of us believe him. He came back telling us how he met the most amazing girl, that he crash-tackled her, and then blew on her."

Heat filled my cheeks as everyone jeered, and I hid my face. "Just like you, we were thinking something dirty. Brad then clarified that Caly got injured in the fall, she grazed her hip and was bleeding. When she lifted her shirt to look, Brad blew, with his mouth, over the wound to help her pain response. He then went and bought her some first aid products instead of flowers to ask her on a date." Aaron turned to look at me. "He was besotted with Caly the moment he met her."

"Weren't we all?" Dwayne announced.

"You see, we saw the difference in Brad the moment they met. As many guys can attest, Caly was pretty picky with guys. There weren't many who hit on her who even got a first date, even Dwayne here tried his luck and failed. So, we knew Brad gained Caly's attention when she said yes to a date. Then we knew he'd won her over when she agreed to another date, and then a third."

"We all lost serious money betting on when she'd ditch him," Dwayne laughed. Brad took my hand in his causing me to smile at him.

"So, as the only person who has known both Brad and Caly independently, I knew the moment these two were in love." There was a pang of sadness in Aaron's voice. "They are both kind-hearted, caring, and fun people. They both have mothers from Eleri, and fathers from Riverside. They have so much in common that you would never pick it from looking at them, but enough difference to make their lives interesting." Aaron raised his glass. "I ask you all to join with me in toasting Brad Meadows and Caly Zilla. To true love."

We all toasted, then Brad and I kissed. When we pulled apart, Rockford had moved to the microphone. "Good evening," Rockford greeted. "Normally, Caly's father would talk now. Caly's mother was going to talk but has asked me to do the speech instead. If that's okay with the Bride and Groom?" We nodded, having discussed it before we left the church.

"I'm sure many of you are trying to guess why I walked Caly down the aisle today?" Rockford smirked at the nodding heads. "To tell this story, I need to give you a bit of background. It is a tradition in the Zilla family to take on a community project at age twenty-one. Caly's father came from Riverside. Through school and university, she developed close caring friendships with people from Riverside. So, Caly decided that's where her focus needed to be."

Brad kissed my forehead. "Relax," he whispered.

"Caly started helping the people of Riverside while she was at school. There was a boy on scholarship who couldn't afford a tutor. Caly volunteered to tutor him for free. Even when Caly went to university, she continued to tutor this boy for free. This week, that boy received his early acceptance to study medicine next year on a full scholarship."

My head swung to find Josh in the crowd. He was grinning ear to ear. He gave me two thumbs up, and I smiled.

"Earlier this year, Caly was talking to a friend at uni. He told her that his degree was a waste of time. You see, he needs twelve months of work experience to become accredited. Because he was from Riverside, he'd be the last picked for placement or a traineeship. That same day, Caly asked her boss to give that boy a chance by letting him fill in for her while she took a holiday."

Freezing like a deer in headlights, I glanced at Aaron. He

raised a brow. "Did you think I didn't know? There is no such thing as coincidence, Caly." Chuckling, Aaron shook his head.

"Her friend now has a full-time traineeship. This will enable him to register for accreditation after graduation. So, how does that put me in the picture? Recently, land zoned for the Riverside college became available for purchase. The Zilla's bought that land for Caly and her community project. They plan to build not only the Riverside College but also the development of a medical center."

My stomach hollowed like it tended to do over the last few months. A moment of anxiety swept over me, and I squeezed Brad's hand, terrified he wasn't there.

"This medical center will benefit Riverside on two fronts," Rockford continued. "All Riverside students of any medical field program will have priority for placement. Nurses, doctors, radiology, allied health, and health services. Whatever their study, they will have a place to learn and become accredited. Secondly, the medical center will have a trauma center. This triage facility will save lives by bringing help closer to the Riverside dead zone. Now, this isn't just a guess. The Zilla foundation looked at the stats of Riverside deaths over the last ten years. Hundreds of deaths will be prevented by enabling residents to reach help sooner."

"Are you okay?" Brad whispered. "You look like you're about to start crying?"

"It's not soon enough," I told him, pressing against that pit in my stomach. "I keep getting this feeling that it's not happening soon enough."

"Caly convinced her husband to involve Sarita hotels. This will provide lodgings for visiting specialists and a longcase care facility. Caly also asked me to partner with her to bring my expertise to the project. I have gladly agreed." Glancing to Brad and me, Rockford gave the nod, and we stood.

"You see, today isn't celebrating the union of two Eleri families. In the joining of these two people, we see the union of Riverside and Eleri. We see the hope for our neighbors across the river to know safe streets, education, and medical care. In this marriage, we see their love for each other and compassion for others. In this joint project, we see a future, for our children, and us." Rockford raised his glass. "To Brad and Caly. To their belief that being born across the river doesn't mean you deserve less." Everyone stood and toasted us, then they clapped.

"The man certainly can talk the talk," Brad whispered. "Do you plan to tell me the real reason you let him give you away?"

Turning my mouth to Brad's ear, I whispered. "Because we aren't just a Sarita-Zilla or Eleri-Riverside union. We are also a Meadows-Rockford combination." Brad froze next to me. "Sinclair Rockford is my father."

Chapter Twenty-Three

"YOUR DAD IS SINCLAIR ROCKFORD?" Brad let the hotel door slam shut behind him. I'd made him wait to discuss it, not allowing him to bring it up at the reception or even in the limo to the hotel. But Brad had been itching since I'd made my confession.

"Yes," I exhaled as I moved my suitcase to the side and turned to face him. "Is that a problem?"

Brad blinked at me. "Does anyone else know?"

"My mother obviously, and Rockford found out when I was seven..."

"Wait, he didn't know?"

"When mum realized she was pregnant, she ended their affair. She decided it would be too dangerous for anyone to know who my father was."

"Is that when you found out?" Brad asked.

"No, I realized it was Rockford three months ago after we married. He found out and dragged me aside to confront me. He said something to me, and it made me realize, they lied to me." Brad looked worried. "Well, not lied to, but misled. I knew mum and Rockford got involved at university, and that he'd asked to marry her, and Granddad said no. Mum led me to believe that was it for them, that my father came along years later."

Lifting the locket out of my cleavage, I admired it. "My mother gave me this when I went to school. She told me my father gave it to her. Rockford found me a year later, and I told him my father gave my mother this locket. That's how he knew," I explained. "Rockford told me he'd made it for my father to give to my mother, and that he protected the wearer."

"Made it?" Brad asked, confused.

"It's a GPS locator," I revealed. "The prototype for Drofkor Engineering's jewelry line. Rockford owns Drofkor."

"That I already knew," Brad told me.

"Rockford told me my father protected my mother from an attempted kidnapping. That's when Gena conceived me. That's when I looked into his eyes and finally recognized mine. I thought back to all the photos of my mother. This locket was hanging around her neck at her graduation, six years before I was born. Gena was with Rockford when she graduated."

"Rockford wanted you to know?" Brad murmured.

"Yes," I admitted. "Rockford always wanted me to know but understood why my mother hid it. He's been protecting me since I was seven, Brad. I wanted my father to give me away."

"So, this shared Riverside project was a cover?" Brad considered.

"Of course not, it's legit. Things were never as bad as they have become since your father crowned himself king of Riverside. Who better to work against him?" Stepping forward, I took Brad's hands in mine.

Brad's eyes softened. "Rockford must hate the idea of us together, Caly."

"He did," I admitted, "until I told him about the prenup."

Brad thought about it, a slow smile emerging as he pulled me close. "He knows the speculation about why he gave you away is going to get back to my father. He did that to stir my old man?"

"He did it because I'm his daughter, and he's always wanted to be a part of my life," I corrected. "This can't leave this room. I'm not ready for everyone else to know yet."

"So, only your mother, Rockford, and us know?"

"And Dwayne, but I'm pretty sure Granddad and Uncle Bryce suspect," I let Brad reel me in closer to his body.

"Dwayne knows everything about Rockford's business. My brother has made a few grabs for Dwayne to try and get that information. So far, Terry hasn't succeeded," Brad informed me.

"You know Dwayne from university?"

Brad placed a kiss on my forehead. "We did our degree together. Dwayne was on the Dean's merit roll. Occasionally, we put our heads together to nut out encryption problems he encounters. Do you remember the encryption model I succeeded in building the morning I met you?" I nodded my head. "I sold it to Drofkor Engineering."

Finding the zip hidden behind the faux old-style buttons in the back of my dress, Brad slowly pulled it down. When I lifted my face, our lips met, merging into a heated kiss. Pushing his jacket from his shoulders, I forced Brad to release me as it fell to the ground.

"I'm dying to be inside you, Caly," Brad murmured, pulling me back into him.

"It has been a month." Undoing his buttons, I slowed my hands. "I hope you still fit."

Brad grinned. "It might be a tight squeeze." The idea made my sex clench. We'd been celibate for a month before the wedding so our wedding night would be unique. We'd still had foreplay, but no actual intercourse. Now, we were worked up, and the foreplay in the limo on the way to reception hadn't helped.

Of course, the limo ride to the hotel wasn't anywhere near as hot. To the point, I worried we'd spend our wedding night fighting because of who my father is. Brad wanted to talk about it on the drive here, but I wouldn't discuss it anywhere we could be overheard.

Taking my mind away from our worries, Brad peeled my dress off and dropped it to the floor. The rest of his clothes followed. Our kissing was urgent, breath ragged with need. Brad picked me up and carried me to the bed. Dropping me on the mattress with a growl.

"I've missed this," I gasped as I scooted up to give us some room.

Brad crawled towards me, Mr. Hyde pointing in the direction he needed to move. When Brad dropped a lick to Mrs. Hyde, I smirked. "Jesus, you're more than ready." Brad licked his lips as he crawled forward.

"I've been dreaming about sex; I'm that horny. This morning I nearly came without touching myself, I was so eager for tonight, for this, for you."

Mr. Hyde twitched hard enough to whack Mrs. Hyde. Groaning, Brad closed his eyes, then we both looked down to watch his precum seep out and drip onto my mound. Brad lifted his eyes to mine. "I may not last long."

"You just have to last long enough," I soothed. "Which in my current state is going to be five seconds. Would you fuck me already?"

Chuckling, Brad eased himself into my niche. "We're doing this?"

Kissing his lips, I smiled. "It's up to fate now."

Mr. Hyde jolted against my opening. "God, the idea that anytime we make love now, we could be making our child." His eyes were full of hope.

"Brad, can you at least be in me while you talk? I'm dying here."

Growling, Brad thrust forward. Opening to him immediately, my fingers raked down his biceps as I cried out. We fucked first, made love later. We did it again in the morning, twice before lunch, and I lost count how many times that night.

By the time we were boarding our flight, I was drinking cranberry juice to prevent any infections. Brad was walking a little awkwardly, as well.

We flew first class, our honeymoon in Tahiti, a wedding gift from our families. We stayed in a beautiful resort, and then we flew home exhausted from a week of fun in the sun, and couple's fun at night.

"Baby, when we get home, can we go straight to sleep?" Brad asked on the drive to Mum's place.

Smiling, I kissed him. "Really?"

Growling his arousal, Brad pulled me closer. "I should have known when I learned your mum named you for a nymph."

Laughing, I encouraged his interest. Arriving home, it surprised me to see the lights on. "I thought mum would be back in Switzerland by now."

"Maybe she wanted to surprise you," Brad hugged me from behind. Smiling, I led the way inside. I regretted it. I should have let Brad go first. That way, he could have saved me from the sight of Gena and Rockford naked and screwing on the kitchen counter. Instead, I stood and stared. For a second, I admired Rockford for the hot older guy he was, then I remembered, that's my dad.

"Oh my god! I cook on that," I yelled as I turned to bury my face in Brad's chest. Cursing, Rockford, and Gena knocked stuff off the counter in their haste to hide.

Backing us out of the room, Brad snickered. "Hi, Ms. Zilla and Mr. Rockford. We're home! Now, we are going upstairs to bleach our eyeballs and look for a new home, so we never have to intrude on you two again."

"I didn't think you were home until later."

Rockford chuckled. "It is later."

"Oh, have we been going for that..."

Covering my ears, Brad moved us up to my room. Once the door shut behind us, we looked at each other and started laughing. "So, you may not end up an only child after all."

"I doubt my mother is looking at starting a family at fifty," I dismissed his concern.

Brad pulled me towards him. "Remember how you riled me up before we got inside?"

"Yeah, then I saw my parents going at it," I grimaced.

"They weren't my parents," Brad whispered against my mouth. "It made me think of us and hope we are still that active at that age."

"They've not dated for twenty years, of course, they are making up for lost time," I rolled my eyes. "You and I, however," I poked Brad in the chest, "we are still going to be married and have teenagers in the house. We won't be sullying our kitchen benches like that."

Cocking a brow, Brad tilted his head as his mouth thinned. "Okay, it looks like we have our first disagreement."

"Why?"

Herding me towards the bed like a predator stalking its

dinner, Brad grinned. Unable to prevent my excitement at the hungry look on his face, I blushed. "Because I still intend to be banging you everywhere and anywhere the need arises in twenty years. Especially when we get the house to ourselves." Picking me up, Brad dropped to the bed with me, his mouth nibbling my neck.

An hour later, we braved returning downstairs. "Is the coast clear?" I called.

"Yes. I've even cleaned the bench and ordered dinner," Gena called back. In the kitchen, we found civilized adults drinking wine at a table, not the fuck bunnies from earlier. I can't explain the relief I felt seeing them both dressed.

"Welcome home!" Coming towards me, Rockford hesitated when he reached me, but I pulled him into a hug. He wrapped me tightly in his arms. "God, I've wanted to hug you so often, Princess."

"How do you know that nickname?" I pulled back with a smile.

"There isn't much I don't know about you." Smiling, he put his hand out to Brad. "We should probably explain..."

"Caly already did," Brad shook his hand. "Do I start calling you, dad?"

Rockford raised a brow. "I would have been proud to have a son like you, Brad, but you can call me Sin or Rockford like everyone else."

"Can I call you, dad?" The few times we'd met since discovering the truth, I'd not been game enough to call him anything but his name.

"Maybe Sin," Gena jumped in, lines furrowing her forehead. "It's still not public knowledge, and we wouldn't want you slipping up."

"How about we sit and discuss a few things?" Rockford

gestured to the table before taking his seat. Giving my mum a hug, I sat beside her. On the table, there were a bunch of magazines. All the covers with pictures of the wedding. It was quite well covered.

"Zilla corporation controlled the photo release as much as we could. So, it only mentions Sin walking you down the aisle in connection with the project," Gena explained. "The conversation mainly focused on your dress. Only the political magazines discussed what a Zilla-Sarita-Rockford partnership could achieve for Riverside. Most of the articles were very supportive."

"Which ones weren't?" Brad asked.

"The ones that worry our partnership could start a war with your father," Rockford answered.

"They are right," Brad suggested.

"Which is why I'd prefer you stay living here for now," Rockford suggested. "Gena isn't in the country that often, but this place is always secure and well-guarded."

"Why does that matter?" I asked naively.

"Because if my father is going to go after anyone, it's going to be you." Weaving his fingers with mine, Brad furrowed his brow. "I'm his son; he won't touch me. Rockford always has bodyguards. You, you're our weakness."

Chapter Twenty-Four

"You look happy," Aaron greeted me at work on Monday morning. "Good honeymoon?"

My body heating at the memory, I nodded, keeping my eyes on the doctor's request as I set the equipment up. "How's everything with you?"

"I've been looking for somewhere to live near the hospital. That way, mum and I are close to work, and it won't be too far for Josh to travel."

"It isn't cheap around here. Why don't you get an apartment in The Fields? It puts you halfway between the hospital and university. It's on the tram route, and if Josh does his placement at the Wish Medical Centre, he'll be close to there too."

"Fields is a nice area, I guess," Aaron considered, watching the machines do their job. It took until we'd finished the test before Aaron walked back into the control room with a shocked look. "Did you say Wish Medical Centre?"

Biting my lip under the bright gaze Aaron was throwing my

way, I turned my focus back to the computer. "I've named it after you and Josh because you were the reason it happened."

"Josh has a different surname."

"I know, but the man your mother lost because he was too far from a hospital was Wish. You are Wish, and you're important to me." Jesus, I had a half-brother. Licking my lips, I looked away from Aaron's intense eat-the-world stare. "It seemed more appropriate to name it after a family I care about who have lost, then some other pathetic option."

"Caly," Aaron whispered my name.

When he stepped towards me, I froze at the hungry look in his eyes. Emotions warred within me.

Looking down at my left hand, Aaron exhaled, withdrawing a step. "You've gone out of your way to help my brother and me so often, Caly. I may have been your watcher, but you've been my family's guardian angel." Aaron walked out.

My heart swelled as my eyes watered. I loved Brad, don't get me wrong, but what I felt for Aaron...was fucking messed up. He was my brother! Smacking that fact into my head still didn't dilute the years of crush that existed. And, he'd wanted to kiss me when he realized I'd named the medical center after him. It'd be a good guess that Rockford never told Aaron I was his daughter. Understandable. Imagine growing up, avoiding getting shot, or stabbed daily. Then knowing you have a sibling living a protected life in Eleri City. It was the definition of suck and a breeding ground for angst.

Shaking off the guilt washing over me, I focused on the thought of getting home to Brad tonight. That set off a swarm of butterflies in my stomach, so it was disappointing when Brad called me halfway home. "Hey, Caly, I'm going to be home late."

"Really?"

"Yeah, I'm nearly finished my write up and am on a roll, so if I can get it done, then it's all edits from there."

While a fair excuse, the annoyance of waiting for him was frustrating. "Okay, I'll leave dinner in the oven for you." Resting my head back on the seat, I closed my eyes once I hung up.

"Ms. Zilla," the driver called. Opening my eyes, I realized I was home. Between all the traveling and excitement of the wedding, I hadn't had a good night's rest in months.

Cooking dinner, I ate, then fell onto the couch to watch some television. Mum had flown out for work and wouldn't be home for a couple of weeks, so the place was all mine. Taking out my laptop, I opened my blog to do this week's update.

Farewell

This blog started as a way of expressing my boredom with the way men go about getting laid. It turned into a dating blog, and I've enjoyed writing about my experiences. Then I met Blow. Dating turned into a relationship, and that grew to love.

I'm out of the dating pool now, and I can't see me going back again soon. Even if I did, I don't want to write about that anymore. There are so many more important things to write about here.

So, this is where I choose to either say goodbye or find another topic to blog. Your ideas are welcome. In the meantime, I think I'll take a break.

Thank you for following all these years. For the comments and support. I found my ever after. I wish you all the luck in finding yours.

Nymph

Pressing the publish button, I sighed. Clicking on the dashboard, I dropped my eyes to the comments preview. Over the past four years, two followers had been with me from nearly the beginning. The Watcher and Sin Rocks.

'*Call me Sin,*' Rockford had told Brad. Covering my mouth, all the fatherly advice Sin had given me started to make sense. My eyes dropped to the following comment from The Watcher on the post about Lancelot breaking my heart.

The Watcher: *I'm sorry*

I thought he'd meant he was sorry because he advised I put myself out there and tell Lancelot how I felt. Aaron's words from this afternoon washed through my head like an antiseptic gel to an open wound.

'*I may have been your watcher...*'

Aaron. He'd even put his number in my phone as Lancelot. My hands were shaking. Not only had Aaron known all these years that it was my blog, but he'd also been aware he was Lancelot.

Slamming my computer shut, I sat trembling on the couch as the tears came pouring out. Aaron had known how I felt about him for years, and he still let me go. Yes, we were brother and sister, but Rockford hadn't told him that, and he'd rejected me. Hugging a pillow to my chest, Aaron Wish broke my heart all over again.

"Thanks, Jack," Brad's voice came from the foyer. Switching the television back on at the news, I swiped at my eyes. "Hey, I'm home." Dropping onto the lounge, Brad studied me as his brows lowered. "What's wrong?"

Shaking my head, I noticed the running headline on the screen. "Just overreacting to the news," I reassured.

That turned his attention to the news about a teenage girl murdered in Riverside. "Another drive-by?"

"She refused to have sex with some guy, so he raped her. She was brave enough to come across the river, get a rape kit done, and press charges. So, he got his friends together, they found her, gang-raped her this time, then beat her to death." I started crying again. This time, for the girl. I had no right to whine about any part of my life.

Pulling me into his arms, Brad held me tight. "Everything okay, Caly? We see this sort of thing on the news daily, and it's only ever made you angry."

"Everything isn't happening fast enough with the Wish Centre. I want it done already. I keep getting this feeling that it's not fast enough."

Brad rubbed my back. "You've been saying that for months, Caly. It's why Sin and Gena agreed to break ground on the trauma center first. We are devoting all the resources towards it and building the college once all the work is internal."

Nodding against his chest, I pulled him closer. "Every time someone tells me the expected completion date, I get filled with dread, Brad. I can't help it." Pointing to the television, I shook my head. "That girl was alive when they found her. By the time the ambulance crossed the river, assessed her, and started back to the hospital, it was too late. She was dead before they got to the river."

Fuming over the insanity of it, Brad patted my hair. "It's ridiculous that there isn't an ambulance stationed in Riverside."

My heart started beating double time. I sat up. "That's right. That's the first point of help. The paramedics are our frontline support. Doctors and a trauma center are only viable if the patient can stay alive long enough to reach the hospital." Out of my seat a moment later, I was picking up the phone while Brad was still blinking at me in surprise.

"Caly, what is it?" Brad asked as the phone connected.

"Baby girl," Sin smiled into the phone. He'd started calling me little girl nicknames.

"Firstly, don't ever call me that again, you sound like a kinky bastard." Rockford chuckled on the other end of the line. "Secondly, Brad's had a great idea. We need to get paramedics stationed in Riverside."

Rockford was quiet for a minute. "I'm finishing up with some business. Can I come by in an hour, and we discuss this?"

"Sure."

"Good. Caly, do me a favor before I get there?"

"Um, okay," I agreed, slightly confused.

"Do a pregnancy test."

Blinking at the change in topic, I stood gaping at the phone. "I don't need to; I'm not pregnant."

"Are you sure? You've been very emotional about this project."

Taking a deep breath, I sagged a little. "Yeah, I'm sure. The human body has a way of telling females they aren't going to be mums. Mine announced itself today."

"Oh," Rockford took a moment. "Well, have a glass of wine and relax. I'll be there in an hour."

Hanging up, I turned to Brad. He was standing behind me, arms opened ready. Stepping into them, I held him tight. "I'd ask you to make love to me right now, but..."

"I heard. How about you read my conclusion while I massage your feet?"

"You know I still understand nothing of what it says, right?" I chuckled.

"That's what Dwayne is for. You are there for the grammar because Dwayne is hopeless at that. He couldn't even spell circuit."

"How can that be?"

"Sometimes the genius is in the doing, not the spelling," Brad proclaimed. Smiling, he kissed me tenderly. "Take a seat."

By the time Rockford arrived an hour later, Brad had massaged my feet to within an inch of their lives. Having read his conclusion, I'd marked with a red pen for all the grammatical errors. Though, I still had no idea what it said.

"Thanks, Jack," Rockford's voice reached us as he stepped inside. For the first time, I was there to see Dwayne pulling two handguns free from their holsters. Removing the chambered bullets and magazines from each, he put them in his pockets. Checking them one more time, Dwayne placed the empty guns on the table. There was a third gun already there, which made me look wide-eyed at my father.

"I'll lock these in the safe until you leave, Mr. Rockford," Jack informed him.

With a nod to Jack, Rockford took my shoulder and turned me from the door and into the kitchen. "Let's talk." Rockford pointed Dwayne to the lounge room. Nodding obedience, Dwayne went to join Brad. "What's going on?"

"I told you..."

"You feel like it's not happening fast enough?" Sin nodded. "We've all heard that version. We've altered this project just for you and that anxiety of yours. Now, tell me the truth."

"It is the truth," I pleaded for him to understand. "Every time I think about it, I get this hollow feeling inside like it's going to go to hell. This sense being able to survive will rely on that trauma center being ready."

Sighing, Rockford took my hand across the table. "Caly, not one person hasn't noticed how your sudden anxiety began with your marriage to Brad. Your mother, your grandfather, and I all talked to you about the risk of getting involved with him. Do you think it's possible that this anxiety of yours, may relate to the fear of Greg Meadows getting a hold of you?"

Peering down at the table, I considered the possibility. My stomach got that hollow feeling again. "Maybe I've got a stomach ulcer," I mumbled.

My dad squeezed my hand. "You've gone from very private life to this project and marriage thrusting you into the spotlight. You have every right to be scared by all this change."

"I can't tell you more than I already have. I need this to happen sooner."

Taking a deep breath, Rockford looked at the door, making sure Brad wasn't there. "Does this have anything to do with what happened between you and Ayah today?"

Tensing, I took my hand back. "What do you mean?"

"I've known Ayah a long time, Caly. I know when he's out of sorts, and this evening he was off-kilter. When I asked him about how you were at work today, he clammed up as if he may say something he shouldn't." Rockford watched me waiting. "What happened between you two today?"

"It's not what you are thinking?"

"Then what is it?" Brad's angry voice came from the butler's entry door. Out of my seat instantly, I watched Brad walk in, his shoulders tense, eyes peering, and mouth in a grim line. For the first time, he looked like his father. Rockford cursed under his breath.

"Were you eavesdropping?" I accused.

"I came to get drinks and didn't want to disturb you," Brad defended. "I didn't realize you would be talking about something I shouldn't hear. Like you fucking around with my best friend!"

"I'm not!" I started blubbering. "I would never. Aaron wouldn't do that."

"So, why does your father think you did?" Brad challenged.

"I never said that," Rockford defended, menacingly.

"You implied it," Brad snarled.

Dwayne was there quickly, moving Brad back a few steps. "Careful, buddy, that's the Devil your confronting."

That's when I realized Rockford was standing next to me, his face peaceable, his eyes glowing with rage. "You've all got the wrong idea. I told Aaron I'd named the Medical center after him and Josh today. He got emotional and started talking about how much I've always helped his family. He didn't even hug me, let alone anything else," I stressed to the three jury members in the room.

They all stood watching me. Looking at the suspicion in Brad's eyes hurt, so I turned my full attention to Rockford. "I want a paramedic station in Riverside. That girl might have lived today if it could have gotten to her sooner."

"Nothing could have saved that girl, Caly," Rockford answered sadly.

"What if it was me?! What if having the paramedics thirty minutes closer may have made the difference?" Body shaking as hard as my voice, unable to contain my emotions anymore, I ran out of the room.

"She's terrified," Dwayne's voice followed me. "Did something happen?"

"Question of the day," Brad grumbled.

Chapter Twenty-Five

NEW BLOG: The Miserable Wife

Trustless

It's been months since I shut down my old blog. But I need to vent, to put my emotions out there somewhere, even if nobody else reads them. I may not stick with the name of this blog, but for now, it's how things are.

It's incredible how quickly things can fall apart. One implied accusation, taken out of context, can shatter trust. I was only married for four months when a simple question implied I cheated on my husband. Despite clearing it up, explaining that wasn't the case, my husband didn't believe me. Over the last few months, our marriage has deteriorated. He's barely home, we have angry sex when he is, and there is very little communication otherwise.

Everything I've done to try and repair the damage sends glares my way and results in days of silence. We were planning a family, but I don't know if our marriage will last much longer. Certainly not long enough for the introduction of another member in the mix. For all I know, if I fell pregnant right now, he'd think it was another man's child.

I don't want to give up on my marriage, but I'm out of ideas. My family wasn't happy with the relationship to start with, so I can't talk to them about it. Right now, I'm so alone, and I've never felt so miserable in my life.

Maybe my cousin was right, and there is a family curse to be heartbroken.

Nymph

🖎

"Caly?" Aaron stood across from me. "Leave that stuff. Our shift finished ten minutes ago. It's Saturday, and your grandparents are expecting you tonight."

"Still watching?"

"My favorite job," he murmured.

"You go, I'll finish these."

Frowning, Aaron dropped into the seat opposite. "You've been working back later and later, Caly. In the last three months, it's like you don't want to leave this place. Is something happening at home?"

My hands froze over the keyboard, the back of my eyes itching. Avoiding meeting Aaron's eyes, I exhaled, shoving my feelings down. "I'll see you tomorrow."

"I'm not leaving until you do. I can't. I have to wait outside until I see you get in your car, so I may as well walk out with you tonight."

"You shouldn't; it would make it worse."

Tilting his head, Aaron assessed me. "Dwayne told me Brad accused you of sleeping with me a few months back. I thought it was all resolved?"

My emotions welled up again, but I choked them back down. "It's not been the same since. Every day I come home, if we make love, it's like he's inspecting me for signs that you had me first. I hate it. It never used to be like this, and all it took was for one person to suggest something happened between us. Brad can't let it go."

Watching me, Aaron's hunger and anger burning in his eyes like always. "You don't look at me the same way anymore either," I mourned. "Both of you make me feel like I've committed some sin."

"You married my best friend," Aaron whispered.

"You didn't want me!" I reminded him, Aaron closing his eyes. "I offered myself to you on a friggin' silver platter, remember? Me, naked, begging you to have me." Swallowing, I looked away, returning to my work. "It was for the best anyway. I could imagine how awkward that would have been knowing what I know now."

Blowing out a breath, Aaron stood and picked up his bag. "We've been together seven days a week for four months. Five days of placement, plus our usual shifts. I can understand if Brad is feeling like I'm spending more time with you than he is," Aaron sympathized. "Go home. Kiss your husband and remind him that placement finished yesterday."

"And when we both start full-time in two months?"

"That's a problem for another time, not now." Stepping up next to me, Aaron caressed a hand down my cheek and wiped a stray tear I hadn't even realized escaped. "I'll talk to him. I've known you longer. I would never have to ask if you were unfaithful."

When Aaron walked out, I dropped my forehead to the keyboard. The computer started tinging alerts like mad. Grumbling, I cleared the warnings and saved the report before sending it.

As I grabbed my bag from the locker, I checked my phone and saw I had a missed call from Brad. Knowing what it was going to be already, I called voicemail.

"Caly, I'm at my grandparent's still. Douglas and I are going over some things with the business. I'm going to have dinner here. Please give my apologies to your family."

Hanging up, I pressed autodial and waited. "Princess?" Kingsley greeted. "Don't tell me you're ditching? I didn't endure the flight back from Switzerland for my mother's company."

"Quite the opposite," I answered, walking towards the exit. "I need to blow off some steam tonight. Can you pick me up and get me drunk?"

"I'm at your place. I was planning on driving my car, so bring it home already." I'd had Kingsley's car four months now, while he was doing his traineeship in Switzerland. I only drove it to work on weekends, when parking wasn't such an issue.

"I'll be home in fifteen. I'm heading out to the car park now."

"Everything alright?"

"Brad isn't coming to dinner. He's stuck at his grandparents," I informed him.

"Again?"

"Again."

"Okay, Princess. We'll see you soon," Kingsley replied angrily. "I think you're right..." I heard him say to someone as he hung up.

Surprised by the accusation in his voice, I didn't notice the black limousine stopped in front of me. Not until something hard and cold shoved in my back. "Get in the car. You scream I'll shoot you," the rough voice hissed in my ear.

Peering over my shoulder, I panicked at the man in the suit

holding a gun against my kidney. With a whimper, I didn't resist. Lifting my free hand to my locket, I clicked it open and pressed the button before I closed it again.

The door opened, and the man behind me shoved me forward. When my eyes met my husband's, in an older and different face, I felt my heart try to escape my ribcage.

"Please, Caly, sit down. I'm not going to harm you," he assured. "We aren't even going to leave this car park."

Swallowing the ball of trepidation in my throat, I tried to relieve the restriction of my airways. It didn't work, but I managed to slide into the car and sit pressed as far from Greg Meadows as I could. When the door shut, I choked down a scream.

Lifting an eyebrow, Greg watched me. "Do you need a paper bag?"

That's when I realized I was hyperventilating. Concentrating on taking even breaths, I shook my head. Pouring two glasses of scotch, Greg offered me one and made another for himself. Mine stayed on the bench. There was no way I was trusting any drink this man put in front of me.

"I have no interest in hurting you, Caly. You are no good to me dead," he tried to assure me. "The news of your marriage to my son filled me with joy. For many years, I thought he'd make a mistake with that cousin of his. The little trollop who wants more than her blood should get her."

"Blood doesn't entitle you. It also shouldn't limit you."

The sides of Greg's mouth tilted up. "A woman after my own heart."

"You have one?" I raised a brow, then remembered who I was talking to and pushed further back in my seat.

"Absolute replica of your mother," Greg laughed, his finger pointing to my face. "Except those eyes. They are a hundred percent your father. Almost to the point that someone cut them out of his handsome face and implanted them into your beauty."

"Much the same as your eyes and Brad."

That seemed to flatter Greg. Taking a sip of his drink, he smacked his lips together. "My point being, I was very happy for you."

"Why are you here?" I braved asking.

"Ah, well, straight to business." Greg placed a card on the bench next to the whiskey. "Despite my son's hate for me, Brad was always my favorite. He reminds me of myself before the world corrupted me. I only want the best for my son. If he feels the best for him is to be free from me, well, I couldn't exactly argue with him. Just look at what he's accomplished without me." Greg's eyes raked over me as his eldest son's had at the fundraiser. I suddenly wanted to shower.

Smirking when I cringed, Greg returned his mind to his visit. "Terry, my eldest, he's always been jealous of the bond and admiration I have for my youngest. He lacks imagination. The only thing he desires is power. My power, to be exact; much like his mother. Breaking free to do his own thing never occurred to him," Greg explained. "I've heard through a reliable source that my eldest is upset that I've let Brad run free. My eldest, it appears, is planning something naughty, and I'm afraid, Caly, it's going to impact you."

"Why does that worry you?" The fear was there in his eyes, and I wanted to understand what scared Greg Meadows.

"Because, Caly, you are the crown. The man who wears you, rules." Watching me take that in, Greg drained his glass of scotch. Placing the empty glass down, he sat back. "Take the card, Caly. If anything happens to my son, call me. If Terry comes for you, call. I can help you."

"Why didn't you go to Brad?" I challenged.

Greg looked bored, but there was something in his eyes that yelled, annoyed. "He won't talk to me. Something about a prenup and putting you in danger."

"Your man, with his gun, just violated the prenup."

"Only if you report it."

Thinking about my necklace and the fact Rockford would know, a thought occurred to me. "Do you keep tabs on your son?"

"I do."

"Where is he right now?"

Greg's face shut down, a hesitation hiding behind anger. "With family."

There was anger in that response. "You don't like that Brad's there?"

"Like me, Brad has made his share of bad choices," Greg answered. "I worry, at times, that he will fuck up the good thing he has."

Looking at my shoes, I considered the venom behind that answer. When Greg offered nothing more, I indicated the door. "May I leave?"

"Take the card, Caly," he insisted.

Picking it up, I went to get out. Greg tapped on the window, and the car door opened. The man, who held the gun, helped me from the car, then slid in and shut the door. Standing there, I watched the limousine drive off, then exhaled in relief.

"Caly?" Aaron's voice came from nowhere. Charged on adrenaline, I screamed. Covering my mouth, Aaron moved me out of sight while I calmed down. Dom stood beside him, putting a gun back in a holster in his jacket. "Are you okay?" Aaron asked, looking me over.

Nodding my head, I gulped for air. "He wanted to talk." The tears came unbidden.

Hugging me to him, Aaron turned to Dom. "Go check her car." Dom disappeared while Aaron pulled out his phone, putting it to his ear. "She's safe, he just wanted to talk," Aaron told who I assumed to be Rockford. "Not physically, just shaken."

Shaking my head against his chest, I stepped back, putting my hand out for the phone. Aaron handed it to me. "Sin?"

"Princess, what happened?" Rockford sounded relieved. Lifting my locket out of my top, Aaron opened it, deactivated the signal, then closed the locket.

"Greg Meadows told me that Terry isn't behaving." Telling Rockford precisely what happened, I fidgeted with the card he insisted I take.

Hearing me out, Rockford sighed. "Looks like Greg has finally admitted he can't control is bulldog anymore. Aaron's going to follow you home. He'll make sure you get there safely. Tomorrow, he'll pick you up and drop you off..."

"No, not Aaron," I intruded. Rockford fell quiet. "Kingsley is in town; he'll want his car. I'll get mum's driver to bring me in."

"Okay, Princess. Put Aaron back on for me."

When I passed Aaron the phone, he put it to his ear and listened. "Yeah, no, I agree with her. Brad still thinks she's cheating on him." Grimacing, Aaron listened to Rockford for a minute. "You're the one who made the accusation, you should have set Brad straight before you left back then, now it's too late."

Closing my eyes, I turned my back on what they said. My marriage was dying all because my father questioned my faithfulness. An idea occurred to me. Turning around, I snatched the phone back from Aaron. "You could fix this. If you tell Brad that Aaron is your son, he'll understand why the idea of us having an affair is wrong."

Rockford was quiet. Mouth dropping open, Aaron stared at me like I had two heads. "Why in hell would you think he's my father?" Aaron almost yelled at me.

"Fuck," Rockford swore on the other side.

"Didn't you know?"

"Caly," Rockford called my name, but Aaron was looking at me like I was insane.

"Of course not. Because he's not. I knew my father, Caly. I watched him get gunned down during a drive-by when I was six years old. Why the fuck would you believe Rockford is my dad?"

Staring at Aaron, my mouth fell open.

"Caly?" Rockford called again. "You jumped to a conclusion. I let you. I'm sorry."

"We're not brother and sister?" I whispered, blinking as the shock hit me like a punch in the guts.

Rockford swore again on the other end of the line as I dropped the phone to the ground.

"Brother and sister?" Eyes narrowing, Aaron tilted his head. "Why would Rockford being my father makes us..." mouth falling open, Aaron's eyes opened wide.

"I need to go." Emotions out of control like a cyclone, I dashed back to my car.

Dom was there, waiting. "You okay? Caly?"

The keyless entry unlocked it for me. Opening the door, I hit the button and gunned the engine. The tires screamed against the car park cement as I drove out of there as fast as I could. It was all too much. I needed to get out of there, and I needed to get seriously drunk.

Chapter Twenty-Six

"COME ON, PRINCESS," Kingsley helped me inside.

"I feel sick," I moaned.

"I'm not surprised," Kingsley muttered.

"Where have you been?" Brad's angry voice came across the lobby.

Kingsley raised his head. "Back off. She's drunk as a skunk, and I expect about to be crook as a dog!"

"That doesn't answer my question," Brad grumbled.

"Really? I thought the answer was kind of obvious," Kingsley muttered. "If you bothered coming to the family dinner, you'd know where she was or why she was upset enough to get plastered."

"I was busy," Brad defended, not even bothering to help Kingsley assist me upstairs.

"Yeah, well, while you were busy, your father thought he'd have a private chat with your wife." Sweeping my legs out from under me, Kingsley carried me upstairs in a fireman's hold. "Thought that would get your attention."

"King, don't," I groaned, not wanting them to fight.

"What do you mean he had a private chat with her?"

"Exactly what it sounded like." Carrying me into the bathroom, Kingsley put me down. Helping me to kneel, he then moved my body to hang over the toilet bowl.

"So, she wasn't hurt?" Brad sounded relieved.

Turning, Kingsley shoved Brad into the bathroom wall. "She had a gun shoved in her back and told she'd be shot if she called for help. The woman you're supposed to love. And where were you while that happened?"

"I was..."

"That was rhetorical," Kingsley dismissed, releasing him with disgust. "Everyone knows where you were and who you were with."

My head was swimming, eyes unable to focus. I'm pretty sure I was suffering travel sickness, but I hadn't moved from the spot. Without warning, the bottle of bourbon I'd drunk, made a surge for freedom and escaped into the toilet bowl.

"It's okay, Princess, let it all out. You'll feel better afterward," Kingsley soothed. Collecting my hair in his hands, he held it back as I groaned and heaved, repeatedly.

"What do you mean, everyone knows where I was?"

Was he panicking? There was a damnable silence above and behind me. Frowning, I tried to puzzle out the conversation. Had I missed something? My stomach didn't care.

Lurching forward, I hurled until there was nothing of dinner, lunch, or bile left inside me. A cold washer pressed to my forehead as I relaxed back. Arms caught me as I fell back, and someone turned out the light.

Most days, I loved natural light. My bedroom windows allowed so much morning light into the room, it encouraged me to get up and outside for a run. Not this morning. My bedroom was a torture chamber, and the sun was the sadistic bastard whipping my ass.

Crushing my head in a vice-like grip with his palms, the sun carved his fingernails into my eyeballs every time I tried to open them. Clutching my stomach, I was sure I'd find an open wound and my insides missing. It felt like they were missing. My tummy cramped, my throat felt raw, and my entire body felt weak and incapable of moving.

Though, I'd been able to move my arm to my stomach. Deciding that my arm was free to move, and that there would be no new torture while my eyes remained shut, I made my break.

Finding my bedside table, I moved my hand back to locate the block-out blind switch. Pressing my finger against the button, I hoped this would work. The bright sun howled as I managed to escape its barbaric abuse and dismemberment of my body.

Once the room was semi-dark, I could open my eyes to only a minor amount of pain. Beside me, on the bedside table, was a bottle of paracetamol, a bottle of antioxidants, and a bottle of water. In front of the two bottles of pills was a Post-it.

'Eat Me.'

In front of the water was another.

'Drink me.'

"Fuck! I've tumbled down the rabbit hole."

There was a small quiet chuckle across the room. Blinking into the gloom, I couldn't focus on anything beyond the bed. Giving up, I opened the paracetamol, took two, then followed that up with two of the antioxidants. By the time I chugged the bottle of water, I felt so much better.

Walking over to my side of the bed, Brad placed a tall cold glass of something bubbly next to the bed. "Sprite, it will replace your electrolytes," he murmured, keeping his voice low.

"Anyone would think you had the medical degree," I teased.

Brad's lips twitched. "Sin came by late last night to see you. He suggested this order of remedy. As the wizened one of us, I took his suggestion." Brad's face fell. "I owe you an apology. Sin explained that you'd thought Aaron was your brother all this time. That you only realized he wasn't last night when you asked your father to reveal that secret to me."

The mention of Aaron reminded me of the time. "Work..."

"I called Aaron and told him you were unwell. I got the same reception that I got from Kingsley," Brad muttered. He shook his head. "I'm an idiot, Caly."

"Yeah, you are."

Brad pouted.

"Let's not do this now, I feel like something the cat dragged in." Slouching down in my bed, I barely withheld a groan.

Pulling back the sheet, Brad roamed his gaze over my naked body.

"Brad..."

"I can make you feel better, Caly."

"You'll make Mrs. Hyde feel better," I debated.

Brad smirked. "One is better than none." Kneeling on the bed, Brad spread my thighs as he lowered his shoulders between them. His happiness sparkled in his eyes. Last few months, I'd missed that look on his face.

Resting my head back, I took a deep breath, then bit my lip at the first flick of his tongue. Yeah, this was a good hangover cure.

*

"It's been ages since we've spent a day together," Brad murmured as he wrapped his arms around me.

Making us dinner in the kitchen, I sighed. Brad's phone rang for the fifth time in the last hour. Picking it up, he looked at the screen and turned it over, so it silenced the ringer.

"You should talk to whoever it is," I offered. It was the first time I'd seen Brad behave like this with a phone call.

"It's Sunday, and I'm with my wife, work can wait," he purred down my neck.

"Since when does work ring you on a Sunday?"

"For the last month," Brad answered, pulling away uncomfortable. "You were working all the time. I made the mistake of answering the phone once, and now it's expected. It's like once I finished my thesis, I became a full-time Sarita executive."

"You know I'm still working weekends until January?" I reminded him.

Brad shoved the drawer shut, only the soft-close mechanism stopping it from slamming. "And I work Monday to Friday, so we still won't see each other," Brad grumbled.

"Hey, I had to do my placement, just like I have to finish my traineeship. Once I graduate, you'll have me every weekend. You're the one who wasted the last three months treating me like an adulteress."

Brad looked down at the knife I was pointing at him. "You have a point," he muttered, "quite literally."

Peering down at the knife I'd been cutting with, I sighed and put it down on the cutting board. "Look, I'm home by two on the weekends. If you had been here for the last three months, we'd have been able to spend time together. I know we rushed into this marriage. If you're having second thoughts, the prenup means we lose nothing if we go our separate ways."

"Except you," Brad breathed. "I would lose you."

My heart was beating hard in my chest as Brad licked his lips.

"Is that what you want?"

My eyes prickled as I thought about not having Brad in my life anymore. I'd had a lot of time to think over the past few months. I'd allowed Brad to sweep me into something I wasn't ready for, all because Aaron broke my heart. I'd rushed into marriage as a reaction to three things. I'd thought Aaron was my brother. Out of anger for my granddad trying to control my life. And, a little out of fear of all the changes happening in my life.

That didn't mean I didn't love Brad. I did. In the six months before one little accusation sent it all to hell, life had been good, and I'd been happy. Being around Aaron had been awkward. I kept thinking, 'what if he ignored Rockford and got involved with me, and then we found out?' All I kept picturing was the night I got drunk and stripped naked, throwing myself at my brother. But Aaron wasn't my brother. Now I knew that I wasn't sure how to feel about it all, but I knew how I felt about Brad.

"Caly?" Grabbing my upper arms, Brad shook me a little to remind me he was waiting for an answer. Jesus, he was crying. Not all out, but there was a tear or two. For that matter, I was too. "Do you want to end this?"

Shaking my head, I choked on a sob. "No. I love you; I always have. I've been trying so hard, Brad. It was like everything fell apart at once. I was trying to cope with everything that happened as best I could. Finding out who my dad is was huge for me. Then, thinking Aaron and Josh were my brothers and not being able to say anything because that would put them in danger. When you started acting as if I betrayed you..."

Swiping the tears cascading down my cheeks, I struggled to breathe. My heart was racing in my chest with all the emotion. "I thought you didn't want me anymore, and when your father showed up last night..." I still felt that gun against my kidney. "God, Brad, I was so afraid and angry, and... I tried to call you to tell you, and you wouldn't even take my call. What was I to think?"

Brad pulled me into his arms. "You are right, I've been an ass and a terrible husband. I'm so sorry. So, very sorry. I've been so, so stupid. That stops today. I love you, and I don't want to lose you."

His mouth moved towards mine, and for the first time in months, I felt butterflies alight in my stomach. I'd missed Brad looking at me like this. Then his phone rang, and Brad pulled back, cursing beneath his breath.

"Let me deal with this, and then we can have some peace." Collecting his phone from the bench, he left the kitchen. "Don't you take a hint...?" He answered on the way out.

Chapter Twenty-Seven

AN UNDERCURRENT *of Discontent*

The last couple of months have been better. So, much better than the previous three. My husband has been attentive, loving, supportive. He buys me random gifts, messages me whenever he thinks about me like he used to. Even more so. I have the perfect marriage.

Yet, there is an undercurrent of discontent. Despite the attentiveness of my husband, quite often, he seems lost in his thoughts. I'll walk into the room and find him staring at his phone, or at the wall looking devastated or, at other times, angry. As soon as he knows I'm there, he forces a smile and returns to his bubbly happy self, but it worries me.

What if he hasn't let go of his suspicion about me? I try to tell myself that he's unhappy with his new role at work since finishing his studies. But a nagging voice keeps wondering if he's regretting marrying me.

At night, I find myself lying awake, watching him toss and turn in his sleep, wanting to know what he's dreaming. I ask, but the answer he gives always feels like it's designed for me, not the truth. I can't escape the feeling that my husband is hiding things from me. I want to be there for him to help him through whatever this is, but how do I get him to let me in, and trust me?

Nymph

The Sinner: *Sometimes, we shoulder weight to prevent burdening those we love. Other times, we do it out of guilt. If you feel your husband is hiding something from you, he probably is. The question is, do you want to know the truth, or will it only make things worse? If you are looking for a way in, I would suggest printing out this blog post and put it in front of him. See how he reacts. Just be sure you can handle whatever is coming if he does open up to you.*

"Smile," Gena cooed before she took another photo.

"Okay, mum, that's enough." Stepping towards her, I held out my hand like she was paparazzi.

"I'm so proud of you." She pulled me into another hug. "Graduating in two years and on the Dean's honor roll."

"Thanks, Mum. Can I have a Maserati as a trophy?"

Rolling her eyes at my less than a subtle hint, Gena snapped another shot.

"Did Caly tell you they've invited her to do a Master's in Sonography?" Brad added.

"Sonography is kind of general, isn't it?" Penny scrunched up her nose.

"Cardiac sonography isn't." Wrapping his arms around my waist, Brad kissed my cheek. "I'm trying to convince her to do it."

"I'd settle with convincing her to go out drinking tonight."

Laughing at Penny, Gena shook her head. "We are having a family dinner to celebrate her graduation, Penny. Why don't you come to that, and you can see why clubs are not needed."

Barely restraining a groan, I almost wished going drinking with Penny was an option.

"I'd love to, Ms. Z." Eyes settling on me, Penny's smile faded as she cleared her throat.

Bunching her brows at Penny, Gena frowned at me. "Brad, can you help me return Caly's gown? Penny wants a private word."

Missing my tenseness, or choosing to ignore it, Brad took my gown and hat. "Sure, she probably wants to discuss Dwayne."

Gena chuckled as they walked off. "Can't blame her. I'd want to discuss him too if I was his age."

Looping her arm through mine, Penny turned us to face the crowd of proud parents and graduates. "If you don't want me at dinner tonight..."

"Why would you think that?"

"You didn't look happy about it?"

"Of course, I am, bring Dwayne as well. I love hanging out with you guys."

We quite often had Penny and Dwayne come over when Brad, Sin, mum, and I all had dinner together. As my best friend, I'd let Penny in on my fraternal heritage. Plus, it was clear my parents were back to dancing between the sheets. So far, it seemed their relationship reigniting wasn't common knowledge.

"Then, why looking so miserable?"

"It's Brad's graduation too, so my grandfather decided to invite Brad's family along to the dinner."

Looking aghast, Penny focused her eyes where Brad's grandparents were talking to mine. "Not Emily?" I nodded. "That's got to be awkward?"

"Remember last month at Brad's twenty-fifth birthday

party? How she kept rubbing her flat belly whenever Brad looked at her. Brad was fuming by the end of the night, and they ended up having heated words over in the corner." My jaw clenched, and I started grinding my teeth, thinking about it.

"I couldn't believe she did that," Penny growled. "So, what if you're not pregnant yet? You're both young and have plenty of time for that to come later. It's ridiculous she's insinuating you're unable to have children this early. Until you start trying, you can't know."

Nodding along, I kept my eyes down. I couldn't believe it when Brad insinuated what Emily was implying with her gestures. She didn't even know we were trying. A stone dropped in my stomach. The hardest part was she was right. Brad and I had been leaving the door open for fate for five months now, and I still wasn't pregnant.

It definitely wasn't for lack of trying. Since we sorted things between us two months back, we were working on it every chance we got, several times a day. Our relationship had been wonderful. Brad was always bringing me flowers and little things to show his appreciation. He took every opportunity to shower me with affection. Still feeling guilty for accusing me of cheating, Brad was determined to make it up to me. And yet, I always felt like he was holding me responsible.

"Anyway, we are both unhappy about her coming. I asked Brad why she was even invited? He said they work together at the family business, so he needed to maintain harmony."

Shaking her head, Penny eyed the crowd. "How about we invite Dom and sketch him on her tonight?"

"We invite Dom, we need to invite Aaron," I reminded her.

"Would that be a problem?" When she turned to face me, I shook my head. "How are things with you two?"

"Good. We've found the balance of being friends and colleagues."

Patting my arm, Penny indicated someone in the mix of bodies. "It's his graduation too. Invite him to celebrate with you."

Sighing, I looked to where Penny was indicating. There stood Aaron with his mum and Josh. Rockford was there talking to them. My father came with them to attend the ceremony. Gena thought it would stop others speculating that he gave me away, then came to my graduation. Giving Penny a smile, I walked over to them.

"Caly," Rockford greeted me with a kiss on the cheek. "Congratulations."

"Thanks, Sin."

Louise Wish congratulated me before Josh gave me a huge hug. As Aaron kissed my cheek, I cleared my throat. "My family is holding a dinner to celebrate our graduation tonight. I was wondering if you and your family would like to join us?"

"Are you sure?" Aaron asked, hesitantly.

"Of course. Sin, you're invited too."

My father gave me a knowing smile. "We'd love that, Caly, thank you."

"It's the same place as the wedding reception. At six." Turning, I went to find my mother.

"You are not balanced friends in the least," Penny smirked as we walked off. "I saw the way you and Aaron were looking at each other."

"That's how we always look at each other."

"I know," Penny sighed. "That's why Brad found it so easy to believe you did the dirty on him."

Reflecting, I tried to remember if we ever did anything in Brad's company that hinted at an affair. The guilt was overwhelming. Trying to convince myself I had nothing to feel guilty for wasn't working anymore. I'd been cheating on Brad in my heart.

❧

"You have got to be kidding me," Penny snarked several hours later. "I can't believe that bitch."

"She's doing it again?" I asked, refusing to turn around and look. Standing with us, Aaron and Dwayne looked over my shoulder.

"Yep, every time Emily thinks Brad's looking," Penny scowled. "She's wormed her way into the conversation Brad's having with your parents and doing it."

Scowling, Penny collected another glass of champagne off the trays carried by waiters. Following suit, I used the action to observe. When Emily threaded her arm through Brad's as if they were here together, I almost crushed the glass in my grip.

"Oh, dear!" Cringing at the cracking noise, Dwayne removed the glass from my hand. "Aaron?"

"On it." Stepping over to the group, Aaron artfully inserted himself between Brad and Emily. My mum used the opportunity to grab Rockford's wrist and walk away. Annoyed with Aaron's move, Emily seethed. As I watched, she turned and said something to him. Aaron, in the meantime, put his back to Emily, blocking her from conversing with Brad entirely.

Rubbing my shoulders, Dwayne dropped his voice. "Relax, Caly. We've been chick blocking since we were teens."

No longer concerned with Brad, but with how pale my mother looked, I slipped out of Dwayne's hands. "Excuse me." Moving over to my mum, I took her hand. "Everything okay?"

Opening her mouth to answer, Gena shut it again when

Rockford cut her off. "Of course. Your mother and I were discussing the idea of marriages, and all the reasons they don't work out."

"Are you two thinking of tying the knot?" My eyes blinked several times, surprised by his answer.

They both looked at me like I was speaking a foreign language. "That will always be up to your mother, Caly," Rockford insisted, no longer appearing as calm. "Excuse me." Eyes tight, Rockford walked off.

"Mum, what happened?"

Peering over to where Emily was standing by herself, Gena's eyes took on a dangerous glint. "That girl is going to destroy your marriage, Caly," Mum sighed.

"She can try," I scowled.

With tears in her eyes, Gena stroked my cheek. "I adore how you only want to see the good in people, but you and Brad have already had one accusation nearly destroy you. You won't survive another."

Was Emily spreading rumors, trying to get Brad to leave me by telling everyone I was unfaithful? "What do you mean?"

Checking over my shoulder, I watched Emily smile as she said something to the boys. Whatever it was, both Aaron and Brad stopped and stared at her, then they looked at each other. "You told her that shit?!" Aaron snarled. "Are you stupid?"

"I was angry and needed someone to talk to," Brad snapped back.

Using the sudden hostility between friends, Emily pressed herself to Brad's side. "Of course, he came to me for comfort, we're family."

My throat was dry. I couldn't swallow if I tried. "Caly?" Mum called my name. "Are you okay?" Aaron and Brad both looked up at the mention of my name and realized the entire party was watching.

Pressing my lips together, I walked towards my husband. After all but shoving Emily away from him, I slipped my arm through his. "It's time to go," I suggested to Brad.

"How dare you?" Emily snapped.

"How dare I? Honey, you need a psychological assessment to deal with your obsession with my husband. Of course, that won't help because we know your obsession is with his inheritance and not him."

"You don't know shit!"

Lifting a brow at the way she spoke down to me, I took a step closer. "Says the woman determined to gain status by using your snatch instead of your brains. They have a formal job title for women like you. There are plenty of rich men in this city eager for a barbie doll, leave my husband alone. Consider yourself uninvited to any joint family events from now on. You can leave."

Emily stepped forward to say something. "Emily!" Douglas snapped, gaining her attention. "Caly is right. You need to leave now."

Pressing her lips together, Emily flicked her eyes to Brad as she stepped back. Composing herself, Emily smiled sweetly. "You'll regret that," she simpered at me, and walked out.

"What was that about?" I grouched at Brad.

"Caly..." Brad looked terrified.

"Brad," Douglas stepped forward, holding his shoulder. "Let's have a word in private."

Kissing my cheek, Brad gripped my biceps in his hands. "I love you, remember that," Brad murmured before he walked away with his grandfather.

Looking at Aaron, I begged with my eyes for him to tell me the truth. "What's going on?"

Scrubbing his hand through his hair, Aaron looked over my shoulder to Rockford. I turned in time to see Rockford shake his head in warning.

Doing a full circle, I found all my family watching me. Kingsley was the only one who would meet my eyes, anger raging in his while Uncle Bryce held him back by the shoulder. "Does everyone here know what the hell is going on, but me?" I asked, frustrated.

"I don't," Penny put her hand up. "Except for some skank trying to steal your husband."

"Great, then you can come out drinking with me. Everyone else can go to hell."

Grabbing up my stuff to leave, I grabbed Penny's hand more for security in case the floor opened beneath me.

"Calypso Claire! What's happening out there doesn't concern us. It concerns Brad and his family. You won't punish us because your husband has secrets."

"For all I know, Granddad, you'd let Greg Meadows take me. That way, you could enforce the prenup and take Brad's inheritance."

"Caly!" Gena stared at me. "Don't you dare think anyone in this room would allow anything of the sort to happen. I had that prenup drawn up to protect you. Everything that we do is to protect you."

Assessing my mother, I knew she felt she was doing the right thing, but keeping me in the dark didn't keep me safe. "Sometimes protecting me makes it worse, mum. Like when you didn't tell me, I owned valuable land, and I found myself on the kidnap list of Riverside's mob bosses. No offense, Sin."

With a shrug, my father waved it off. But his eyes told me I'd offended him, but he'd let it slide this once.

"She has a point," Aaron offered. "She deserves to know."

"Then she can ask her husband," Granddad grumbled. "I'll get the bill. This celebration is done."

Tugging on Penny's hand, I moved towards the door. "Let's go. I'm over this bullshit."

"Caly," Aaron tried to stop me from leaving.

"Thank you for trying," I murmured. With one last glare at my family, I walked out the door.

Penny took me home. Getting plastered when I wanted to talk to Brad and find out what was happening didn't seem like a good idea. When Brad finally came back, that was. Which he did, two hours later.

Excusing herself when Brad walked into the kitchen, Penny left. "You left the party without me?" Brad approached slowly.

"I was sick of everyone lying to me. I needed to get out." Moving to the dining room table, I met Brad's eyes. "Are you going to stop lying to me?"

Hesitating, Brad sat on a chair opposite and watched me. Eventually, he let out a massive sigh, and his entire body deflated.

"Emily's pregnant."

My insides hollowed out as an abyss of massive proportions appeared beneath me.

"The baby is mine."

Chapter Twenty-Eight

You know how people say it was like a slap in the face? That's what I felt like. Slapped in the face with a cold, wet fish. Hell, a frozen fish. Jolting back from his words, I blinked at Brad, my eyes already itching. "Your baby? But you hadn't had sex for ages before we got married?"

Adam's apple bobbing, Brad met my eyes, his glassy. "Caly, I thought you were cheating on me. It was stupid, I was angry, and she was there. I fucked up."

No, no, no, this wasn't happening. "You fucked her!" I corrected him as I stood up. "And then you came home and fucked me. You treated me like the adulterous when all the while, you were the one who cheated on me. With her!" I felt dirty and used and betrayed. "God, I'm going to need to get tested. Who the hell knows what that bitch has?"

"I'm clean, Caly, you know that," Brad argued.

"You were clean when we got tested before we started trying for a family. Since then, you've stuck your dick in the local dumping ground," I scowled, glaring at him. "You fucked her without protection, then came home and fucked me. Do you understand how fucked up that is? You were meant to be having a child with me, not her."

Standing up quickly, Brad tried to pull me towards him. "Caly..."

"No," I backed away, angrily, "don't touch me."

Grimacing, Brad swallowed hard. "You have every right to be angry with me. Hell, you should hate me, but I didn't do it to hurt you. I didn't even intend to cheat on you. It just happened."

When I shook my head, tears fell down my cheeks. This felt worse than when he accused me of cheating on him. "I can't believe we've been trying for months, but you fuck her once, and she gets pregnant. Are you sure it's yours?" Inside, I was praying it wasn't. I wanted Brad to tell me it wasn't.

His hesitation tore me apart. "We agreed to keep the pregnancy quiet until a paternity test could happen. I wanted it done sooner, but it puts the baby at risk. Since, if it is mine, it will inherit the Sarita fortune one day, Douglas decided we'd have to wait for it to be born."

"But, my family knew about it?"

"No, but your mum worked it out tonight."

Studying Brad, the puzzle pieces started coming together. "But they all knew you cheated on me?"

"Apparently, I'm not as subtle as I thought."

"God, even your father knew." Exhaling in surrender, I sunk into the dining room chair. Greg Meadows' reaction to me, asking where his son was playing in my head. "For them to all know, it wasn't just the once, was it?"

"Caly-"

"How long?"

Looking at his toes, Brad did nothing as his tears dripped

from his chin. "From the day after I thought you cheated, until the day after my father visited you."

"You were with her when it happened. Weren't you? You were with her while your father's man shoved a gun in my back and forced me to meet with him."

"Yes."

My heart shattered on the floor. As if that ended the heartache, the room calmed, and I could breathe again. Rolling back his shoulders, Brad looked like the pain was less than a moment ago. Meeting each other's eyes, I knew that he knew that wasn't the case. The hurt was too deep even to express now.

Brad's phone rang. We both looked at the number. ESME flashed on the screen. All those times I saw that name ringing, I'd thought Esme was someone from work. Brad even told me it was work. "Emily Sarita's Mobile....what's the E stand for?"

"Executive." It stopped ringing then started immediately again. "She won't stop until I answer," Brad explained, picking it up. "Let me get rid of her." Taking the phone with him, he walked out of the kitchen area.

The revelation wrenched, twisted, and yanked my stomach out. My chest ached, and I shivered from the cold. When Brad walked back in, I expected him to sit down and try to plead his case for making us work. Boy, was I expecting too much.

"I have to go," Brad announced as he came in to collect his jacket and keys.

"What?" I stood up. Now, I was pissed.

"Emily's on her way to the hospital. They think she's having a miscarriage," Brad explained, pulling on his jacket.

"Wait, Emily called you and told you that?" I asked, confused. Who the hell can make a phone call while going through a miscarriage, and why was I a little relieved?

"Yeah, I'm going to meet her," Brad told me as he headed to the door.

"Hold up? Are you leaving me for her?" Was this seriously happening?

Brad turned to look at me, wide-eyed. "Of course not, but if that baby is mine, it's my responsibility."

"Now you want to be responsible? How about being responsible and using protection when you fucked her. Or, I don't know, not cheating on me in the first place?" I yelled at him.

"I get that you're angry, but she's upset and in pain," Brad tried to explain.

"I'm upset and in pain," I argued, "and I'm your fucking wife!"

"You're not pregnant!"

As far as punches went, that one was a king hit.

"Look, I get that I've hurt you, but this can wait. Emily needs me right now." Looking at me like I was selfish, Brad started for the door.

Maybe I was selfish, but he dumped this mess on me and was running off to comfort the other woman. The seething inside of me demanded this was all wrong. "You walk out that door, Brad, and you walk out of our marriage," I warned beyond angry.

His hand on the handle, Brad hesitated. Looking me over, he shook his head. "You don't mean that." He stepped out into the entryway.

"Brad, don't leave." Following him out, I grabbed Brad's jacket sleeve to try and stop him. Jack sat there, pretending to see and hear nothing. "We both know this is a ploy to bring you to her. If you go, there is no undoing this." If he were willing to choose her now, it would tell me exactly where I stood in the pecking order.

Yanking his sleeve out of my grasp, Brad kept walking. Rage

surged in me. Picking up the water glass on Jack's desk, I threw it at the wall. It hit and smashed right by the door Brad was opening. Turning back, Brad looked at me, wide-eyed. My heart pounding like fists thumping a punching bag, I glared at him. "We need a few hours to cool down," Brad declared before slamming the door after him.

Those fists escaped the confinement of my heart and started pounding my chest. Breathing became painful, and my chest hurt horribly as I collapsed to the ground crying. My blood was rushing in my ears, the erratic pounding of my heart filling the silence that Brad left behind him.

Helping me up, Jack walked me back inside. "Can I call someone?"

"No, thank you, Jack," I sobbed. "Call me if he comes back, please? No matter the time."

"Of course," Jack stepped back out to the entryway. Slowly making my way upstairs, crying all the way, I collapsed on my bed and let it all out.

Waking early, I looked around my room for any sign Brad had been home, then checked my phone. Nothing. Picking up the phone, I called the security line. "Yes, Ms. Zilla?" Keith, who was on duty, answered.

"Did Brad come home last night?"

"No, Ms. Zilla." He was young and had only been with us a few years now, but Jack would have filled him in at shift change.

"Thank you." Hanging up, I looked at the wedding rings on my finger. Would I forgive him if he came back and swore he loved me? Could I forgive him for choosing her over me last night? What if last night was a ploy, and he went and slept with her again?

God, I curled over myself; I didn't trust him anymore. Never once did I consider Brad cheating before. Even the months he'd barely spoken to me, we'd had sex regularly, so why would I have thought he was cheating? Swiping at my eyes, refusing to cry again, I got dressed and met mum downstairs for our run.

"Jack told me about last night," Gena greeted me with sympathy.

"I don't want to talk about it." I kept walking past her. "I just need to run."

Sparing a look of worry for Rockford, who stood in the kitchen doorway, Gena followed me outside. After the usual length, Mum stopped to stretch, but I kept running. By the time I came back, she was gone.

After showering, I came down for breakfast to find Gena and Rockford waiting for me. Still nothing from Brad. "Caly, you can't internalize this."

"You were all quite happy not to talk to me about it last night," I responded, dryly while I poured coffee. "How long did you know he was cheating?" Silence. Gripping the bench, I told myself I couldn't cry.

"Princess," Rockford took over. "No one told you because we love you, and everyone could see how hard you were trying to make this marriage work. Over the last few months, things had been good. Brad stopped the affair, and you two seemed happy. We left the past where it belonged."

"Every relationship has rough patches, honey," Mum reassured.

"Did Sin cheat on you?" I snapped. Looking at each other, they both shook their heads. It made me sick. Tipping my coffee down the sink, I walked to the door. "I'm going out."

"Where?" Rockford asked, concerned.

"To see my lawyer," I rounded on them. "There is a prenup, and I remember there being a clause about infidelity. I want to reread that document and see what my options are if this marriage ends." Wisely, they both stayed quiet as I walked out.

Granddad's lawyer saw me immediately. Giving me his copy of the prenup, he left me alone to read it. There was a million-dollar settlement involved in the case of either of us being unfaithful. No wonder Douglas had been keen to keep Brad's cheating under wraps.

Continuing reading, I kept notes in my head of the options, especially if I wanted to be a bitch about it. Not that I wanted to end on bad terms. But he'd chosen her over me. Was I overre-acting because of the affair? Or were my feelings of playing second fiddle justified?

Closing the document, I grabbed my stuff to leave. "Is there anything you need, Caly?" The lawyer asked.

"Not yet." Rechecking my phone, I left. Giving in, I texted Brad that we needed to talk. Three hours came and went with no reply. I texted Brad again. Night fell, I crawled into bed alone, with still no response, and cried myself to sleep again.

"Caly?" Aaron answered the phone. "It's early."

"I've just got back from my run," I explained. "Have you seen or heard from Brad in the last couple of days?"

"Not since the graduation dinner. Why?"

Closing my eyes, I tried to block the images of Emily and Brad shacked up, making more babies - an impossibility. Still, it was there, none the less. "I know about Emily."

"Oh," Aaron exhaled slowly. "Is everything okay?"

"No. He left me for her two days ago. I've been trying to contact Brad to talk, but he's not answering his phone or responding to my messages."

Aaron was very quiet. "He's a fool to give you up for her, Caly." My breath hitched at the emotion in Aaron's voice and the unsaid, *'I'd never give you up.'* "I'll call him and see if he'll talk to me."

"Thanks, Aaron." Holding back a sob, I disconnected the call.

It was near dinner time when Aaron called back. "I've left him a voicemail and message. Dwayne did too. Neither of us has heard back from him. I'm working tonight at the bar, but I'll keep an eye on my phone."

"Thanks, Aaron."

Another night came and went. Trying a different approach, I called his office. "I'm sorry, Ms. Zilla, Mr. Meadows, is on leave this week."

"Did Brad inform you of that?"

"Well, no, I haven't heard from Mr. Meadows, but his cousin came in on Tuesday and advised us he'd be on leave."

"Wait, Emily was at work on Tuesday?" I asked, surprised.

"Yes," the secretary answered as though I'd asked a ridiculous question.

Hanging up, I was even more depressed. Emily hadn't lost the baby, not if she was at work the next day. But Brad hadn't come back to the house to get any of his stuff.

My next call went to Douglas, who told me the same thing as his secretary. His responses were a little more trimmed as if he were restraining, telling me where to go.

Holding myself back from yelling, 'hello! I wasn't the one who cheated', I expressed my concern that Brad disappeared, and no one seemed worried.

"He's gone to the beach house," Douglas replied. "Brad swung by Monday night and collected the key."

"So, you saw him?"

"No, Emily got him the key. She stayed the night. We were already in bed," Douglas answered impatiently.

"Wasn't she at the hospital? Brad left because Emily called and told him that she was having a miscarriage."

There was an awkward pause on the other end of the line. "I know nothing about that. I wasn't aware you knew about Emily's situation. Still, as far as I'm aware, the pregnancy is continuing with no issues. Perhaps, Brad made an excuse to leave."

"Well, it wouldn't be the first time he's lied to me to be with her, but I know she called, I was in the room when she did," I assured him.

"I'm sure Brad is giving you the space you need, Caly," Douglas soothed. "He might need the time out to get his head in the right space as well."

"Yes, I'm sure this can't be easy for Brad. Of course, if he'd kept it in his pants..." Taking a breath, I calmed myself. "If you hear from him, even if he doesn't want to talk to me..."

"I'll let you know," Douglas assured.

Hanging up, I stared at my phone. Why did I find it hard to accept Brad would up and leave me? He'd cheated on me and got another woman pregnant. Was Brad just up and going that hard to believe?

Yeah, it was. So, I spent my third night tossing and turning. That feeling of dread about the hospital wrenching at my insides.

In my dream, I stood by a fresh grave, watching all my friends and family cry as a coffin lowered into the ground. Worried it was Brad, I pushed through the crowd until I saw him, lamenting the way that men do. That made me turn my attention to the headstone.

Calypso Claire Zilla
Beloved daughter and wife.

Dancing around my grave with a daisy, Emily pulled the petals one by one. "He loves me, he loves me not, he loves me, he loves me not, he loves me!" She sang as she picked the last petal. She put her hands under her dress and pulled out a baby. "And I've got the child to prove it."

Lifting her hand, Emily pointed a gun at me. "He loves you?" Cocking her head, she smiled. "He loves you not." She fired.

Flinching as the air rushed out of me, I stumbled forward and fell into the grave. They started throwing the dirt in as I screamed.

Chapter Twenty-Nine

Betrayal

It turned out that gut feeling that something was wrong was right. The entire time my husband was accusing me of infidelity, he'd been the one cheating. To say the revelation crushed me, would be an understatement. Not only was he unfaithful, but he also got the other woman pregnant, and he told me just before he left me.

He left me feeling betrayed, confused, and dirty. We were trying for a family, so we weren't using protection, and as it turns out, he wasn't safe with her either. The day after he left, I paid a visit to the lawyers and followed that up with a visit to my doctor for an STI screen. I must have showered five times in that first twenty-four hours. He left me feeling physically dirty.

So, why do I want to hear from him? To talk to him? And understand how and why this happened? He told me and left, with no time for me to process it, or even time to get angry about how he made me feel. He doesn't deserve five more minutes of my time. But that niggle is there telling me we aren't over yet. That his behavior, walking out and not talking to me, is out of the ordinary for him.

My concern isn't hung up on the man who betrayed me. I'm worried about the man I loved. No one has heard from him. Not even his best friends. That is what worries me the most.

Am I stupid?

Nymph

Pierced My Heart: *Not stupid. You sound like a kind-hearted woman who can't see the bad in people. Even when they crush your heart, they can't kill the kindness of your soul. What worries me is that this man betrayed you in the worst way, and it sounds like you'd forgive him and take him back. Don't. He doesn't deserve you after what he's done.*

ஃ

"What's this?" Aaron asked as I put a bag at his feet Thursday night.

"Some of Brad's things," I answered, managing to hold back the sniffles. "I finally got a reply from him an hour before I came to work. I told him I'd drop some of his stuff off with you, so he didn't have to see me if that's what he wants." Tears threatened to spill. "He replied, 'thanks.' That's it, nothing else."

Taking my arm, Aaron moved me down the hall to our manager's office. Most of the afternoon staff had left, and it was only Aaron and me now. "Caly, are you okay?" Aaron asked, throwing the bag I'd given him aside. When I shook my head, Aaron cupped my cheek in his hand. "Jesus, Caly, I'm sorry."

Pulling me into him, Aaron held me while I cried on his shoulder. I blubbered about how I know we'd rushed things, but I did love Brad and thought we had a great future. Emily destroyed it all. Then I sobbed that Brad just upped and left. That the most response I'd gotten after four days was a 'thanks.'

"I deserve more than that," I bawled. "I put up with months

of crap. I didn't even get that mad about him cheating until he left me for her."

"She's carrying his baby. Sometimes that makes men make bad choices," Aaron explained.

"His father said Brad made a lot of bad choices. Greg worried Brad would fuck his life up with those bad choices," I confessed, finally calming.

"I've been more worried about Brad fucking your life up. We all have been."

The bell rang at the back door, telling us we had a patient from Emergency. "Get yourself cleaned up. I'll get everything started." With a final eat-the-world-whole glance, Aaron left me alone in the office to deal with work.

Wiping my eyes, I took deep, calming breaths. Once I shut down my emotions and cleaned my face, I went to do my job. It was good to be here and take my mind off everything. Focusing on the detail of my work, I ignored the empty feeling in my stomach. Of course, I hadn't eaten much this week, so that empty feeling may have been hunger.

Mum offered to stay a few weeks after Brad left, but I assured her she could get back to work. Rockford came to visit last night to check on me. I'd kept us focused on discussing the joint project, and he'd let me keep us on topic. "Hi, Caly," a young voice called for my attention.

"Hey, Sabrina, how are you feeling?" I asked the ten-year-old girl wheeled in from the pediatric ward.

"I wouldn't be here if it were good," Sabrina mourned. "Doctor thinks it is bad, but he doesn't want to say it. His eyes give him away, though." She closed her eyes, then jolted awake. "I'm tired, Caly."

Squeezing her hand as we walked into the room, I gave her a mild smile. "We'll make it as quick as we can then." Taking the request slip from the wardsman, I waited for them to move Sabrina onto the scan bed. While setting everything up, I talked to Sabrina about school and music. Since her diagnosis with terminal cancer, she'd been coming here. Almost a year. Her foster parents put her through every treatment to try and save her.

Foster parents? Yeah. You see, the reason Sabrina was dying was that her mother was an abusive bitch. Just one of the things Sabrina's mother did was blow cigarette smoke into her baby's face. It stopped her from crying, or making noise, or talking, or breathing. Last year, when Sabrina collapsed breathless at school, cancer already riddled her lungs. By the time they found it, it was spreading elsewhere. That's how the child abuse Sabrina endured became public knowledge.

"You want the music on?" I asked Sabrina when she was ready.

"I'm too tired today. Can you talk to me?"

"Of course." Giving her hand one last squeeze, I walked into the booth to start plugging in the settings.

Stepping up, Aaron explained the procedure. When Sabrina acknowledged him, Aaron administered the radiopharmaceuticals to make her tumors glow. "Do you have any questions before we start, Sabrina?" Aaron asked as he double-checked my set up.

"Why is Caly so sad tonight?" Sabrina asked, not realizing I could hear.

Looking at the window, Aaron hesitated. "Marital problems. Any questions about the procedure?"

"This isn't my first rodeo," Sabrina gave a tired chuckle. "I hope in my next life, I get to marry a guy like you."

Blushing for the first time I'd ever seen in my life, Aaron cleared his throat. "Let's get this done so you can get back to the ward," he soothed. Joining me in the booth, Aaron avoided my eyes. "Good to go."

Pressing the mic, I avoided looking at Aaron. "Here we go, Sabrina. Nice even breaths for me," I reminded as she slid into the machine. "Are you doing anything over the summer?"

"We were going to Disneyland. I've always wanted to go to Disneyland."

"Which one?" The answer made me sad. The likelihood was she wouldn't live through the summer.

"Japan."

"It's great, you'll have a good time."

"You traveled a lot as a kid, didn't you?"

"Yeah. My mother travels the world, so the summer for me was traveling with her and sightseeing with the nanny. My mother always took the time out to do the big stuff like Disneyland with me, though." The stretcher stopped sliding. "The bad drumming is about to start," I informed her, using Sabrina's term for the noise, before turning off the mic.

"You don't resent your childhood happening on a plane?" Aaron asked.

"No, that's who my mum is." Both of us kept watching the screen.

"Why didn't you go into the family business? Why this?"

Considering Sabrina in the machine, I felt a pang of regret. "When I was five, I got very sick. I could barely breathe. It wasn't asthma, so I had to have a bunch of scans done. The procedures and technology intrigued me, and it fascinated me from then on," I explained. "If I want to, I can take this knowledge and go to work in the research sector of Zilla Corp Medical with my mum. But I wouldn't work on the business side. I'm too honest to be in business." Hitting the mic button, I checked in on our patient. "Okay, Sabrina, halfway there. You still awake in there?"

"Yeah," a feeble response came back. "I just want to sleep."

Frowning at her response, I noticed her oxygen saturation was lower than usual. "Okay, Sabrina, give us a minute," I assured as I turned off the mic. "Call up a nurse, and let's pull her out."

"We haven't finished the test," Aaron looked at me, confused.

"Look at her sats, Aaron?" I pointed to the screen. "I want to pull her out."

"I'll call up the nurse, but we need to finish the test because we can't inject her again tomorrow," Aaron pulled rank.

With a sigh, I told Sabrina we were starting again. There wasn't any response, but her vitals were stable, so I could tell she was sleeping. Aaron called the nurse to come up while I started the next test.

"Everything okay?" The nurse asked when she knocked on the door.

Explaining my concern as the machine finished the last run, I stepped back to the mic. "Sabrina, we're all done. You okay?" No response. "I'm pulling you out now."

Going in, Aaron used the manual button to slide the stretcher out. As he did, Sabrina's vitals glitches. "What was that?" I asked, checking the screen. "Did you knock the monitor?"

"No," Aaron answered as the vitals glitches again.

Glancing at the nurse, she was already hurrying into the room. A moment later, the machine alarmed. By the time I got into the room, Aaron had Sabrina out of the scanner and was getting ready to perform CPR.

"No," the nurse stopped him. "She's NFR."

Aaron looked up, surprised. "You're sure?"

The nurse nodded, a tear shining in her eye. "She went through all the requirements to ensure she knew the choice she was making. She wanted to die on God's terms. We can't perform resuscitation."

My breath hitched. Aaron turned to look at me. I couldn't help it, seeing Sabrina lying like that. She'd gone through so much and hadn't even got to experience life.

"Excuse me," I murmured and rushed out of the room before I started blubbering in front of everyone.

Ten minutes later, Aaron found me. "You okay?"

Having finished crying five minutes ago, I gave him a small nod. Now, I sat there, trying to focus on the report.

"First death?" Sitting down beside me, Aaron placed his hand over mine.

"Yes," I chocked. "You?"

"I watched my dad shot down in front of me, remember?"

Cradling my head in my hands, I tried not to start crying again. "I'm sorry, that was a stupid question. I'm so fucking stupid."

Aaron patted my back. "You're in shock, not stupid."

Pushing away, I stood. "Not just that question. Everything. I let Brad talk me into marriage before we'd had a relationship. I was still in love with you, upset that you rejected me, thinking you were my brother. Of course, Brad was able to see that. I'm not an actress for a reason. Do you know how fucked up I felt thinking I was in love with my brother?" I raved. Getting up, I walked into our manager's office to try and hide, but Aaron followed.

"Caly-"

"That's why I didn't see he was cheating, and everyone else did. Being here with you, I wasn't giving Brad the attention he needed. The fuel was already there: Emily's ambition, my feelings for you, and Brad's jealousy. Rockford's accusation was the spark to burn our relationship down."

Moving towards me, Aaron took my shoulders in his hands to stop me pacing. "Caly, this isn't your fault. You didn't make Brad cheat on you. He chose to leave and not contact you. I saw you trying. He can't blame this on you because you never did anything wrong."

"How didn't I see it?" I mourned. "If he loved me, how could he give me up?"

Cupping my cheek, Aaron's froze me with his eat-the-world eyes in front of my boss' desk. "Because he's stupid." Moving forward, Aaron stopped just shy of my lips. "I'd never be with anyone else if I had you," he whispered. "I've always been in love with you." He kissed me, hard and passionate, the back of my thighs hitting the edge of the desk.

Accepting the kiss, I held back from losing myself in it. Placing my hands on Aaron's chest, I pressed, and Aaron withdrew. "I'm married," I reminded him.

"Not tonight, Caly," Aaron murmured, leaning me back beneath him. "Please? We've been good for so long. You always choose him, and he's left you. Choose me, even if it's just for this moment. Choose me."

My heart was thudding in my chest, my body warming to the touch of his fingers under my shirt. Electricity followed the kiss of his lips along my neck like a plasma globe. "Aaron," I breathed his name, not pushing him away.

"Choose me, just once, Caly. Be mine."

When Aaron's mouth pressed to mine, I didn't hold back. I kissed him with everything I felt for him. From the moment he came to our school, Aaron enamored me. By the time teenage hormones kicked in, I was besotted.

This wasn't about revenge, or hurt, or spite. There was none of that as Aaron pulled my top over my head and removed my bra. All I cared about was Aaron, that he was touching me, kissing me, and he wasn't saying no.

Tugging Aaron's shirt over his head, I ran my hands over his body and purred at how my fingers tingled touching him. As he rubbed his hardness against me, I moaned his name. Unbuckling my belt and work pants, Aaron yanked them down and off, his pants were gone a second later. Then, he was between my thighs, naked and hard, and already dripping precum.

Kissing me deeply, passionately, Aaron shoved into me. My breath caught in my throat. Lifting my ankles around his tight ass, I encouraged him deeper. Not that Aaron needed much encouragement. He was pushing as hard and deep as he could, as fast as he could. One of his hands was pressing down on my hip, which drove me wild.

Rising to climax fast, I fed on Aaron's moans. Repeating my name like a sacred prayer, with every thrust of his hips, Aaron forced me to call his name. My body responded as adamantly. My hips were rising to meet Aaron's forward momentum. He was so deep inside me, so thick, and getting bigger with every penetration.

When Aaron started throbbing, I was about to orgasm. "Don't stop," I whispered when he froze within me. "Please don't stop," I begged.

"Caly," Aaron hesitated, he closed his eyes, trying to focus. "Caly, do you love me?"

Meeting his eyes, I knew this answer would never be a lie. Straining up, I sucked his bottom lip, loving the groan from his throat, and the hard pulse of his cock buried deep. "I love you, Aaron. Always have."

Pupil's dilated, Aaron kissed me hard as he pulled his hips back and drove forward. There was no restraint now, and I was tipping close to climax when Aaron broke from the kiss and came hard. Grabbing his ass, I encouraged him to keep going, lifted my hips, loving the feeling of him deep within me.

Panting his name, I bit my lip as my eyes folded back in my head, and I came. Aaron didn't stop thrusting until I couldn't form words any longer. Clinging to him, I trembled from the extreme sensation of my orgasm.

Laying me back, Aaron released my legs from around him and kissed over my heart as we steadied our breathing. "Don't go back to him," Aaron murmured. "When Brad wants you back, tell him it's too late."

Tears prickled the backs of my eyes, but as I opened my mouth to respond, the bell rang at the back door. Remembering where we were, we stared at each other, then down at how naked we were and swore. Pulling away, we dressed as quick as we could. Using tissues from the desk to clean the mess, Aaron threw it in the bin then ran out to answer the call.

Fixing my hair, I tried not to look like I'd just been deliciously boned in my boss' office. Staring at the reflection of my wedding rings in the mirror, I felt guilt churn in my stomach. Tears fell unbidden. My hands were shaking as I slipped my rings off and stared at them a moment longer. He left me. For her. I'd done nothing wrong just now. Had I?

Confused about everything, I gazed back to the desk. The one thing I knew was that I loved Aaron Wish, and I was never going to regret what happened. Even if it never happened again.

Chapter Thirty

"CALY?" Aaron called beside me, making me jump. "Are you ready to go?"

"He wants to see me," I whispered, staring at the phone in my hands

"Who does?" Aaron frowned, taking my phone from me. "Of course, he does," Aaron grumbled. His eyes lifted to mine. "You don't have to go, and you shouldn't be feeling guilty."

"I'm not..."

"You are," Aaron huffed, handing me my phone back. "I know you. I know that look on your face. It's the same look you gave me when you threw two questions in the finals so that I could beat you and get Dux of our year. Or, when Josh got in that fight in year ten. You shoved him away and threw some punches, so it looked like you'd beaten that shit up. All so, Josh wouldn't get expelled." Aaron stared down at me, eyes intense. "The same look you had arriving at work last week when you scratched your cousin's car," Aaron finished.

Biting my lip, I wondered how the hell did he know I did

all that? Kingsley hadn't even realized I'd scratched his car yet. Throwing his bag on his back, Aaron stared me down. "I know you better than anyone, Caly, so I know you are feeling guilty as hell right now. You shouldn't. We did nothing wrong."

"Aaron, we had sex, and I'm married. Albeit, not for much longer, but currently, I'm married, and I slept with a man who wasn't my husband. Two wrongs don't make a right," I pleaded for him to understand how hard this was for me

Shaking his head at me, Aaron looked disappointed. "Don't meet him. Tell him I have his stuff, and you'll get your lawyer to arrange the divorce. Don't go to meet him."

"Why?"

"Because he will turn this around on you," Aaron snapped. "He will see your current guilt and use it to manipulate you into taking him back. Two people will regret it if you do that, Caly, and neither of them will be Brad."

My eyes were stinging from crying so damn much. "Brad made a mistake, but I still care for him, Aaron. I have to hear what he needs to say. Then, we'll go our separate ways."

"That's what you say now," he muttered, pissed off. "I bet you five thousand dollars in the morning, you'll be crying and regretting you went and met him."

"He's still my husband, and my friend."

Aaron's eyes filled with rage. "Really? If you still believed you were married, why is it my cum swimming inside you right now?"

The comment staggered me back. "What?"

"You heard me," Aaron huffed and started to walk off.

A shiver went through my body as I closed my eyes. "We didn't use protection."

"Of course, we didn't. I don't carry condoms around in my

pants in the hope of scoring at work." Aaron turned back angrily. "I'm clean, and I know you are, so it doesn't matter?"

Gripping my stomach as it twisted in knots, I blinked fresh tears. Aaron's eyebrows lifted then dropped low over those intense eyes. "Caly, Jesus, you're on the pill, right? I mean, you were when you offered yourself up that night, so I thought..." Aaron was watching me, his pupils dilating. "Oh, you dumb fuck!"

"Excuse me?!"

"Not you. Your husband. You've been trying for a baby, and he knocks up his cousin." Aaron swept his hand through his hair in frustration. "No wonder you've been more moody than usual when your periods are due. Of all the stupid ass things to do." Gritting his jaw, Aaron turned and walked towards the door. "If you forgive him, you're a fool. He doesn't deserve you."

Standing there, watching Aaron leave, I pressed my lips tight to hold myself together.

"And, get your ass back on the pill," Aaron called over his shoulder. "The last thing you need is for him to get you pregnant too."

The door slammed shut behind him. Not sure how to feel, I stared after him blinking. My phone went off in my hand. Jumping a little, I stared down at the screen. Brad said he'd see me in forty-five minutes. With a sigh, I slipped my phone into my back pocket, grabbed my bag, and headed out to where my driver was waiting. Talking to Dom by his car, Aaron looked caught between rage and emotion so deep he didn't know how to express it.

Sucking in a breath, I refused to cry. Opening the back door of my mother's town car, I slid in without paying attention.

"Hello, Caly." Turning to the deep voice coming from beside me, the first thing I saw was the gun. My heart raced as my pupils unfocused from the weapon to see Terry Meadows sitting in the back of my car.

Checking for the driver, I felt a scream building in my chest. That wasn't my driver. "He's in the boot," Terry advised. "Dead. If you don't want to join him, then, I suggest you be a good girl and swallow that scream you're working towards."

The fact that he knew what a person about to scream looked like told me more than I needed to know. Closing my mouth, I cringed back into the corner of the car and reached for my necklace.

"Hand down, Caly." Terry moved the gun closer. "I'm not stupid. A rich kid like you, there will be one of Rockford's devices planted somewhere on you. I'll need it intact to test it later. For now, sit on your hands."

Trembling like anything, I slid my hands behind my back as we drove away. Aaron and Dom were returning to their cars, not even watching to make sure I was in the car.

"Enough of the sobbing," Terry directed. "It's a forty-five-minute drive from here. If you annoy me, I'll have to amuse myself."

Pressing my lips together, I tried hard to quit my crying.

Putting his gun away once we were out of the car park, Terry sat back watching me. "Well, I have to say, my little brother has good taste."

"What do you want?" I dared to ask as he went to touch me.

Smiling, Terry leered at me. "Well, I need you to do some convincing for me, then, we should get to know each other better."

"Over my dead body."

"I love a challenge, Caly. So, be careful what you dare me to do," Terry warned. Interrupted by his phone ringing, Terry answered it. Turning his head to the window to talk, I couldn't hear more than his monosyllabic answers.

Using this distraction, I slipped my phone out of my pocket behind my back and moved it to the side to text. Putting the phone on silent first, I used my peripheral vision to open a message. Selecting my mother, father, and Greg Meadows as recipients, I sent four simple words.

Terry Meadows has me.

My phone lit up immediately with a call from Rockford. Pressing the answer button, I put it on speaker and turned the screen off.

"...do it now," Terry ordered as he turned to look at me. "All the pieces are in place." Terry hung up the phone.

"Where are you taking me?"

"Somewhere safe."

"Anywhere with you isn't safe."

"Well, you can thank your husband for the pleasure of my company," Terry grumbled.

"Brad? Why?" I chocked. Had Brad realized that divorcing me would cost too much and went to his brother for help?

Terry huffed. "Look, I would have left you well enough alone, except for a roll in the sheets, you had nothing to offer me. Why do you think I hadn't come for you by now?"

When I shrugged, Terry shook his head. "You are innocent, aren't you?" He sounded disgusted at the idea. "Look, the plan was quite simple. You divorce my brother, he marries Emily, she has the baby, and then Brad dies, leaving everything to the kid. I marry her and take over as the child's authority." When his phone lit up, Terry dropped his eyes to check it. "Then you went and pissed that bitch off, and she made you part of the deal."

Wait! Was he telling this correctly? "You and Emily are in cahoots?"

"That girl was desperate to come to me, but she's a nasty schemer, I tell you. This entire plan is hers. Originally, you were to be left alone. No one wants to piss off the Zilla's. Then she calls me Sunday night, telling me the plan changed. She's good, but it was still messy to change direction last minute."

"So, now, I die, she marries Brad, he dies after the baby is born, and she screws everyone over?"

Lifting a brow, Terry smirked. "You've got the gist of it, though, she won't be screwing me over. If she thinks I'm stupid enough not to know a double-cross when I see one, she's wrong."

"So, what is your plan?"

Appraising me, Terry blew out a breath. "Relax, Caly. You won't be dying anytime soon. I have plans for you. Emily's plan, while good, was only beneficial to me until I was able to snatch you. Now, I'm the king of the castle."

His words made me swallow hard. How did he know what his father said to me?

"In all honesty, until I heard my father's conversation with you, I wouldn't have chosen this way forward. It took a lot of digging to understand what he meant. Your mother's will alone was enough to change my plan, but when I found your grandfather's... Baby, I was trading up the moment I saw that sweet piece of inheritance."

At the blank look on my face, Terry smirked. "You don't know?" When I shook my head, Terry's grin grew. "Well, it's not important now. First, tonight, you're going to get a front-row seat to the Riverside riot. Then I'm going to crown you queen."

The car came to a halt. The driver got out, opened my door, and yanked me from the vehicle. Managing to grab my bag from the floor, stumbled as he forced me forward. Dragging me across the movie theatre carpark, he opened the door to the waiting vehicle.

"You're leaving my car with my dead driver here at the cinema?" I asked the thug manhandling me.

He didn't answer me. When he took his eyes off me, I quickly stashed my phone down the side of my bra. Having boobs helps hide some fantastic things. I also used that moment to activate my locket. Seeing my movement, the thug turned to say something. Swinging my bag at his head, I was grateful for the heavy textbook I had in there to get ahead on my master's work.

Letting me go as he bent over in pain, clutching his head, I turned to run. My feet stopped, fear filling my heart. Terry clicked off the safety on his gun, which was pointing straight at my head. My mouth was too dry even to swallow.

"You're a feisty one." Grinning, Terry backed me up against the car. Grabbing my throat, Terry lowered his gun. Hard metal pressed against my inner thigh, making me jolt before it slid up to the junction of my legs. Holding back the tears, I felt stinging the backs of my eyeballs, I held my breath.

"I'm going to enjoy you," Terry murmured.

Forcing a kiss against my lips, I gritted my teeth, refusing to let his probing tongue inside.

Pulling back, Terry laughed. "I have a ring gag at home that will force that pretty mouth open to whatever I want to put in there," he threatened. My whimpered made Terry smile more. "But that's later. Now, we need to get moving. I'm on a tight schedule tonight. Performing a hostile takeover," he informed without explaining. "Tie her hands behind her back," Terry ordered his thug.

Yanking my arms behind my back, the thug cuffed me at the wrists with a zip tie. Cringing at how tight it was, I cried out at the man's grip as he shoved me into the back seat of the car.

Terry's phone rang as he slid in beside me. "What is it? What do you mean someone tipped him off?" Terry listened, getting angry. His eyes came to me. "Find him and do it already. I want them all dead by sunrise."

Hanging up, Terry picked up my bag, emptying the contents onto the seat between us. "Unusual for someone not to have a phone these days." He lifted his eyes to mine. "Where is it?"

"It was in her hand when I pulled her out of the car," his thug informed him. "She shoved it in her bra."

Terry tilted his head to appraise my breasts. "Caly, you're making this too easy on me."

Reaching forward, Terry slinked his hand under the bottom of my shirt and slid it up my abdomen to grope my breast. I kicked out with my leg at his knee. Terry pointed his gun at me again. "Behave," he warned.

Copping a feel, he smiled, eyes getting glassy. I wanted to vomit. Shifting his hand, Terry found the phone. "While I realize your hands are tied, I'll take this now. Save you being tempted to warn your family of their imminent death."

"What?" I gasped as he slid my phone free.

"What did you think hostile takeover means?" Terry smiled. "Tonight, the Sarita's and Zilla's will cease to be. That will leave everything to you since you're married to the heir of one and will be the heir of the other. My father will also not live to see the dawn. Then we'll marry, which will give me full control of this city's wealth.

There was no holding back the tears now. "You can't, my

mother and Kingsley aren't even in the country. They'll inherit before me," I argued his theory. "Plus, you'll be in jail."

Terry shook his head as we crossed the river. "No, I won't. My father will die as a result of the Riverside riot. The Sarita's death will get pinned on that crazy bitch and her pregnancy hormones. She'll turn the gun on herself before its done. Your family? Well, they were nice enough to get into bed with Rockford, literally, in your mum's case, so he'll take the fall for that."

It was my turn to smile. "You might have to rethink that," I suggested, my eyes going to the phone in Terry's hand. "Your dad wasn't the only one to get that alert."

Frowning, Terry tried to wake my phone. When he saw the pin code lock, Terry scowled. Removing the protective cover, he snapped his arm back and broke my phone against my temple.

My head roared with thunder from the hit. It was more than the phone, but the strength behind it. Brad wasn't the only one in his family to work out. Dropping my chin to my chest, pain searing, my vision scattered for a moment.

Lowering his window, Terry threw my broken phone out of it while bringing his to his ear. "The Zilla's have been forewarned. Forget them and take care of the Sarita's."

I could only hope Rockford heard enough to warn everyone.

Chapter Thirty-One

THIRTY MINUTES LATER, the thug hauled me into a building in Riverside. Bloodstained my work shirt from the laceration the phone caused at my temple. Shivering, despite the late spring warmth, I tried to huddle in on myself.

Terry used that as an excuse to wrap his arms around me in the elevator. "I'll warm you up, Cupcake."

"Get off me," I yelled, trying to get away from him.

Holding me easily, Terry dug his fingers in when I tried to squirm away. "Hmm, I like it when they fight," Terry laughed, pulling me tight to the front of him while he groped me. The thug chuckled.

"Oh, my god, get your dick away from my ass," I squealed when I felt him rubbing his semi-hardness against me.

"Don't worry, Cupcake, you are going to scream for me when I shove it in there," he teased. Clenching at the idea, since it wasn't something I'd ever considered trying, I whimpered. "We'll work up to that." Terry pinched my nipple hard.

Hissing, I shoved my hips back, forcing him away. Dropping my cuffed hands, I blocked him from rubbing himself there.

"Want to cop a feel, Cupcake?"

He gave me an idea. "Sure?" Grabbing his bulge, I dug my nails in and twisted as I pulled away.

Roaring in pain, Terry shoved me forward, ramming my face into the side of the elevator. A moment later, his gun was at my temple. "Do that again, Cupcake, and I won't use any lube when I fuck your ass."

"Probably a good thing," I hissed against the elevator wall. "At least then, I'd be able to feel you. You're not half the man your brother is."

The gun was going to leave a bruised impression on my head with how hard he pressed my face into the shiny metal of the lift.

"Keep mouthing off, Caly. You're not doing yourself any favors," Terry murmured in my ear. "I've learned from my father's mistakes. Kidnapping the rich bitches and knocking them up doesn't get you anywhere. Marry them and knock off the family, and you get everything. So, get used to me touching you, Cupcake. I'm going to be doing a lot of it from now on. A man has rights when it comes to his wife, after all."

"You're deluded and living in the fifties," I snarled. "These days, a woman can still charge her husband with rape, especially when you kidnapped her. That's not mentioning that there is no way I will agree to marry you, so no celebrant would wed us."

The elevator doors opened. Pulling me away from the wall, Terry shoved me forward for the thug to manhandle again. "You'd be surprised what you'll agree to when drugged off your face, Caly." My eyes went wide as I was dragged from the elevator. Terry's smile was villainous. "Now, you're getting it,

Cupcake." An apartment door ahead of us opened. Terry turned his eyes to the man standing there. "Has he done it yet?"

"No, still telling us to get fucked," the guy growled. "Who's the dish?"

Grabbing the guy by the neck, Terry rammed him into the wall. "This is my future wife, show some respect."

"Sorry, who's the hot bitch?"

Laughing, Terry released him. "This is Caly Zilla. Current sister-in-law, future wife. Caly, meet my best friend, Bozo," Terry introduced casually.

"Have to be, to be your friend," I muttered.

"Ooh, she's got a mouth on her," Bozo smiled. "Can't wait to see her brought to heel."

"Neither can I." Focusing on a man waiting in the lounge, Terry held out his hand while the guy handed him another phone. "Take her to the room, Caps. Let her get reacquainted with her husband."

My stomach dropped. "What?"

Striding forward, Terry held up Brad's phone. I swallowed. "You said you'd meet with him. I told you he'd see you in forty-five minutes."

"What if I'd refused?"

With a shrug, Terry waved me away. Dragging me through the furnished apartment, Caps took me up the hallway to the bedrooms. At the end of the hall, another guy stood guard. "Open it," Caps ordered. The guard unlocked the door, and Caps hauled me inside.

"Brad?" I whimpered when I saw him lying on the bed. He was shirtless, and his upper body and face showcased bruises all over him.

"Caly." Sitting up, Brad cringed over his abdomen before he

was off the bed and moving toward me. "What are you doing here?"

"Obvious, isn't it?" I asked, turning so he could see my hands cuffed.

"What is she doing here?" Brad yelled at Caps as he pulled me out of his grasp and into a hug.

"Boss thought you needed some motivation," Caps told him. "Since beating you isn't working, your wife has become your collateral damage. She's here because of you. You've got an hour to do what your brother asked, or he changes the game." Stepping out, Caps shut the door.

Stepping back, Brad looked me over, assessing me, starting with the blow to my head. "How bad did he hurt you?"

"I'm sure it's nothing compared to what's coming," I grumbled. "What are you doing here?"

"They snatched me on Sunday night. Emily's phone call was a setup," Brad explained as he walked into the adjoining bathroom. Returning with a wet cloth, Brad started wiping the blood off my face. "How did they get you? Dom follows you everywhere."

Blinking at the revelation, Dom's constant presence in the car park made a little more sense. I'd thought he had a grandmother who was sick or something. "They texted me from your phone to meet and talk," I admitted. "I don't know how they lost Dom. I saw him with Aaron in the garage. They killed my driver, and we're waiting in my car."

Brad closed his eyes as if hearing that hurt. "Fuck!" Brad opened his eyes. "Did you activate the device your father gave you?"

"Yes, but not until they dumped my car. I managed to get a message out to him and your father. Rockford heard most of what your brother's plan is. He should be able to stop him."

"You think Rockford will give a shit about my family?" Brad growled. "His concern will be protecting your mother and getting you back unharmed." Brad's eyes went to my head. "Well, as unharmed as possible."

"He will warn them, and the police," I assured. Sitting down on the bed, I felt exhausted. "What do they want from you?"

Brad pointed to the desk in the corner, on which sat a laptop. "That belongs to your dad. It's his personal computer and has the codes for all those GPS devices on it. With it, they could find any of you they want," Brad revealed. "I wrote the encryption. They want me to unlock it."

Eyes focused on the desk; I studied the laptop. "The encryption you created for your thesis? The one you sold to Rockford?"

Sighing, Brad nodded. "I've refused until this point."

"You're going to keep refusing."

"I can't sit here and watch them hurt you, Caly," Brad caressed my face. Moving away from his touch, I put some distance between us. Brad froze.

"You can, and you will," I scowled. "You could cheat on me behind my back, so you can damn well stand there and act like you don't care if your brother hurts me. You aren't giving them the information on that computer."

"Caly, I love you. You can't expect me to-" Brad tried to move towards me.

Again, I stepped back. "It's not just the GPS information on that computer, Brad. All the security information for the medical center and the college is on there. Plus, every other project Rockford has. He had me under surveillance since I was seven. Do you think that might be on there?"

Brad paused to consider me. "You're saying, I'm putting your life in danger if I do unencrypt that computer?"

"Your brother isn't going to kill me, Brad. I'd prefer that. But my parentage is a huge leverage for him. Him finding that out, it puts more than my or your life in danger. If Terry gets that information; you could be killing hundreds or thousands."

Wiping his hands over his face, Brad looked at me with tears stinging his eyes. "You're asking me to stand here and watch them hurt you, probably..." Brad turned away.

"I'm telling you, you have to." I started crying too. Jesus, I didn't want to get hurt, or worse. Watching Brad beaten wasn't on my to-do list either, but I knew the work Rockford did to save lives.

We'd spoken a lot over the months. There were projects in Riverside that never had his name on them, which the media didn't even know about. If that information was on my father's computer, Terry would find out about them. I couldn't live with that on my conscience. I'd already watched one child die tonight. If it meant condemning the lives of children, I'd prefer to give up my life or suffer whatever Terry dished out.

The door opened as Terry came in with Bozo. Curious as I was, my brain told me I didn't want to know why he had that nickname. "Are you ready?" Terry asked Brad.

Looking at me, Brad closed his eyes. "Go to hell."

The response raised his brother's eyebrows. "Well, from what I'd heard, you adored your wife. I truly didn't expect that answer."

"He cheated on me, Dickwad," I grouched. "Was it that big a jump?"

Eyes narrowing, Terry's lips formed a straight line. "I was under the impression you were unaware of your husband's infidelity?"

"I told her Sunday night," Brad admitted. "Emily made the being pregnant thing kind of obvious, and it all came out."

Quirking that singular brow, Terry eyed his brother. "You still came when Emily called?"

Brad closed his eyes. "He chose her," I answered for him. "I told him if he left Sunday, our marriage was over. He still left anyway." I glared at Brad. "Told you, you would regret it."

Surprised, Terry looked between us. "Well, that doesn't change things now, does it?" Striding towards me, Terry yanked me off the bed and turned me to face Brad. "Time to do your thing, Little brother."

"Not going to happen," Brad folded his arms across his bruised chest.

"Really?" A knife appeared in front of me, making every muscle in my body tense.

Brad's jaw tightened. "Yes."

Moving the knife behind me, Terry released my hands from the cable tie. The instant relief caused my body to heave forward. "Undress," Terry directed, sliding his knife back into his pocket.

"Excuse me?"

Terry made a gesture to Bozo. Before I could register the move, Bozo punched Brad in the solar plexus. Brad tried to dodge, but his face grimaced in pain, and he moved stiffly. Falling to the ground, Brad struggled to breathe, while Bozo kicked him in the ribs. Gritting my teeth, I held in my plea to stop hurting him for as long as I could. When Brad turned blue with the inability to breathe, I couldn't keep standing there.

"Stop!" My modesty wasn't worth watching Brad get beaten to death. Kicking Brad a few more times, Bozo stepped back and cocked a brow at me, his feet staying ready to start up again. Understanding the threat, I lifted my shirt over my head and dropped it to the ground. Unbuckling my pants, I let them fall before kicking my shoes off.

Appreciating the scenery, Terry moved closer. "Everything, Caly," he murmured, lifting the chain of my necklace until it pulled my locket free from my bra.

Reaching behind me, I unclasped my bra, letting it fall, then squirmed my hips until my knickers were at my feet.

"This is beautiful," Terry assessed the locket. "Who gave it to you?"

"My father gave it to my mother, and my mother gave it to me."

Opening the locket, Terry slid his thumb over the depressed blue stone. When he didn't disengage it, I realized he didn't know it was a GPS. Drofkor's jewelry was either earrings or watches, so of course, it wouldn't occur to him.

"The stone matches your eyes," Terry observed. "You look like your mother in every way, except your eyes, so I'm guessing they come from your dad. Your father gave her this, so she'd remember his eyes. A very nice and thoughtful gift."

Keeping hold of the locket, Terry used his free hand to pull my hairband out, making my hair fall around my face. "You're beautiful, Caly. I don't want to hurt you, so I need you to convince your husband to unencrypt that computer for me." Scooting his face under the waterfall of my hair, Terry licked my ear. "Please?" He whispered before placing a kiss over the pulse of my neck.

Trembling with fear when his hand grabbed my hip, I bit my lip against talking and shook my head.

Sighing against my skin, Terry blew against my ear. My entire body tensed at the feel of his breath. "Stupid, Caly." Stepping back, Terry yanked my locket from my neck.

"Ow!" Rubbing the back of my neck, I grimaced. 'If anyone ever makes you fear for your life, I want you to pull the chain from your neck. Pull it hard, so the links break. An army will come to save you.' Resisting a smile, I watched the broken chain dangle from Terry's hand, where he held the locket.

"I'll keep this as a souvenir," Terry shoved it in his pocket. When he grabbed my hair in his fist, I cried out at his grip, then he pushed me forward. "Get on the bed, Caly. Let's see if you can feel me."

Stumbling forward, I caught myself on the bed. Trembling there for a minute, I couldn't bring myself to get on the bed.

Brad was getting to his feet as Bozo returned to the door. "Don't," Brad growled at his brother.

"It's your choice, Brad," Terry threatened. "The computer is right there. In the meantime, since you couldn't get your wife pregnant, I guess your big brother will need to do the job for you."

Using his eyes to plead with me, Brad bit his lip.

"He's going to do it anyway. Don't worry, he's only a little prick," I assured Brad. It was a lie from what I felt in the elevator, but Greg told me Terry was jealous of Brad. So, anything I could do to delay the inevitable was going to be part of my playing deck right now.

Hissing when he grabbed my hair, Terry moved me sideways to ram my body into the wall. "Caly, Caly, Caly. We've discussed that mouth of yours. It seems you're not as meek as previous reports suggested." Terry looked over his shoulder. "Bozo," Terry gestured with his head.

Walking across the room to a locked cupboard, Bozo removed a key and opened it. My eyes widened at the things hanging inside. Collecting a long black stick, Bozo closed the closet again before handing the cane to Terry.

"Shit! I'm sorry," I screeched as Terry used my hair to reposition me, forcing me to bend over the bed. "Please, I'm sorry. I'll behave."

The cane looked evil, even in its presentation. It may have been weak, but I'd prefer him to stick his dick in me then find out how much that was going to hurt me.

Bending over me, Terry made me feel how much my current situation turned him on. "I'm going to make sure that you never talk back to me again, Caly. Another thing I learned from my dad. If you tame bitches the moment you get them, you never have to worry about them stepping out of line again."

"God, Terry. Don't." Brad stepped forward, worried. "She's never even been belted as a child."

Releasing my hair, Terry used the stick to point at the laptop. "Computer is right there when it gets too much for you, Little brother." Taking a few steps to the side, he made sure I could see him in my peripheral vision before he stroked the stick. Tears were already cascading down my cheeks.

"I had this specially made. I used to use car aerials, but you can only beat someone with an aerial so long before it breaks. This beauty is the bastard child of an aerial and a cane."

Breathing was difficult, my heart pounding in my ears, my vision blurry from the flood of fear. Flexing the black metal a little, Terry released it, so I could hear the way it whistled.

"Keep your legs under you, Cupcake. Caning isn't so bad on the rump, but it can split the skin if it hits over bone." Pulling his arm back, a whistle sung through the air.

There was a loud snap as it connected right across my bare bum. A microsecond later, pain seared around the impact site. Eyes wide, voice lost, my knees bending, I nearly collapsed then and there. Then the second hit landed, and I screamed.

Chapter Thirty-Two

FIVE HITS. That's all it took for my legs to crumble and to fall to the floor in agony. That didn't stop Terry. The next strike caught me right across my back. Arching back away from the pain, the one after that struck my side.

"Terry, stop!" Brad yelled over my screaming.

My hip, my thighs, my arms. I'd curled into a defensive ball, buried my head in my knees, and jolted with each impact. Something was dribbling down my back. As Terry hit me again, the wet seemed to insulate the pain a little, but the noise changed to a thwack.

An animal growled. The hitting stopped. It took me a while to hear the sounds of fighting over my crying. Trying to lift my head to make sure Brad was okay, I screamed as pain seared along my spine. At one stage, the cane hit the back of my neck, and now I couldn't look up.

Managing to unclench my fingers from around my knees - though, I couldn't feel one of my hands - my legs fell away from my face. That small movement was agonizing. Blinking away the tears, I saw Brad and Terry rolling around, punching the shit out of each other.

The door opened as Caps entered. His brows jumping at Bozo unconscious on the floor, Caps looked to where Brad and Terry were fighting. "Shit!" Caps ran forward, grabbed Brad in a headlock, and pulled him away from his brother. "What the hell happened?"

"My little brother grew some balls," Terry grumbled. Stumbling to his feet, he watched Brad struggle against a much bigger Caps. "He took out Bozo while I was caught up in my fun. Didn't bloody see him coming."

"Damn lucky I came in," Caps grunted. Struggling to keep hold of Brad, Caps held out a phone to Terry. "It's Spade."

Taking the phone, Terry put it to his ear. "Tell me the jobs done?" He asked as he went into the bathroom and checked his bleeding nose and lip. Brad got a few good hits in on his brother.

"Let me check on her?" Brad asked Caps.

With his eyes finally coming to me, Caps released Brad, stepping back. Not liking what he saw, Caps cursed and turned away.

Crawling to where I was shaking and sobbing on the floor, Brad hesitated to touch me. "Jesus, why didn't you let me do it?" Brad murmured. Moving my hair out of the way to check my face, Brad then followed a few trails of blood back to their sources.

"Get him away from her," Terry ordered, coming back into the room. Grabbing Brad, Caps dragged him back.

Yanking his torn shirt off, Terry threw it aside. "You should know, Dad's dead. His businesses are mine now. You got an issue with that?"

Swearing under his breath, Brad shook his head. "I have no interest in that shit; you know that."

Reaching down, Terry forced me to stand. Whimpering and keening, I gritted my teeth with the pain flaring like white-hot fire over ice. As I got my feet beneath me, I steadied myself.

Finger combing my hair out of my face, Terry observed me. "Still not going to unencrypt that computer for me?" Terry asked, placing a kiss on the tip of my nose. "Cupcake can't take another beating." Turning his eyes to Brad, Terry stepped forward as he took the gun from his back.

My eyes lifted to my husband. "Brad, do it," I urged, no longer fearing anything but his surviving the next few minutes.

Meeting my eyes, Brad shook his head. "You were right. It is more than you and me. If Terry kills me, he'll never get that encryption broken."

"That is frustratingly accurate." Terry turned his gaze on me. "You may want to look away, Cupcake." Still gazing at me, Terry clicked off the safety, raised the gun, and turned his head back at the last second to fire.

"No!" Trying to move forward, I watched Brad's mouth fall open as the room filled with a loud bang. The man I'd once promised to love until death crumpled.

Catching me around the waist, Terry put his gun to my head. "Shh," he whispered to my ear. That's when I realized I was sobbing Brad's name. "Caps, I need to comfort my sister-in-law. Why don't you get Bozo out of here."

"You're sure you'll be right with him?" Caps indicated Brad, where he lay groaning on the floor, holding the bullet wound in his abdomen. Caps' face was a little pale as if he was going to be sick with what he was witnessing.

"He's dead," Terry shrugged. "Slow, but the outcome is the same."

White as a sheet, Caps dragged Bozo out the door, his eyes flicking to me with fear as he left me alone with Terry and Brad.

Walking us to the bed, Terry nibbled down my neck as he did. "Shh, Cupcake. I know you're hurting. If you fight me, you're going to hurt more," Terry guaranteed as he encouraged me to move over the bed.

Sobbing, I kept my eyes fixed on Brad, tears rolling down his face as he watched on in agony. Trying to move, Brad cried out in pain and collapsed back, panting to the ceiling. "It's okay, Caly," Brad soothed, turning his face to mine. "Don't fight him, and you'll be okay."

Dislodging a raging river of tears when I shook my head, I knew that was the worst lie Brad ever told me. "No, I won't," I admitted, moving back on the bed. "I love you, despite what you did."

Swallowing with difficulty, Brad gazed at the ceiling. "You weren't going to forgive me, though, were you?" I closed my eyes as Terry leaned over me, tears falling faster. "I'm an idiot, Caly," Brad admitted. Leaving his gun on the bed, Terry stood straight to remove his pants. "But I'm not as big an idiot as Terry," Brad half-laughed, blood spluttering from his lips.

Glaring at his little brother, Terry turned his way as he unbuckled his belt. He didn't notice when I grabbed the gun and clicked off the safety. Agonizing as moving was, I let my brain go into autopilot.

"Why am I the idiot?" Stepping forward, Terry kicked his dying brother in the side. Crying out, Brad coughed up more blood. "Hey? I didn't cheat on her. I didn't put her in the position she's in, so why am I the idiot?"

Aim.

"Because... you left a loaded weapon next to a champion shooter," Brad coughed. Terry turned wide-eyed towards me.

Fire.

Staggering back against the wall, Terry was already dead before his body fell to the ground. My ears were ringing from the gunshot, but I noticed the door opening in my peripheral.

Turning, I fired again. The guard fell to the ground in the hall. The reverberation of the gunshot killed my hearing. Relying entirely on my sight, which was blurry from crying, I watched the entrance. Someone stepped in front of the door, saw me aim at them, and fell back out of shot.

"Caly!" Someone yelled my name like they were a distance away. My body was in agony, my heart decimated, but I dared not trust a word anyone said while I was still naked and hurting.

"It's Dwayne. Put the gun down." A head peeked around the corner, and I aimed again, unsure. They ducked back. "Caly, can you hear me?" the voice more familiar now as the ringing in my ears died down. "Caly, I need you to put the gun down. Damn it! Ayah, get your arse up here."

More distant thunder, more shadows outside the door, then Ayah's face peeked around at me.

The gun grew heavy in my hands.

"Caly," Brad coughed my name. "Put the gun down. Your dad's here."

Clicking the safety on out of habit, not from conscious thought, I lay the gun on the bed. Crawling to Brad's side, I covered his bloody hands with mine. "Brad," I sobbed.

The pain became negligible in my need to keep Brad alive. Everything was secondary as I looked for something to help stem the bleeding.

Brad lifted his hands to my face. "It's okay, baby. We're safe," he coughed up more blood.

"Caly, Jesus!" Entering the room, Aaron grabbed the sheet from the bed and wrapped it around me. "What did he do to her?"

Brad let his eyes move to Aaron. "Take care of her, Ayah. Promise?"

"I promise," Aaron assured, putting his hand on Brad's shoulder. His other arm was around me.

Brad's eyes fluttered, and my heart stuttered.

"No, you hold on," I yelled at him, not willing to accept this was how I lost him. "I can't forgive you if you're dead. You need to hold on."

"It's okay, baby," Brad repeated. "You already did." With blood smearing his lips, Brad smiled. His pupils contracted and became fixed, then Brad's head fell to the side.

My heart tore open in my chest. "No!" I thumped his chest. Pain searing through odd places on my body, but I didn't care. "No!"

Paramedics burst through the door. Grabbing me up, Aaron moved me back. Dwayne was there, helping hold me as I thrashed and kicked and screamed.

My father came through the door with more paramedics. They were trying to get a look at me, but I fought to get back to Brad.

"She's hysterical. We need to put her out before she does more damage to herself."

Something jabbed in my thigh, a sharp sting followed by all my muscles going limp. The paramedic loomed over me as I dropped in Aaron's hold, and my eyes started to shutter. "Easy does it. No one is going to hurt you now," the paramedic assured.

My tongue tangled, trying to point out the flaw in that logic. Every beat of my heart was torture. The blackness stole me away, the pain fleeing with my consciousness.

§.

Opening my heavy eyelids, I had to blink a few times before I could focus. A hand squeezed mine. "Mum?"

Turning my head to that side, the nerves in my neck lit up like electricity. Instead of Gena, my father was sitting beside me, holding my hand. "Your mum is on her way home. I promised I'd stay until she got here."

"Brad?" My throat parched, I licked my lips to try and relieve it.

Rockford shook his head. "I'm sorry."

My throat hurt, my body throbbed, and my heart ached. "I shot Terry Meadows," I whispered. Everything on slow action replay in my head.

"Yes," Rockford stared at my hand. "I should have gotten there sooner. I wanted to make sure storming in there wouldn't put your life in danger. I waited those extra minutes until my guy on the inside gave me details. I'm sorry, Princess. My spy assured me Terry wasn't going to hurt you. When the vital alarm went off, I came as fast as I could."

Rockford's gaze went to my other hand, and tears fell down his cheeks. Following his eyes, my neck hurting to turn, I found my left hand bandaged and I couldn't move it. The memory of the cane slamming against the top of my hand and unimaginable pain jolted me. With one sob, I started crying.

Rockford stood up. "It's okay, Princess. You're safe now," he comforted, putting his forehead to mine. "I'm proud of you for doing what you had to do to protect yourself. I promise you, though, that you will never go through that again. I'm going to make sure that everyone knows if they hurt you, they'll be dancing for the Devil afterward."

A clearing of a throat got our attention. A man in scrubs standing there. "Miss Zilla, I'm nurse Mack. I need to check your wounds."

With his lips in a grimace, Rockford looked at me. "You okay about this?" Shaking my head, I bit my lip as my eyes unleashed a flood. Rockford turned to the nurse. "Come back later."

"Sure." Nurse Mack hesitated. "Are you in pain, Caly, would you like me to get you some paracetamol?"

"Something a little stronger," I rasped. My throat was killing me.

Frowning, the nurse hesitated to move any closer to my father. "On a scale of one to ten, ten being unbearable, what's your pain level?"

"My back and neck are killing me, and my hand feels like it's crushed," I offered. "Eight."

Nodding, the nurse took a step closer. "Has anyone talked to you about your injuries yet?"

"It's the first time she's woken up and not become hysterical, so no," Rockford answered.

"I'll get the Doctor on shift to speak to you," he assured. Then looked at Rockford. "The doctor still needs to do that other test, and her Grandfather has been calling hourly."

"I'll call Mr. Zilla and let him know she's awake. Everything else can wait."

Withdrawing, the nurse nodded. "I'll page the doctor."

When he walked out, Rockford pulled out his phone. "What other tests?" I asked.

"Give me a second, Caly. When the doctor comes, we'll

answer any questions you have," Rockford assured as he went to leave the room.

"Dad," I chocked. Rockford looked back at me, eyebrows in his hair. Swiping at the tears on my cheeks, I tried to stop crying, but they kept falling. "Don't leave, please?"

He didn't even hesitate. Taking my hand in his, Rockford made the call. "It's me. She's awake," Rockford informed the person on the other end of the line. "They are finding the doctor now, and then the police are going to want that statement." Rockford looked at me while he listened. "In one word, delicate. We'll see you later." Hanging up, he checked a few messages on his phone before putting it away.

"How long?"

"Thirty-six hours," Rockford quantified the time I'd been unconscious. "It's all over the news, so I don't want you watching it. The media don't have the full story, so they are speculating, and some of the ideas would upset you."

"Greg Meadows is dead," I murmured.

"Yes, all the Meadows are dead, including his third wife. Brad was the last to die," Rockford informed me as if that should mean something, but he didn't elaborate. I gave him points for not singing hallelujah.

"The Sarita's?"

"Alive. Grieving the loss of their grandson," Rockford answered shortly. "There is a bit of tension there, not aimed at you, but it will impact. But I've told them they'd have to wait for a decision on that matter."

"Emily and the baby?"

"Yes," Rockford replied. Eyes angry, and voice clipped.

Trying to turn my head away in shame, I winced. "Aaron must hate me. He told me not to agree to meet Brad."

Tilting his head, Rockford considered me, then exhaled.

"Hate? No. He spent the last two days here but had to leave for work. I expect he'll be back when his shift ends." Rockford squeezed my hand. "They were already in your car, Princess. He doesn't blame you for what happened."

"It would have happened anyway," I breathed understanding.

Eyes avoiding mine, Rockford cleared his throat. "Caly, the way you were when we found you, they had no choice but to do a rape kit. They found evidence of recent sexual activity."

"Terry didn't rape me," I revealed with relief. "I shot him when he tried."

Rockford's brow went up. "I was hoping that was the case. They only found one person's sperm, but it didn't match your husband's blood type."

My body tensed without warning, which made me cringe in pain, and I had to force myself to relax.

"Aaron told me what occurred between you two before Terry abducted you. We had to tell the police. They've made Aaron give a sample and are waiting to talk to you before they take action," Rockford warned me.

"They think Aaron...?" I asked, confused. Rockford gave a gentle nod. Blinking away a fresh set of tears, I felt a new level of humiliation. "God, as if things aren't fucked up enough."

Someone knocked at the door and came in. "Caly, I'm Doctor Childs. How are you feeling?"

"Like I'm Frankenstein's bride."

"Yes, I can imagine so." Doctor Childs came forward with my chart. "Caly, you suffered some severe injuries during your abduction. Most of the damage is severe bruising or minor lacerations that required cosmetic treatment, but there were three deep ones. The one on the back of your neck required a few stitches, the two across your spine were quite deep and required a lot more attention. A plastic surgeon performed the stitches for you, so there should be minimal scarring."

Well, that explained the pain. "What about my hand?"

Placing the chart aside, the doctor came around to examine my fingers. "Three of your metacarpals suffered crush fractures, the skin torn up, and a few veins opened. Luckily, nothing should be permanent. It's going to take some time to heal and then physiotherapy. Because of the open wound, we can't put it in plaster." Picking up the clipboard again, the doctor wrote some notes. I swear they did that to avoid making eye contact. "I'm going to have a trauma counselor come and talk to you. The police will insist on it, but I know a good one who is more targeted towards victims of your situation."

"No one raped me," I assured him, hating what he was suggesting.

Lowering the clipboard to his side, the doctor met my eyes. "I was referring to the torture, Caly." His sharp eyes assessed my defensiveness.

Oh.

"Knock, knock," Penny's voice called out as a big bloom of flowers walked through the door with four sets of legs. Queenie and Penny materialized from behind the orchards as they set them down.

"I'll check in on you again later," Childs excused and left.

"You're awake and not screaming," Penny yelled, relieved, and ran forward to cuddle me. "Oh, my God, you scared the living shit out of me." Penny pulled back, smiling and hiding her glassy eyes. "Need anything?"

"I'd kill for a pizza." Everyone froze. "What?" They all looked at each other, warily. Terry Meadows' face as I shot him playing over and over in my head, but nowhere near as much as Brad's as he died. "Oh. Well, if you want something else, I guess that will do."

"I'll call one of my men and have him go get enough for us." Taking out his phone, Rockford sent a look that told me my pretense of being okay wasn't fooling him for a second.

Queenie started telling me about some hot doctor who fell over himself, checking them out. Already having tuned them out, I closed my eyes for a minute, and when I opened them, the room was dark and quiet.

"Dad?" I whispered, panicked.

"Right here, Princess," his tired voice reassured as he squeezed my hand.

"Where'd everyone go?"

"They left hours ago, when you fell asleep again," Aaron's voice came from the other side of the bed. "Your Granddad came to see you. He said he'll be back in the morning and to tell you he loves you." Standing up, Aaron moved by the bed and touched my arm.

"Your mother will be landing at six in the morning," Rockford murmured. "I'd like to go meet her at the airport, calm her down, but if you need me here...?"

I didn't answer straight away. Admitting the fear that I'd open my eyes and be back in the room with Terry Meadows and Brad's dead eyes staring out at me was something I couldn't verbalize. Instead, I started bawling.

Chapter Thirty-Three

"...DON'T AGREE," my father's voice argued in the kitchen. "She needs to stay and to deal with this."

"The specialist in Switzerland will ensure her recovery," Gena disagreed. "She needs time away from this, Sin. The media are hounding her. We had to bring her home early because they were finding ways to sneak into her hospital room. She won't even sleep in her bedroom."

This morning was my second day waking up in the guest bedroom. The doctors weren't happy. They worried I'd pull my stitches, but they couldn't guarantee my safety at the hospital. So, Gena countered by having a nurse come in twice daily to check my wounds and treat my hand.

"Running away never solves anything, or haven't you learned that yet?"

"Jesus, what did you want me to do? I fell pregnant to you!" Mum snapped. "I wasn't putting my child's life in danger."

"It wasn't me that put her in danger. It was her husband and his jealous mistress. That's all over for Caly now. She needs to be with those who love her, and she needs to stay here and face what's happened."

"I'm her mother, and she's coming to Switzerland. That's final."

"I'm her father, and I've not had a say in anything in her life," Rockford hissed. "If Meadows knew he was messing with my kid by taking Caly, he would never have touched her. Like twenty years ago, you're making the wrong decision. You're encouraging Caly to do what you did, and that didn't turn out so great in the end did it?"

A smack sounded in the kitchen, and then the room fell quiet. Using the break in the war, I stepped into the doorway and cleared my throat. My parents looked at me, a bright red bloom the size of my mother's hand on the side of Rockford's face.

"Caly, you look lovely," Gena forced a smile. It dropped when she looked over my clothing. "Isn't that dress backless?"

"I have a cardigan. I hate not being able to wear a bra, but this dress is tight enough to support me," I explained my choice. The black dress was sexy from behind, but the knee-length skirt made it passable for a funeral. At worst, I'd be a sexy widow. My breath hitched at the thought.

My mum hesitated. "Hap..."

"Don't," I warned, meeting my mother's eyes. "There is nothing happy about today."

Gena flinched. "Why the Sarita's chose your birthday for the funeral..."

When I cringed, Rockford stepped forward. "Douglas wasn't concerned with birthdays when he organized the funeral for his grandson." Placing a reassuring hand on her shoulder. "They've lost enough this past week," Rockford reminded her.

Stepping by my mother, Rockford gave me a gentle hug. His palms cupped the back of my head, so he didn't touch my back. When he pulled back, he looked at my bound hand. "Nice accessorizing," he complimented the black lace ribbon I'd wrapped over the bandage. "The cars waiting, if you're ready?"

"Yes." Turning carefully, I limped to the door. Mum hadn't wanted me to go to the funeral. Rockford argued I needed to for closure. Plus, not going would fuel the rumors that Brad worked with his brother. That it was my assassination gone wrong.

Outvoting mum, I'd agreed with my father. Saying goodbye was essential to me. Setting the story straight was equally important.

Despite Rockford telling me not to watch the news, I'd turned it on once. The media weren't sure if Brad was in cahoots with his brother, or we were both victims of an overzealous mob boss. The one point they could all agree with was the money.

Greg Meadows died first. That meant his wealth split between his sons. Terry died next with no dependents or wife, so his half went to Brad. I was Brad's wife.

Before you get excited about me being the new mob boss of Riverside, I only inherited the money and estates. Over the last week, the news reported many attempts to seize the power vacuum left by the Meadows' deaths. Each one was resulting in more bodies. By the snippets I'd overheard, I suspected Rockford was ensuring no one took the crown.

The first funeral on today's list was in Riverside. Rockford's security cleared the media frenzy and kept close guard around their boss. Brad wasn't our only casualty. Rockford lost some of his employees, trying to get me free. Most of them buried already. But the funeral today was important to me.

This man was dead because of me. I'd insisted when I found out that I attend. Rockford, who was already paying for the funeral, moved it to this morning, so I didn't have multiple days of death.

"Kingsley, why are you here today?" A journalist called ahead, catching my attention.

"The young man we are here for today died trying to protect my cousin who I adore. Why wouldn't I be here? The more pressing question is, why are you here? Is it to honor the memory of this young man's self-sacrifice? Or, to get another photo of Caly to splash across the media with another fictional headline?"

"Let him in," Rockford directed as we came even with Kingsley.

The wall of protection cracked long enough to absorb Kingsley and his bodyguards. "King!" I gasped, inner eyes itching with tears of relief to see him.

Cuffing the back of my head, Kingsley hugged me to his chest and kissed the top of my head and made sure we kept moving. "Don't stop the wall of flesh, Princess. The war Terry Meadows started is still burning on this side of the river."

"I'm surprised Granddad let you come."

"He wasn't happy, but if you could be here, so could I. Once I won that argument, he went all out. Did you notice the body armor on the guys he sent with me? This damn suit I'm wearing is bulletproof."

No, I hadn't noticed the body armor, and I didn't care. After the shadow of the narthex fell over us, the doors shut out the media, and the small army around us took a breath.

"Kingsley," Rockford greeted my cousin with a handshake. "I appreciate you coming. Your welcome to sit with us."

Smirking, Kingsley raised a brow at the man in front of him. "I appreciate that you're the person to fear on this side of the river, Mr. Rockford. But Caly's my cousin. Don't think you can tell me if I can sit next to her or not because you're banging her mother."

Lifting a brow, Rockford assessed Kingsley. "One, I don't bang Caly's mother. That's what you do to women. I have sex or intimate relations with them. Two, you're on my turf. I'll tell you whether you can sit with my daughter whenever I like, especially when you are on my side of the river."

"Dad," I pleaded. Kingsley's eyes like saucers after the genetic revelation.

"You didn't know?" Rockford snickered at Kingsley. "The Zilla's sure are good at keeping their secrets." Rockford took my hand, ready to enter the church proper.

Kingsley's stare tracked to our hands, then to my face. "You knew?"

"For several months now. It's why Rockford gave me away at the wedding."

"Granddad is going to have a coronary."

"By the end of today, more than likely. It's time for some Zilla secrets to come out." Signaling his men, Rockford took the step forward. "We'll meet you inside, Kingsley."

Walking into the church hand in hand with Rockford, the place became quiet. Mum wasn't with us for this funeral. Rockford asked her to stay behind, and we'd meet her at the church for Brad's. Focused on his path, Rockford ignored everyone as they stared. Dwayne was on my other side, and two more bodyguards followed behind.

My face still bore the marks of last week. One was the bruised impression of Terry's gun, shining like a purple and black sun from my temple. I'd tried covering it, but no amount of makeup was going to hide it. Thinking about it made me jolt and whimper. My face was pressing into the side of the lift, Terry Meadows breath and hands on me.

"Caly?" Rockford pulled me a little closer, Dwayne stepping to block people's view of me. "Another flashback?"

When I nodded, breathing through the tears trying to escape, my dad squeezed my hand a little. "I know it's hard, Princess. Being here today is important, for you, and for the family of the boy who died for you."

"Don't guilt-trip me. I insisted on being here. Things are still fresh, and every time I feel an injury, or see someone who looks like..." I exhaled.

Observing me, Rockford lifted his eyes and scanned the crowd. "Aaron is here." Stepping aside, Rockford opened a gap for me to locate Aaron and his family. My feet started moving toward him like two magnets drawn towards each other.

Like everyone else in the church, Aaron stood watching us walk down that aisle. When Josh saw me, he went pale and leaned in to say something to Aaron. For the first time, Aaron didn't give me the usual ravenous for the world look. As he shook his head and answered his brother, Aaron looked as tortured as I physically felt.

Since I left the hospital, Aaron and I hadn't spoken, but we were going to have to. The police had been kind when I gave my statement. They charged me with Terry Meadows' death, but then dismissed the case as self-defense. I'd never see the inside of a cell or courtroom. Then they'd asked about Aaron. I'd explained that when Brad disappeared, I'd thought he left me. I'd turned to Aaron for comfort. Brad's disappearance opened a whole-nother can of worms.

"Mrs. Caprica, this is my daughter, Caly Zilla," Rockford

introduced. That one introduction is why Rockford didn't want my mother here. He'd decided to make a move, and he didn't want her knowing about it until it was too late. Everyone around the woman looked shocked, and then the gossip took off. "Caly wanted to be here today to show her appreciation for your son in his efforts to prevent her abduction."

"Hello, Miss. Zilla," the woman curtsied as if I was royalty.

Frowning, I grabbed her hand before she could lower herself further. "Please, don't," I begged as she straightened surprised. "Dom was a friend, not an employee to me. I didn't even know he was working when he was always there. I'm here today to mourn my friend with my friends." I looked at Dwayne, including him in that vital role. He gave me a kind smile, tears in his eyes.

Stepping forward, Dwayne kissed Dom's mother's cheek. "Patricia," he greeted.

Patricia looked us over, a small smile on her lips. "Dom was a good boy. I'm grateful that if he had to die as part of this, it was in doing the right thing. Thank you for coming."

Handing her an envelope, Rockford stepped back. "Our sympathies, Patricia. Dom was a good boy."

Taking my hand, Rockford led us to the seats left for us. Penny was there, already crying. Dwayne wrapped her up in his arms, and I swear I saw him tear up. Big softy he was.

Greeting Louise Wish, I flinched a little when she brushed a bruise on my cheek. "Good to see you up, Caly," Louise embraced me tenderly. She'd come to visit me in hospital after her shift a few times. Aaron was there when he wasn't working, so it was the only way she got to see him for the last week.

"Josh." I kissed his cheek.

"Don't touch her back," Aaron warned when Josh went to hug me. "Or her ass."

Chuckling at Josh's attempt to cop a feel, I pulled back, cringing a little in the movement. Stepping to Aaron next, I moved in to kiss him. "We need to talk," I told him before my lips touched his cheek.

"I know."

"Can you come over after the funeral this afternoon?" Pulling back, so it didn't look like I was lingering.

Aaron's eyes were fierce storms of hurt and anger. He knew I was saying goodbye, but not why. The 'why' was important, and I wanted him to hear it from me, not someone else. "Of course." There was misery in his reply, which caused the tears I'd been holding in to escape.

Swiping them away, I turned without meeting his gaze. If I'd looked up and seen my heartbreak reflected in his eyes, I would have kissed him to make it go away. That wasn't something that would put either of us in the right place.

Brad's infidelity was already out there as media fodder. One of Terry's men who survived told them Terry used Brad's mistress to lure him out, then used Brad to get to me. Kissing another man would only add fuel to the rumors.

Dom's service was lovely and straightforward. Rockford talked about his sacrifice, and Aaron gave the eulogy. While Aaron discussed growing up with Dom, and some of the stuff they got up to with Brad and Dwayne, I cried quietly. Penny linked her elbow with mine above my injured hand. Rockford held my other, freeing it when I needed to wipe my nose and eyes.

"We all have those things we want to say to the people we care about if we knew it would be the last time." Starting his wind up, Aaron swiped at the tears on his cheeks. "I was talking to Dom only minutes before Terry Meadows men murdered him in cold blood. We were talking about girls and how they drive us crazy. We were talking about love.

"We tell our families every time we see them or say goodbye, how much we love them. Why don't we do that with our friends? Why, when we share our deepest secrets with our mates, don't we farewell them with love?

"I lost two of my best mates on the same night, and I had never told either of them. I love them. So, why don't we all turn to our mates, our friends, our confidants, and tell them what they mean to us?"

Turning to Rockford, Dwayne gave him a bro hug. "Love you, Sin."

"Love you too, Dwayne."

All around the church, friends embraced. Kissing cheeks, Penny and I told each other how much we loved and appreciated our friendship. Kissing Josh's cheek, I said to him I loved him, and the same with Kingsley. Then, gingerly, I walked up the podium to where Aaron was watching. His eyes widened when I approached. "You've been a great friend to me, Aaron. You already know I love you, but I wanted to remind you, I still do," I whispered tearily.

Cupping my head, Aaron hugged me to him, my arms gripping the back of his suit. "I love you too, Caly."

Dwayne touched my shoulder, and I hugged him next. "Thank you for risking your life to save me," I whispered.

"I always wanted to be the prince who saved the princess," Dwayne smirked in an answer.

With a chuckle, I kissed his cheek. "My prince." Returning to my father's side, Rockford embraced me. Dwayne and Aaron hugged and cried on each other's shoulder.

Waiters were circulating with trays of shot glasses. Rockford took two, handing one to me. "Riverside tradition for those who die young," Rockford explained to Penny and me.

Pulling back from Dwayne, Aaron cleared his throat as he lifted a shot glass in the air. "To Dom. He was a friend to some, and a guardian to others. To another Angel of Riverside," Aaron announced, then he threw his shot back.

"Angels of Riverside!" Everyone around us cheered and drank. Penny and I followed suit. The vodka burned down my throat and heated my insides. I'd heard the term Angels of Riverside before. Now, I knew it was those who died too young.

"The ones shot down before their time," Dwayne clarified as we did it again at Brad's church service.

During Brad's service, I sat at the front, crying my heart out, my mum comforting me as best she could. Kingsley took my other side at Brad's funeral and stayed there through the burial at the grave. Blocked out by my family, Rockford sat in the pew behind me and put his hand on my shoulder when I broke down completely.

It was that photo that the papers printed the next morning when they revealed my parentage to the rest of Eleri.

At the burial, I restrained my tears because opposite me, not crying, was Emily. Acting the part of the grieving widow, Emily caressed her tummy while she stared at me.

When Emily kissed the red rose she held and threw it on Brad's coffin, I started to cross the grave to strangle the bitch. Holding my shoulders, Kingsley held me in a comforting hug to stop my forward movement. "Soon, Caly. Your revenge will come soon."

When the funeral finished, I stayed standing by the grave. Everyone came to give me condolences before doing the same for Douglas and his wife. They'd distanced themselves from Emily, who the tabloids named his mistress.

"If she loves him so much, I could push her in the grave with him," Queenie offered.

"And ruin Brad's afterlife? Nah, he deserves peace," I allayed. Kissing my cheek, Queenie walked away. My family gave me some distance, leaving me alone by the grave, but within a few meters reach.

"I wish I could say I was sorry for your loss," Emily approached when I was alone, "but you were always going to lose him."

"And always to you." Emily looked at me, suspiciously. "Terry told me your part in this."

Jaw tensing, Emily raised a brow, but her eyes were darting around. "I don't know what you are talking about," she denied sweetly. Looking down at her flat belly, Emily started rubbing it. "So, you got the Meadows fortune, and I'll get the Sarita?"

"Why do you say that?"

Smirking, Emily lowered her face to look at me through her lashes. "I know the prenup stopped you from getting a cent of the Sarita money. That means this baby is the heir. Douglas will have no choice but to leave it all to me. Of course, since I have Brad's child, I'm going to be lodging a lawsuit to take the Meadows inheritance also. You understand?" She batted her eyelashes.

Restraining clawing her manipulating eyes out of her head, I took a deep breath. "You should have asked to read the prenup before you put your plan into action. Then you would know how wrong you are."

Emily watched me, still sure of herself, but hesitant.

"You see, any children were only entitled to ten percent each," I explained. "So, that baby will only get ten percent. I will set up a trust to ensure it receives it on his twenty-first birthday, but you won't get a cent."

Part of me filled with mixed rapture and misery as I watched Emily's smile start to fade. "There were two clauses in the prenup which you made Brad break. The first was the infidelity clause. That baby proves Brad cheated on me after both of our marriages took place. That's a five percent payout right there. My lawyer tells me that's around eight million dollars, so I'm set for life."

Emily's eyes were growing angrier by the minute. "The second clause was the one where my marriage to Brad put my life in jeopardy. When you organized for Terry to take me, so you could have my husband, and or his money, you activated that clause." I waited for a heartbeat to see if she would deny it again.

"Can you guess the penalty for that, Emily? Remember, you're dealing with a Zilla here."

Emily stayed quiet, her eyes menacing.

"Everything went to us, to the Zilla's," I clarified. "Minus your child's inheritance and my payout, of course."

Emily bristled. "Douglas would never allow that to happen."

"He already did," I assured her. "Yesterday, Douglas signed everything over. As of Monday, Queenie became CEO, leaving Kingsley to inherit the Zilla foundation." Nothing about this made me happy, except watching Emily's world getting torn down. Yeah, that was worth a small twitch of the lips.

"You bitch!"

"Me? You're the one who seduced a married man. You organized to have me, and my husband kidnapped and killed, so you could inherit everything. You got greedy, and it has cost your family everything. You were always in the Sarita will. You would have inherited a percentage and had a corporate level job for life, but you had to have it all. Now, you will get nothing, not even my husband's child."

Emily froze, her eyes wide. "What do you mean?"

"You can't keep babies in jail, Emily. His great-grandparents will raise your child. I will ensure he's provided for like Brad would have wanted, but you'll never see your child from the moment it's born."

"You have no proof!" Emily spat.

My eyes wandered over her shoulder to the police who had been waiting to arrest her. Convincing them to hold off to the funeral had been hard, but they'd used the time to gather more evidence. Logs of her phone calls with Terry, and other stuff. I didn't want to know the details.

"Emily Sarita, you are under arrest for felony murder of Brad Meadows, and as an accessory in the kidnap and assault of Calypso Zilla," the detective stated loud enough for everyone to hear.

"Felony? I didn't touch anyone."

"We can charge accomplices with felony murder if they were working with the murderer. We have the proof that you were."

Now, Emily was crying as the detective read her rights to her. I allowed my mouth that small twitch once, as I turned and went to join my family.

There was no happiness. Not while losing Brad was still fresh, and not while every breath made me cringe. Nothing would ever bring justice for the lives Emily ruined out of greed. Brad and Dom were only the names I knew. There were at least five more that worked for Rockford, and the others who worked for Meadows.

Thinking about the war Emily and Terry started on both sides of the river, made me remember Jean-Paul Satre.

'When the rich wage war, it's the poor who die.'

It wasn't Eleri mourning its lost sons today. Brad might have been the grandchild of a Sarita, but even in his heart, he was a Riverside boy.

Tonight, Riverside would come together to mourn everyone lost. Tonight, they'd praise the Angels of Riverside.

Chapter Thirty-Four

"You didn't even ask me..." Gena's yelling traveled into the lounge room. Each of Rockford's replies was gentle rumbles that were unintelligible through the wall.

Sitting in the lounge, I sipped herbal tea while looking out the windows as the sunset over the Eleri river. That one sentence at Dom's funeral traveled through Riverside at high speed. It made it to the media before we'd even left the graveyard after Brad's burial.

Emily's arrest was getting most of the media coverage as the truth was finally leaked. So, the news that I was Sinclair Rockford's daughter was secondary right now.

Yet, it hadn't stopped a journalist shoving a camera in my mum's face and asking if Rockford raped her. Considering Rockford was a meter away at the time, I'd thought the journalist suicidal. Let's say my mother's reply wasn't PG-rated, and there was no chance they would be able to air it on television.

"You look exhausted," Aaron murmured as he took the seat beside me.

"I feel like I haven't slept in weeks."

"Have you been sleeping?"

"On and off."

"Nightmares still?"

"Yes." We both sat drinking our tea.

"You don't want me, do you?" Aaron braved finally. Turning back to the room, I met his eyes. "Caly, I know you. You're scared and hurting and..."

"I'm moving to Switzerland tomorrow." Aaron's eyes bugged out of his head. "Mum thinks it's best. There is a specialist there who will make sure I don't lose the use of my hand," I explained. "When I come home, we can have this talk again. See where we both stand then."

Aaron observed me. "You're scared."

"Of making the same mistake? Yes," I admitted. "When I come home, I don't want to rush into anything. We'll date, then, a couple of years from now, you may manage to make an honest woman of me."

"Caly, I'm not Brad. Both in that, I won't risk losing you, and also because I'm never going to have the money to keep you like this." Aaron indicated my mother's apartment.

Picking up the Manila envelope on the table, my hand trembled as I did. "In case you missed the news, money is the least of my problems right now." I handed Aaron the envelope.

"What's this?"

"The title deed to Greg Meadows' penthouse apartment here in Eleri. It looks over the river and is smack bang in the middle of town. A hop, skip, and a jump to the Uni for Josh, and walking distance to work for you and your mum."

Aaron looked at pages then to me. "My name is on this?"

"I don't want it." My stomach churned in disgust, just thinking of that man and the trauma his sons put me through.

Focusing on the decisions I'd made with regards to the estate I'd inherited, I pushed my emotions aside.

"Everything in Riverside will go towards much-needed resources for the community. Either through the profit of sale or redistribution. Greg Meadows only owned the penthouse and a beach house that wasn't in Riverside. Your father died because of Greg Meadows. Your family never received compensation for that."

"You're giving me a penthouse as compensation for my father's death?" Aaron looked at me like I was insane.

"I'm giving you a penthouse for you and your family to make a home," I answered, uncomfortable with the whole thing. Aaron told me he was struggling to find a place he could afford on this side of the river. It made sense to give this to him when it fell in my lap. "You'll still need to pay utilities, etcetera, but it should do for what you need."

"Caly, you've given my family a lot, and sometimes unaware, but this is too much." Aaron chucked the envelope on the table. "This isn't why I'm here."

"Then sell it and give the money to a charity of your choosing. I don't want it, so I don't care what you do with it." Standing up, I started to leave.

"Caly." Taking my hand, Aaron kept me in front of him. With a gentle tug forward, he turned my hips to bring me to him, guiding me to straddle his lap, careful not to hurt me.

"Aaron, I'm not ready. I feel guilty over Brad, and I spook easily. I can't even step outside this apartment without Rockford and his men around me. It's all too much, too soon. I need time and space to heal."

Eyes filling with worry, Aaron wiped away the silent tears trickling down my cheeks. "Caly, I need you to know two things. One. I don't want your money or name. Give it all away.

I only want you," Aaron whispered, his mouth hovering over mine. "I just need you." He brushed his mouth across mine, the ghost of a kiss. "Two. I can give you time. If you promise me that you will come home when you're ready. I'll wait."

The tears ran faster. My body hummed with tension, and as Aaron's lips kissed along my jaw, I knew I needed him too. Not just in the physical sense. I'd been in love with Aaron for as long as I could remember. He'd always been the guy for me. We both knew that.

"I know you knew it was my blog."

Hovering over my lips, Aaron met my accusation. "I hated every one of those guys. I wanted to hurt Ego."

Sighing, I leaned my forehead against his. "Knowing Rockford was reading my blog, I'm surprised a few of my worse dates are still breathing."

Smirking, Aaron kissed my nose. "When you started writing about Lancelot, your dad had Dwayne track down who it was in real life. When he found out it was me, your dad nearly ditched me as your watcher. It took some very fast-talking and a promise I would never pursue you to keep my job. Of course, that still allowed for you hitting on me. I was going to come up to your room that night I drove you home from the Pitstop. The chance of having one night with you was enough to make me forget your dad's warnings. Then Sin called freaking out about the blog post, and I had to let you go."

Closing my eyes, my tears falling faster in regret. "Is it bad that I wish you'd never turned me away? I've felt guilty about how much it hurt me every day. I loved Brad, I did, but I still wanted you."

"Everyone knows you cared for him." Slipping the cardigan I was wearing off my shoulders, Aaron kissed along my jaw. "Society's obsession with only loving one person at any one time is wrong. If that were the case, no one would ever have love affairs." His lips tasted my neck.

"I can't stop seeing him lying there; the way he looked at me." My heart rate sped as Aaron's hands moved my skirt from between us.

"Then, look at me." Touching my chin, Aaron encouraged me to focus on him. "Just see me."

Meeting his eyes, I drowned in how blue and full of life they were. That hunger wasn't for the world; he wanted to devour me. Releasing his fly, Aaron shifted himself free, before his eyes widened a little. "Are you okay with this?" He checked, suddenly very concerned.

Using my uninjured hand on his shoulder to lift myself over him, I moaned when he filled that space in me. It was passionate, gentle, and the physical connection I needed. When I came, I bit Aaron's shoulder to stop anyone rushing in or Aaron realizing I was in pain. Trembling in Aaron's arms afterward, we regained our breath, and I held the sorrow of leaving him inside. "Your parents have stopped fighting," Aaron breathed in my ear.

"I noticed. I'll order takeout for dinner."

"Your mother said she was cooking."

"Yeah, but that's not what is happening in that kitchen."

Aaron stopped to listen. When he heard the heavy breathing and something clatter to the floor, he chuckled. "The best way to end a fight." He rubbed his nose against my cheek. "Let me stay with you tonight? I don't have to hold you, but I want to be here with you."

"I'm leaving in the morning."

"Then let me have tonight with you."

"I may cry, or worse, if I have nightmares."

"Loving someone is being able to handle them at their worst

and helping them up when they are ready." Clearing the hair from my face, Aaron met my eyes. "Let me hold your hand through the night."

A spark of happiness glowed in the clouds of sorrow around my heart. "I'd like that."

When we went to bed that night, we made love again, slow and gentle; then, we slept holding hands.

&

The next morning, I left Aaron sleeping in the guest bedroom. I couldn't go into my bedroom yet, let alone take Aaron in there. "You don't have to go," Rockford murmured as the chauffeur packed my bags into the car.

"You were right about the funerals and letting people know. Mum's right about this. I'll come home, I promise, and I expect to be part of your life," I insisted. Looking towards the elevator, I rubbed my chest as my heart ached. "Say goodbye to Aaron for me."

With a sigh, Rockford hugged me. "I've always been proud of you, Princess, but you are right when you say you need time. Aaron will understand." God, I hoped Rockford was right.

The plane ride was torturous. Both for leaving everything behind, but also because I had to sit side-on. My back still hurt too much to sit straight. Mum reached out at one stage and held my hand. I didn't even realize I was crying until she did. "You were right, you know. You said Lancelot would remind me of your father. He does."

"How did you know?" I asked, wiping the tears from my eyes.

"The eyes. You described them very well." Closing my eyes, I remembered his eyes last night. "He'll wait for you, Caly."

"How could you know?"

"Because your father waited twenty years for me."

"I'm so happy for you both, mum. Will you transfer home to be with him?"

"No," She answered very sure. "Not yet, anyway. We are happy with our lives how they are. We'll be together when I'm home and focus on our businesses when apart."

"He's upset about me leaving."

"He thinks I'm taking you away again," Gena countered with a sigh. "He's only been in your life for a short time. He feels like he's losing you again." I was quiet for a moment. "He wants the best for you," Mum reassured. "He knows you need this."

"Did you ever love anyone else, mum?"

Slumping in her seat, Gena took a breath. "No, honey, but I was never Guinevere." I looked up at her, confused. "Guinevere loved Lancelot first. When their love wasn't permitted, she gave her heart to Arthur. She never stopped loving Lancelot. A familiar story? Two best friends, a King and a knight, and the beautiful girl who stole both their hearts."

Smiling through my tears at her, I took her hand in mine. "You are such a romantic, mum."

"And you have a big heart, Caly." Mum tapped my chest. "Never doubt you couldn't love them both enough."

Wondering if she was right, I cuddled into my mum's shoulder. It didn't matter now. I'd lost them both. Hopefully, my Lancelot would still want me when I came home. "And you, Mum. I love you so much too."

Chapter Thirty-Five

*Healing & **Forgiveness***

My husband broke my heart. He cheated on me and left me for another woman whom he'd given the family he promised he'd give to me. That was nothing to the pain of watching someone I care about die.

Loving my husband put me in a situation that left me scarred. I need time to recover. I have to learn how to go outside of my house without fear first. Then learn to trust my heart again after his reck-lessness mangled it.

I can't blame my husband for all the pain. It wasn't his fault. Not most of it. But his actions led me there, and for that, I'm strug-gling to forgive him. I hate myself a little for being foolish enough to love him, and I still grieve losing him. He wasn't just my husband; he was my friend. I lost two people in my life when he left. More-over, because of him, I lost a third. The man I fell in love with long before my husband, who broke my heart by choosing only to be my friend.

I'm seeing a Psychologist because hating myself for loving someone isn't healthy. I have to deal with this in my time, in my way, or I may never move on.

Over the last two months, I've cried a lot. Nightmares haunt my sleep, to the point I've woken to scream in reality. I've only now gone my first week without screaming in my sleep. The nightmares are still there, but I can wake crying now without waking everyone else with my fear. My mother has aged, caring for me, holding me while I sob uncontrollably in the middle of the night.

The pain inside me is still burning like an oil refinery, and I'm struggling to see the light at the end of the tunnel. Instead, I wait every night, eager for the sunrise. I find myself standing at my bedroom window, searching for that first beam of sunlight. There is nothing quite like waiting for the light to eat the darkness and swallow the world.

Even writing that reminds me of him. Not my husband, but my friend whom I loved, and who I now know loved me too. Choosing him would have broken my heart, but I could have healed from that one. Some secrets are hard to hear, but they are justified. My husband's secrets proved fatal and cost people their lives.

So, while the night feeds my pain, I find myself more and more staring out the window during the day. I daydream of the man I love, that I left behind, and didn't even say goodbye. He promised he'd wait for me. I'm scared to use that as my beacon, but at the same time, it's the only way I can survive the dark.

Nymph

Recovery was long and hard. Physiotherapy was one thing, therapy was another. The nightmares lasted for months, Gena coming in most nights to hold me. When mum went home, Kingsley stayed to be with me. I wasn't ready to go back to Eleri yet. I didn't want to go back until I knew I could stay there. Aaron deserved more than my coming and going. The idea of going back and not seeing him, or letting him know I was there, seemed worse. So, I stayed away.

"Have you told her about him?"

"Who?" My gaze turned from the window to Kingsley, slouching in my bedroom door.

"Who?" Kingsley echoed humored. "The man you watch the sunset pinning for is who. Who else?"

"When did you get back?"

"Don't avoid the question. Have you told your therapist about Aaron Wish?"

Sighing, I dropped onto my bed. "No."

"Why not?" Kingsley eased himself down beside me.

"It's too soon."

"It's been months, Princess. You haven't woken up screaming for three months now. Your wounds are healed, and your physiotherapy is going well. When do you think it will be time to deal with the fact you are in love with someone who wasn't your husband?"

"When I've gone a month without crying over Brad."

Kingsley raised a brow at me. "Did you seriously mark X in the calendar and set a date for when you had grieved for your husband for an adequate time?"

"No! I just don't think I have the emotional capacity to talk about Aaron until I've reached a point of stability. That point happens to be when I can go a set period without thinking about my ex-husband and cry."

Sitting, Kingsley observed me. With a deep breath, he leveled me with his gaze. "It's time, Princess."

"Why?"

Taking my hand in his with care, Kingsley watched me.

"Because, you not only mentioned Brad without crying, but you referred to him as your ex-husband."

Blinking rapidly, I went back over my words. "I did."

"Perhaps, the therapist isn't to who you need to talk," Kingsley offered. "You should try calling Aaron. Say hello."

"You used to hate the idea of me with a Riverside boy."

Kingsley released my hand. "That was before he spent days beside your hospital bed, looking like his world was crumbling. Before I knew he fell in love with you while keeping you safe. Don't get me wrong, I still hate the guys from Riverside, but that's my issues. Since your mum and dad have been seeing each other again, I've gotten to know Dwayne and Aaron better. I kind of like them."

"Well, that was unexpected. Does one of them have a sister you are trying to score with?"

"Simmer down. Do I look stupid enough to seduce Dwayne's sister? The guy would beat me to a pulp. I'm just mindful of how everyone is cautious talking about you when Aaron is in the room. You need to call him. He lost his best friend and the woman he loved when that shit went down. He deserves to have a sunrise to smile at too."

"This has to be the weirdest conversation we've ever had," I muttered.

"I agree. So, let's not have it again. Now, you have time to kill until your therapist arrives. Why don't we go for a walk outside? Maybe across the road and see if we can make it to the fountain this time?"

"I'm just going to make breakfast and relax."

Standing up, Kingsley took my right hand and tugged me towards the bedroom door. "Come on, your dad flew back with me. Your mother met him at the door, so I'd say the kitchen is out of order, Why don't we go out for breakfast. There's that cafe on the other side of the park."

"King!"

"Part of your recovery is facing the outside world again, Princess. You're meant to be spending at least five minutes outside each day."

"I do."

"Standing on your balcony doesn't count. It's time."

"You're saying that a lot this morning."

Smiling at my grumble, Kingsley grabbed my jacket and handed it to me. "Because it is. Breakfast, and I'll bring you straight home afterward."

Huffing, I followed him out to the apartment door. "What is it with those two and the kitchen?" I hid my face in my hands.

"Weird, isn't it?" Opening the door, Kingsley looked as disturbed as me. "I'm learning very quickly not to go into the kitchen unless I can hear talking."

Stepping outside was scary. Three steps onto the footpath and my chest tightened, making breathing hard. Wrapping his arm around my shoulders, Kingsley urged me towards the road. "I was speaking to Penny yesterday. She's keen to visit soon. It'd suck for her to come all the way here to see you and be stuck inside the entire time."

"True."

"You can do this. There is no danger here. Just across the park and back."

It felt like I was walking the plank. My chest restricted, the ground beneath my feet was uncertain, and the world around me was spinning out of control.

"Just think about Wish."

Imagining Aaron waiting on the other side of the road helped, but it wasn't enough to distract me. When Kingsley urged me forward, I forced myself to think about other things.

"I'm surprised Rockford came to visit. Does that mean things have settled down in Riverside?"

"Rockford says they have plateaued. He dealt with all those wanting to occupy the vacant throne. Now, it's the matter of letting the villagers settle into the new way of things."

Making the other side of the road, Kingsley smiled at me. "Queenie is loving being a twenty-five-year-old CEO of a billion-dollar company. She's already making the rounds of their businesses and making herself known. She's settled down a bit more with the position, which is surprising. I've only heard of her banging the VP of Infrastructure for the Sarita corporation these past few months."

It made me chuckle. To know Queenie was still the girl she'd always been. Wild but ambitious. "How are the Sarita's?"

"Good. Granddad has made sure they will maintain their level of comfort for the rest of their life. They lost their grandson and business. That's enough."

Flashes of Brad gasping for breath on the floor made me close my eyes and look to the side. Counting in my head, I breathed through it, as my therapist taught me. A month ago, I'd be in tears remembering Brad that way. I was getting better.

"Granddad has offered me her old role when I finish my internship, but I don't know. I kind of like it here in Switzerland."

"You like the women here."

The smirk was wicked, lighting up Kingsley's eyes. "Yeah, I do."

"But if you stay, you could take over from Gena, and she could come home."

Lifting a brow, Kingsley shook his head. "I don't have her bio-science knowledge, Princess. Besides, Aunt Gena and

Rockford are working out their own relations. They don't need any help from us."

"Good point."

A phone ringing drew our attention to Kingsley's pocket. "Speak of the devil. Hi, Aunt Gena. Yeah, I know. Caly is with me. We decided to duck across the park to the cafe for breakfast."

The smile grew on Kingsley's face as we reached the street on the other side of the park and stepped us out to cross it. "Furthest yet. Why don't you come to join us? Okay, we'll see you soon." Hanging up, Kingsley slipped his phone away as he turned to face me. "Well done, Princess. You made it to the cafe."

Looking around, I checked back over my shoulder and the building across the park that had become my new home. Facing Kingsley, I stepped into him and wrapped him in a hug, a few tears escaping. "Thank you."

Arms tightening, Kingsley held me a minute longer. "I'll always be here for you when you need me, Princess. Even if you don't know it. I'll always have your back. Now," he pulled back, his eyes watery before he turned away, "breakfast."

Gena and Rockford joined us, looking a little messed from their passionate reunion. My dad wrapped me up in the biggest hug the moment he saw me. It'd been four months. But, despite talking on the phone all the time, it felt like forever since I'd seen him. Dwayne was pulling me into a bear hug the moment after Rockford released me.

After breakfast, Gena and Kingsley went to work, and Rockford and Dwayne walked me home. "It's our first visit here, so we're going to do some sightseeing," Rockford explained. "We could come back after if you wanted to join us? I know you haven't done any sightseeing yourself."

"I'm not sure if I could do it."

"You'd have me and Dwayne, Princess. We'll protect you." My father brushed his fingers along my chin. "Be brave. The effort will be worth it."

Sucking in a breath, I felt my heart rate surge as I told myself I could do this. "I'd like to try."

"Good, we'll be back to get you in two hours."

"I've got an hour until the psychologist arrives if you want to hang out?"

"Actually, Dwayne and I were going to go do something. Just us guys. We'll see you soon, okay?"

"Have a good time, dad."

Rockford's eyes softened like they did every time I called him that. Throwing me a smile over his shoulder, they left to get up to whatever mischief they were planning. When I made my way upstairs to my room, a piece of paper with Aaron's name and number, including the area code, sat on my bed. "Subtle, King."

Collecting the phone, I dialed the number. "Hello?"

"Aaron?"

There was a moment of silence. "Caly? God, I've been dying to hear your voice. Wait, do you have facetime?"

"Yeah, but-"

"Then put it on, damn it."

Humored, I took my phone away and pressed the button to turn on the video. Aaron's handsome face filled my screen, in his work shirt, and what looked to be his car. "Were you driving?"

"Just waiting for Josh to finish at the university, and then I'll drop him to work. Jesus, look at you. Just as beautiful."

My hair was a mess, and I wasn't wearing any make-up, but the compliment fired against my skin and filled my cheeks. "How is Josh going?"

"Good," Aaron grinned, knowing it wasn't why I called, but as happy as I was to talk to each other. "Your dad is there, isn't he?"

"Yeah. They arrived this morning. Dwayne and Rockford left to go sightseeing."

"You must be happy to see your dad again."

"I am. I'm safe when Dad's around."

"I bet. Rockford's not someone you exactly want to mess with at any time of day, especially with Dwayne beside him."

"How's work?"

"Not the same without you there," Aaron admitted. "Michael brought in a new trainee for both our positions. They've finished the training and now work at the weekends."

"How's the nine to five treating you?"

"Good. I'm liking having my weekends and nights to myself. I wanted to tell you, I did something with the penthouse."

"Oh?" My tongue felt too big in my mouth.

"Are you okay?"

Damn video calls. "Yes, of course. What did you decide?"

"I sold it and purchased a place in the Fields for mum, Josh and I. You were right, it's a good location for us and well-priced. Rockford gave me advice on where to invest the rest of the money."

"That's good. I'm glad you could use it."

We sat there for a moment. "When are you coming home?"

"Not yet." Another moment of quiet. "So, Dwayne and Penny are still going strong?"

Laughing, Aaron filled me in on Penny and Dwayne, and how she was so dramatic, but Dwayne was utterly infatuated with her. We talked until the car door opened, and Josh joined Aaron. Then Josh held the phone while Aaron drove him to work. They both told me about their new place, and Josh talked about how demanding medicine was turning out to be. Then he said bye and disappeared from the car, leaving Aaron and I smiling at each other until my doorbell rang.

"I have to go. It's time for my therapy."

"How is your hand?"

"Good, but it's not physical therapy. I'm seeing a trauma specialist for the psychological side of things."

"Of course." Aaron's face dropped. "Caly, can we talk again. Even if it's as friends?"

"I'd like that." The doorbell rang again. "Can I call Sunday night?"

The smile in Aaron's eyes highlighted his hunger. "I can't wait. Talk to you soon."

Hanging up, I let my psychologist in, and we settled in the lounge room. "You look happy today?"

"Kingsley and I walked across the park and had breakfast in the cafe there this morning."

"Caly, that's good." We continued to discuss it. Walking through my fear and how Kingsley and I talked the entire way, so I wasn't focused on my surroundings. "While that's great progress, I get the feeling there is something else behind that smile this morning."

"I just got off the phone with a good friend who I've really missed. His name is Aaron." She watched me for a moment. "I'm in love with him," I admitted.

The therapist's eyebrows went up. She sat back. "Do you want to tell me about him?"

"God, yes!"

Chapter Thirty-Six

Home

I'm going home. It's been six long months since everything came undone, but I can't keep hiding from my life. That's what it feels like I've been doing. Don't get me wrong; I needed this time away. To heal, to trust me, to accept the changes to my body, and me as a person. Shutting off and focusing on me was necessary, but now I'm ready to go home. More so, I'm prepared to move on from the hurt and try loving someone else again.

Who am I kidding? I've loved someone else before it all fell apart. I loved him so much it hurt. We've been talking more these last two months, almost daily these previous two weeks, and now I'm keen to do it face to face.

We won't be rushing into anything. Just friends to start and hanging out. We will work ourselves towards more if it feels right. There won't be my father in his ear telling him he's not good enough. My family will need to think twice if they think of doing anything similar. It will happen, or it won't, but that will be our choice this time around.

Wish me luck. The plane is about to board, I've left my mother at the gate, choosing to make this journey home alone. It's my first test to make this trip alone. So far, so good. Without a doubt, it will be exiting the gate at the other end that will be the hardest, but I already know my dad will be there. So, there is a safety net ready to catch me. That awareness makes this trip a little easier.

Nymph

Pierced My Heart: *Travel safe. I hope for you to know that the safety net is there makes moving on smoother for you. You can do this, Nymph. Even if you take baby steps, you are still stepping forward. Once you get that forward momentum, there will be no holding you back.*

The Sinner: *Don't doubt for a second that you have more than one safety net ready to catch you. I'm glad you are willing to give your first love another chance. If you let your husband's betrayal stop you pursuing what chemistry you have with this guy, you'd regret it. Take your time, set your boundaries, and move forward with hope, no doubt in your heart. He's the luckiest guy in the world to have you love him.*

Nymph: *Update. I'm off the plane and in my dad's car heading home. I'm' anxious and excited and can't sit still. My dad is laughing at me.*

Pierced My Heart: *You probably look like a child on its way to the zoo. A smile is covering your face, bouncing in your seat. Your dad is most likely enjoying seeing you smile again. Let him enjoy the experience.*

"Welcome home, Miss Zilla," Jack greeted as I came into the nook of mum's apartment.

"Thanks, Jack."

"You're looking better."

"I am much better. Ready to get my life back on track," I answered determined.

Rockford walked in with one of my bags, Dwayne, right behind him with the other. They'd met me at the airport with huge hugs and kisses. Jack opened the door for me. As I walked into the apartment, the first thing I saw was Aaron. He smiled at me.

"Surprise!" a bunch of voices yelled, scaring me, causing me to run back through the door.

Dad caught me. "Deep breaths, Princess."

"I told you a surprise party wasn't a good idea," Aaron shook his head at Penny and Queenie. They looked horrified by my response. Yes, it had been six months. I'd dealt with most things, but some things needed time. A lot of time.

"Sorry," Penny apologized from within her shoulders.

Heart still racing, I hugged her. "Don't be. Give me a second?" With a nod and knowing smile, Penny allowed me to walk to Aaron. We'd started speaking online after I called him. For the past month, we'd been talking nightly.

Smiling as I approached him, Aaron's eat-the-world-whole eyes were full of hunger. "You look beautiful."

"It's so good to see you." My cheeks were burning, and my heart was pounding with excitement.

Closing the distance between, Aaron considered me, his eyes glassy, and pupils dilated. "Tell me that you're home to stay?"

"Home to stay," I susurrated.

Cupping my face in his hands, Aaron kissed me passionately, until my toes curled, and I forgot how to breathe. Cheers erupted throughout the room. Hands pulled me away from Aaron's smiling face as the rest of my friends and family hugged and welcomed me home.

When I got to Granddad, his eyes flicked to Aaron. "I hope you know what you are doing, Calypso?"

"Back off, Granddad."

Opening his mouth, Granddad paused, considered, and lowered his voice. "Are you happy, Princess?"

"I will be," I promised.

Pulling me into a firm embrace, my grandfather held me tight. "Then I'm happy for you."

Aaron and I didn't happen straight away. He went home that first night, and every other night we hung out or went on dates. When I'd told him I wanted to take things slow, he understood and didn't push for anything. Most of the time, it was like hanging out with a hot friend who you want to get naked, but don't want to ruin the friendship.

A few weeks later, my attempt to return to work at the hospital failed. The moment we drove in the car park, my hands started shaking, and I began hyperventilating. There was no way I could get out of the car.

Taking my hand in his, Rockford sat forward and told his driver to head home. Tucking me into his side, he let me fall apart on his shoulder.

It was the first time I got to see my dad's house in Riverside. It was on the banks of the Eleri river and on the edge of the ghetto part of Riverside. The building was an old factory that Rockford had renovated into a stunning split-level home. The former carpark and work-yard were now a beautifully mani-cured landscape. It also had more security than the airport. The simplicity and beauty of it took my mind off my failed attempt.

Handing me a glass of bourbon, Rockford lifted a brow. It

was only nine in the morning, but I hadn't stopped shaking. Sighing, I took the drink. "I guess there are some things you can't get over."

"It's called post-traumatic stress. There are two treatments. Face it and push your way through it, or avoid what triggers it." Rockford took a sip of his coffee.

"I thought I could do it, that going back to work was fine."

"It could be the carpark. We could try asking permission to enter via emergency and take away that exposure." When I sat contemplating the pool and waterfall out the window, Rockford set his mug aside. "Or, you accept that you've come a long way in your recovery, and we don't push this button for another year."

"You're suggesting I take a year off?"

"You are registered, thanks to your traineeship. You have options, Princess. Kingsley will be moving home this month to take up Queenie's old role at Zilla Corp. You could intern under him, or I could find a use for your skills with Drofkor." Picking up his phone, Rockford stepped up to me. "Speaking of which, I'm due in the office. Would you like to hang out here for the day, or come to see where I work?"

Setting my empty glass aside, I smiled up at my dad. "You have a nice place, and I'd like to see more of it, but I'm very aware I missed out on shadowing my dad for a day at school. I'd like to see what your life is like away from mum and me."

Kissing my temple, Rockford guided me out to the car with his arm wrapped over my shoulders. "We should talk about getting you a car."

"Mum has never wanted me to have one."

"We've discussed your mum can be wrong. You would feel safer and more secure getting around in your car than you are with a driver."

"Because of the way Terry abducted me?"

"Don't think I haven't noticed how you won't hop in the car with me until you check who's in it. Let's schedule some time tomorrow to look at cars. Aaron told me you loved driving Kingsley's while he was away."

"Are you offering to buy me a Maserati?"

"Not if you are going to be driving into Riverside to stay with me when your mum is out of town. We could do a Mercedes. The bulletproof one." Glancing up, I caught the smirk on his face. Giving him an elbow, Rockford laughed.

It was great to see what my father's life was like on a day to day basis. I spent the day attending meetings with him. After he finished, Rockford took me to his place for dinner and convinced me to stay the night in his guest room.

The fact Gena was in Switzerland was a huge selling point for me not going home. Gaming with my dad - he was a total geek under that debonair business suit - we talked about the Riverside project. It was during this conversation I made up my mind about what I wanted to do.

A few weeks later, I began my role as the Joint Community Projects Officer for both Drofkor and Zilla Corp. Collaborating with Rockford and Kingsley was a perk of the job that I loved. When working with Sin, I'd stay at his house. That way, we could extend our time together and stay up all night problem-solving project ideas I had.

Riverside wasn't safe, by far, but it was so much better than it used to be. It was a long road to changing the mindset of the residents and to removing the crime.

Our most significant benefit was the Meadows' money was gone. There was nothing there to bribe the authorities or government officials anymore. That created a change in itself.

The residents who wanted to see a difference were the

driving force. Things had improved enough that Rockford deemed it safe for me to drive to his place, with the doors locked.

"Mum wants you to join us for dinner when she gets home this week," I read the message on my phone. Aaron was driving me home after dinner with Louise and Josh. I always let Aaron drive when we were hanging out. There was safety to being in his car that I didn't have anywhere else. Maybe it was the inability to fit a body in the trunk.

Aaron and I quite regularly joined his family for dinner at their new three-bedroom place in The Fields. Aaron used the extra money from selling the penthouse to pay Josh's uni fees, and the rest he invested. Aaron went to Rockford for advice on how to handle his finances. While Aaron wasn't rich, he was sensible with what he did have; that impressed my grandfather.

Looking down to where I was responding to mum's text, Aaron lifted a brow. "Double date with your dad?"

"Yes," I smiled at him. "You okay with that?"

"I love your dad, Caly. He terrifies the shit out of me when he's angry, but he's a good man."

When we pulled into the carpark for my building, I slipped my phone away. "Want to come up?" I tried to keep my manner casual. For four very long months, we'd dated, held hands, and done nothing more than hug and kiss. Past ready; I was close to begging.

"Are you sure?" Aaron parked the car.

"You've been in my place plenty of times, Ayah. It's not a big deal." Who was I kidding? It was going to be a huge deal if I got my way.

"Caly," Aaron shook his head, his devour-the-world eyes lighting up. "You and I both know that was a loaded request.

We've taken it very slow. I want to make sure you are sure before anything happens."

Leaning across the handbrake, I kissed his lips. Pulling back enough to open my eyes, I watched his pupils dilate. He was ravenous. "I'm ready."

Opening my door, I hopped out of the car. Ever the gentleman, Aaron locked his car and took my hand as we walked to the elevator.

Removing something from his pocket, Aaron turned to face me. "Don't freak," he warned. Those words seemed to bring automatic anxiety with them. "I bought this for you." He held up a sweet ring with a blue stone that matched his eyes. My hand went to my chest, where my locket used to be. I'd wanted it back, but the police said it was evidence and wouldn't return it.

"It's a friendship ring. I'm serious about you, and my mum said this is how guys used to stake a claim with intent to propose one day." Observing me, Aaron took my right hand and slid the delicate metal onto my ring finger. "I know it's too early for marriage, but I want you to wear this and never take it off, okay?"

A thought flickered in my mind. "It's a GPS, isn't it?"

Aaron's lips quirked. "Designed for you. It doesn't need activation. Rockford can find you from his cell phone anytime, day or night."

Laughing, I grabbed Aaron's shirt and pulled him close. "That's called stalking," I breathed against his lips.

"That's why only your father can access that location, not me."

Lost in those hungry eyes, I lifted on my toes and kissed him hard as the elevator doors opened. Dancing into the foyer like we were in a kissing tango, Aaron turned and pinned me against the wall. Taking my hands above my head, Aaron caressed down to explore. His palm had just brushed my breast when there was a rather loud and noticeable yawn.

Pushing Aaron away, I felt the heat in my cheeks as I met the middle-aged guard's eyes. "Shit! Sorry, Jack." Taking Aaron's hand to lead him inside, I tried to restrain my grin from reaching my ears.

"Welcome back, Miss. Zilla. Mr. Wish," Jack greeted. Standing, he tapped the table at Aaron. Sighing, Aaron removed the gun from his back, removed the clip, and cleared the chamber, then put it on the table.

Observing his ease with the gun, I frowned. "When did you start carrying?"

"I got my license in high school when I used to shadow your father. I've carried every time we've been together except at work, Caly. If you were an ass-girl, instead of shoulders and abs-girl, you'd know that already," he winked.

Surprisingly, I felt safer. Tugging Aaron towards me, I smirked up at him. "When it comes to you, I'm a give it to me now girl."

"Lame, Caly. Cute, but lame."

"For the love of God, go inside," Jack groused. "I've known her since she was a child. I can't be hearing or seeing her do..." he gestured to the wall Aaron had pinned me to, "...that. Your mother and father are bad enough."

Laughing, I pulled Aaron inside. "Speaking of shoulders and abs." Smiling, I shoved his jacket to the ground, then worked his shirt buttons open.

Cuffing the back of my neck, Aaron captured my mouth for the most delicious and sinful slow kiss. His tongue spread my lips and explored my mouth in a way that made me think of a different type of oral. Drenching my knickers by the time he let me take a breath.

"Shit," I breathed as he peeled my jacket off, backing me towards the stairs. "That was the best kiss I've ever experienced." Winking, Aaron did it to me again.

Losing a shoe on the first stair, I dropped the second somewhere further up the stairs. Aaron's pants dropped halfway down the hallway. Then Aaron was kicking his shoes off to prevent tripping over. Considering he wore work boots; it was quite amusing to watch.

Leaving my dress at my bedroom door, we were in my room, no lights, feeling our way over each other. Aaron's mouth found my nipple through my bra, causing me to cry out with how hard and sensitive they were. Sucking was painful, but when he flicked them with his tongue, I prayed like a sinner on Sunday.

When Aaron flung his boxers across the room, his hardness tried to tear through my knickers and get wet. The only sounds were our heavy breathing and kissing. Gripping his hair as Aaron licked and sucked his way south, I bit my lip. The intense sensations of desire took over.

Strong fingers caressed my hips, gripping my ass as Aaron nuzzled my mound. "Please tell me you like a guy eating you out?" Bunching my brows at the interruption, I peered down at him, surprised. "Doesn't everyone?"

"No," Aaron kissed over my hip bones. "I guess it's something you either love or hate."

"Ayah, I love it, go to town."

Grabbing my knickers, Aaron peeled them down my hips, kissing every inch of revealed skin, he finally slipped his tongue into my slit. Grasping his hair, I cried out with relief and eagerness for more. I'd forgotten how wonderful that felt.

Sitting back to yank my knickers down, Aaron spread my thighs and dived in like I was the best meal in town. Delivering me to the verge of climax, Aaron found one of the scars on my hip with his wandering hands. A jolt of discomfort seized me when he caressed it. Trying to hold onto the mood, I brushed his hand away and went back to enjoying his administrations.

A few seconds later, his hand found that scar again and played over it. Groaning, I moved his hand to my breast for him to play. "Not ready for that, Ayah. Let me enjoy this, and you can explore that stuff later."

Grunting an agreement, Aaron took back his hand to lift my thighs over his shoulders, so my feet rested on his back. My eyes went wide, only made so much more engaging when he pulled my knees open to the side, butterflying my legs. No guy had done it like this before, but seconds later, I gripped his head and screamed my orgasm into the dark.

Crawling over me, Aaron let my legs fall to the side. "Condom?"

"I'm on the pill," I panted.

Even in the dark, I could see Aaron smile. "You say the sweetest things."

Rolling us, Aaron helped me align his pelvis with mine. "Take your time, Nymph," he breathed as I started to sink over him. "Nice and slow. I want to feel you."

"You say the sweetest things," I mimicked.

Aaron thrust up, surprising me. "Don't tease, Caly, or I'll make you scream for mercy."

"God, that sounds so good." Leaning forward, I eased him further inside me.

"Later." With his hands on my hips, Aaron controlled my speed. "Slow now. Hard and furious later."

Moaning, I circled my hips as I lowered down. Arching beneath me, Aaron gripped my ass, kneading my bum cheeks, adding to the sensation. Biting my lip, I slid down the last few inches until our pelvises met. Buried deep inside, I could feel him rubbing against my cervix as I circled my hips.

Groaning, Aaron caressed my breasts and played with my nipples. His expertise sent bolts of pleasure to my sex, making me clench. The sensation was too intense, and I froze. "Ayah."

"Caly?"

"If I move again, I'm going to cum. " Biting my lip, I moaned.

Laughing, Aaron grabbed my hips as he thrust into me from below. Placing my hands over his, I threw back my head and thanked the stars for sending me my Wish. Then he threw me on my back and pumped into me slow but hard. Singing his name, I climbed towards orgasm again.

Lowering his mouth to my nipple, Aaron bit, just enough to make me feel it. My eyes widened when he swelled inside of me. Moaning my name, Aaron shoved forward and came. The spurt of his climax, making me cry out as my eyes rolled back in my head.

"I love you," Aaron breathed as he kissed me deep and slow. "I'm never letting you go." Holding me to him while our breathing returned to normal, Aaron started laughing.

"What?"

"If your mum came home, she'd find a trail of clothes leading to your room." Aaron nipped my shoulder.

"Well, at least we are in my room," I grumbled. "If I walk in on my parents having sex in the kitchen one more time, I'm going to need counseling for a different reason."

"Again?"

"I'm not game enough to ask what the obsession with kitchen sex is, in case the answer relates to my conception." When Aaron snickered, I elbowed him.

"Okay, so I'd like to broach a subject then." Wrapping his arms around me, Aaron cinched them tight in a restraining nature. "Do you want to find a place, or could we look at finding our place?" Turning my face to him in the dark, I contemplated his question. "We've been dating four months, Caly, but we've known each other for a long time."

While he had a point, I wasn't sure I was ready to take that step yet again. "Two more months," I suggested. "I'll stick it out here another two months. You still feel the same; we'll start looking for a place."

Aaron kissed my nose. "Deal." Moving his hand to the scar on the side of my ribs, Aaron caressed gently. "Now, let's talk about your issue with me loving every bit of you."

Chapter Thirty-Seven

Happiness is...

There were moments when I believed I could never be happy again. I was wrong. I am. I'm only a few weeks out from the first stage of my very first community project reaching completion. Still, the memory of what I lost to get here dampens the excitement. As a result, my nightmares have gotten worse again, the closer it gets.

Life is a rollercoaster ride. You are always going to have highs and lows. Hitting bottom and doing that slow torturous climb to the top only makes you appreciate the view. That is what it felt like over the last year. A slow torturous climb.

Moving on hasn't been easy, but it's happened. There are days I look in the mirror, and the scars will reduce me to tears. There are still nights I wake from the nightmares, crying, and barely holding back my scream. Moments when I am out, and I find myself alone and terrified and start to panic that I'm not in a safe place. But those days when my scars seem too obvious, my boyfriend takes me to bed and loves them while he loves me. The nights I wake in a crying mess, he holds me and lets me know I'm safe with him. When I have a panic attack, my family and boyfriend are on speed dial to talk me back to myself. They remind me that I have a safety net. I'm loved, and that's what gets me through the worst days.

It's taken me a while to understand that moving on doesn't mean forgetting. You can't. Trauma becomes a part of you. Whether it's physical scars, you see in the mirror, or the psychological toll it takes on you. What you suffer embeds itself in your very being. Surviving entwines with the fibers of your soul, and it makes you and breaks you for the rest of your life. Anyone who tells you to move on and ignore the past has never genuinely suffered. If they had, they'd know you can't. It's not about forgetting. Surviving and moving on is about accepting.

I accept that my husband made a mistake, and it hurt me.

I accept that a jealous woman collaborated with a greedy man to hurt me.

I accept that I was tortured and left scarred.

I accept that I killed the man who was harming me to save my life.

I accept that a man I loved, who was my best friend, died in my arms after another man killed him.

I accept that there was nothing I could have done to prevent the events from that night.

That one. That last one is my killer. The guilt that burdens me for still being here, for still breathing, when he doesn't, is a weight of stone in my heart. I must accept it was all out of my control. Nothing I could have done would have saved him. Saying that is both heart-breaking and a weight lifted from my shoulders.

My counselor said one of the most significant impacts of trauma that we need to overcome is survivor's guilt. Even for rape victims, the first step to healing is acknowledging that others make them feel guilty for someone else hurting them. But the blame isn't theirs. It never was, and it never should be. Guilt is the blanket wrapped around you at the scene to cover your nudity, and to hide your shame. So, the days I find the guilt unbearable, I look in the mirror, I trace my scars, and I tell myself the following words.

'The guilt is not mine. The shame does not belong here. Not on my body. Not in my heart. It is not mine to carry.'

One day, I hope those words have sunk in enough not to need repeating. Until then, the mantra unburdens me long enough to ride to the top of the rollercoaster and see the view from the top. It's a beautiful sight. One of friendship, family, love, and potential.

I've found my reason for going forward. I've taken on a new job where I get to work with people I admire and care for, and I get to help those less fortunate. I'm giving back to the community, and I'm better for it. I'm moving on, but I haven't forgotten.

Yesterday, I told my boyfriend and father I plan to visit my ex's grave on the anniversary of his death. They took it well and will go with me. Afterward, I'm going to tell my boyfriend I'm ready to move in with him. It's time; at least, that's what my cousin tells me. The thing is, he's right, as always.

Nymph

🝔

"Happy anniversary," Aaron murmured as he cuddled into me. "It's been six months since we started dating."

Six months since I got back from Switzerland. A week since we'd found a lovely small estate to live in, only ten minutes from mums. We were moving in together in three weeks. Sweaty and in desperate need of a shower, I lay languid and happy and very satisfied. I could quickly go to sleep and...

"Hey," Aaron poked my bum, "you told me you had a surprise for me. No going to sleep until I get my present."

Smirking, I reached into the bedside drawer to get the card.

Handing it to Aaron, I rolled over so I could watch his face while he opened it. Taking out the Father's Day card, Aaron frowned. Opening it, he looked at the pathology confirmation. "You're shitting me?"

"You're upset?" Anxiety was eating away my insides now the sex high was dropping away.

"Just surprised. I thought we'd marry first and all that." Observing me, Aaron pulled me close.

Peering between us, I laughed at how the news seemed to have reinvigorated him. "Trust me, I was as surprised as you, but I guess accidents happen." Kissing across his chest, I prayed Aaron was okay with this. While unplanned, I'd had the week waiting for the confirmation to become attached to the idea. "I guess you're stuck with me now."

"Like you were ever getting rid of me," Aaron cooed, his hand drifting down to caress my tummy.

"You're not angry?"

Laughing, Aaron pulled me on top of him, settling me where he wanted me. "You make me happy, Caly." Kissing him, I made him show me how happy.

Afterward, I lay in his arms content. "If it's a girl, I want to name her Sabrina Louise."

Shifting closer to me, Aaron sighed. "My father was Louis."

"I know, and your mother is Louise." Happy, I leaned my forehead against his.

Kissing my nose, Aaron took a deep breath. "If it's a boy, Dominic Bradley Wish. They were my best friends."

Closing my eyes, I blinked my tears free. Focus on what you can control. "Zilla-Wish," I corrected. They'll need to keep the Zilla name.

"You'll be taking mine when we marry, Caly." Aaron's hands caressed me.

"I'll be hyphenating."

"Did you just agree to marry me?" Back muscles tensing beneath my hold, Aaron waited, his body frozen.

"Not yet."

Exhaling, Aaron kissed my head. "Do you think that's right?"

Cuddling him tighter, I prayed he understood my reasoning. "Having a baby together is not the right reason to marry."

"I want you to marry me when you're ready, Caly. If you say you're not ready, I can accept that, but once there's a bump, the media are bound to take notice."

Well, he had a point there. The journalists were still hanging around. So far, my relationship with Aaron seemed to have gone unremarked. Then again, I'd kept a pretty low public profile over the past six months. Tomorrow would change that. It would be my first time in the spotlight since the abduction. I was nervous as hell, but I needed to be there.

"I know."

The next morning, Rockford, Queenie, and I stood outside my community project. Sharing the scissors, we cut the ribbon to declare the Wish Medical and Trauma Center open.

It took me months to accept that had the medical center been open, Brad still wouldn't have been here. The media asked me to talk on the matter. Instead, I spoke about the reason's the medical center was essential to me.

"Miss Zilla," a reporter asked when I called for the last question. "Do you have a close relationship with your father?"

This again! Forcing a smile, I told the truth. "Yes."

"How long have you known Rockford was your father?" Another jumped in, taking the opening.

Swallowing my annoyance, I didn't want to give them something else to speculate about. "My father has always been there for me."

"So, there is no truth to the rumor your mother hid the pregnancy from him?"

Right, that was it. "My father is standing right here. Look at us, side by side, and tell me there was any way he wouldn't know?" Everyone chuckled.

"Do you still think about the night Terry Meadows kidnapped you?"

My hand shook on the podium. Ready to intervene, Rockford placed his arm around me, his jaw grinding audibly. Putting out my hand, I stopped him.

"Do you think about it?" I asked. The journalist blinked at me. "Don't you think that question to the person who sees the scars every time they look in the mirror is insulting?" The journalist who asked it bowed his head.

Taking a breath, I used the silence to get ahead of the situation. "The focus of today is the benefits this joint project will bring to Riverside. The media outlet that focuses on my private life instead will be struck from any further news events. Is that clear?" There was a lot of bobbing heads in the audience, along with grumbles about me being like my parents.

"Wow, Princess! You grew bitch in your old age," Queenie laughed as we walked to the side. Aaron was there waiting among the other attendees.

Approaching him with a smile, I took a deep breath. "Are you ready for this?"

Stepping into me, Aaron smiled, his eyes guarded despite his joy. "Just been waiting for you, Caly." His eyes on me, the shield slipped away, and Aaron's eat-the-world truth shined over me as he lowered his face and kissed me. We'd discussed the media reaction to our relationship and decided to get it out of the way.

Cameras flashed behind us. Slipping his hand into my lower back, we followed the others inside, leaving the nosy media behind.

Epilogue

"IF YOU THROW up on my wedding dress, I'll kill you," Penny muttered.

"Sorry, I'm fine, I'll be over it in a minute. It's your fault for serving fish at your wedding. Who the hell does that?"

"Speak to my mother. I wanted chicken and steak. I told the caterer chicken and steak. I also told the decorator cream and gold, so why am I looking at cream and rose gold? It clashes with my dress." Pressing my lips together, I shifted out of harm's way while Penny gestured in her annoyance.

"Anyone would think this was my mother's wedding with all the changes made by her. Dwayne's already offered to knock her off for me five times before we even got to the reception."

Placing my hand on hers, I tried to ease her frustration. "It could be worse."

"The night isn't over yet, Caly. There are still speeches and cake to go."

"Wait, you're not letting your mother do a speech, are you?" I asked, panicked.

"No, thank god," Penny relaxed a little. "Daddy is doing the speech. We are traditional, which means your father is doing the groom's parent's talk."

"You've seen him do speeches, Penny, you know you're safe in his hands."

"Speaking of which." Penny wiggled an eyebrow. "Have you noticed where your father's hands are right now?"

Scanning the room, I located my parents dancing in a way that was inappropriate for their daughter to see. "I swear those two can't keep their hands off each other. Since they got married last year, it's not safe to visit them unannounced." Don't get me wrong; I liked that they were happy. I just wished they'd be content in their bedroom and not the kitchen, lounge room, and dining room. Argh, the last was still making me cringe. I saw more of my dad than I ever needed too.

"Sabrina, stop running around the tables," Aaron called, catching my attention. Snatching her up in his arms, Sabrina giggled as he tickled her.

"I can't believe she's two," Penny smiled, watching as Sabrina ran to Dwayne for protection.

"I know. The time has flown. Have you and Dwayne agreed on a name yet?"

Peering down, Penny cupped her slight tummy. She was three months along, and Dwayne and Penny were already fighting over names. Dwayne told Aaron that he didn't care, but Penny got riled up about it, and they always ended by having scorching hot sex. For the last month, Dwayne was bringing up the baby's name nightly.

"No. Two nights ago, Dwayne was suggesting Herbert for a boy. Herbert?" Penny hissed appalled.

Chuckling, I shook my head. "Well, remember, if it's a boy, I've already chosen Dominic. Dwayne can't have it."

Studying me, Penny reached out and brushed a loose strand behind my ear. "You still having the nightmares?"

"Nowhere near as bad as it used to be, only enough to feed my anxieties."

"Maybe it's time you stop going to his grave, Caly. It's got to annoy Aaron that you visit Brad still?"

"He understands. He even comes with me for the anniversary," I reminded. Rockford came with me sometimes, Dwayne, once or twice. The understanding was that if I needed to go, I let them know, and they went with me.

They'd closed ranks after I went by myself, and a journalist cornered me to ask questions about the attack. The photos of me by Brad's grave balling my eyes out made that journalist my family's public enemy number one.

"Caly, it's been over three years," Penny touched my hand. The scaring was minimal; the surgeon had done a great job. "You and Aaron should be married by now. I'm worried he's waiting for you to let go of Brad."

"Penny, that's not why Aaron hasn't asked yet. He's waiting for me."

"Then why are you making him wait?"

"Because he made me wait. Because I blamed him a little," I confessed.

Penny looked ready to cry. "Because if he hadn't rejected you, you wouldn't have fallen in love with Brad?"

God, it was ridiculous that I even thought this way, but it was there lurking in my subconscious. No matter what I told myself, there was a part of me that looked at the man I loved and blamed him. "I don't want to. I love Aaron, always have. But sometimes, his hands caress the scars, and it brings it all back. I can't let it go."

Penny tilted her head. "Honey, you know he stayed away because of your family. You can't blame him."

Right as she was, those niggles that people have were hard to suppress for a reason. That's why focusing on the positives was so vital to me now. If I let the negative voices in, I'd lose everything again. "All the projects I've been doing with Sin, rebuilding Riverside and making it a safe place to live, it's helped." I looked across the room to Aaron laughing with Dwayne, Sabrina asleep on his shoulder. "I'm ready now."

At that moment, Aaron turned his head and saw me watching him. Winking at me, he said something to Dwayne. With a loud laugh and slight blush, Dwayne nodded, herding his groomsmen back to the bridal table.

Carrying our daughter to me, Aaron smiled. "Speech time, are you right to take her?" Letting him place Sabrina in my lap, I lifted my cheek for a kiss before he walked off.

My eyes went to our little girl. Sabrina had my mother's coloring with her blonde hair and olive skin. But our little girl had Aaron's eat-the-world-whole crystal blue eyes. I adored her. As the only grandchild and great-grandchild so far, Sabrina got spoiled rotten. For that reason, we had to limit our family sometimes. Even Kingsley came over to spend time with her, bringing her presents all the time.

The speeches went well. The staff wheeled out the cake as Penny gulped her water before forcing a grin. "If it's not the salted-caramel apple cake I ordered, I'm going to slit my mother's throat with the cake knife."

"Just make sure she attacks you first so that you can claim self-defense." Penny's eyes widened. No one ever talked about what I did that night. They tiptoed around the subject.

If I made the off-handed comment like 'I'm going to kill

him,' everyone turned into living statues. It was annoying, and it was time to stamp that shit out.

Yes, I killed someone in self-defense after that person murdered my husband. It was the only thing I could do at the time to protect myself. "Too soon?"

Eyes growing wider for a moment, Penny burst out laughing. Giving me an awkward head in boobs hug - on account of my sitting with Sabrina in my lap - Penny went with Dwayne to cut the cake. The bottom two tiers were, in fact, the correct cake. The top-level was not. Cursing under her breath, Penny scowled at her mother.

Throwing his hands in the air as if to cheer, Dwayne knocked the top layer of cake flying across the room. It landed in a fruitcake mush at Penny's mother's feet. Everyone went quiet when Penny's mother screamed as if she'd seen a murder.

Watching her mother try and repair the mess, Penny started laughing. Bent over cackling, I thought she was going to wet herself. Give her nine more months and childbirth, and she probably would. "I love you so much," Penny declared to Dwayne. "I'd fuck you right now if I could."

Grinning like a Cheshire, Dwayne lifted a brow. "I was thinking, what about Rover for a boy?"

Arriving home that night, Aaron seemed lost in thought. Last year, I encouraged him to go back to university for his medical degree. He was loving it. I'd never seen Aaron so happy, apart from the first time he held Sabrina in his arms.

"Penny for your thoughts?" I finally asked as I unlocked the door.

"Your mother isn't traditional, is she?"

"No. Gena wouldn't care what flavor cake we had, as long as we have some form of dessert."

Seeming relieved, Aaron smiled. "I'll get the munchkin into bed, and then I want to see you out of that dress."

"I'll meet you in the bedroom." Tossing the bride's bouquet on the sideboard, I kissed Sabrina's head before he took her off to her room.

In our bedroom, I undressed. Still feeling a little queasy, I let my curiosity get the better of me.

"Where are you?" Aaron called from the bedroom.

"Bathroom."

"Still feeling unwell? Please say no. I've been imagining doing naughty to you all night, and my hardon is killing me."

Opening the door, I walked out, enjoying his reaction to my naked body. I wasn't the only one naked, and Aaron wasn't lying about being hard and ready.

"Come here," Aaron growled, tackling me to the bed.

"Wait, wait, I have something for you," I laughed as he ducked his head between my legs.

"It better be an orgasm."

Cursing as his tongue darted out to taste me, I surrendered. "Okay, surprise can wait, eat away."

"Now, you're talking."

Gripping his hair, I arched back, thrusting up into his mouth. When I started pumping my hips, Aaron slid two fingers in and coaxed me the rest of the way to climax.

"God, you're delicious. Now, the main course." Crawling over me, Aaron prepared to submerge.

"Mummy!" Sabrina called out as our door flew open.

"Shit!" Rolling off me, Aaron pulled up the sheet to cover himself.

"What's up, sweetheart?" Laughing, I wrapped my robe around me and picked her up.

"I had a nightmare," Sabrina was rubbing her eyes as she cuddled in.

"Oh no, what about?"

"A bad man was running around killing cakes," Sabrina murmured, resting her head back on my chest. "He killed the cake with fruit, and it screamed like a girl."

Trying not to laugh, I soothed her that she was safe, and no cake murders were in our house. The next time I saw Dwayne, I'd have to tell him he's a cake murderer. Settling Sabrina back into bed, I made sure she was asleep then went back to our room.

Aaron was lying there staring at the ceiling, a broad smile on his face. Lowering his eyes to me as I came back in, Aaron threw his sheet back.

Squealing a little with joy that he was still ready to go, I jumped on the bed prepared to mount him, but Aaron held up his hand. "Hold your horses, Nymph Queen. Care to explain this?" He held up the pregnancy test I'd been hiding behind my back when he tackled me to the bed earlier.

"Oh, I forgot about that. You distracted me," I purred, licking up Aaron's defined abdomen to flick his nipple. Aaron loved nipple play, his or mine; it was always part of foreplay. I'd made him orgasm once by licking and sucking his nipples and rubbing my body over his groin.

Grabbing a fistful of my hair to stop me, Aaron checked himself when I cringed, and he released me a little. While I didn't mind mild hair pulling, it could act as a trigger after Terry used it to move me around a lot. "Let's focus for a second, Princess." Aaron waved the stick again. "This says you're pregnant."

"That's because I am." Squeezing my breasts together around his shaft, I rubbed back and forth.

Groaning, Aaron pushed me back. "Stop distracting me, Caly," he chuckled, then his voice got stern. "You're pregnant?" Loving the light in his eyes, I nodded.

Kissing me, furious and deep, Aaron shifted his body and was inside me seconds later. Crying out, I dragged my nails down his arms. Aaron was over-enthusiastic.

"Ayah, you've already got me pregnant, calm down a little."

"God, Caly, knowing my baby is inside you, it makes me so horny."

Wide-eyed, I jolted as Aaron came. He'd never finished before me, and if he did, it was just before, so I went over straight after him. "What the hell?" I blinked at him. Aaron blushed. "You are going to make that up to me, Mr.," I scolded.

"You know, I will." With a smile and peck on the lips, Aaron went into the wardrobe. "I'll excuse my poor service by saying I was nervous," he called back to me.

"About what? I thought you wanted another baby?"

"Oh, I do. I also want to do this right this time." Coming back into the room, Aaron dropped down on one knee. "I've been carrying this around for years, waiting until I knew you were ready, Caly." He held up a simple ballerina solitaire. "Will you marry me, make an honest man of me?"

My mouth dropped. Can I say, Aaron naked, on bended knee, asking me to marry him...I forgave him instantly for the poor showing just now. Not that I was going to tell him that.

"Are you fucking kidding me?" I raised both my brows at him. Aaron's face dropped as I crossed my arms. "I'll say yes, and let you put that on my finger if you remind me how you got me pregnant. Because, Ayah, if what just happened was a preview of our married life, then we are going to have major issues."

With his brows rising, Aaron stood to loom over me. God,

he was gorgeous, but when he got that ravenous look in his eye, I melted faster than ice cream in summer. "Did you demand sexual satisfaction before you'll agree to marry me?"

"Damn straight, I did. I am not marrying some two-second preppy. I expect a lot from my husband. He needs to be a great father, caring, loving, honest, faithful, and an overachiever."

"Caly, I'm not superman," Aaron laughed, moving towards me.

"I'm not expecting you to be perfect. Failures are acceptable as long as we learn from them; better ourselves; try harder." Moving back on the bed, I spread my legs. Aaron started to harden. He loved it when I got a little demanding. "Now, let's consider what happened foreplay, and you remind me what an overachiever you are."

Knowing I was teasing and winding him up, Aaron shook his head. "I hope you slept well last night, Nymph."

"If you do your manly duties, I should sleep very well tonight." Smiling wickedly, I knew Aaron enjoyed this side of me. It was time to marry him. Not because I was pregnant with his child, or because it felt wrong to say no. We'd had over two and a half years together. We weren't rushing, we weren't proving a point. We loved each other, and we were a family. It was time.

"Jesus, you know I love it when you look at me like that." Aaron took a deep breath, his hand stroking his engorged shaft.

Biting my lip, watching him, I swung my legs playfully. "Prove it."

THE END

Holly's Trilogy

BOOKS 1-3: HOTEL SERIES

THERE'S DESIRE, AND THEN THERE'S LOVE. SOMETIMES TELLING THE TWO APART CAN BE VERY DIFFICULT.

Holly thinks she has it all, a successful career and steamy relationship and her dream job about to become a reality.

Without warning, it all falls apart. Then a chance meeting changes Holly's life completely. Sometimes a little goodwill really does go a long way.

The complete Holly Claire Trilogy in one compilation that will leave you fanning yourself and swooning.

Available February 29, 2020

Join the Beautiful and Deadly

Join Ebony's Mischief List

Sign up to Ebony's mailing list for the following perks:

- latest news on new releases
- heads up on upcoming promotions
- exclusive freebies like coupons to read Ebony's stories on Radish for free
- first chance at Giveaways
- get a free book

Go to https://ebonyolson.com for more information

Also by Ebony Olson

Hotel Series

Holly Claire Trilogy

Henderson

Cassidy

Holmes

Jess Butler Trilogy

Best Man

Black Mark Series

Black Mark's Resistance

Black Mark's Secret

Black Mark's Heart

Black Mark: The Complete Saga (Compilation)

Eleri Royals Series

Calypso

About the Author

Ebony lives in Sydney, Australia, with her husband, daughter, and six cats. She loves to read fantasy, thrillers, and paranormal romance, spending most of her free time with her nose in a book or writing.

Having always possessed an over-active imagination she spent her younger years regaling friends with fantastic stories, holding her audience captive with the passion and suspense of her characters plights.

Now in adulthood she has numerous published works and shows no signs of stopping her imagination from spreading across as many pages as it can find.

If you'd like to follow Ebony or simply say hi you can find her here:
Website: http://ebonyolson.com/

facebook.com/EbonyOlson.Author
twitter.com/Ebony_Olson
instagram.com/ebony_olson
amazon.com/author/ebonyolson
bookbub.com/authors/Ebony_Olson
goodreads.com/Ebony_Olson